MURDER ON THE CAMINO

WILL BIDDER

'Where yousa from?' he asks, following me with his stench of piss and sweat.

Aware that now is not the time to give him my brother Alistair's London address where I spent the last four months unemployed, I say St-Jean-Pied-de-Port, the town where I started this disastrous Camino de Santiago.

'Me from Roma,' he says in broken English.

I'm too tired to deal with this guy. I've walked twenty kilometres since breakfast. I'm exhausted. And impatient. And there's something odd about the way he keeps turning back to the cabin.

The man steps in front, blocking the path with his scarred feet. Up close, he's taller than I thought, towering over my six-foot height. He must have shaved his head with a blunt razor as the cuts are still raw. I step back, but the cliff edge isn't far behind.

'Me Massimo,' he says, leaning forwards. 'Watsa your name?'

His breath smells like he's eaten raw fish or something rotten from a bin, even though the last village was hours ago.

He stares down at me, hardening his eyes. I try to stay calm, but he's standing so close that I can see mucus in his beard.

'Watsa your name?' he says again, his voice more a growl.

My chest is pounding but I refuse to give him my real name. It's already late. And the longer we spend talking, the more likely he's going to follow me on the trail.

'Michael,' I lie.

He points his finger at my face. 'Gimmie cigarette, Michael.'

I shake my head. There's no way I'd give him one even if I did smoke.

Massimo looks back to the cabin, scratching his finger-nails into his arms. 'Mio Dio,' he says, gazing up at the sky.

I step back but the ground feels unsteady. I turn around, careful not to lower my guard in case he tries to grab me. I'm less than five steps from a huge drop.

Massimo breathes heavily. His arms are full of grazes, some already bleeding. 'Gimmie cigarette,' he says. 'Massimo *need* cigarette.'

'No cigarettes,' I say, trying to move away from the cliff.

He raises his hand. I flinch, convinced that he's going to hit me, but instead he starts slapping his face. I step sideways but then his eyes stare at my shorts.

'Cigarette,' he says, pointing at my waist.

Instinctively, I look down at the money belt tucked under my shorts; the same place where I've hidden the six hundred euros.

Massimo lunges forward. I block with my hand but his fingernails catch my skin. 'No cigarettes,' I say, gritting my teeth.

His eyes remain fixed on my shorts.

'Aspetta, Michael,' he says, pointing at my feet. 'You no move.'

Massimo turns around, revealing a tattoo that covers his entire back. Its depiction of the crucifixion could pass for a lost Michelangelo, except Jesus was a carpenter, not some semi-naked, aggressive religious fanatic. Christ's mournful eyes gaze back at me until Massimo reaches the cabin. The metal door screeches against its hinges. And then he disappears inside.

My legs are trembling. I have to get away from him but I don't have the energy to run. I'm an obvious pilgrim target — if pilgrim is the right word to describe myself, considering I've only just started the Camino. I would never have attempted this trek across Spain if it wasn't for my so-called friends back in London. How am I in this situation? I knew I should have woken up earlier or tried to catch up with the other hikers. But if this man wants to steal my money, he'll have to fight me for it. I didn't start this journey just to run away again.

Massimo returns from the cabin. His figure casts a silhouette against the fading light but there's something else in his hand. Christ. He's carrying a wooden staff; the type which might have parted the Red Sea or at least battered down an abandoned cabin door.

He walks towards me, pointing the staff's metal-edged tip at my head. I move back, until the sharp end presses against my neck. He stares into my eyes before slowly lowering the staff. Then, to my amazement, he pushes it into my hand.

The wood is almost the length of my body and about three inches wide. God knows how he's carried it this far, as the thing weighs a ton.

Massimo steps backwards, kicking up dust until he's measured twenty paces. He stands straight and moves both legs apart.

''It me,' he says, raising his voice, 'an' you walk away. But miss an' me 'it you.'

He wants me to throw this staff at him? Is he actually being serious?

Massimo bows his head. He seems to enter a trance, whispering what sounds like a name under his breath. Finally, he lifts his chin, wipes his eyes and makes the sign of the cross against his chest. He turns around and stretches out his arms, as though imitating the tattoo on his back.

Everything falls silent.

This has to be an act. How many other pilgrims have encountered Massimo out here on the trail? Did any of them throw the staff, or did they just hand over the money, their egos bruised but with a good Camino story to tell?

'Adesso!' shouts Massimo, looking back over his shoulder. 'You musta do it, Michael. God punish you if you can't be a man.'

Sweat runs down my armpit. He's standing too close. A half-decent throw will almost certainly hit him. But what happens if I miss and it's his turn next? Forget my six hundred euros. Massimo could actually kill me.

'Don't be a fool, Michael,' he shouts. 'You musta respect the Lord. This is what 'e wants. What 'e *demands*.'

The metal tip is sharp enough to impale him. Does he want to die?

'Throw the steek,' yells Massimo. ''it me, motherfucker!'

My chest is beating so hard I can barely think straight. This is the only way he's going to let me past. I stare ahead, trying to measure the distance. All I have to do is throw the staff far enough to miss him.

Massimo starts chanting in Italian.

I grip the middle of the staff and lift it over my shoulder. It's heavy but I can balance the weight. I take one last breath and start to run forwards. After five or six steps I gather enough momentum to turn side-on. And then, no longer thinking about what I'm about to do, I release the staff from my hand.

The staff is still soaring through the air when I finally look up. It seems as though it's easily going to clear the giant's head, but then its trajectory peaks and gravity starts bringing it down. Massimo stands rooted to the spot, still chanting, still blind to the staff hurtling towards him. I shout, terrified at what's about to happen, but Massimo refuses to listen. And then, before I can release the scream trapped in my throat, the staff crashes into the back of his head.

Massimo staggers forwards.

For a few seconds, he appears to have miraculously retained consciousness, but then his knees buckle. He starts to fall sideways. The rest of his body follows. And then his head hits the ground with a sound that turns my stomach.

I run towards him.

Blood is pouring from the gash in his head. I drop to the ground and press my ear against his beard but he's not breathing. My fingers touch his neck but I can't find a pulse.

Jesus Christ. What have I done?

My hand is shaking so much I can hardly type the emergency services number. I hold the phone to my ear, but there's no dial tone. 'No network' says the message on the screen.

Massimo's eyes gaze at the sky. The wound has stopped bleeding but there's no point trying to resuscitate him. No one could have survived that blow to the head.

This isn't happening. Ten minutes ago, I was just walking the Camino, worrying about problems which all seem so pathetic right now. Why did I throw the staff? All I had to do was refuse to play his game. He would have probably attacked me and stolen the money, but at least I would have been the victim. At least I wouldn't have killed a man.

I lift Massimo's head, shouting at him to wake up. I beg him to listen, but the whites of his eyes stare at the sky. I place his head on the ground, my hands covered in blood.

I stare at the staff lying beside him. Did its maker craft the object knowing it might one day be used as a weapon — a weapon to end human life?

As far as anyone else is concerned, I could have just walked up behind Massimo and smashed him on the back of the head, no motive, no cigarettes, just cold-blooded murder.

The only chance I have of a defence is if there are any other pilgrims who also came across Massimo and his staff-throwing dare, but I haven't spoken to anyone except Joseph since I started walking two days ago. The police are going to come looking for me. What do I say when they interrogate me about what happened? I hardly speak a word of Spanish. And it's not like Massimo's still here to confess that he made me do it — that throwing the staff at him was his idea.

Fuck. I only wanted to walk the Camino to get away from everything; London, my failed career, and Jessica. If I'd bothered to look for another job instead of wasting all those months in Alistair's house, none of this would have happened. I'd be sitting in some other recruitment office, still hoping to hit some impossible monthly target, but safe in my own boredom.

A breeze whips up the leaves around the cabin, sending a chill down my spine. It's getting late. I don't have anywhere to stay tonight. And what if there's still another pilgrim walking behind me? What if they turn up and find me kneeling over a dead body? How will I explain what happened — that it was all just an accident — an accident that went horribly wrong? But if I walk away this moment, no one will ever know it was me.

I have to get out of here.

TUESDAY 10 JUNE
(TWO DAYS EARLIER)

Gatwick cleaning machines wake me on the floor. I've barely slept in my sleeping bag liner, which true to its name, is no more than a thin sheet sewn together at the bottom. Other early morning passengers roll up their real sleeping bags. It's not even 4am.

I chose an early flight for two reasons. The first was cost. The 7am cheap seat — or should I say 'cheaper' seat, considering it's June — was the best I could find at such short notice. Secondly, a dawn flight meant I had to sleep in the airport, thereby eliminating the risk of waking up late on Alistair's sofa, because once again, motivation deserted me. The fact that I bought a one-way ticket from London to Bilbao was probably a combination of both.

The departures board seems determined not to update its information. I can't even kill time in the airline queue, as that would involve having baggage to check in. The electronic screen finally changes. The flight's been delayed. We won't be leaving until 10am.

I remind myself not to get impatient. After all, it's not like I have anywhere else to be right now.

What I am upset about, however, is the intervention which Greg and Dev staged last Thursday evening. They were so quick to storm the living room that I had no time to change out of my pyjamas or hide the newspaper weekend supplement; the inspiration behind my 'age-old pilgrimage to Santiago de Compostela'. There was nothing strategic about their attack, my best friends since childhood both dismissing my intention to walk across Spain as a complete waste of time. When I managed to slide the magazine under the sofa with my foot, they were already ranting about how I risked 'derailing a promising career' in recruitment all for the sake of another gap-year. This must have pinched a raw nerve as I then accused them of making me depressed. Greg seized on this immediately, diagnosing my condition as boredom from not leaving Alistair's house — that and an addiction to Instagram, Facebook, TikTok and everything else on my phone.

'Addiction?' I said, trying to laugh this off, but Greg was well into his speech, claiming that I was always online every time he checked, which means I need to review my privacy settings. While I tried to explain that it was quite normal to spend three hours a day online — five being more realistic in my case — he retaliated, arguing that social media was killing my brain cells.

Dev then took over, just as they probably planned on the walk from Clapham North tube station. Despite playing down suggestions that I was entering a quarter-life crisis at the age of twenty-seven, his probing implied little support for my trek. How far was the journey? I wasn't sure; possibly five hundred miles — and yes, I did remember giving up half-way through our Duke of Edinburgh Bronze Award expedition at school. What was I taking? My black backpack, trainers — yes, I was aware that those shoes were for skateboarding and not long-distance hikes. Did I have a guidebook, compass and maps? No, you just follow the yellow arrows on the trail, at least according to the magazine article. How was I going to communicate when I didn't speak Spanish? I assured them that my GCSE Grade C would stand me in good stead. What was I going to do if I broke my leg in the middle of nowhere or got attacked by wild animals? And most importantly, what would they say when they received panic-stricken calls from my mum when she hadn't heard from me for weeks?

'I just can't understand why you left your old job,' Greg interrupted. 'You've got to start focusing on your career. Waste any more time and you'll be unemployable. Before you know it, you'll have no profession, no stability and no future. You don't want to be one of those people who life just happens to, do you, James?'

At this moment I lost it, calling Greg a boring accountant, materialistic and everything else I could think of to hurt him.

'There's no way you're going to finish this Camino,' he said, clearly offended. 'You haven't left the house in months. Who's going to arrange your itinerary or book all the accommodation? There's not a chance in hell you can do this all by yourself.'

'Want to bet?'

From the smile on Greg's lips, I knew I'd fallen into a trap. 'Alright,' he replied. 'How about we pay you a thousand pounds if you complete your pilgrimage —'

'And with no Instagram,' interrupted Dev.

'Let's say no social media at all,' added Greg curtly. 'You walk this Camino, all five hundred miles, or however long it is to Santiago de Compostela, and you get a grand. But if you give up at any point, or we catch you online, then you work for Dev as his personal assistant for the next three months. Do we have ourselves a deal?'

After that, everything happened quickly. From the way

Alistair and my parents had been urging me to work for Dev's property agency these last few months, I should have known they were planning an ambush. But I hadn't expected to start the Camino so soon, or actually walk all that way. And with no socials for an entire month? Was that actually possible? The money, however, was alluring to say the least. It had been months since my last pay cheque and I was well into my overdraft. If Greg and Dev had been cruel, they would have confiscated my mobile phone. All I had to do was change my settings and they'd never know when I went online.

'Deal,' I said, rather unconvincingly.

'Now hand over your mobile. Don't want you having any temptations, do we?'

Greg smiled as he snatched my phone. 'So what are you going to do once you've found yourself on this walk, James? Move to Andalusia and write your life story?'

'Exactly,' I said, watching him place my phone in his suit pocket. 'And you can tell my brother you failed to talk me out of this. I'll send you bastards a postcard from Santiago.'

I wake with a jolt. I'm still in the airport entrance hall except there are hundreds of people pushing suitcase trolleys. I check the screen. 9.35am. Christ. Grabbing my backpack, I run towards security. The electronic gate accepts my boarding pass but the line of passengers in front is never-ending. I push through the queue to the x-ray machines where my backpack somehow appears on the other side without raising any red flags. I run through the waft of perfume in duty free, weaving between the pushchairs and airport selfies.

Whoever's in charge of departures has given me a gate which requires a shuttle across the airport, but I just scrape inside the closing doors. The shuttle ambles along leaving me plenty of time to calculate the ten hours and fifty minutes I've spent in the airport only to still miss my flight. The door opens and I bolt up the escalators. A final boarding call is announced on the loudspeakers as I race past the other gates. I throw my boarding pass at the desk attendant and board the plane, passing rows of scowling passengers. And before I've barely had time to shove my oversized backpack under the small seat in front, we're jetting down the runway.

Had I researched my travel options in more detail, I would have learned that Biarritz was a far more convenient airport to fly into, considering the Camino starts in France. Instead, however, I travel from Bilbao airport (where I accidentally withdraw six hundred euros from the cash machine instead of the sixty I'd intended) into the city centre, and then on to San Sebastián, Biarritz, and finally a nauseating bus ride through the mountains to St-Jean-Pied-de-Port, during which the man opposite me throws up into his hands before he can find a sick bag.

My relief on finding accommodation in the small French town is short-lived after the woman behind the desk asks me for something other than my passport. 'Credentials?' I repeat, wondering if I've said the word correctly. She switches to English, explaining that this is the official pilgrim's booklet to collect stamps after every stage on the Camino. I didn't realise you needed pilgrim documents to stay in an albergue, as this place is apparently called. In the end, a photocopy of my passport is enough for a bed, although I can't help sensing something ominous about the way she laughs when I ask for a regular room.

I'm starving after travelling all day on an empty stomach, but the albergue has a nine o'clock curfew so there's no time to find a restaurant for dinner. The owner shows me the communal area which is filled with hiking boots, walking poles and other types of Himalayan-esque expedition kit. She then leads me into a large room which is also the only room in the establishment.

While I'm no stranger to hostels, I've never experienced anything quite like this. It's difficult to see with the lights out, but there have to be as many as forty people all lying cheek to jowl. I walk through the aisles of bunk beds, past faces lit up by mobile phones, with not a single window in sight.

The last remaining bed is a top bunk and the whole frame rattles as I climb the ladder. The plastic sheet rips when I stretch it over the bed, so I lie on the bare mattress, too tired to climb back down for my sleeping bag liner. I then take out the mobile phone I found in Alistair's wardrobe; not that he'll ever find out.

Unlocking the screen with the same 'M' shaped password I guessed on the flight before the tenth failed attempt locked the handset, I log into Facebook, still wondering why my brother chose this letter for his security code.

Within moments, a new message arrives. My chest starts beating. I recognise the profile picture immediately; her tanned cheek bones smiling on the steps leading up to The Ritz.

'*Missing you already darling. Saw you on Facebook earlier but won't tell a soul. Still thinking about you under the sheets. Kisses J. Xx.*'

Jessica. My brother's girlfriend.

The other reason why I'm walking the Camino.

WEDNESDAY 11 JUNE

I wake after the deepest sleep I've had in weeks. The other hikers must have all left as the bunk beds are empty and their equipment has disappeared. I take advantage of the facilities, which with its three toilets and showers would have been a squeeze when everyone else was still here. Five minutes into my shower, I'm hit by the smell of bleach. The foreign words behind the half-transparent curtain sound like curses and I emerge in my traveller's towel which barely covers my waist. The cleaner waves his watch at me as if I've overstayed my welcome. His hostility is surprising. 9.30am is not exactly late by anyone's standards when you're on holiday. Sensing that now's not the time to argue, I change into my hiking clothes and go off in search of the Information Centre.

The woman at the main desk has the patience of a saint as she explains how the Credentials work before issuing my first stamp which she marks in my booklet with today's date. Discovering that I don't have a Camino guidebook, she gives me an itinerary for each stage and a list of all the albergues where I can stay. Today is tough — 'the foothills of the Pyrenees,' she says in English — and she advises me to take lots of water.

'Wait,' she says, calling me back from the door. 'This is for you.'

She hands me a white shell with string looped through two holes at the top. 'Tie it to your backpack,' she says. 'It's the sign of a pilgrim.'

Starving after missing dinner, I find the nearest cafe outside on the cobbled streets. The wedge of potato omelette is surprisingly tasty despite the barman's decision to recook it in the microwave. I order another, trying to resist the temptation to check Alistair's phone. Jessica still hasn't responded to my message from last night. She's certainly opened it. '*Seen 7.48am*,' says the notification under my eight lines, which on reflection was a little excessive, especially the part about how I couldn't imagine being with anyone else except her. Maybe she was just in a rush and didn't have time to respond. Last Friday seems like an eternity ago. But I can still smell the perfume on her neck; still see the look in her eye as her legs pulled me towards her.

The screen suddenly lights up. I reach for Jessica's message but there's a different notification; one I haven't seen before.

'Professional Misconduct claim', says the subject line, followed by my brother's full name. Alistair's mobile must still be connected to his London law firm's account.

It's a short email, stating that he hasn't responded to the Preliminary Notice of Claim which they sent twenty-one days ago. I wonder if Alistair's seen the email, but if I message him now, I'll have to confess that I took his spare phone.

I'm sure it's nothing important, probably just one of those spam emails lawyers are always receiving, even if it does directly refer to my brother in the claim. Alistair isn't the type for malpractice. Bill enormous hourly rates and make rich people richer, yes. But professional misconduct? Not a chance. He lives for his career. And the last time he brought up work — which is mostly all he ever talks about — his head of department said that they would make him a Partner before the year's end.

I put the phone away, pay the bill and set off on my first stage of the Camino.

The trail goes up and doesn't stop climbing. I was surprised yesterday by the greenery from the bus window, but the landscape has grown wilder, still not a palm tree in sight.

When there's no sign of the top after two hours, it finally dawns on me that I should have done some training before starting a five-hundred mile trek across Spain. I could have got in shape without even leaving the house. All I needed was a disciplined routine of push-ups every time I watched one of those CSI murder series I got addicted to during my life of unemployment. I'm sure Jessica wouldn't have minded if I'd borrowed the plastic exercise step she keeps in Alistair's wardrobe — the same place where I found his work phone. What's worse, I'm all alone up here and I can't remember the last time I saw one of those yellow arrows.

I stop climbing and try to find one of the Camino markers, but the fog makes it impossible to see more than ten feet ahead. I have no idea if I'm still on the trail. Those forty professional hikers from the albergue have all vanished into thin air. Perhaps they heard a storm was coming and decided to stay behind in St-Jean. I just wish Dev hadn't mentioned the wild animals.

At last, a tall headstone marker with 'Navarra, Nafarroa'

chiselled under a sideways sunrise appears through the mist. I was convinced I'd lost the yellow arrows, but the sign assures me that I've crossed into Spain — or the 'Basque Country' as the wall graffiti explains.

The sun starts burning through the fog. Red-tiled roofs are just visible in the valley below. Ponies graze the hillside, horned rams with blue circles painted on their coats move in herds and a bird of prey circles overhead.

'Buen Camino,' says a man sitting on a stone wall at the top of the climb.

I'm surprised to find him all the way up here, considering he must be well into his late sixties. He has a thin face with grey stubble and is carrying the same equipment everyone else had in the albergue.

'Pilgrim?' he asks, watching me carefully. I say I'm walking the Camino, to which he replies 'then you must be.'

It turns out that we both stayed in the same albergue last night. When I say how surprised I was that so many people were sleeping in our room, he explains that it was one of the better ones in town. Camino accommodation apparently ranges from municipal albergues which charge six euros for a bed in a dorm with eighty others, to the private albergues which cost twelve euros a night with fewer pilgrims and more bathrooms. It feels so long since I had a conversation that I'm happy to listen to his speech about how the sideways sunrise on the Navarra marker represents the same shell on my backpack, with all the lines symbolising the different places where pilgrims start their Caminos — like Stuttgart, where he's from — before finishing in Santiago de Compostela.

'So what do you do when you're not a pilgrim?' he asks, dropping from the wall with the agility of someone half his age.

I'm reluctant to answer; even more so when he points out

the next yellow arrow as though he thinks we're going to walk together. 'Not much,' I eventually reply. 'I was made redundant a few months ago. And now I don't really have any plans.'

'How old are you?' he asks.

'Twenty-seven.'

I can practically hear what he's thinking — that I'm incapable of holding down a job or making plans for the future, just like Greg and Dev said.

'Lucky you.'

'Lucky?' I interrupt. 'Why?'

'Because you're about to start your next seven-year cycle.'

It transpires that this man, whose name I don't even know, believes my life is about to enter its next stage, one defined by 'creativity'. I try to hide my cynicism from him, who at sixty-nine is also about to enter his next stage, but he sounds like he's dropped his marbles and watched them roll all the way down this mountain straight back into France. Ignoring my obvious lack of interest, he asks about the last seven-year cycle I supposedly started when I turned twenty-one; something about building a nest and becoming financially independent.

'What is this you keep checking?' he asks, staring at my phone. 'I think you will enjoy the trail more if you just see everything instead.'

Just see everything instead? Easy for him to say — this retired man who's making light work of the climb compared to the sweat patches under my arms. Jessica still hasn't responded. And I'm tired of listening to this grandad with leg muscles the size of a marathon runner. There must be some Camino etiquette for situations like these. Does he expect us to walk together for the rest of the day? Even if I could overtake and find the stamina to stay in front, knowing my luck something terrible would then happen to him; something that would plague my conscience for the rest of this trip.

'Sehr gut,' he says, as the next slope appears ominously in front. 'It was nice to talk. Sure you know the way?'

I wave my itinerary pages from the Information Centre.

'I'm Joseph,' he says, shaking my hand in a strong grip.

'James,' I reply.

'You know this pilgrimage is called the Way of Saint James?' he says grinning.

I didn't. Clearly, I'd missed that as well.

'So see you in Santiago, Saint James,' he says, tightening his backpack straps before disappearing ahead.

After twenty-five kilometres, my legs reach Roncesvalles, the end of the first stage. Twenty-five kilometres over a mountain. I've never walked so far in one day, or plan on ever doing so again.

It's gone seven o'clock when I find the albergue inside an old monastery courtyard, but instead of monks or another religious order, it's a woman's toned stomach which greets me in the entrance. I ask if they have any beds, following which she falls out of her handstand. 'My, my,' she says, still staring at me. 'It's super late of you to turn up now.'

Impatient and exhausted, I ask if she works here, but the woman's just a pilgrim from California; one with enough energy for handstands after a full day's hike.

'You're not seriously walking in those?' she says, staring at my trainers.

Thankfully, the albergue owner — or 'Hospitalero', as Joseph explained — arrives, but then I have to tell him why I got here so late. It seems like he's going to turn me away until he finally says there are a few beds still available. He stamps my Credentials and tells me to leave my trainers in the storage rack which is stacked from floor to ceiling with hiking-boots.

I follow his instructions up to the third floor to a main room which must be hosting all of last night's pilgrims as well as everyone else on the stage. Apart from Joseph, wherever he is right now, I didn't see any other hikers all day, so it comes as a shock to find so many people here. My feet ache as I hobble towards the bed. I check the bed number and open another set of plastic sheets, wondering why these albergues have such little faith in their guests having dry nights.

'Bonsoir,' says the woman in the bunk below. She scratches her arms and runs a hand through her hair, revealing a line of marks stamped across her forehead. 'Bed bugs,' she says, responding to my stare. She starts showing me other bites which she apparently got in St-Jean. 'Hospital gave me Cortisone,' she says, making an injection sign.

I look at her face, wondering if we stayed in the same albergue last night. I slept on the bare mattress after tearing the sheets, which I now realise aren't for weak bladders but a deterrent against bed bugs. She smiles, oblivious to her risk as a carrier. For a second, I see what looks like an insect hanging off her fringe, so I go to the bathroom and wait until she's gone.

The albergue must have an agreement with the restaurant over the road, as it's packed when I arrive. Careful to avoid my French bunkmate, I choose a table in the far corner. The waiter hands me a *Menu Peregrino* which has a three course Pilgrim meal with a complimentary bottle of wine.

While hesitant about the refrigerated red wine, I'm a convert by the time the waiter returns with my *primero* which comprises chunks of meat covered in black beans. *Segundo* is grilled cod, and for *postre* I have yoghurt served in a porcelain jar.

Eating alone is surprisingly enjoyable until someone behind says there are wild boar in these parts. I'm grateful to have finished pudding when their conversation moves on to the couple who got lost on the mountain we climbed earlier and had to survive for days eating from animal troughs until the rescue services found them.

I can't help feeling that today's been a success, but then the table starts talking about the pair of skate shoes in the albergue boot rack. 'Good luck to him is all I can say,' says someone laughing. I finish the wine and ask for my bill.

Lights-out has already been enforced when I stumble back to the monastery. I knock into various bunks on the way back to mine, only to remember that I'm sleeping on the third floor and not the second; thankfully before I wake the stranger sleeping in what I thought was my bed.

The phone screen blinds my eyes. Jessica still hasn't replied, even though she had time to post a picture of the bottle of Moët & Chandon which one of her clients couriered straight to her desk, probably because they've fallen in love with her as well. No one else has messaged, not even a one-liner from Greg and Dev like 'EMERGENCY — OPEN IMMEDIATELY' before saying that I'd lost the bet and had to work as Dev's PA for the next three months.

Sore from Jessica's rejection, I start scrolling through Instagram. The usual suspects are all there. Friends I haven't spoken to in years but who are still broadcasting promotions, bonuses, holidays, engagement rings, house keys, and syphilis, although that last account was probably hacked. It's been so long since I last went public that I feel an urge to share a photo of my hike through the Pyrenees, just to prove I'm doing something with my life.

The news feed refreshes, uploading a close-up of an Ethiopian dish with all the standard London foodie hashtags. I recognise the profile picture immediately — that eye-brow raised selfie he took in Spitalfields Market.

Greg's online.

Fuck. I still haven't changed my settings. It won't be long before his message arrives; no words, just a line of faces crying with laughter over how I lost the wager on my first day of the Camino.

I finally discover the privacy option, only for the whole application to crash. I reset the phone, banging it against the mattress until the screen reloads and I can move the cursor to make me invisible.

'*Waste any more time and you'll be unemployable,*' I can still hear him saying. '*You don't want to be one of those people who life just happens to, do you, James?*'

Greg's green light vanishes and he's finally ready to start his meal now that he's achieved his ten likes.

I click on Alistair's work emails. His inbox must be ordered into separate folders for every case he's working on, but there's one email he hasn't opened yet — another headed 'Professional Misconduct', only this time with an attached Letter of Claim.

My thumb activates the sensors without touching the screen. An automatic message appears, confirming receipt of the email at 22.46 on Wednesday 11 June.

It's a long document, letter-headed by what I presume is the other law firm and outlining a chronology of the allegations. I'm so shocked that I have to scroll all the way back to the top to check that my brother is actually named as 'the defendant'. It's full of legal jargon, but from what I gather, they're accusing him of stealing a suitcase containing confidential documents which their barrister lost in a west-end pub — and how they have CCTV footage to prove it was Alistair. Someone called the Ombudsman is investigating the claim, and my brother has to inform his firm's professional indemnity insurers unless he wants to be financially liable. But it's the last paragraph which is most concerning. Not only does it threaten to have Alistair struck off the roll which would end his entire legal career, but it also states criminal charges, including a prison sentence.

My brother, a criminal? Impossible. They must have made a mistake.

The room starts spinning from all the wine. Where are you, Jessica? Tell me you're finding this as difficult as I am. Last night's kisses aren't enough. I need to know you love me. Like I love you.

DAY THREE
THURSDAY 12 JUNE

My back's so sore I can hardly get off the mattress. I lean over the top bunk but the woman with all the bed bugs has left, along with the pilgrims from dinner who laughed at my trainers. I check my messages but there's still nothing from Jessica. I wish I'd never found Alistair's phone. Doesn't she realise her silence is killing me? Did last Friday really mean nothing to her?

I must have slept on my itinerary as the pages are all crumpled. Yesterday was exhausting, but there are still seven hundred and fifty kilometres to Santiago. Was I really that stupid to think I could walk this whole Camino? I can just imagine Greg and Dev's faces when they realise I gave up on the second stage. Maybe they were right. Maybe I am one of those people who life just happens to.

Take my only real job, which I applied for in the last week before graduation, when three years of drinking cheap pints in the student union finally came to an end. Initially, I was thrilled to receive the acceptance letter, even though I hadn't intended to commit my life to a career in recruitment, let alone start the following Monday. While nowhere near as prestigious as Alistair's law firm, the office was on the edge of Aldgate East and the status as a graduate trainee became part of my identity. I was seduced by the perks, such as free rein of the Operations Director's credit card for work drinks every Thursday; The Hanging Bell in the middle of the open plan office which we rang every time a client was placed in a new role; subsidised meals in the work canteen where the daily menu arrived in an 11am email from Mrs Hand, resulting in endless puns about 'the Hand that feeds'; and a new suit for the employee with the highest commission at the end of every month.

Much to my amazement, beginner's luck helped me get a few placements, but then the winning streak dried up. After six months, doubts started creeping in and I soon realised I'd never reach the heights set by Alistair, Greg at his accounting firm, or Dev, whose property business had started to take off. In the three and a half years that followed, I only rang The Hanging Bell seven times, after which even the bell clanger knew I was never going to earn a fittings appointment for a new suit. And then we merged — or were rather swallowed by an older, more aggressive firm of city recruiters. In came weekly one-to-one appraisals with the new Managing Director who evaluated our performances with cold statistics and a worrying lack of eye-contact. If my figures were bad already, they sank from a collapse in confidence. The strain on the Director's face became a permanent feature of our meetings and the Thursday drinking clique started avoiding me completely.

While redundancies were inevitable, I took the humiliation of the first bullet. Naturally, they called me into a meeting late one Friday afternoon after they'd squeezed every drop of productivity from me before delivering the fatal blow.

In five short minutes, the Managing Director explained why they had no other choice but to let me go. His eye spent most of the time watching the clock and he didn't even ask me to sign any restrictive covenants, which really showed his confidence in my recruiting abilities. And so after four tortuous weeks of turning up to work every morning when everyone knew I'd been given the boot, the notice period finally expired and I left the office with a half-empty box of possessions and not so much as a team farewell.

As the shock wore off, it was a relief to know I'd never have to walk through those doors again. In many ways their decision was justified. My organisation was woeful, I was never proactive, and I foolishly believed that my cold-calling evoked a certain charm, even though that had also given up on me by the end, if having ever existed at all. But most importantly, I knew that the job and its motivation to make as much money as possible wasn't what my first day at school and every day afterwards had intended for my life. What I hadn't expected, however, was how lost I'd become over the next four months.

―――――

After hours of walking on the trail, numbed by woodland scenery and Jessica's rejection, Alistair's professional misconduct claim returns to my mind. My brother lives for his career, but he's always desperate to hit his monthly billing targets set by the firm's equity partners. Could this explain why he stole the barrister's suitcase and all those documents?

I still can't decide if I should call him or at least check that he received yesterday's email with the attached Letter of Claim. But Alistair will kill me if he discovers I took his spare work phone. And when Greg and Dev find out that I'm walking the Camino with access to social media, I'll lose the thousand-pound wager. No. It's safer just to keep quiet. Besides, even if Alistair has done something wrong, he'll never trust me with confidential information, or God forbid actually seek my advice.

Alistair and I have always had a strained relationship. Even before I was born, I was destined to be the runt of the litter. The stories about our childhoods always centred around my brother, like when mum pushed his pram into a shop and he started singing along to Handel's Water Music on the speakers while the customers all crowded around baby Alistair as if he was some Messiah.

Everything I owned as a child was a hand-me-down from Alistair, except of course his reputation. My teachers at school couldn't disguise their disappointment at how I'd failed to inherit the intelligence gene, which the other kids all noticed as well, including Greg and Dev who started calling me 'number two'. Naturally, Alistair excelled in his exams and then won a music scholarship to some prestigious boarding school for his A-levels, turning down a place at the Royal Academy of Music so he could read law at Oxford instead. If things weren't bad enough, the world then decided that Alistair had suddenly become cool; not because of who he was, but because he graduated from the best university, and qualified at the best law firm in London, before buying a house in Clapham where he could live his best life. And then, to rub salt into the wounds after I flunked my school exams, went to an ex-polytechnic and failed to discover any passions, Alistair beat me again by finding Jessica.

It's as though life has always been playing one cruel trick and forgotten to deliver my brother's real fate. But what if this is the moment Alistair's luck finally runs out?

Even if his misconduct accusation is a mistake, it

wouldn't be the first time his morals were compromised. As a trainee, he lied to his Head of Department, claiming to have booked a weekend trip to Tuscany when his whole graduate intake was asked to spend the weekend working on an urgent due diligence assignment. He even had the nerve to bring in a box of Biscotti that following Monday which he just bought from some deli in Soho. And then there was the time Alistair phoned in sick and said he'd eaten bad oysters when he'd actually overslept and missed an essential client hearing at The Royal Courts of Justice.

Maybe dishonesty runs in the family. Just look at what happened between me and Jessica. My whole family is going to disown me when they find out I slept with Alistair's girl-friend. But what if she's the one I'm supposed to spend the rest of my life with?

I knew I should have stayed in London to see if there's a chance of us being together, instead of walking along some Camino cliffside as the sun's setting and I still don't have anywhere to sleep tonight —

'Hey you, pilgrim!'

And it's here, late in the evening on Thursday 12 June, where I meet Massimo and kill him.

———

Jesus Christ. What have I done? I threw a metal-tipped staff at a man's head and then fled the crime scene. What if another pilgrim behind me has already found Massimo's body? How will I explain that I just abandoned him — unless I lie and say I went looking for help until I realised there was nowhere else around for miles? I can't leave him on the trail. I have to go back, call the police and then explain everything that happened.

In reverse, the woodland is barely recognisable to the route I walked an hour earlier. It's too dark to find the yellow arrows and the birds have all disappeared, the silence broken only by creaking trees.

All I can think about is what I'm going to say to the police. My Spanish is so bad that I'll never be able to explain what really happened. Even if I do speak to someone who's fluent in English, it's going to take hours for the police to come all the way out here. Did I really think I could spend the night alone with a dead man?

The moonlight finally illuminates the cabin in the distance.

I retrace my steps, waiting for Massimo's corpse to appear in front of me. It's eerily quiet, not a sound except for my feet on the gravel.

The cabin gets closer until I reach the door. Fuck. I must have missed him.

I scan the ground with Alistair's phone, moving away from the cabin until I'm sure I passed the place where his head struck the ground.

I try a different route, then another, but Massimo is nowhere to be found.

Where is he? Surely the police couldn't have arrived so quickly, even if another pilgrim managed to get phone reception and reported what they'd found. There's no way forensics would have examined the whole area and removed the body in such a short time. They would have set up tents, lighting rigs and cordoned off the whole cabin with police tape.

What if an animal dragged him away into the woods; a wild boar, or something bigger, like a bear if they have those out here. But where's his staff? It was right outside the cabin. My fingerprints must still be all over the wood.

There's direct evidence that I held the weapon which killed him.

Christ. Why didn't I wipe off my prints while I still had the chance? The wood was completely smooth. The murder investigators will almost certainly get a perfect sample from all the dirt and sweat on my fingers. I've ticked all the classic mistakes from those CSI programmes I binge-watched on Alistair's sofa. The detectives won't waste any time identifying his corpse when it does finally turn up. After all, how many people have a Michelangelo tattooed across their back?

And then I find something — not the body, but stains on the gravel. I kneel down, holding Alistair's phone inches from the ground.

My chest is pounding. It's blood. Massimo's blood. I knew this was the place he fell. But where is he? Did he somehow regain consciousness and limp away? Is it possible that even with a gaping wound in the back of his head, Massimo is still alive?

Before I realise what I'm doing, I start calling out his name. I have to find him. What if he's lying on the cliffside, bleeding to death? He needs to get to a hospital. And fast.

My calls echo down into the valley but there's no response. The adrenaline makes it impossible to think clearly. But if Massimo pulled himself up from the ground, there's only one other place he could have gone. The cabin.

I trip on a root which sends the phone flying out of my hands. Crawling forwards, I feel through the darkness until I finally find the handset. The screen is completely cracked but the phone doesn't seem to be damaged. Scanning the area one last time, I walk towards the cabin, covering my hand with my t-shirt to avoid leaving any fingerprints on the handle.

The door grinds against its hinges.

'Massimo?' I whisper into the darkness.

No response. Fuck. He must have passed out.

I step slowly inside the cabin. The stench makes me hold my mouth, but then the door swings shut behind me. I kick something heavy; a bucket from the sound of the liquid spilling around my shoes. I point the phone screen to the floor, retching from the smell of whatever was in that bucket. The cabin is full of blankets, old newspapers, food packaging, bottles and firewood, but there's no sign of Massimo or his staff.

What if he watched me walk into his cabin? What if he lured me inside just to trap me?

I creep back towards the door but trip in the darkness. I fall forwards, landing against something sharp. An old nail on the wall goes straight through my t-shirt, cutting the skin above my right arm.

Something moves outside.

I run towards the door so he can't lock me in. My hand grips the cold handle. I twist it sideways but the door refuses to budge. It must be jammed; either that or Massimo is on the other side, refusing to let me out. I yank it towards me using all my strength. The door flies open, crashing against the wall.

I step back, waiting for his giant, half-naked figure to appear in the doorway, but seconds pass without any sign of him.

I inch forwards, hands raised to protect myself. I check both sides outside the door.

The silence returns. I reach down and grab the nearest rock. I'm not afraid of hitting him again; not if this time it's in self-defence.

Something clangs against the wall sending up the hairs along my neck.

I step outside, waiting for Massimo to come charging through the darkness.

Another sound comes from the back of the cabin. My hand drops the rock. And before I know what I'm doing, I've started running down the hillside.

I don't dare look behind. Not even when I reach the woods.

FRIDAY 13 JUNE

I f the situation wasn't bad already, things only got worse last night. Alistair's phone ran out of battery before I escaped the woods, so I had to feel my way through the darkness until the lights of what turned out to be an albergue appeared in the distance. My relief from not having to sleep outside disappeared when the Hospitalero unlocked the entrance. Peering behind the half open door, she demanded to know why I'd arrived so late. Still trembling from what had happened outside the cabin, I tried to give her my Credentials but then she stepped backwards.

'Qué es eso?' she said, staring at my hands.

I looked down, only to discover the cause of her alarm. After trekking through the darkness and scared witless that Massimo was stalking me on the trail, I'd had no idea I was carrying evidence from the crime scene. But standing in the doorway, I suddenly realised my hands were covered in Massimo's blood.

Instinctively, I pointed at my shoulder where I'd cut myself inside the cabin, but then she stared at my arm, shaking her head as if to challenge how so much blood could have come from such a small wound. Convinced she was going to turn me away, I opened the page with my albergue stamp from last night's monastery.

'James Pollock?' she said, still standing behind the door as she read the details on my Credentials. 'Y tu pasaporte?'

The Hospitalero checked both documents carefully, her eyes finally settling on the pilgrim shell hanging from my backpack. 'Entrad,' she said, at last opening the door.

Desperate to wash my hands, I put everything down and asked to use the toilet. She pointed across the hallway, still staring at my clothes. I shut the door quickly, but as I switched on the bathroom light and saw my reflection in the mirror, I realised Massimo's blood was not only all over my arms but also on my white t-shirt. I ran the hot tap, scolding my hands as I tried to scrub everything off my skin, but I couldn't remove the stains.

When I finally returned after cleaning all the blood from the sink, the Hospitalero was copying my name and passport number onto a page in her register. I asked what she was doing but her eyes remained fixed on my wet t-shirt. I must have frozen as she told me twice to collect my documents from the table.

'Tu cama,' she said, pointing to a fold-out camp bed in the corner. And then, before I had time to panic that she was going to call the police, she walked away and turned the lock behind her door.

I lay there for hours, still dressed in my clothes, waiting for a police car to arrive at any moment. The mattress springs dug into my back as I stared into the darkness, trying to piece together everything that happened outside the cabin. It was already a blur, but the more I remembered, the more convinced I became that Massimo had survived.

To any other person, a blow from that metal-tipped staff

would have surely resulted in instant death, but Massimo was enormous. His thick skull must have absorbed the impact, despite all the blood pouring out of the wound. Maybe he never died. Maybe I was too shocked to check his pulse properly. Or maybe he did die, but miraculously came back to life, stood up and then walked off with his staff, all before I returned to that cliffside. It had to be Massimo making those sounds when I was trapped inside the cabin. He probably heard me shouting his name but didn't respond because he was still furious with me for nearly killing him. Either that or he was waiting in the darkness, ready to exact his revenge.

The chances that another pilgrim found Massimo's body are highly unlikely. No one else was on the trail that late and even if someone had discovered his corpse, they would have contacted the police and waited for the forensics and detectives to arrive. But there was no network coverage up there, so they couldn't have called the emergency services. And I would have seen lights through the darkness. The only other possibility is that a wild animal got to him first, but I was only gone for an hour at most; hardly enough time to devour an entire body.

No. Massimo is still alive. He has to be.

The trail this morning has flattened, making it easier to concentrate on Alistair's cracked phone screen. I wish I hadn't charged the battery in the albergue last night. Jessica still hasn't answered, even though it's been days since I confessed my feelings for her. No one else has messaged either; not even Greg or Dev who must know by now that I've started my pilgrimage. Then again, it's no surprise I haven't heard from them considering how little we communicate with each other these days.

Before their intervention, the last time I saw Greg and Dev was at an old school friend's wedding in central London. By that stage, I'd been unemployed for three months and hadn't left Clapham since April. It had taken two whiskeys in the pub across the road to give me the courage to walk into the hotel ballroom, and then two glasses of champagne before I found the nerve to speak to anyone. It didn't help that my suit seemed to have grown two sizes since I last wore it, or that my white collar had a yellow mark from where I burned it with Alistair's iron, but after my first interaction with another guest — some stone-faced banking uncle on the groom's side — I knew I was in for a long night.

The problem with not doing anything is that it's not a problem until someone asks what you do. My explanation that I was in the process of changing careers was immediately interrupted by the balding uncle, who asked what exactly I was going to do. His glare intensified as I tangled myself in knots, the combination of booze and shame making me more discouraged than I'd been five minutes earlier. Greg and Dev, who were hovering on the outside, then leaped at the chance to sell themselves. Dev was in his element after brokering the sale of a four-million-pound property off Kensington High Street and from the way he regaled the event, you might have believed that it was Dev who'd acquired the plot of land, drafted the architectural plans, built the mansion from the ground upwards, furnished its walls with Pre-Raphaelites and then personally chose the buyer himself, thereby taking his own net-worth to the princely sum of four million pounds. But the uncle was impressed enough to place a gold-leafed business card into Dev's hand and invite him to a business lunch at The Ivy the following week so they could discuss future investment opportunities with Dev as his personal acquisitions advisor.

The rest of the wedding was equally disastrous. In hindsight, I should have used the free bar as inspiration for the next time anyone asked what I did for a living. There was nothing to stop me from lying about being an arms dealer, or an influencer with thousands of followers, or just some modern-day flâneur who sauntered around London observing daily life, as long as I said it with confidence. But instead, I stuck to the fringes of the ballroom until the first of the under-thirties left, after which I also made my excuses to leave, just ones that didn't involve a babysitter.

The worst part about being angry with my friends is knowing that I'm wasting my energy thinking about them. How could they have bet on me not finishing the Camino? They couldn't have made it more clear how they thought this trek was a complete waste of time, but it would have been nice to feel some support, or at least not have my phone confiscated. I can just imagine them laughing about all the menial tasks they'll make me do when I work as Dev's dogsbody for three whole months. But there's not a chance I'm losing this bet. I have my pride to protect. And telling them about what happened with Massimo outside that cabin is the last thing I'm going to do.

Late in the afternoon, I'm caught up by two sisters from Holland who don't look a day older than fifteen. I try to push on but my feet ache and I don't have the stamina. The girls trap me in conversation, telling me how they're walking with their aunt, who may or may not have stopped in the last village, and their tiny poodle which has been yapping every night in the albergues, not that the girls consider this a problem for everyone else trying to sleep in the shared dorms. I try to make my disinterest more obvious, but then they start talking about their couch-surfing adventures around Europe, even though their combined age has to be less than the required age to do anything legal.

The next albergue is full, but according to my itinerary there are other places to stay. The three of us walk on until we pass an old house set back on a drive with the type of exterior Dev would describe as 'French-Quarter chic with a seven figure price-tag'. The girls are already reminiscing about the time they had to sleep rough while cycling through Albania, when a young man dressed in a white linen suit walks out of the house and waves from the terrace. He's clearly mistaken me for someone else, but I use the opportunity to ditch the sisters.

The property grows more impressive as I walk along the drive, past apple trees and a gazebo with vines crawling up its sides. The man comes down the steps wearing the kind of leather moccasins my brother has. He's no older than me and deceptively tall, with a face so gaunt that it doesn't seem to have cheekbones. 'Welcome,' he says, somehow already aware that I speak English.

While it's clearly no albergue, I ask if he has any rooms for the night, just to put some distance between me and the Dutch girls before I'm turned away. 'Come inside,' he says smiling. 'We always have places for pilgrims.'

I ask how much he charges for a bed, but he pretends not to hear, instead leading me through a high-ceilinged dining room decorated with candlesticks and silver cutlery. Intimidated by the elegance of his family home, I again ask for the room rate.

'We can discuss money later,' he replies, waving away my question with his hand.

The small issue of my Camino budget weighs heavier as we walk through the house. There are no parents around and he speaks about the home as if it's his to do as he pleases. For all I know, it could be some fancy rehabilitation centre or a country club with an introductory fee more than all the euros stuffed inside my money belt. We reach a mahogany staircase with tapestries hanging from the walls. Again, I say that I need to know the price per night, but his thin smile implies I'm overcomplicating things. At last, he taps his finger on a small wooden box resting on a table at the foot of the stairs.

'Just put your donation inside before you leave in the morning,' he says, still holding my eye. 'But then again, you might decide to stay longer.'

The man leads me up the staircase into a large communal area. He shows me the laundry room and says I can leave anything here that needs washing. Without thinking, I open my backpack and take out the plastic bag containing my dirty laundry. 'Just give that to me,' he says, as I realise the seriousness of my mistake. I try to pull the bag from his hands, but he refuses to let go, even when I say there are other dirty clothes in my backpack.

'What's this?' he says, staring into the bag. 'Your t-shirt's covered in blood.'

I try to describe how I cut my shoulder but he quickly interrupts. 'It must have been a deep cut for this much blood.'

For a few terrifying seconds, I think he's going to reach inside and take out the t-shirt, but then he closes the plastic bag. 'Surely you went to the hospital for stitches?' he says, a frown falling across his face.

I try to explain how I patched the wound with a medical kit, but his eyes stare back. 'You must go to the hospital tomorrow to check it's not infected,' he interrupts. 'Are you sure it was just a nail?'

I nod, forcing myself to look into his face. 'Well then,' he says, placing the plastic bag on the floor. 'I suggest you put the rest of your clothes into the machine after you've showered. Let me show you where you're staying tonight.'

The room has a double bed, views of the garden and a large marble-surfaced ensuite bathroom, but despite the luxury, I can't help wishing I was staying at a municipal albergue in an eighty-person dorm. I shower for ten minutes, wasting enough time until the owner has surely gone downstairs. I then quietly return to the laundry room, throw all my clothes inside and select a wash at sixty degrees. The washing machine starts a two-hour cycle as soon as I close the door.

Three men dressed in linen shirts are sitting outside at a table in the courtyard. Relieved that I'm not the only pilgrim staying here, I ask if I can join them. The eldest looks at me slowly then nods at an empty chair. From the silence that follows, I can't help wondering if I've interrupted something important — maybe family news, considering they all share the same hair and certainly look like brothers. I consider standing up and leaving, but I don't want to be alone again with the owner, who was clearly suspicious of all that blood on my t-shirt. Aware of my intrusion, I ask the men where they started walking from this morning.

'We are not pilgrims,' replies the same brother, who must be their designated speaker. 'This is our home.'

I say how nice it must be to live here, but his eyes remain focused on the table. Committed to my seat, I stare at the trimmed hedgerows and gravel garden where not a single stone seems misplaced, until the silence forces me to speak again. 'We are a community,' the man responds, after I ask what exactly they do here.

'Nice,' I reply, wondering when the other two are going to acknowledge me. 'So are you painters, musicians —'

The man's chair legs scrape against the gravel. 'The world must be purged of its sins,' he says, standing on his feet. 'We pray our work will be enough to earn the Lord's salvation.'

I stare across the garden, past the gazebo and vegetable allotment to where the trail continues beyond the trees. I knew it was a mistake to stay here the moment I walked through the door. The fact that it's not even listed on my Camino itinerary should have been enough of a warning, but now I'm trapped in some cult community and my clothes, including that white t-shirt covered in Massimo's blood, are all locked inside the washing machine for another two hours. The only people who know I'm here are those two Dutch sisters, who've probably forgotten all about me after checking into the next albergue with their long-lost aunt and yapping poodle. Unable to sit any longer with the brothers, I make my excuses and return upstairs to the bedroom.

Alistair's phone is fully charged but there are no message notifications. The lavender scent in the room has a sickly quality which traps in my throat. I try airing out the smell, but when I open the window one of the brothers stares straight up from the courtyard. I go back downstairs, take one of the community's flyers just to show willing, and walk across the lawn towards the gazebo, wondering how the hell I'm going to survive a whole evening in this place on Friday the thirteenth.

'Hello, James,' says a voice behind my back.

The young owner smiles as if oblivious to the fright he's just given me. I don't remember giving him my name. Perhaps I didn't. Maybe he entered the bedroom while I was showering and found the Credentials in my money belt.

'So how are you progressing with our literature?' he asks, looking at the pamphlet.

I lie and say it's interesting, even though I've spent the whole time on Alistair's phone and not read a single sentence of their mission statement.

The man enters the gazebo and sits opposite, our knees almost touching. 'We don't normally host pilgrims,' he says, refusing to blink. 'However, I sensed… a connection when I saw you walking on the trail. You were tired. You needed rest. That's why I waved from the house. You felt the connection as well,' he says, widening his eyes as he starts nodding to himself. 'That's why you arrived here when you did.'

The man picks up the leaflet and starts turning through the pages. But just as I expect him to test me on their ideology, or worse, ask again about the blood stains on my t-shirt, the three brothers walk past with books under their arms.

'They will continue their search this evening,' he says, watching them reach the end of the drive. He sighs wearily. 'Unfortunately, we've had some sad news, James. One of our friends who was staying here, decided to leave unexpectedly. It's been a shock for us all.'

I feign sympathy but the man raises his hand. 'He was a troubled soul,' he says, staring blankly across the garden, 'but he was making progress. He assured us he would only be gone one night — that he needed the trail to clear his head. He set off in the opposite direction back towards France. But that was three days ago.'

The young man suddenly looks up with his piercing eyes. 'Tell me, James. When did you start the Camino? I presume you came from St-Jean-Pied-de-Port?'

'Yes,' I say, swallowing the lump in my throat.

He seems to give my answer great thought.

'You didn't meet an Italian, did you? He's very tall, has a

shaved head and was walking barefoot with nothing except my staff; something he became very attached to. He's not the kind of person you easily missed. His name is Massimo.'

The man continues to talk but I can't process anything he's saying.

'Is everything alright, James? Your face has gone white.'

He reaches forwards and touches the same shoulder I cut myself on the nail. 'Tell me, James. What's troubling you?'

I try to say that it's exhaustion from all the kilometres I walked today, but my words don't make sense. The man tightens his hold, pushing his thumb into one of the nerves near my armpit. I stare back, refusing to give in. Who does this creep think he is? We're practically the same age. Does he really think he can control me?

'Well then,' he says, finally releasing his grip. 'You better go upstairs. What a shame. I was looking forward to your participation this evening.'

I walk down the gazebo steps. My legs carry me across the grass but they can't hold a straight line.

'James?' says the man, calling back across the garden.

Slowly, I turn around.

'You would tell us if you remembered anyone matching Massimo's description, wouldn't you? We won't be angry. We just need to know he's safe.'

SATURDAY 14 JUNE

I wasn't thinking straight after yesterday's interrogation with Charles Manson, but everything now seems much clearer. Massimo had no intention of getting trapped with these people so he left without telling anyone. Why he decided to walk backwards on the trail isn't clear, but someone who makes you throw a metal-tipped staff at their head shouldn't be expected to make rational decisions. But like Massimo, I also have my escape plan; although one that's far more practical than walking five hundred miles to Santiago. I'm going to quit the Camino.

According to my itinerary, it's just two stages to Estella, the next main town after Pamplona. By the time I get there, I'll have either run into Massimo again, or met another pilgrim who's seen him alive, so this whole nightmare can end. But there's no way I'm going to fly back to London, lose the bet and have to work as Dev's PA. Instead, I have a better idea. I'll take a bus to Bilbao, find a cheap hostel and spend the next few weeks living off my six hundred euros until I've wasted enough time to have realistically walked the whole trail.

After five days on the Camino, I'll have experienced enough situations to lie to everyone back home about my journey. Besides, I'll have plenty of time in Bilbao to research the well-known pilgrim landmarks and invent stories about all the fascinating pilgrims I met along the way. Greg and Dev won't part easily with the thousand pounds, especially when I have to call them and pretend that I've reached Santiago, but the fact they confiscated my phone means I won't have to provide any photographic evidence of my final destination. If I'm feeling inspired, I'll fake some spiritual awakening and act like a changed man. And when I finally return home, Jessica and I can break the news to Alistair about how we're in love and going to start a new life together. But first, I have to leave this house.

I turn the bedroom lock, careful not to wake anyone. A pile of laundry neatly folded inside a new plastic bag greets me in the hallway. My white t-shirt is visible through the bag; the same white t-shirt that was covered in Massimo's blood which the cult leader almost touched with his bare hands. I stuff the clean clothes into my backpack and quietly close the door.

It's difficult to keep my balance in the darkness but I reach the main staircase without the floorboards giving me away. The descent is mostly silent until I reach the last step which creaks loudly enough to test the foundations of the building. I freeze. Nothing moves except for the flickering candle next to the donations box. I quickly calculate a real-istic contribution for my stay. The ensuite room would have easily cost three-figures if this was some boutique bed and breakfast in the Cotswolds, and the owner provided a personal laundry service. But what exactly am I supporting? Is money even important to these people?

The zip clinks along my money belt. I reach inside, only

to realise I must have spent my last ten euro note on lunch yesterday as all the remaining notes are fifties. There's no way I'm paying that much for one night here. I've got my exile in Bilbao to think about and I doubt there'll be many places in the city offering beds for the standard six euros municipal albergue rate. My fingers find some loose change at the bottom of the money belt. With any luck, I'll be long gone before anyone discovers I paid for five-star treatment with three euro coins.

My hand hovers over the money slot, hoping that the tissue I wrapped around the coins will soften the fall. I let go. The coins clunk loudly against the bottom of the box.

'Thank you,' says a voice from across the hallway.

I shudder.

Footsteps walk towards me and the young owner's face appears in the candlelight. His forced smile demands an explanation for my miserly contribution, but I try to act like I've done nothing wrong. His eyes dart between me and the donations box as he asks why I'm awake so early and how far I plan to walk today. I respond briefly but it's difficult to sound convincing with his relentless gaze. He considers my answers as though determined to find faults. Was my plan to walk thirty kilometres in today's heat sensible? Was I sure I didn't have time for breakfast or to join them for morning prayers in the garden? I use every excuse I can think of until the man finally accepts that this is the last he's going to see of me. But then he steps closer. 'There's still something I don't understand,' he says, hardening his eyes.

The man clears his throat, holding his clenched fist across his mouth. 'You see, James, it was only last night as I lay in bed, that I started thinking about how you cut yourself. Where exactly were you, when you ran into this nail?'

I try searching for an answer that doesn't involve Massimo's cabin but nothing comes to mind. The man continues to watch me. I shake my head as though the question is of no significance, but I can't leave any clues, not after the mistakes I made with the Hospitalero in Zubiri. 'It was on a tree,' I finally reply.

'A tree?' he repeats. 'A nail on a tree?'

I step backwards but the staircase blocks my heel.

'There's something else I don't understand,' he says, frowning. 'The cut on your shoulder. It was the right arm, am I correct?'

I nod.

'Yes,' he says, staring at my shoulder. 'That's what I thought.'

He exhales slowly. 'You see James, yesterday evening when we were sitting in the gazebo, I touched your right shoulder; the same one you just confirmed you'd injured. And yet you barely showed any sign of pain, even when I squeezed it.'

I step sideways but he follows me.

'I checked the right arm of your t-shirt,' he says, his smile starting to fade. 'There's a tear in the cotton, presumably from this nail you mentioned. But the tear is hardly big enough for all that blood.'

Again, his eyes return to my shoulder. 'Lift up your sleeve. Show me the wound.'

I shake my head.

'Show me,' he repeats.

'Why?'

'Because I don't believe that was your blood on the t-shirt.'

'This is ridiculous,' I say, but he cuts me off.

'Last night, you changed the washing machine setting to sixty degrees, didn't you?'

He steps towards me. 'Did you think I wouldn't notice, James?'

'Look,' I say, raising my voice. 'I don't know who you are, but I'm leaving right now. And if there's a problem, we can just call the police.'

'Call the police?' he says, nodding. 'Yes. That's always an option.'

I walk through the darkness searching for the main entrance. His footsteps follow. I quicken my pace, trying to remember the way through all the rooms and corridors. Hairs stand on the back of my neck as I finally see the door. What if it's locked? What if the man behind me is holding the key in his hand? I twist the handle. Somehow, it opens. I wait for his long fingers to grip onto my shoulder or for something heavy to land on the back of my head, but nothing changes except for the cold air that rushes into the building. My front foot steps outside.

'And James?' says the man's voice behind me.

I don't turn around.

'Like I said yesterday, if you see Massimo, tell him all is forgiven. We just want him to come home.'

I walk out onto the driveway, convinced that the three brothers are waiting for me outside. My knees are stiff, my chest still pounding. The main gate is still twenty metres away. Any moment now and Massimo's half-naked outline could come staggering through the trees, his staff clunking on the gravel as he returns from the wild. What if he tells the cult leader that we met two days ago? What if he says I'm responsible for the gash in the back of his head?

The gate screeches as I lift the bar, but I don't dare look back. I walk towards the trees and then break into a run. I refuse to stop until I reach the first yellow marker, back on the safety of the trail.

After hours of walking, I reach the top of a climb filled with wind turbines. A row of iron sculptures marks the summit, below which lies Pamplona whose streets I got lost in at lunchtime. I drop my backpack and shelter from the wind.

I can't help wondering if I should have escaped earlier today. According to my itinerary, Pamplona has a train station and I definitely saw buses with signs for other cities, including Bilbao. I could have bought a ticket on Alistair's phone and got the hell out of there. But part of me wasn't ready to give up on the bet with Greg and Dev. And anyway, I still don't know for sure that anything bad happened to Massimo, even if the cult leader has made me completely paranoid.

I hurl a rock over the iron figures and curse my bad luck. I would never have walked into that place if those Dutch girls hadn't been so annoying. I should have just put up with them until Pamplona and then checked into a normal albergue with normal pilgrims walking the Camino. At least that way I wouldn't have stayed in Massimo's old home. For all I know, I could have slept in Massimo's old room, my head on his old pillow. And now I can't stop thinking about what that man said in the gazebo yesterday.

You didn't meet an Italian, did you? He's very tall, has a shaved head and was walking barefoot with nothing except my staff; something he became very attached to. He's not the kind of person you easily missed.

And it's true. Massimo wasn't easy to miss when I threw that same metal-tipped staff straight at the back of his head.

Fuck. The cult leader must know that I lied to him about not seeing Massimo. He knew all that blood on my white t-shirt wasn't mine. And he accused me of washing my clothes at sixty degrees to try and destroy all the evidence.

What if he's already told the police I arrived with a t-shirt covered in blood stains just days after his friend went missing? And what if he's not the only one? What if the Hospitalero from Zubiri also reported how I turned up late at her albergue, desperate for a bed and with hands covered in blood? It won't take long for the police to connect both events and realise they involve the same man. Me.

Desperate to avoid these thoughts, I take out Alistair's phone and start scrolling through Jessica's latest social media updates. A notification appears at the top of the cracked screen. It's another of Alistair's work emails, marked with the same 'Professional Misconduct' subject heading. I open the link, triggering another automatic email receipt.

The message must be from the other side's lawyers as it confirms the time and date for an off the record meeting. Alistair, according to the email trail, finally responded to their Letter of Claim and requested a meeting at nine o'clock on Monday 16 June at his firm's offices in London. There's nothing in Alistair's response that denies the accusation. If anything, his tone implies a confession. To think my brother stole confidential documents from a barrister in a London pub almost beggars belief. He's never been caught out in his life. And now they're threatening him with prison. How will he last one day behind bars, let alone survive a full sentence?

The wifi loses connection, but then a new notification appears — an email from Alistair, sent to himself.

'Who is this?' it says. 'How have you accessed my account?'

Fuck. The email confirmation receipts. He must have realised someone else was opening the emails before him.

The screen lights up with another message but I switch off the phone and hide it in my backpack.

What am I going to do? If I confess that I borrowed Alistair's phone, he's going to hit the roof. He'll accuse me of not only putting his whole career in jeopardy, but also threatening his firm's entire client network by wandering around Spain with a phone linked to their business accounts. I know he's freaking out that someone's hacked his emails, but I can't handle a confession right now. When I get to Bilbao I'll reconsider my options, but now's not the moment. If I was a decent brother, I wouldn't let him suffer all by himself. But if I was a decent brother, I wouldn't have slept with Alistair's girlfriend.

Jessica Jackson. I knew I was in trouble the moment I met her.

Alistair had never had a serious girlfriend so it came as a shock when he announced that he'd invited someone to spend Christmas in Hampshire with the whole family. The information he revealed was limited, although we learned that Jessica worked for a large media company in Mayfair, had a History of Art degree from Edinburgh University, and had been in Tatler's society pages twice.

'How wonderfully boring,' I remembered telling mum. 'Sounds like the workaholic has found the girl of his dreams.' What I hadn't expected, however, was that Jessica was the girl of my dreams.

The first thing I noticed when I picked them up from the train station was Jessica's eyes. They were so perfectly green that I couldn't stop looking at them — along with the brown curls hanging below her Alpaca bobble hat. She'd embraced me like an old friend, kissing me on both cheeks before unbuttoning her long camel hair overcoat and diving headfirst into the back of my Volkswagen Polo.

After that, things didn't get any easier. Jessica proved an equal match for our family competitiveness, thrashing everyone at Monopoly, Scrabble and Charades, before announcing how she'd signed up for the London Marathon that April and was going on a ten kilometre run around the village, even though it was snowing outside. Everyone was smitten, including Beans, our black Labrador, who immediately abandoned my bed where he normally slept in the holidays and scratched the paint off Alistair's door until Jessica welcomed him inside, where the traitor spent the rest of the week.

On the last night of their stay, Alistair had to negotiate some important acquisition with clients in New York, so Jessica suggested we opened a bottle of wine. The thirtieth of December. The best night I'd had all year — all two hours of it. As she snuggled up to Beans, the three of us sharing a blanket on the kitchen floor, Jessica confessed how she'd never intended to work in media and always thought her life would be more adventurous than a one bed flat in Battersea Park. After graduation, she'd set off on a gap-year she never intended to finish. She rode a motorcycle across Argentina, backpacked through Latin America, and then moved to New Orleans where she started a fling with some American twice her age who sailed her around the Caribbean on his yacht until he unexpectedly proposed and she realised it was time to come home. I listened in awe, wondering if Jessica had ever disclosed her history to Alistair with such intimacy, but then my brother's face appeared at the door and announced that it was time for bed.

The following morning, I waved them off from the platform and returned to my freezing Polo. I was so sad that I couldn't turn the key in the ignition. It felt like Christmas had never happened. That Jessica's cold lips had never touched my cheek before they whispered goodbye.

The next year, I avoided Jessica at every opportunity. I turned down invitations for Sunday roasts, barbecues, house parties and weekend trips back home. I waited impatiently for news that Jessica had finally come to her senses and broken things off, but she and Alistair only grew closer; to the point where no one could imagine them apart. And then I was made redundant. Unable to afford rent, I slept between Greg and Dev's sofas until there was no option but to accept Alistair's begrudged invitation to move in — no doubt thanks to mum's persuasion. My brother tried his best to arrange his life around Jessica's flat in Battersea, but she was determined to spend weekends in Clapham, tickling my toes awake on the sofa before the smell of her blueberry pancakes came wafting out from the kitchen. And then, when things weren't already awkward enough, she got tickets for the sold out Eddie Vedder show in Shepherd's Bush, or 'Shey-Boo' as she called it.

Jessica knew I was obsessed with Eddie. We'd bonded over our love for Seattle bands and I knew I couldn't pass on seeing my hero for the first time; even despite my anxiety which had stopped me leaving the house. Jessica said cocaine always lifted her spirits when she was feeling down, so we did lines on the kitchen table after I promised not to tell Alistair. Before I knew what was happening, Jessica showed our tickets to the doorman at Shey-Boo, who glared into my eyes, unaware that my date, dressed in her leather jacket and Dr Martens, was the one person in the world I couldn't be with. We pushed our way to the front just as Eddie came on stage. For the next ninety minutes, nothing else existed except Eddie and Jessica. And then he sang Last Kiss, Jessica's favourite song. Our cheeks touched as Eddie sang about the car swerving off the road, but I didn't dare look at Jessica's face. Her fingers touched mine. Then her hand. And then her lips. I don't know how long it lasted — possibly all the way to the taxi outside, or to the stairs of her apartment where we started pulling off each other's clothes. That was last weekend. Almost one week to the day.

Where are you, Jessica? Why haven't you messaged? What about all those things we promised each other?

———

Exhausted, I walk through a field of allotments until I reach Puente La Reina, the end of the stage. The Hospitalero gives me a glass of water which tastes of salt. He says my light-headedness is probably dehydration and shows me to the last bed in the albergue.

While a park bench would offer more privacy, it's a relief to be back with other pilgrims. I shower and then kill time on Alistair's phone until everyone else leaves the dorm. Finally, I open my backpack. I was desperate to check the white t-shirt earlier, but I was too afraid after what the cult leader had said about the stains on my clothing. This time, however, there's no excuse.

Lifting the item up by its arms, I stretch out the white cotton which has shrunk to a third of its original size. No wonder that man was suspicious. Even after a sixty degree wash, the thick splodges are still obviously made of blood.

'You alright, mate?'

I shove the t-shirt back into my backpack and look up at the top bunk where a handsome face and thick curly hair has emerged from under the sheets.

'Did you hurt yourself?'

I say it was just a small cut, but the man jumps down

from the bed. He walks towards me in a pair of tight underwear which must be two sizes too small for him.

'You coming to the fiesta tonight?'

I try to think of an excuse, but the man is too quick for me. 'Everyone's going,' he says grinning, 'my brother also. We're walking the Camino together. You should meet him.'

I accept the invitation before he can ask anything else about my white t-shirt.

'I'm Enzo,' he says, gripping my right hand.

'Nice to meet you,' I reply, stepping in front of my backpack. 'I'm James.'

There must be as many as thirty pilgrims waiting outside the albergue, including Enzo's brother Bruno, who's older, hairless except for his beard, and has arms filled with tattoos. We follow the backstreets, past some gothic-looking church and into a small plaza where long tables filled with people line the cobbles. It seems like the whole town is dressed in white except for the red handkerchiefs around their necks. The brothers find another group of pilgrims who've reserved some seats, although not enough for everyone to sit. Wary of avoiding Enzo, I help a tall man called Shay find other chairs in the street. Apparently, the brothers have a reputation for drinking; tonight being their fourth consecutive night out. Shay takes delight in explaining how Bruno is a master at defying albergue curfews, usually with a flip flop wedged in a window or back door. 'He's like that guy in Prison Break,' he says. 'Except Bruno's tattoos show how to break back inside.'

I keep my distance from the brothers, afraid that Enzo might ask more about my stained t-shirt in front of everyone. I still can't believe my carelessness. I was convinced I was alone in the dorm earlier, but it didn't help that I then hid the t-shirt as soon as Enzo asked if I'd hurt myself.

Overwhelmed by the need to be sociable, I check Alistair's phone to see if Jessica's finally responded, but cheers fill the table as Bruno returns with jugs of red wine mixed with Coca-Cola.

'Where are the brothers from?' I ask, after downing my second glass of Kalimotxo.

'Not sure,' says Shay, raising his voice over the marching band entering the square. 'Napoli, I think.'

The band starts a conga through the old town, leading all of us in tow. Enzo borrows a trumpet and improvises a solo in front of the main drummer, while Bruno, not to be outdone, runs with a herd of small bulls and reaches the end of the fenced-off route without being gored. By the time we stagger home, the ten o'clock curfew has long expired and the albergue is locked up for the night.

Bruno goes off in search of his window while the rest of us wait outside the main entrance. The alcohol must have gone to my head as I can't stop myself from asking other pilgrims if they met a barefooted Italian from Rome. No one confirms my description when Bruno returns through the darkness. 'Che cazzo,' he says, shaking his head.

Someone has moved his flip flop as the window is locked from the inside. The meeting continues in Italian. From what I gather, Enzo thinks we should wake the Hospitalero, but Bruno demands more time. We huddle together, sharing body heat as Bruno again disappears. Tired from today's walking, I start to doze on my feet, but then someone says a word that startles me.

'What did you say?' I ask, interrupting the conversation.

'Just some guy we were going to meet tonight,' says Enzo.

'*Massimo*?' I reply.

'Yes. You know him as well, James?'

My whole body tenses. I try and avoid the question, asking when exactly they last saw him.

Enzo shakes his head. 'I can't remember. Thursday maybe?'

'In the afternoon or that night?' I interrupt.

'Fuck, man,' says Enzo, lighting a cigarette. 'I don't remember. Why's it so important to you anyway, James?'

'No reason,' I reply, snatching too quickly at the words to sound natural. 'I guess I was just worried about him. He was drinking wine and standing outside some cabin on the edge of a cliff. I tried talking to him — more to make sure he wasn't going to do something stupid — but he was really drunk, so in the end I just kept walking. Maybe I shouldn't have left him there. I suppose that's why I asked when you last saw him.'

'I think it was the afternoon,' says Enzo. 'But there were no shops that day so I have no idea where he found wine. What about you?'

'Me?'

'Yes,' he says, throwing the cigarette butt into the street. 'When did you see Massimo?'

I flinch at the sound of his name. 'That afternoon as well. Probably not much later than you.'

'It's just strange he didn't come,' says Enzo, as though not processing my answer. 'Massimo was really excited about the fiesta. We arranged to meet here tonight.'

'You don't think he fell, do you?' I interrupt. 'It was a really steep drop.'

Enzo stares at my arm. I try to move away, concerned by his reflective manner, but then he looks straight into my face. 'Your t-shirt,' he says. 'It was covered in blood. How did you cut yourself?'

'It was a nail,' I reply, glancing behind to check if anyone else is still listening.

'A nail?'

'Yes.'

My head is spinning. Why did I check my t-shirt right there in the dorm? And to hide it so quickly when Enzo stared down from his bunk. Christ. I spent the whole fiesta thinking I'd got away with it, when Enzo must have been wondering about those blood stains all evening.

'Let me see.'

'See what?' I reply.

Enzo stares again at my arm. 'Where you cut yourself.'

Before I can respond, the lock turns behind the albergue door. We all step back, expecting to see the Hospitalero, furious at having been woken up, but instead Bruno's face emerges from behind the entrance.

'Told you I could get inside,' he says, grinning with his white teeth. 'Just like Prison Break.'

SUNDAY 15 JUNE

How could I have been so stupid last night? I hadn't even drunk that much at the fiesta before the words came spilling out. There was nothing subtle about the way I kept asking those other pilgrims if they'd seen anyone matching Massimo's description — and that was before I heard Enzo say his name outside the albergue.

Why was I so insistent on asking when he'd last seen Massimo? I should have known better, especially after what had happened earlier when the two of us were alone in the dorm. But instead, I pushed Enzo until he lost his patience. *'Why's it so important to you anyway, James?'* he'd asked, those his precise words.

After that, my memories all muddled together. I don't know why I lied about Massimo drinking wine but Enzo challenged my story, wondering where his friend could have bought alcohol considering there were no shops around for miles. And then Enzo asked again about my white t-shirt, as if he knew the blood stains were connected to Massimo's disappearance. It was foolish to use the same excuse about my cut shoulder, but like the cult leader, Enzo also disputed how one nail could cause so much blood. Thank God Bruno unlocked the main door when he did. Terrified that Enzo would again ask to see my wound, I walked quickly through the albergue until I was the first to reach our dorm. But as I lay in the darkness, it was not so much my paranoia that Enzo would tell his brother and everyone else about what I was hiding in my backpack which stopped me from sleeping, but another detail which was far more concerning.

Thursday afternoon. The last time Enzo saw Massimo. The last time anyone saw Massimo on the Camino.

Except me.

———

I spend the morning walking through fields along the trail. The hangover fills my head but I'll never outwalk the Italians if I keep stopping for breaks. Both brothers were fast asleep when I crept out of the dorm before sunrise, but it won't be long before they and everyone else start catching up.

The route is mostly flat except for a steep hill which takes ages to climb. Even with the pain in my body, the view from the top is impressive. I don't bother to check for any non-existent messages from Jessica as I take out Alistair's phone. The camera focuses, reaching as far back as yesterday's wind turbines, beyond which lies Pamplona, and further still, Massimo's cabin.

'You don't think he fell, do you? It was a really steep drop.'

Fuck. Why did I say that? What if Enzo knows I was the last person who saw Massimo on the trail? I literally gave him the exact location where I threw that staff straight at the back of Massimo's head.

What if something terrible happened to Massimo that night before I went back to the cabin? What if he woke up on the ground, lost his footing in the darkness and fell straight over the edge of that cliff? I've spent days trying to convince myself that he's alright, but now nothing seems certain. Those men in the religious cult were clearly concerned enough to send out a search party. Even if he had just escaped their community, this doesn't explain why he was a no-show last night. '*Massimo was really excited about the fiesta,*' I can still hear Enzo saying. '*We arranged to meet here tonight.*'

What if I'm the reason why Massimo didn't make it to the fiesta? What if I spent the whole night celebrating with his fellow Italians, when I was responsible for his disappearance?

The dots of other pilgrims appear below. I have to get rid of my t-shirt, but I haven't seen any bins since leaving town and the ground's too hard to dig a hole deep enough to bury anything. Even if Massimo is safe, I can't walk the trail carrying a white t-shirt covered in his blood stains.

Voices carry up to where I'm standing. I hear laughter but then someone calls out my name. Whoever's down there — Enzo, Bruno or anyone else from last night — it won't be long until they reach the top. I have to get to Estella, the town at the end of today's stage, and then find a bus to Bilbao. It's the only way I can escape what happened to Massimo.

The yellow arrows lead into a small plaza. The temperature gauge reads thirty-four degrees but the heat on the cobbles feels much hotter. I should have filled my bottle before leaving the albergue as the few shops and bars I've passed have all been shut, today being a Sunday. My hangover feels worse, or maybe it's dehydration, combined with paranoia that I'm being followed by the Italians.

An industrial-sized bin appears on the far side of the plaza. Instinctively, I drop my backpack, unclip the fastening and reach through the drawstring opening. I open the bin, ready to finally dispose of the evidence, when a voice calls across the square.

I look up, still clutching the white t-shirt in my hand.

Three pilgrims are sitting with their backs to the church wall. They must have been watching me this whole time, hidden under the shade of the tower. I wonder if it's not too late to throw away the t-shirt and walk on, but then one of them waves in my direction. 'Come over,' shouts the same voice from before.

A tall, broad-shouldered man, no older than early thirties, gets up and walks towards a rectangular box shaped like a tombstone. He tilts his bottle and presses a button which sends water pouring from the spout.

I hide the t-shirt in my backpack and walk towards him. My mouth is so dry I can barely ask if the water's safe to drink. 'Must be,' he replies, running fingers through his hair. 'I've been drinking from these all week but haven't gotten sick yet.'

He soaks his head under the water and then drinks from his cupped hands.

'British, right?' he asks, as if this explains my reluctance to drink from the copper pipes. 'Go on. It won't kill you.'

The water tastes fresh despite the mineral aftertaste. I take large gulps until the cold temperature hurts my head.

'Come join us when you're done,' says the man. 'You don't want to be out here alone — not after what they were saying last night. I'm Eric by the way.'

He walks away before I can ask what exactly he means.

'You!' says the taller of the two women as I join them in the shade. It's difficult to see her face behind the frizzy hair and large sunglasses, but I can't remember if we met last night at the fiesta. Maybe we did. Maybe I also asked her if she'd seen Massimo on the trail.

'You know everyone's calling you *the guy in those shoes*, right?' she continues.

'I'd say Red Coat's doing just fine,' Eric interrupts, splashing water from his bottle across her legs. 'Better than you, anyways,' he says, laughing. 'Go on, Carolina. Show him what's growing on your foot.'

Carolina throws him a glare and then unstraps her sandals, revealing a bubble of pus large enough to pass as a sixth toe. Still wary of how they saw me trying to hide my t-shirt, I ask how she managed to get a blister this big after only five days of walking. 'Thanks to these,' she says, tugging on a pair of leather hiking boots tied to the straps of her backpack. 'They're Grampy's old boots,' she adds, still staring up from behind her dark sunglasses. 'He wore them on Camino back in the seventies. My plan,' she says, pausing, 'had been to wear them all the way to Santiago, but there's not a chance I'm going to walk all that way in these guys now.'

Thankfully, the discussion moves on to how Carolina should treat her blister. Eric offers to pierce the skin with a needle before stitching it up with thread, but Amy, their other American friend, is convinced this will infect Carolina's foot and end her pilgrimage. But what they do agree on is that she can't keep walking in her family heirloom. 'It's why you see all those hiking boots left behind in the albergues,' Eric continues. 'The humidity makes your feet swell up, so if your boots are tight already then you're in real trouble.'

My 'strategy' to wear broken-in trainers was apparently

the best decision I could have made, at least according to Eric, who then reels off a list of all the people who've already given up because of blisters.

'There was this one British guy,' he says laughing, 'who started every morning with fifty press-ups, before he limped off to the bus station in Pamplona crying about his feet.'

'You can talk,' Carolina interrupts. 'Who else on the Camino pays a hundred euros to sleep in a tree house with an ensuite bathroom?'

Eric retaliates with some argument about a hereditary sleeping condition, but Amy accuses them of bickering like an old married couple. 'Anyway, it's getting late,' she says, checking her phone. 'I don't want to stay out much longer.'

The two women take the lead, Carolina walking mostly on her back heel. Still worried that Eric's going to ask why I walked straight towards that bin in the plaza, I ask if he knows the girls from back home in the States. He shakes his head and describes how he met them in Roncesvalles on the first day, but then frowns when I ask if they plan to walk the whole way together. 'Who knows?' he says, lowering his voice. 'They were both pretty shaken up after last night's news.'

I ask what exactly he means.

'You haven't heard?' says Eric. He motions with his hand to slow down. 'Let's just say there was an incident,' he continues, making sure the girls are out of earshot. 'Everyone was talking about it in our albergue. Carolina and Amy were terrified. They weren't sure if they wanted to walk today. How the hell haven't you heard about this, James?'

'What do you mean, an incident?' I ask, barely processing anything he just said.

'Nothing's been confirmed,' says Eric, as though

searching for the right words. 'But apparently some pilgrim got attacked on the trail a few days ago.'

'Attacked? What happened?'

'No one knows,' he replies, shaking his head. 'But they're saying it happened outside Zubiri. Can you imagine coming all the way here to walk the Camino, only to get attacked by some maniac on your second day?'

'Do they know who did it?'

'That's what they're trying to find out.'

'They?' I interrupt.

'The National Police,' says Eric, staring into my eyes. 'They didn't turn up at your albergue this morning?'

I shake my head.

'Two officers walked straight into our dorm demanding to see everyone's Credentials. They wanted to know where we stayed on Thursday night. Turns out we walked the same stage when the attack happened. That's why the girls are so worried. No one knows if it's safe to keep walking. And the police said we had to stay in groups. That's why we were surprised when you turned up on your own.'

'Do they know if he's alright?'

'He?' Eric interrupts. 'Who said the victim was a man?'

I'm shaking so much that I can't respond. I try to breathe slower but Eric must sense that I've lost my composure.

'The girls keep checking their phones,' he says at last, 'but no one's posted any updates. Guess we'll find out more tonight. I just hope they catch this psychopath so we can all go back to enjoying the Camino again.'

Estella appears sooner than expected. It would have been too suspicious to stop walking with Eric after what he said about the attack, but I can't believe I've left it this late to escape. It's already seven o'clock and I still haven't booked my bus ticket or found accommodation in Bilbao.

A stone bridge crosses the river into the old town, but Carolina leads the way down a narrow street, following the app on her phone until we find a group of pilgrims waiting outside the albergue. I try to see if I recognise any of them from last night, but then a blue armoured truck with a yellow and red stripe parks next to the building. I strain my eyes until the white lettering on the vehicle becomes legible. 'Policía Nacional.'

'Everything alright, James?' says Eric, calling back to where I've stopped.

I stare at the truck. Whoever's inside must have heard Eric say my name. I tell the Americans I'm going back to the bridge for a photo, but Amy interrupts and says the beds will all disappear unless I join the queue. I try another excuse about buying food but she says I won't find anywhere open on a Sunday evening.

The truck is less than twenty metres away. Who knows who's watching from behind those blacked-out windows.

'Let Red Coat find his bottled water,' says Eric. 'I'll tell the Hospitalero to hold your place. But don't expect a bottom bunk tonight.'

I climb the cobbles to the top of the bridge. The reception must be weak as Alistair's phone still hasn't loaded. I sit on the stone ledge as the river drifts slowly below. Finally, the cracked screen lights up. According to the search results there's only one bus going to Bilbao and it leaves at eight o'clock — one hour's time. I select the option, ready to pay with my card. A curser swirls in the middle of the screen. Again, I look down to the street, hoping the police haven't followed me.

The Americans must have noticed how I bolted at first sight of the truck. Why didn't I just tell them today was my last day on the Camino? I had every intention of saying this earlier but then Eric started talking about the incident, which I haven't stopped thinking about all afternoon. What if something really did happen to Massimo? What if he's the reason why the police are now involved?

The webpage continues to load. My bus has one change and doesn't get into Bilbao until midnight, but I'll sleep in the bus station if I have to and then find somewhere more permanent in the morning. At least by then I'll be miles away from the trail.

The screen refreshes. Red letters appear next to the eight o'clock bus. 'Completo.'

'Hey, James!' shouts a voice below the bridge. Eric leans against his knees catching his breath. 'Other pilgrims just turned up. I convinced the owner to hold your bed, but you need to come right now.'

Eric walks me back to the albergue, talking about some monastery on the other side of town which has a free wine fountain. I can't believe the bus to Bilbao is sold out. I'm almost tempted to go to the bus station and ask if there are any seats still available, but then the blue truck appears at the end of the street.

Sweat runs down my spine. Why did I come back? I could have easily told Eric I'd found somewhere else to stay — anywhere, a hotel if I had to, just so long as it didn't have the Policía Nacional waiting outside.

Up close, the vehicle is enormous. I can hardly breathe as our faces reflect off the glass. I'm convinced the doors will slide open and someone will step out, but somehow, we reach the albergue entrance.

The Hospitalero turns me away but Eric then explains in

Spanish that he's already reserved my bed. The man strikes a match, lights his cigarillo and exhales smoke across the room. 'Twelve euros,' he says, more to Eric than me.

I place a fifty euro note on the desk, desperate to get to the dorm before the police arrive. The man stares at the money and asks if I have anything smaller. I shake my head. He snatches the note and disappears into the back office. Eric laughs at the lack of hospitality and tells me to find him upstairs.

The door opens. I turn around, paranoid that Enzo and Bruno have followed me here, but a pair of black lace-up boots with steel toe caps step inside the albergue. A pistol fills the man's holster, along with a baton which hangs from the other side of his waist. The officer leans against the desk and looks at me through his aviators. 'Credenciales,' he demands.

I flinch.

I can't show the officer my documents. As soon as he sees the stamp dated Thursday 12 June, he'll know I stayed at the first albergue after Massimo's cabin. He won't waste any time calling the Hospitalero. There's not a chance she'll have forgotten how I woke her up late and then walked into the albergue with blood all over my hands. Christ. She even wrote my full name and passport number in her register.

I pretend to look for my Credentials even though they're hidden in the money belt under my shorts. The officer watches as I start removing objects from my backpack. The blood-stained t-shirt appears at the bottom but I hide it under my itinerary. How am I still carrying evidence from the attack? I've had days to throw away that t-shirt, but it's still there, still covered in Massimo's blood, and right under the police officer's nose. I stare at the badge sewn onto his blue uniform. 'Perdido,' I say, shrugging my shoulders.

'Credenciales,' repeats the officer.

My face reflects back in his aviators. Again, I say that I've lost the documents.

The Hospitalero returns from his office. I understand little of their conversation which then comes to an abrupt end. 'The officer needs your Credenciales,' says the owner. 'You cannot stay without documents.'

I hold up my backpack and say I must have left the booklet at the last albergue.

'Where did you stay on Thursday night?' asks the owner.

'Thursday?' I repeat, pretending to think backwards.

'Thursday 12 June,' he adds, breathing cigarette smoke into my face.

'On Thursday, I stayed in… Pamplona.'

'Pamplona?' the officer interrupts. He turns to the Hospitalero and says something I don't understand.

The owner leans over the reception desk. 'Why did you need three days to walk here from Pamplona? It's only two stages away.'

My face starts twitching as though I've strained a nerve. Terrified they're going to search my backpack, I explain how my blisters were so bad that I stayed in Pamplona on both Thursday and Friday night.

The officer puts his phone on the desk and pushes it towards me.

'Where did you stay in Pamplona?' says the Hospitalero.

My hand shakes as I scroll through the images. How is this happening? Did I really think I could get away with lying? Both of them must know I've been dishonest. What if it's a crime to lie to the police?

The officer stares back until I choose the largest albergue from the photographs. 'Aquí?' he asks, covering the photo with his thick thumb.

I nod.

The officer puts the phone on loud speaker.

Any moment now and he's going to find out I lied about my chronology. Even the Hospitalero seemed sceptical when I said I spent two nights in Pamplona to rest my feet. Do albergues even let you stay that long? What if the officer tells me to remove my shoes? I don't have a single blister on my feet.

After the ninth ring the officer finally hangs up.

'Pasaporte?' he says, pointing at my booklet on the floor.

I give it to him with my trembling hand. The officer turns to the photograph page. He studies my details as if memorising them and then slaps the front cover against the desk.

The Hospitalero disappears into the back office with my passport.

The officer watches as I put everything into my backpack, but I ignore his stare, hoping he hasn't noticed Alistair's phone or my Credentials hidden under my shorts.

At last, the Hospitalero returns. 'Photocopy machine broken,' he says. 'I give you passport later.'

I lift the backpack onto my shoulders. It's not as if I'll need my passport until tomorrow. Desperate to act naturally, I stand upright and try to walk towards the staircase.

'James Pollock?' he says, calling me back. 'One more question.'

I can barely swallow the lump in my throat.

'An Italian pilgrim was attacked on Thursday,' the Hospitalero continues. 'He was tall, had a shaved head and was carrying a long walking stick. He was from Roma. Do you remember him?'

My chest is pounding. I pretend to consider the question then finally shake my head. 'No. I met two brothers from Italy, but they were from Napoli, not Roma.'

The officer watches me through his lenses. Fuck. Did I answer too quickly? What if he's already interviewed Enzo, Bruno or anyone else from last night? I was so desperate to know if they'd seen Massimo still alive that I couldn't keep my mouth shut. What if someone has already told the police I saw Massimo on Thursday? What if this police officer already knows that I'm lying?

'Is he alright?' I ask, my voice starting to crack.

The officer takes a hard look at me then speaks to the owner.

'He says that's enough for now,' says the Hospitalero.

I turn to the staircase, trying to ignore the way both of them are still watching me.

'James?' says the Hospitalero, before I reach the first step. 'I think you're forgetting something.'

Hairs climb on the back of my neck. Slowly, I turn around.

'Your thirty-eight euros,' he says, pointing at my change on the desk.

DAY SEVEN

MONDAY 16 JUNE

I t was a mistake to go out last night. I should have
stayed in the albergue but Eric convinced me to join
them for dinner. Still shaken from the police officer's
questions, I was reluctant to go anywhere near the old town,
but the girls ignored my suggestion to find somewhere
authentic and chose a restaurant in the main plaza instead.

Our table at the front of the terrace was the least conspic-
uous place in all of Estella. I spent most of the time paranoid
that Enzo and Bruno would walk past and ask if I'd heard any
more about Massimo, but the brothers thank God never
appeared. By the third bottle of wine, we all seemed to have
been distracted from the attack. Eric took more abuse for
staying in his ensuite tree house, before ordering 'polla' when
the waitress took our orders. Carolina — feet propped up to
rest her blisters — then explained in a fit of giggles how Eric
had asked for dick instead of chicken, which accounted for
the waitress's swift departure. 'Oh shit,' she then said, hiding
behind her menu. 'Just don't look up right now.'

'What?' said Eric, still defensive after his faux pas.

'It's that French guy,' Carolina whispered. 'The one we

met in Zubiri who wouldn't shut up about this being his seventh or eighth Camino.'

'Who, Luc?'

'Ey!' shouted a voice across the plaza. 'It's the Americans.'

Before anyone could respond, a tall wiry man wearing a 'Climb Kilimanjaro' t-shirt pulled up a chair at our table. Ignoring how his knee knocked into mine, he laughed at Carolina's feet, reminding her that there were still seven hundred kilometres to Santiago. I stared at the thin hairs on his chin, waiting for Luc to introduce himself, but then he reached across the table and took Amy's half-eaten mousse, oblivious to the looks of horror which the girls exchanged.

'So did you 'ear the news?' he asked, licking chocolate from the spoon. No one answered, not that this dented Luc's excitement. 'The Italian 'oo got attacked,' he continued, loud enough to attract people on other tables. 'Guess what? They found 'is body.'

'His body?' interrupted Eric. 'What do you mean?'

'Ee's dead.'

My knee crashed into the table. Amy moved back, but a hand caught the bottle of red wine before it rolled off the edge. 'Lucky I'm 'ere,' said Luc, acknowledging me at last. 'Clumsy boy.'

Before I could retaliate and tell him to annoy some other table, Luc took an empty glass and filled it with our bottle. Fingers pinching the base, he swirled the wine, watching our reactions. 'French media is already running the story,' he said, looking straight at me. 'Apparently, the investigators are tracking everyone's phones. And the worse part,' he said, finally turning to the others, is that they're saying it was no accident. But murder.'

I don't know how many seconds passed but the next thing

I remember was Eric asking how the French website had already published their article.

'Do they know anything about the murder weapon?' I interrupted.

I couldn't just sit there in silence, but from Luc's laugh I knew I'd made a mistake.

'Maybe you can tell us?' he said, shaking his head.

My whole face must have turned red, but I didn't break eye-contact as I asked what exactly he meant by his comment.

'English, non?' he replied, scratching the hairs on his chin. 'You must know Agatha Christie.'

His eyes stared into mine until I realised it was a joke. 'But imagine,' he said, turning to the girls. 'Imagine if the killer is — 'ow do you say in English — a psychopathic and wants to —'

'Shut up, Luc!' said Amy. 'You're freaking everyone out.'

'I'm just saying,' he said, smiling across the table. 'Maybe it's another pilgrim. If you wanted to kill someone, then 'ere's a perfect place to do it.'

'Alright Luc,' said Eric, as the girls stood up from their seats. 'I think you've said enough.'

Not long after, the four of us split the bill and walked back to the albergue in silence.

The bed frame creaks as I climb down the ladder. Eric is still asleep, the girls too from the sound of their breathing. I feel around for my clothes and step outside, quietly closing the door. No one else seems to be awake in the albergue, including the Hospitalero who's not at his desk. I turn the key in the main door and step out into the cold air.

The bus station across town is just a small waiting room attached to the side of an old building. The entrance is still locked, even though the first bus to Bilbao leaves in forty minutes. I have to buy my ticket with cash. Thank God I didn't use my debit card on the website yesterday when I sat on the bridge. Whatever happened to Massimo, I can't risk leaving an electronic trail of my escape.

Careful to avoid other pilgrims, I find a small cafe tucked away from the Camino markers. The barman tells me to sit as he prepares the coffee and tortilla. It's a quarter past six on Monday morning. Six days ago, I was still in Gatwick airport, still yet to board my flight. Still yet to throw that metal-tipped staff at Massimo's head.

I start searching for hostels in Bilbao, unable to ignore what Luc said about the police tracking everyone's phones. He probably meant hacking, but who knows how the police operate here. Alistair's phone has a British SIM card which must stand out from all the other numbers in the area. What if the Policía Nacional are already following me through cell towers or satellites? What if they know I've been searching for every available bus route out of this town and plan on heading straight to Bilbao?

The man places my order on the bar, along with two biscuits and a newspaper. I thank him, still staring at the results on the cracked screen. The cheapest room available costs thirty euros a night and the rates double at weekends. I lift the cup to my mouth, just as the newspaper headline catches my eye. Scalding coffee burns my hands. The barman asks if I'm okay, but I can't speak.

'*Muerte en El Camino*,' reads the large black letters on the front page. '*Un Italiano de treinta y dos años de Roma encontrado muerto en peregrinación religiosa cerca de Zubiri. La investigación continúa.*'

Jesus Christ.

Italian. Thirty two years old. Found dead outside Zubiri.

Massimo.

He's dead.

I killed him.

The cafe starts spinning before I can read the next paragraph.

Everyone I've met over the last week is going to read this headline and realise what happened. The albergue owner in St-Jean who took a photocopy of my passport when I didn't have Credentials. The Hospitalero in Zubiri who copied all my details into her register after I turned up late with blood all over my hands. The cult leader at the religious community who washed my t-shirt covered in the same blood; blood which he'd refused to accept had come from the small cut on my shoulder. And that's not to mention Enzo, Bruno and every other pilgrim I met at the fiesta and asked if they'd seen anyone who resembled Massimo.

Fuck. Why did I have to lie and say that Massimo was drunk and stumbling around the edge of that cliff? If just one of them comes forward and reports what I said, then I'm in serious trouble. Between them, these people all know everything; the day I started the Camino, the day I killed Massimo outside his cabin, and every day since when I've tried to hide what happened.

Maybe one of them already went to the police before the newspaper printed the story. Maybe the Policía Nacional already know I lied to them last night when I said I stayed in Pamplona on Thursday. It's too late now to change my story, or God-forbid, actually make a confession. No one is going to believe me if I finally come clean and tell them what really happened — that Massimo made me throw that staff straight at his head.

'Trágico,' says a voice behind me.

I shudder and turn around. The barman leans over my shoulder and stares at the newspaper. 'Muy trágico,' he repeats, mopping up my spilt coffee with a cloth before he returns to the bar.

I leave five euros next to my untouched tortilla and walk outside.

Jesus Christ. What am I going to do? My fingerprints are all over the staff. Why the hell didn't I wipe off my prints instead of just staring down at his body? I gripped my hand so tightly that there's no way I didn't leave perfect prints on the wood. Even if the police haven't yet found the murder weapon, they wouldn't have missed the other evidence I left inside the cabin. That old nail contains traces of my DNA from the blood on my shoulder. And forensics won't miss the marks I left on the door handle when I thought Massimo had trapped me inside. My hands were covered in his blood. They would have made a perfect print on that metal handle.

And my skate shoes. Fuck. The grip on their soles must be all over the trail — and not just the trail, but also all around that cabin where no one else walked except Massimo with his bare feet. There's not a chance anyone covered my tracks or that the wind blew them away. The detectives must have reconstructed my whole route from my footprints alone — and not just where I killed him, but also when I returned later that night to search for his body. No one else on the Camino has been wearing anything remotely resembling my trainers. They've been the only pair I've seen in every albergue boot rack. For a whole week, I've been known as 'the guy in those shoes', at least according to Carolina. I was so proud to be one of the few pilgrims who didn't have a single blister, but everyone out here must know me from my footwear.

How could I have been so stupid? It's bad enough I threw that staff at Massimo's head, but the police must already know that I went into his cabin that night. And why would anyone, let alone a pilgrim walking the Camino, enter that place unless they didn't have something to hide?

What if forensics have matched the blood on the cabin door with the traces of blood I left on the albergue sink in Zubiri or in the cult leader's washing machine? What if they've matched my samples with Massimo's corpse? My hands were all over Massimo's neck when I checked his pulse. It's all incriminatory evidence. The police have everything they need to convict me. It's like they say in all those CSI TV series; science always catches the murderer.

I wander the streets, replaying what happened outside that cabin again and again in my mind until I realise there's only one option available. I have to escape. Right now.

A queue has already formed inside the bus station. Seven people stand in front but only one sales window is open. The clock hands on the wall move closer to seven o'clock. A man in a grey suit bangs on the glass, after which the second booth opens. The line surges forward with no respect for the order of priority. Those previously at the back find their positions improved, much to my infuriation as well as the other customer still waiting second in line at the first window.

Finally, I reach the front. I ask for a ticket on the Bilbao bus that's leaving in three minutes but the employee doesn't understand my accent. I repeat my request in Spanish, but then he leaves the booth, resulting in more huffs from those waiting behind.

A hand touches my shoulder making me flinch. A backpack is visible in the screen's reflection but the Policía Nacional could already have detectives working undercover dressed as pilgrims. I turn around, still clutching the money for my bus ticket.

The man's face has darkened since we met on the first day; a thick beard replacing the grey stubble which had last covered his chin. 'I hope you're not cheating, Saint James?' he says, lowering his backpack.

'Cheating?' I repeat, still in disbelief that Joseph of all people has found me. 'No. I'm just asking for directions.'

The lines on Joseph's forehead thicken. 'Directions in the bus station?'

'Yes. I got lost and couldn't find anyone to ask.'

'Thank goodness for that. You know there are some people who say they walk every day when sometimes they travel by bus. Bad pilgrims,' he says, smiling.

I look away but then a figure appears behind the ticket booth.

'You want to buy a ticket to Bilbao?' asks a voice through the loud speaker.

I tell the employee that she must have made a mistake, but she can't hear over the microphone feedback. 'These are the bus times for Bilbao,' she says, sliding a printed schedule under the window. 'You lost the first bus, but the next one leaves at ten o'clock. Does your friend also need a ticket?'

Again, I explain that I only want directions, after which the next customer pushes forward and takes my place at the window.

'Come on,' says Joseph. 'Let's go.'

My backpack catches on the door as we leave the waiting

room. Unaware that I'm attached to the handle, I pull harder only to tear the strap's stitching. Joseph unhooks me and then leads the way outside.

A coach with a 'Bilbao' sign pulls out of the parking bay, but not before an old lady with a shopping trolley steps in front of the vehicle. The brakes screech and the driver then climbs down the steps to where the lady's waving her ticket at him. Hands on hips, he checks her ticket. The woman protests at having to stow her trolley in the downstairs compartment and so the driver carries the wheeled bag up the steps. Rows of passengers look down at us from behind the tinted windows. The electric doors press together and the driver turns the engine, filling the bay with exhaust fumes. My only means of escape then pulls forward, leaving the bus station ten minutes later than its scheduled departure.

'You know,' says Joseph, staring at the bus as it disappears into the distance, 'it's true that we carry our greatest fears in our backpacks. Sometimes they feel too heavy so we feel like giving up. It's completely natural. Happens to everyone at some stage. But if every pilgrim gave up, no one would reach the end. And isn't that why we are here — to reach the end?'

Why is Joseph doing this? It was bad enough having to listen to his lecture about seven-year cycles, but that was before I met Massimo. Before I killed a man.

'Did you remember to pray for forgiveness, James?'

'What?'

'Don't look so nervous,' he says, placing his hand on my shoulder. 'Alto del Perdón. You know, the big hill after Pamplona?'

Joseph opens his guidebook to a photograph of the same iron sculptures I saw on the day I escaped the religious cult. He translates the paragraph from German, explaining how it's called 'The Mount of Forgiveness'. Joseph starts describing how the figures represent different pilgrims over the ages, but I don't care about mediaeval people who walked the Camino with donkeys and other items to trade.

I can't believe my bad luck. If Joseph hadn't turned up in the waiting room, I'd be sitting on that air-conditioned bus heading straight to Bilbao. I could have left all of this behind. But instead, I couldn't think clearly after seeing the newspaper headline in that cafe.

Muerte en El Camino. La investigación continúa.

'And these,' says Joseph, pointing at two figures on the right of the photograph. 'These are modern pilgrims. Like us.'

He sighs, finally acknowledging my lack of interest.

'I suppose you heard about that Italian,' he says, closing the guidebook. 'I can't believe it either. He was just a young pilgrim, walking the Camino.'

Joseph looks straight at me. 'The police are asking for anyone with information to come forward. I don't suppose you know anything, James?'

I shake my head. I think I'm going to throw up.

'Well then,' he says, tucking the guidebook into his back-pack. 'They say we should walk in pairs — you know, for safety. Do you want to walk together?'

I make an excuse about sending postcards to my family, although I can't help sensing his disappointment.

'Sehr gut,' he says, smiling faintly before finally breaking eye-contact. 'See you in Santiago, Saint James.'

Joseph walks down the street until he disappears back onto the trail.

I drop my backpack and sit on the floor. I can't leave the Camino today. Not now. Not after Joseph caught me trying to buy a bus ticket to Bilbao. If I suddenly disappear, everyone's going to ask why I gave up on the same day Massimo's murder made front page news. It's far too suspicious, especially after Enzo saw my white t-shirt covered in blood; the same t-shirt I still have to get rid of.

A notification sounds from Alistair's phone. Sunlight reflects off the cracked screen but instead of another work email it's a Facebook message — one I've been desperate to receive.

'*Darling, there's something I need to tell you...*'

The message doesn't look real, as though the phone has mistakenly written her name across the screen.

Why has it taken Jessica so long to respond? I've been thinking about her this whole time. She's possessed my every thought, even when I didn't realise I was thinking about her. I've yearned for her attention. For her affection. But now she's finally here.

I stare at the message, desperate to read what she wrote after that first line, but instead I drop Alistair's phone into the bin and walk back towards the trail.

TUESDAY 17 JUNE

W hat the hell was I thinking throwing away Alistair's phone? I know I was in shock after the newspaper headline, but what possessed me to believe that dropping the handset into that bin outside the bus station was ever a good idea? Maybe I felt empowered by rejecting Jessica's message after tormenting myself all week that our affair was over. But thanks to some reckless impulse, I have no way of following the investigation. And I've left more clues connecting myself to the murder.

That phone is full of photographs, most of them selfies with close-ups of my face next to every recognisable landmark on the Camino. Why did I even document my pilgrimage? It's not as though I could have posted anything on my socials without losing the bet with Greg and Dev. Every picture has a date and time stamp. And now, thanks to my stupidity, I've left evidence of all the places I passed before I found that cabin on the cliffside.

Christ. I can't remember if I even switched off the phone. Anyone could have found it by now; the Policía Nacional, Enzo, Eric, Luc or any of the other pilgrims who thought I was acting strangely or had something to hide. It was just a normal street bin with no cover. And it was barely full. I heard the handset hit the bottom. The screen would have been visible to anyone who just leaned over and looked inside.

Fuck. If another pilgrim finds the handset, they'll give it straight to the police. Who wouldn't be suspicious of an expensive phone dumped in a public bin during a murder investigation? It won't require a codebreaker to crack the 'M' password. Anyway, the police must have every method under the sun to unlock a mobile phone. They can probably bypass the whole security system by just plugging it into some app. And when they do, the first picture they'll see will be me.

How could I have been so foolish? I thought going off-grid might ease my paranoia that the police were following me, but without that phone I have no idea what's going on in the hunt for the murderer. Images of Massimo's face could have been released days ago. What if the Hospitalero in Zubiri gave a statement to the police, explaining how I arrived late on Thursday night with my hands covered in blood? What if the cult leader or Enzo told the police about my bloodstained t-shirt? That thing's still hidden in my back-pack because I was too afraid to throw it away yesterday. What if the police find me and then demand to search my bag? I'm literally walking the Camino carrying evidence from the crime scene. A crime involving a dead pilgrim.

The Policía Nacional weren't at last night's albergue, but who's to say they won't turn up again tonight? The murder was the only thing people were talking about in our eighty-person dorm. I even heard a young woman crying on the phone as she told her family she was so frightened she'd booked a flight home. The whole pilgrim community is in shock. And all because of me.

Why am I still here on the Camino? I should have stayed

behind in Estella after Joseph left and then taken the next bus to Bilbao. At least that way I could have flown back to London before facing criminal charges in my own language, under my own country's jurisdiction. But I couldn't think clearly. And instead, I just aimlessly followed the yellow arrows on the trail.

I didn't see Joseph for the rest of the day; not at the wine fountain outside Estella; not in the next village where Luc was showing a group of pilgrims where he'd taken shelter last year when it rained golf-ball sized hailstones; and not at the vending truck in the middle of a field where I found Eric, minus the girls, sitting under a tarpaulin tent with thirty other pilgrims.

The American spent most of our conversation praising the truck owner's entrepreneurship in selling cold drinks in the middle of a field, but after he downed his beer, he suggested walking together for the rest of the stage. Still in shock from the newspaper headline, I said I wanted to spend the day alone, however then he took out his phone and asked for my number. 'But I saw your cell phone the other night,' he said, after I claimed to be walking without a mobile. 'You were on it that whole time in Estella.'

The best excuse I could think of was that I'd thrown away the handset for more isolation on the Camino. 'You ditched your phone?' Eric replied, loud enough for others to hear. 'But that thing must have cost six hundred bucks.'

Paranoid that all those other pilgrims knew I'd abandoned my phone, I tried to explain that the money wasn't important, not that Eric seemed convinced. 'No disrespect, James,' he said, 'but you're not exactly ready for an eight-hundred kilometre trek. I mean your clothes aren't for hiking, that backpack must be wreaking your spine, and those sneakers... well let's just say you've got a reputation for them already.'

My trainers. Fuck, I still had to get rid of them. But until I found a sports shop or a pair of old hiking boots in an albergue, I was going to have to keep walking in those same trainers.

'James?' Eric said loudly. 'Did you hear anything I just said?'

I looked up to see him shaking his head.

'Look,' he then said, lowering his voice. 'I didn't want to ask, but the girls brought it up again this morning, so I have to say something.'

'What is it?' I said, still trying to decide what to do with my trainers.

Eric stared over my shoulder as if he was going to drop the subject, but then he pulled his chair towards me. 'Do you remember when we first met?'

'It was in the plaza outside that church. You told me it was safe to drink from the water fountain and then called me Red Coat.'

'Yes,' said Eric, frowning. 'But we saw you do something before then. You walked over to a bin and took something out of your backpack. It was a t-shirt.'

I flinched.

'The girls were convinced you were going to throw it away,' he continued. 'But when I shouted and you realised you weren't alone, you then put the t-shirt back in your backpack and walked towards us.'

'I don't think I understand,' I said, trying to laugh. 'A t-shirt?'

'It was white. And you haven't worn it since.'

'Oh, that one,' I said, trying to fake realisation. 'What about it?'

Eric's face remained unchanged. 'Why were you throwing it away?'

'This is going to sound strange,' I said, snatching at the first thing that came to mind, 'but that t-shirt had some weird stain on it.'

'That's what the girls said,' Eric interrupted. 'They thought it was blood.'

'Blood?' I said, laughing. 'No, it wasn't that. It was actually something worse.'

'Then what was it?'

I could barely think over my pounding chest.

'It happened when I was showering in one of the albergues,' I said, still trying to decide what to say. 'The t-shirt fell on the floor and when I picked it up, it had this horrible stain on it. I don't want to think what it was,' I added, cringing.

'So why didn't you throw it away?' said Eric, looking at my backpack.

'I did,' I replied. 'I threw it away that night we stayed in Estella.'

'But you didn't throw it away before then? Even though you thought the stain might have been something nasty?'

'I thought I could wash it in one of the sinks. But that was impossible.'

'Why?'

'Because when I took it out of my bag, I realised it was worse than I thought.'

'Okay,' said Eric, nodding. 'It's just that first you throw away your expensive phone and then your t-shirt, so I guess I thought...'

He shook his head before he could finish his sentence. 'I guess we're all on edge after what happened to that Italian.'

I stared across the field, unable to think of anything to say.

'Is everything alright, James? You've been out of it ever since we sat down. Is something else bothering you?'

Again, I lied, saying the heat was probably getting to me.

'Are you sure you don't want to walk together? You don't want to get heatstroke and collapse out here. They're saying it's only going to get hotter.'

'I'm fine,' I said, firmly.

'Okay then,' he said, staring at my trainers before he stood up. 'Maybe see you in Los Arcos. But if not, have a great Camino.'

Thankfully, that was the last I saw of Eric.

———

A footbridge emerges through the trees. Except for the last town with its one main street filled with pilgrims eating lunch, I've managed to avoid everyone else on the trail, but the sound of traffic is a reminder of life beyond the Camino.

A juggernaut stacked with three levels of cars flies past, dislodging air that almost knocks me sideways. I climb higher up the bridge, the yellow fields stretching all the way to the horizon. Transfixed by the speeding vehicles, I stare down until something further along the walkway catches my eye. I approach the flickering pages. It's a pilgrim booklet; one that looks just like mine. Another truck hurtles underneath, rattling the wooden slats. I try catching the booklet but the wind lifts it away from my hand. The pages land on the edge of the bridge, inches from the barrier and the dual carriageway below. With one hand on the rail, I stretch out with my trainer. The booklet slips through the gap, but somehow, I trap the corner under my shoe. I drag my foot backwards, careful not to lose grip of the booklet.

I sit back against the bridge, feeling its vibrations against my spine. The booklet has the same front cover as my one, with 'Credencial del Peregrino' written under a shell next to a bearded pilgrim. I wipe the footprint off Saint James' face and open the first page. The handwriting is barely legible, but I can make out the scrawls of its owner's name. Michael Evans.

Gimmie cigarette, Michael.

Massimo's face flickers in my mind — not the unconscious face I left on the ground, but the one that stared down at me as he pushed the staff into my hands.

A car races under the bridge, its blaring horn changing pitch as it disappears into the distance. According to the Credentials, Michael Evans is English. There are albergue stamps from every stage, including the last one from Los Arcos — the small town I reached last night before I decided to keep walking — dated 16 June. That was yesterday. Michael must have dropped his documents earlier today without realising.

I stare down from the bridge but there are no other pilgrims in the distance. If Michael left Los Arcos this morning, he's probably staying in Logroño tonight. And if there's anything I've learned about albergues, it's that they won't give you a bed without seeing your Credentials.

My intentions to return Michael's documents end the moment I cross the river. Logroño is larger than I expected, its old town dominated by a Gothic cathedral and a long wide boulevard. I try to find a shop selling hiking boots, but it's already getting late and all the albergues have '*completo*' signs on their doors. I eventually find a pensión, but a small room costs four times the price of a private albergue.

Concerned about where I'm going to sleep, I follow signs to the Tourist Information Centre. The man at the main desk calls other albergues listed on my itinerary pages, but again, these are all full. 'What about here?' he says, pointing to the last option on the sheet. The albergue has a religious cross beside its name — the reason I've been avoiding it. He dials the number. The conversation is too fast to understand, but from the smile on his face I know the news is bad.

'Good news,' he says, ending the call. 'They have a bed for you.'

The man circles the albergue's location on a large fold-out map of the city. 'It's an old convent,' he says, handing me the page. 'A donativo. Do you know about these?'

I explain how I've stayed in one of these already, choosing not to mention the cult leader or my measly three euro donation.

'They lock their doors at eight o'clock, so get there quickly,' says the man. 'The nuns are looking forward to your arrival.'

After several wrong turns, I finally reach the building marked on the map. There's no one in the narrow street except for an ugly gargoyle which stares down from its perch. I look for somewhere to dump my white t-shirt until I realise there are probably hundreds of CCTV cameras all around the city. I should have dug a hole earlier when I walked through all those fields. But once again, I lost my nerve.

I walk slowly to the main door. This is the last place I want to be, but it's either here or sleeping rough in the city. I just hope no one else I've met is also staying the night.

The iron knocker breaks the silence. I flinch, haunted by

the sound of the staff striking Massimo's head, until a heavy bolt slides back.

The door opens, revealing a wrinkled face in the entrance. 'Español, Français or English?' asks the old lady, touching a crucifix around her neck. 'Where did you begin?' she asks, continuing in my native language. I ask if she means St-Jean-Pied-de-Port or where I started this morning, but she moves on to the next question. This is the first time I've heard of her religious order, but I lie and say I read about it in my guidebook.

'Enter,' she says, her frail hand beckoning me inside.

The building is eerily quiet except for occasional foot-steps on the marble floor above. The nun lowers herself onto a wooden chair and asks for my Credentials. I reach into my backpack. A smile fills her face as she opens the most recent page. 'I see you stayed with our friends in Los Arcos,' she says, warmth in her voice.

I nod, grateful for the trust I seem to have earned, even though I don't remember anything religious about last night's albergue, which come to think of it was actually in Torres Del Río and not Los Arcos.

'You are walking the Camino for your faith?'

'Yes.'

My lie seems to echo around the hallway. The nun presses her stamp firmly onto the page. 'Vespers start in a few minutes but there's time for a glass of water if you're thirsty, Michael.'

Michael?

I stare at the booklet in her hand. A bell chimes down the corridor but it's too late to explain how I accidentally gave her the Credentials from the bridge instead of my own pilgrim documents.

The nun leads me down a passageway, past dormitories,

reading rooms and a large kitchen where the other sisters are preparing dinner. We reach an arched door at the end of the cloisters. 'The service is just about to start,' says the nun, looking up to me. 'Why don't you join the others at the front?'

Unease fills my body. Not only have I cheated my way inside, but I also lied to the nun about my identity. What if the Policía Nacional turn up and ask for everyone's Credentials and passports? They'll see immediately that my two documents contain different names. It won't take them long to connect my movements to the other albergues where I stayed, all the way back to the cabin on that cliffside.

I walk into the chapel, watching the back of everyone's heads until I'm sure I haven't met them before. There are five pilgrims in the congregation: one resting against the font with his eyes closed, another murmuring what must be prayers, and three men sitting on the front row. I sit alone and watch the dust motes float across the twelve disciples in the stained glass. The first notes of the organ welcome the choir who walk at a glacial pace down the aisle. The organist plays a medley of mostly missed notes until the last sister reaches her pew. The same nun who vetted me earlier then slowly climbs the lectern. Her face barely visible above a hymn book, she clears her voice and releases a warble which threatens to shatter the stained glass. Ten torturous minutes follow, but then, just when it seems that we've endured the worst, the other nuns take to their feet and deliver high-pitched wails which sound more like small animals being neutered with hot irons.

The nun finally descends from the lectern and calls us to the front.

'Now it is your turn,' she says, her eyes moving around the circle — all of us men, and all double her height. 'I would like you now,' she says, enunciating every word, 'to say why you are walking the Camino.'

A shudder fills my spine. Massimo hasn't left my conscience the moment I entered the building. I shouldn't be here. I should never have entered God's home.

'Speak with honesty,' she continues. 'This, after all, is the only thing the Lord asks of his followers.'

No one responds.

'Iñaki,' she says, turning to the thin man who was asleep before the organist woke him up. 'Perhaps you could begin — in English, if you don't mind. Then we can move clockwise around the group.'

There are three others before me: Iñaki, then two-thirds of the group who I assume are friends walking together. Between them, they should cover enough material before it's time for my contribution.

Iñaki pulls down his sleeves so that they cover his hands. Tucking his chin between his shoulders, he starts shaking until he eventually opens his mouth. I stare at his black gums and the gaps between his missing teeth. 'I am here,' he says, scratching his arms, 'because of heroin.'

He looks straight at the nun as though she is the only person present.

'For three months I was dying. But my friends make me go to hospital.'

He pulls on his sleeves. For a brief second, I see peeling scabs of skin until he stretches the jumper back across his arms.

'I was lying on that bed thinking, why am I here, wasting my life, hurting everyone I love? So I got up, removed the tube connected to my body and left the hospital. That was three weeks ago. Today, I am here.'

'Thank you, Iñaki,' says the nun, bowing her head. 'And

what about you?' she says, moving to the next man in the circle, who has a thick jaw and dark eyebrows.

'I'm here,' he replies, 'because I was invited.'

'Invited?' repeats the nun. 'You felt a vocation? A calling from God?'

'No,' he says, pointing to the two men either side of me. 'Their friend dropped out at the last minute, so they asked me to come instead.'

The next person steps into the circle but I can't hear what he's saying. Why am I still here on the Camino? The wager? My lack of purpose? Jessica? None of these seem relevant anymore. How can I pretend it didn't happen? Massimo is dead. A family in Rome is grieving their son. A son who was murdered on a pilgrimage. At some point the police will find out it was me. I'll carry this burden for the rest of my life. It will follow me all the way to the grave.

'Michael?'

I look up. Everyone in the circle is staring at me.

'Don't be afraid to speak,' says the nun. 'Nobody here is going to judge you.'

Massimo's pulped face fills my mind. I bow my head, but this can't stop the tears in my eyes. Someone puts their arm around me, but the contact only increases my desperation.

'Don't worry, dear,' says the nun. 'The Lord forgives all his followers.'

The Lord forgives all his followers.

Except me.

I am beyond forgiveness.

WEDNESDAY 18 JUNE

I wake in the darkness, sheets stuck to my chest. I try to breathe slowly, still haunted by Massimo's eyes as they gaze up at the sky.

How am I still carrying my white t-shirt? After the newspaper headline, I was too frightened to throw it away in case anyone caught me, but I'll be in serious trouble if the police stop me and demand to search my backpack.

Christ. Why didn't I wear my black t-shirt that day or another colour which wouldn't have made Massimo's blood stains so obvious? Eric didn't seem convinced by my lie about dropping it on a filthy bathroom floor. Like he said, why would I have kept carrying a soiled t-shirt if those marks were really what I thought they were? Even from across that church plaza, the Americans thought the stains looked like blood. And they saw me trying to drop it into that bin before Eric shouted at me. Fuck. What if one of the girls reported me to the police? Or Enzo? He knows my t-shirt was smeared in blood. I even admitted that when he caught me inspecting the t-shirt in our dorm. How could I have been so careless? But I can't keep walking with it hidden at the bottom of my back-pack. I have to dump that t-shirt somewhere far away from the trail.

The bedroom door slowly opens. A figure drifts past the foot of my bed. I lay still, pretending to be asleep as the footsteps continue towards the window. The blinds lurch upwards, flooding the room with light. I cover my face and sit up. The nun smiles weakly and turns to the other beds which are all empty. 'Time to get up,' she says, disapprovingly.

The others are downstairs eating porridge and freshly baked bread. Iñaki, I learn from the sister pouring coffee, left before sunrise after a sleepless night. My mind fills with images of all those scabs on his arms until one of the boys asks if I want to join them this morning. I can't think quickly enough to make an excuse. 'Great,' says the tallest man, placing a white Panama hat on his head. 'See you outside, Michael.'

Instinctively, I almost correct his mistake, but something stops me before the others leave the table.

I sit in silence, trying to decide what to do. It's bad enough that I broke down during last night's chapel participation, but it's too risky to tell them my real name now, even if using Michael Evans' Credentials was completely unintentional. Everyone on the trail is talking about the investigation. I can't let the boys know I lied about my identity. That one stamp dated Thursday 12 June in my pilgrim documents proves I was in Zubiri on the night of Massimo's murder. It could pin me straight to the crime. The more I think about it, I was actually fortunate to discover Michael's Credentials. Maybe it wasn't coincidental. Maybe it was serendipitous. There's nothing to stop me from pretending to be Michael, at least until I reach Santiago. No one would ever know — not if I walked ahead of all the other pilgrims who already know me as James.

A bell rings loudly through the cloisters. The same nun who woke me earlier enters the refectory and says it's time to leave. I place twenty euros in the donativo box and pick up my backpack.

Whatever hopes I had of switching shoes end when I see that mine are the last pair in the boot rack. 'You ready?' asks the man with the Panama, as he laces up his hiking boots. 'Nice trainers,' he adds. 'We were wondering if those were yours.'

Outside, the other men are also wearing headwear; a baseball cap and leather cowboy hat complementing the Panama. 'So how far you walking today, chief?' says the man in the cowboy hat, who sounds Scottish.

Unprepared for the question, I say I'm walking the whole stage.

'Aye, us too,' he replies.

'Right,' says Panama, stepping out into the street. 'You ready, Michael?'

We walk all morning, past 'first breakfast', 'second breakfast' and 'elevenses' — expressions I suspect they borrowed from Tolkien. The boys explain how they hadn't planned to spend the night at the convent; their night of tapas and wine also derailed by fully booked albergues and the nuns' eight o'clock curfew. 'But now's not exactly the time, is it?' says the man in the baseball cap. 'Has there been any news since yesterday?'

'Naw,' says Cowboy, shaking his head. 'Last I read, they were still waiting for the autopsy results.'

'So they still don't know who did it?'

My voice seems to hang in the air.

'Stupid question,' I say, staring ahead. 'I hope they catch him soon.'

———

After olives and wine for 'second lunch', I start feeling like an honorary, although hatless, member of their group. Relieved that none of them mention my behaviour in last night's chapel service, I realise my concerns were unnecessary. I'm safer with the Hats instead of walking alone. All the pilgrims we've overtaken since Logroño seem to think we're friends. And if I keep this up, maybe I can hide until the end of the stage where I'll leave the boys behind.

As conversation finally slows, I start wondering which of the Hats I'd choose if I could only walk the Camino with one of them. Cowboy seems most willing to socialise ('nae vino, nae Camino') which doesn't make him the best choice for keeping a low profile. Panama, however, is fluent in four languages, including Spanish, making him invaluable when translating Menu Peregrinos and reserving beds in albergues. But it would be a mistake to drop Baseball, who's not only happy to lead from the front as though he's 'Point' in some old Vietnam War movie, but also surprisingly knowledgeable about the trail considering he was only invited at the last minute.

It's hard to walk with the Hats and not think about Greg and Dev. The three of us have been friends for as long as I can remember. My adolescence is literally inseparable from theirs. And yet unlike the Hats, the thought of walking the Camino with my best friends is the last thing I'd want to do. Greg would spend hours boring everyone about his big accounting career and Dev would be so stressed about losing clients that he'd spend the whole pilgrimage on his hands-free, keeping tabs on whoever was in charge of his property business while he was out of the country. These five hundred miles would only confirm what the three of us already know but are too afraid to admit. That maybe we're just not close anymore.

I can't pinpoint when our friendships started to fray. Even after A-levels when Greg's three As put my academic results to shame, we still visited each other's universities every year. Of all those trips, nothing beat the first time Dev and I went to Cambridge. We hadn't even seen Greg's eighteenth-century College or the bar downstairs before he revealed the plan for the weekend. 'Here,' he said, throwing three black cassocks onto his bed. 'I spoke with the College Chaplain and he said we could borrow these. But get changed now. We're leaving in fifteen minutes.'

There was barely time to process what was happening as we thumbed down our first car in the rain. 'So where to, gents?' said the bloke, grinning as the three of us squashed together on the back seats. 'Or should I say *fathers*.'

Greg's explanation that it was a College-sponsored fancy dress hitchhike to Amsterdam was quickly interrupted. 'Nah lads,' said the man. 'You can do better than that. This ain't some fancy Cambridge University ball or whatever you lot do. Dress it up, literally,' he said, laughing. 'Say you're trainee priests, travelling to some religious convention. But just don't say Amsterdam, for fuck's sake.'

Roused by our travelling salesman's pep talk, we went all in with the next stranger who picked us up. 'I know one ought not to ask questions of a personal nature,' said our elderly driver, whose three-metre eyesight should have prevented him from owning a licence or driving on a motorway in the dark, 'but what exactly inspired you all to join the clergy?' Dev's description of the moment he accepted 'the call' prompted a period of silence from the old man, who might have briefly fallen asleep at the wheel. 'I must hand it to you,' he said, swerving around the car in front. 'It's admirable that three men your age have committed themselves to the Lord's work so early in life. Oh look,' he said, pointing at the next motorway sign. 'That's the turn off for Canterbury. We can pull off here if you want to visit your boss.'

Any guilty consciences from deceiving our last driver ended when he left us at the ferry terminal. 'Fuck,' said Greg, taking everything out of his backpack. 'I don't believe it. I must have left my fucking passport behind.'

The reality of what he'd done was still sinking in as we reached the front of the queue. 'And there's no way you can make an exception?' Greg asked the employee behind the desk. 'I'm afraid not, sir,' the man replied, staring at our cassocks. 'Every passenger must show their passport before boarding the ferry. It's the law.'

Desperate that our whole trip was about to end in Harwich, Greg asked to speak to the Manager. 'You can try,' said the official. 'But she'll only give you the same answer.'

Dev and I held back as our robed friend explained the situation to the Manager who'd come downstairs from the main office. 'Hurry the fuck up!' said Greg, running back as he straightened his dog collar. 'We've got five minutes before the boat departs.'

The overnight ferry descended into carnage after we found other students from Greg's College, including John Lennon, Julius Caesar and Cleopatra. We spent most of the night between the dancefloor and the toilets, finishing the bottle of Jägermeister that Dev had smuggled onboard, much to the barman's confusion at how we'd got so drunk on free glasses of water. Hungover and seasick after a sleepless night, we were too tired to hitch when we docked in Hoek, so we jumped on the train to Amsterdam and started our celebrations early.

Who knows what the other visitors in the Sex Museum thought when they saw three men of the cloth perusing the most vulgar pornography any of us had ever seen, or what was going through the waiter's mind in The Grasshopper coffee shop when he served us space cakes with complimentary joints 'on the house', which he said raising his eyes to the ceiling, but after wandering around all afternoon we finally realised we hadn't booked any accommodation. Hours later, and still no closer to finding beds for the night, we found Julius Caesar in the Red Light District, who was too stoned to explain where he'd lost Cleopatra and his missing purple cape. Christ-like in all white, he led us, his three disciples, through Plaza Dam to the last hostel in the city. Preparing for a night on the street, we watched Jesus speak to the person at the desk, behind which hung an enormous cross. 'Good news,' said our saviour, confirming that it was indeed a Christian youth hostel. 'There's room at the inn.'

What followed was mostly a blur, but we did all make it to the Rijksmuseum the next morning. Miraculously, everyone else from Greg's College was also at the rendezvous point, including Cleopatra, who'd spent the night with King Arthur, much to Caesar's disappointment. Greg, still dressed in his cassock and dog collar, was unusually quiet as we boarded the coach back to Cambridge, but he became visibly anxious as we approached the ferry terminal.

'Now then,' said the driver's voice on the microphone, after we stopped unexpectedly on the side of the road. 'Dutch customs all know where you lot have been, so if you've got anything in your pockets you shouldn't have, then now's the time to get rid of it.'

Most of the bus disembarked to dispose a river of drugs down the drain, but Greg's anxiety about his missing passport had escalated. Dev and I tried to calm him down, telling him to say that he just lost it in Amsterdam, but Greg's face had turned red. 'You don't get it, you morons,' he interrupted. 'They're going to kick me out of Cambridge. And this will be on my record for ever. I'll have to explain it at every job interview. My whole career is fucked.'

Finally, we managed to make him explain why he was so distressed. 'It's what I said to the ferry Manager in Harwich,' said Greg, shaking his head. 'That fucking travelling sales-man. I should never have listened to him.'

'What did you say?' said Dev, getting impatient.

'I told the ferry Manager I was starting my priesthood at the Vatican,' said Greg, trembling. 'And that if she didn't let me onto the boat, I would never fulfil my life's vocation. Fuck,' he said, punching the seat in front. 'She said she'd put a note on her file to pass on to Dutch customs. They know everything about me; my name, address, university, every-thing. What am I going to say when the custom officials realise that I'm here, hungover on a coach travelling back to Cambridge, instead of taking my vows with the Pope?'

'Right everyone,' said the driver, clearing his voice on the microphone. 'We have two guards who are going to check all your documentation. And they've asked for you to remove any fancy dress covering your faces.'

We watched from the back seats as the uniformed offi-cials boarded the coach. They moved slowly down the aisle, checking everyone's passports. I felt Greg shaking as the men approached, but then they stopped next to a bloke with hair below his shoulders who was carrying an old sleeping bag.

'You,' they said, clearly taking a dislike to his appearance. 'Get off the bus with your bags.'

The whole coach watched the officials search the man outside. Greg was convinced the hippie wasn't even a student, let alone someone from his College, but then the passenger finally returned with his sleeping bag under his arm. The driver then received the signal and we drove onto the ferry, Greg's degree and future career still safely in-tact.

I can't imagine my friends doing anything fun these days. It's almost as inconceivable as realising I've actually killed someone.

The next time I see them will probably be during visitation hours, providing I can serve my prison sentence back home. And when I finally get released, Greg and Dev will have long moved on and probably started families of their own. We'll have nothing left in common, except who we used to be.

Late in the afternoon, an abandoned sofa turns up on the trail. The Hats, it transpires, have amassed a following on Instagram with their 'Camino shot of the day', which has so far included them running with their backpacks from plastic bulls in Pamplona and an Abbey Road-indebted photo of them walking between the iron figures at Alto del Perdón.

Cowboy orders everyone into position as he balances his phone on the backpack. Concerned about them having a record of my face, I say that I don't want to crash their photograph, but Panama is too busy listing all the reasons why we shouldn't sit on the sofa, including fleas, pensioners' incontinence, and everything else festering inside the fabric. 'Come on, Michael,' shouts Cowboy, running back into the frame. 'You're one of us, today. It's on a ten second timer.'

I reluctantly move into the gap they've saved for me.

The light flashes less than ten feet from where we're sitting. It's too late to avoid the photograph now.

'Five seconds,' says Cowboy.

I shouldn't be here. I've been lying to the Hats all day, flinching whenever they call me Michael — the same name I gave Massimo when he demanded to know my name outside his cabin. It's only a matter of time before the boys find out I lied. This is all my fault. I could have easily corrected the nun last night when she first called me Michael. All I had to say was that I'd found those documents outside Logroño and that my real name was James. But instead, I let the paranoia get the better of me.

'Three seconds.'

I have to lose the Hats. There are too many pilgrims who already know my real name. What if someone's at the next albergue when I arrive with my new friends? It won't take long for the Hats to realise I've been lying about my identity. That I'm a fraud.

'Ready?'

And a murderer.

The phone flashes.

Cowboy checks the photograph. Our faces are all visible, mine even more so without the protection of a hat. Within seconds the photo is posted online.

'So, Michael,' says Cowboy, after a round of notifications fill his phone. 'We're going to stop in the next town. And seeing as we've hit it off, we wondered if you wanted to join us for the week, or maybe all the way to Santiago.'

'Obviously we'd find you a hat,' adds Baseball. 'Maybe a

sombrero, or one of those flat caps from Italy. What are they called again?'

'Coppolas,' interrupts Panama.

'Aye, like the film director. Who was Al Pacino's character in The Godfather?'

'Michael Corleone.'

'Michael!' says Baseball, punching my arm. 'Just like you.'

'Thanks guys,' I say, trying to ignore the pounding in my chest. 'I really appreciate it, but I think I'll just walk alone.'

Cowboy frowns. 'We've almost finished the stage, pal, so we might as well stay in the same albergue.'

'Actually, I'm just going to keep walking.'

I check my itinerary pages, trying to ignore the awkward silence.

'Well, it would be a shame to lose you,' says Panama, 'but I understand if you need to crack on. We can add each other on Instagram and stay in touch that way.'

'Thanks, but I don't have Instagram.'

'You don't have Insta?' interrupts Cowboy. 'You're not one of those people who have something to hide, are you?'

I try to laugh this off.

'Then what about your mobile number?'

'Look guys, I didn't bring my phone, so let's just see what happens.'

'Fine,' says Cowboy looking away. 'Nae pressure. Do what you have to do, Michael.'

Not long afterwards, I say goodbye to them at the next bar.

I walk on until the last town fades in the distance. The white t-shirt feels like it's burning a hole in my backpack, but I can't find anywhere to hide it. And I'm nervous after my awkward goodbye with the Hats. They were clearly suspicious of my disappearing act, especially after we were getting on so well. What if they mention me to another pilgrim who knows my real name? I already stick out a mile in these trainers I'm still wearing. I can't afford any more mistakes; not with the murder investigation which is impossible to keep up with without Alistair's phone. Michael Evans' Credentials will only create more problems. I can't use his documents again. I have to go back to being James.

Signs for an ecological albergue appear on the trail. It's not listed on my itinerary and the location, tucked away down a pot-holed lane thick with brambles certainly adds to its appeal. I've walked further than today's official stage, so with any luck I'll be ahead of all the other pilgrims I've met so far.

I follow the handmade green arrows to a door behind a tall fence. I turn the handle and peer inside. Hammocks sway between apple trees, blankets lining the well-kept grass. Some pilgrims sit cross-legged playing guitars, while others chase a frisbee, none of whom I recognise from before.

'Welcome,' says a woman wearing orange striped trousers. She smiles with perfect teeth and leads me towards a staircase covered in blossom. I follow her upstairs, dragging the strings of the beaded door with my backpack so that they clatter into each other.

Meditation music fills the reception which also doubles as a kitchen where other pilgrims are peeling potatoes in the sink. Beanbags line the floor, some of their occupants reading, while others snooze under patchwork quilts.

The Hospitalero, a man in his late-fifties wearing a loose vest, cut-off shorts and a red bandana, appears from behind the reception desk. He reaches out with his bracelet-filled wrist and grips my palm. The smile under his bleached hair, however, drops as he studies my face.

'Hey, Michael?' says someone across the room.

I flinch and turn around. It takes a few moments to place the skinny man curled up in the corner. We barely spoke after the chapel service, but I couldn't not be moved by what he said about using the Camino to overcome his heroin addiction. This place is miles away from the convent. How did he walk all this way? He's literally skin and bones. Trust my luck to run into him again. I was ready to drop Michael's name, but with Iñaki here, that's no longer an option. Reluctantly, I wave back across the room.

The Hospitalero asks for my Credentials, so I take out Michael Evans' documents. 'How do you know Iñaki?' he asks, studying my previous stamps.

'We met yesterday in Logroño,' Iñaki interrupts.

'Okay then, *Michael*,' says the Hospitalero. 'There's free yoga in the garden and a communal dinner at eight. It's fifteen euros for the night. You're downstairs in bed fourteen.'

He returns the Credentials, pinching the corner of the booklet as I try to take it back.

Laundry is as good as any excuse to avoid the free yoga. I dump everything into the garden bucket, including my Lycra shorts which turn the water black. Trying to ignore how the Hospitalero stared at me, I hand-wash my clothes, which is surprisingly therapeutic until I remember the white t-shirt at the bottom of my backpack.

The clothes line is almost full so I hang my wet items in the few places still available. But as I reach up to peg my shorts, I see the same pair of lacy red underwear that Jessica was wearing that night I went back to hers. Fuck. Alistair's professional misconduct hearing. It was on Monday — two days ago. What if he pleaded guilty to stealing the barrister's suitcase and all those confidential documents? I have no way of reading his emails and finding out what happened. What if he's already been struck off or prosecuted as the other lawyers threatened? Despite our difficulties, he's still my brother. I still love him, even if I stupidly slept with his girl-friend. And what about our parents? How will they cope if their golden child has been arrested? How will they manage with both sons behind bars?

I look back to the garden, wary that someone might have seen me staring at the underwear, but they're all too busy wrapped up in blankets and making OM sounds in the grass.

The communal meal is surprisingly tasty even though it's mostly seeds and vegetables. The Hospitalero seems intent on gazing at me from across the table, so I pretend to be part of the main conversation. I feign interest as the woman in orange trousers discusses the three stages a pilgrim has to endure before reaching Santiago: first the physical endurance ('the feet'); secondly, the inner struggle ('the head'); and then finally surrendering your emotions to come through to the other side ('the heart', which she says clutching her chest). Everyone around me seems convinced by the theory, but if anything, I've been fighting all three stages together ever since I killed Massimo.

'And that's why we're all one big Camino family,' says the woman, linking the tips of her fingers together. 'Because we're all enduring the same struggle.'

It's already late when dinner finishes. I head back to the room, but then remember how the dew soaked my clothes last time I left them hanging outside overnight. Even in the dark, I can tell the clothes line is mostly empty. I feel my way alone the line until I reach the end, still one item short. I check the bundle again, but my black Lycra shorts are still missing. Apart from the skinny jeans I'm wearing, those shorts are the only walkable clothes I have to wear from the waist down.

I walk back along the line, but my shorts are definitely not there. I know I hung them next to the lacy red underwear. Come to think of it, I even borrowed half of her clothes peg. Fuck. Whoever owns the underwear must have accidentally taken my shorts. I think back to all the pilgrims at dinner, trying to decide who would have chosen such a risqué pair for a five-hundred mile trek. At least twenty-five people sat at the table, more than half of them women. There was the mother and daughter from Arizona, both of whom were attractive, although I doubt either of them would air their sexy laundry in public. No, the red lingerie has to belong to someone walking alone; someone who's definitely up for some debauchery, or not fussed about hiking in tight underwear.

I return to the dorm, anxious to find my shorts. Everyone is already asleep, except Iñaki, who's reading a few bunks further along. 'Come with me,' he says, after I explain what happened. 'I got all my clothes from lost property. If your shorts aren't there, we'll find something else instead.'

The reception area is dark except for a lavender-scented candle burning on the balcony. Iñaki hobbles up the stairs and opens the beaded door. He switches on the light. A naked couple lying on the far beanbag grab their clothes and disappear before I can ask if they've seen my lost shorts.

Iñaki is still laughing about the used condom on the floor when he finds a wicker basket full of lost property. He removes all the objects, including a torn Machu Picchu t-shirt, a Camino guidebook from the eighties with half its pages missing, earplugs, a pocket knife, and a pair of worn hiking boots which he puts to one side, but no black Lycra shorts.

Iñaki suggests writing a note asking everyone to check their backpacks before they set off in the morning. He then leans against the desk and starts scratching the scabs on his arms.

'What you said last night was really inspiring,' I say, looking up from my handwritten note. 'I can't imagine what you're going through. But you're doing so well.'

He shakes his head. 'Sometimes it feels like hell, but we all have our struggles, don't we. What about you, Michael?'

'Me?' I ask, distracted from the words I was trying to write. 'What do you mean?'

'Your struggles.'

My hands are shaking so much that I drop the pen. 'I don't understand what you're asking.'

Iñaki crosses his arms and looks straight into my eyes. 'Sorry, Michael. I know it's private. But from your reaction last night in the chapel, it was obvious you have trauma in your mind. That you're carrying something heavy. Do you want to talk about it?'

'No,' I say quickly, before lowering my voice. 'It's just something from back home. Nothing serious.'

Iñaki stares back. He must suspect something's wrong. Or that I'm obviously in denial.

'A few days ago,' he says, again scratching his arms, 'I saw this blind pilgrim walking the Camino. She had a thin white pole but couldn't see exactly where she was going. Now that's amazing. You finished your note? I think I saw a message board somewhere around here.'

Iñaki walks behind the reception desk but then stops

abruptly. 'Hey, Michael,' he says, his voice now a different tone. 'Come look at this.'

I follow him to the message board. A printed page is pinned to the cork, the Policía Nacional's emblem at the top of the page. The notice is in Spanish, below which there is a black and white photograph of a passport picture.

'He looks just like you,' says Iñaki, turning back to compare my face. 'Except his name is James Pollock.'

I stare transfixed at the notice. From what I can translate, it gives my full name, date of birth, and a description of my appearance, including height and hair colour.

Jesus Christ. No wonder the Hospitalero was suspicious when I arrived. He would have seen my face before I even stepped foot inside his albergue. Maybe he spoke to the police officers when they came to issue the wanted notice. If Iñaki hadn't been in the reception room earlier and called me Michael, I would have given the Hospitalero my real Credentials and told him my real name. I would be in police custody this very moment, being interrogated over Massimo's death, and probably confessing to murder.

'So he's definitely not you?' says Iñaki.

I shake my head, incapable of any other response.

'Weird,' he says, leaning closer at the notice. 'He's like your doppelgänger. Your evil twin.'

I flinch from Iñaki's short laugh. It's difficult to tell if he's challenging me, or if it's just his twisted sense of humour.

The Hospitalero must know I lied about my name. Even from the black and white photocopy, the image is undeniably me — James Pollock. What if he's already notified the police and told them I'm here?

'What does it say?' I ask, trying to sound composed as I stare at my face on the page.

'Not a lot,' Iñaki replies. 'Just that the Policía Nacional are looking for him.'

Iñaki yawns and turns away from the message board. He stares at the pocket knife on the desk and steps back, as if realising there's a weapon in the room.

'Time for bed,' he says, still avoiding eye-contact.

The warmth has left his voice. He wasn't tired before. He said he couldn't sleep. That he was an insomniac. He doesn't want to be alone with me. The murderer.

Iñaki walks to the door, forgetting the hiking boots he left on the desk.

'Good night, Michael. I hope you find your shorts.'

THURSDAY 19 JUNE

The Policía Nacional know I killed Massimo. They must have interviewed the Hospitalero in Zubiri. What if forensics have matched the blood in her sink with my DNA from the cabin? The detectives would have already reconstructed all my movements at the crime scene. They must know that I lied to the police officer in Estella when I said I spent two nights in Pamplona. The police will have inspected all the pilgrim registers. It won't have taken them long to discover that James Pollock never stayed in any of the Pamplona albergues on Thursday 12 June — the last day anyone saw Massimo.

I dress quickly in the dark, careful not to wake anyone. My jeans feel tight but I'll soon find a bus stop or another way to escape the trail. At least the dorm leads straight out into the garden.

Light filters through the gaps in the balcony floorboards overhead. Someone must be awake; probably the Hospitalero still wearing his ridiculous bandana. If he contacted the police and told them I was here, they would surely have arrested me in the middle of the night. Either that or they're waiting for me outside.

I step quietly under the balcony, wary of casting my shadow across the grass. The gate is twenty metres away. If it's locked, I'll jump the fence and hope there aren't any brambles on the other side. I look up one last time at the balcony and then set off across the garden.

'Michael?' calls out a voice from above.

Hairs climb the back of my neck. I stop and turn around. The Hospitalero is standing with both hands on the balcony ledge and gazing down at me. 'Come upstairs,' he says.

This is it, the moment it all ends. The Policía Nacional must be there as well. They'll only need a few seconds to read my rights before they lead me away in handcuffs.

I'm almost halfway to the gate. If I run now, I might still be able to escape. But what if it's not too late to explain what really happened — that Massimo made me throw that staff at him.

My legs are shaking so much I need the banister to climb the stairs. The lavender incense drifts across the balcony. I push through the beaded door, scattering black flies which were asleep on the strings. The reception area is empty except for the Hospitalero who's lying on a beanbag in the corner. 'I think you've forgotten something,' he says, gesturing towards the notice board.

'What?' I ask, my voice trembling.

He lights a cigarette, letting the smoke curl from his mouth. 'Go see for yourself.'

I can barely cross the room. All the other pilgrims must have seen my wanted notice yesterday. I'm amazed only Iñaki asked about it.

'Not there,' says the Hospitalero, annoyed at how I've strayed into the private area. 'The main desk.'

A sheet of paper rests on top of an item folded so neatly that I don't recognise it as mine. It takes both hands to hold the handwritten note.

'*Sorry for taking your shorts. My bad. Kisses Sky xx.*'

I walk towards the door holding my black Lycra shorts. I can feel the Hospitalero's eyes boring into my back. I have to get out of here. Right now.

'By the way,' says the Hospitalero, gazing at the notice board before turning back to me. 'Please remind your boyfriend that lost property is for people who've lost their possessions, not a place where they can take whatever they want.'

I open the beaded door, but not before the man clears his throat.

'And next time, please throw away your condom so someone else doesn't have to. That's my room over there,' he says, nodding at the far corner. 'I hear everything.'

'Yes,' I say. 'It won't happen again.'

The Hospitalero leans back into the same beanbag where last night's couple were having sex. 'Good,' he says, stretching his hands behind his head. 'Buen Camino, James.'

I turn back, clattering the beads in the door. 'Michael,' I say, emphasising the two syllables. 'My name is Michael.'

'Of course,' he says, still watching my face.

I get as far as the bottom step before I have to sit down. Fucking hell. No wonder he was staring across the table last night. He must have recognised me from my photograph on the police's wanted notice.

My foot kicks something hard under the bench. I reach down and find the same hiking boots from the lost property basket. Iñaki must still be here.

I untie my trainers.

The hiking boots are one size too big and so worn out that

they barely hold together, but I have to cover my tracks. How have I taken this long to change shoes? I should have done this the moment I left Zubiri, long before the detectives found my footprints around that cabin. And yet I wasted all that time, hoping he wasn't actually dead. Even after the newspaper headline, I still couldn't think clearly enough to make a plan. But now, a whole week after Massimo's murder, I finally have replacement shoes.

I hide my trainers behind the wooden boot rack. It's a narrow space, but I push the shoes into the gap until they disappear from sight. I then move quickly across the garden, crushing the wet grass with my new hiking boots until I reach the main gate.

The sun beats down from the sky. I have to escape but I'm stuck in the middle of these fields. That ecological albergue wasn't even on my itinerary, so if the Policía Nacional drove all the way out there with my wanted notice, they would have targeted all the main albergues as well. Christ. My face must be plastered over every notice board on the Camino. Iñaki recognised me straight away from the black and white photograph, so there's nothing to stop Enzo, the Americans, Joseph or anyone else I've met from doing the same. The Hats must have seen my face on the notices. Maybe they've already told the police how they spent the whole of yesterday with me on the trail and how I was calling myself 'Michael'.

Fuck. The photograph they took on the abandoned sofa. I was the only person not wearing a hat — the only person whose face was visible. If the police see that photograph, they'll have a direct match. The Hats know everything about me: where I grew up, my last job, and where Alistair lives in London.

Too much time has passed to hand myself in. If I'd gone to the Policía Nacional sooner, I might have had a chance to explain what really happened. But that's not an option now I'm a wanted man. I'll never clear my name without Massimo here to admit that he made me throw that staff at his head.

I have to leave the Camino before the police find me. But even if I do escape and go into hiding, they'll turn their search into a full-scale manhunt. Fleeing the country will be impossible with all the airport security. And even if I do manage to get home — by boat, car or any other means — who says I'll be safe there? The Spanish police could already be working with British intelligence. What if that image of my face has been released in the media back home, explaining how I'm wanted in connection with the murder of an Italian pilgrim on the Camino? Without Alistair's phone, I've completely cut ties with the outside world.

I can't carry this burden much longer.

Even if Massimo did threaten me, I still killed him.

I have to speak to someone; someone who isn't going to flip out when I confess what happened outside that cabin. I've got to give my side of the story before the evidence starts mounting against me. But even if I did have a phone, who would I call? There's not a chance I'd contact Greg or Dev; not after their pep-talk ridiculing what I thought I'd achieve by walking the Camino. Alistair's got enough on his plate with the professional misconduct accusation. That leaves just one other person. The same woman whose face refuses to leave my mind —

Gunfire throws me to the ground.

White noise rings in my ears. I lie face-down, my chest pounding against the soil until it finally seems safe to move. I raise my head through the corn. Two cartridges explode in the sky, sending me back to the ground.

What the fuck is going on? Did I lose the yellow arrows or take a wrong turn? Or are they aiming at me? What if the Hospitalero only let me go this morning because the police already knew my location? What if they lured me into this field instead of arresting me in the albergue? Out here, hidden from view, they can do whatever they want with me. And I'm still carrying that white t-shirt.

Scrambling to take off my backpack, I unclip the straps and reach inside. More shots fire overhead from what sounds like different parts of the field. The police officer in Estella was carrying a pistol, but who's to say they don't have shotguns? My hands are shaking so much I can barely reach into the bag. I have to move quickly, either forwards through the crops, or back to where I came from. But I can't hide the t-shirt here. Whoever's standing above the corn would have marked my location the second I dropped to the ground.

Adrenaline carries me through the field. With the backpack pulled tightly around my shoulders, I crawl on my elbows, careful not to reveal my position. The straight lines between the crops seem to leave me exposed, but I convince myself that the corn is still hiding me. My arms tire, my wrist too from clenching onto the t-shirt. I'm caked in mud, but I haven't moved far away enough to bury the evidence.

Black boots step into the channel ahead. I freeze. The footsteps change direction and start walking towards me. I close my eyes, pretending this isn't happening, but then the boots stop inches away from my face. They're neither polished or steel toe capped like the officer's pair in Estella. A glove reaches down through the corn. There are holes in the fingers revealing calloused skin underneath. The hand flattens, ordering me to keep low. Ants scurry around the laced boot. I wait for the next shot — the one that's intended for the back of my head. The silence lasts for ever, but then the hand pulls back the stalks of corn, revealing blue sky overhead. 'Levanta,' says a deep voice.

I emerge from the field.

The man stands with a rifle cocked over his arm. He's old enough for wrinkles across his jowls. I try to speak, but his hand stops my words. He turns to another man across the field who's also dressed in tweed. The shotgun follows its target across the sky. It fires, scattering a flock of birds overhead. The silence is so perfect it sings. Something heavy falls to the ground. Lines hurtle towards us, parting the crops like torpedoes until three Springer Spaniels race past, leaping through the corn as they track the scent.

The old man's eyes remain fixed on my face until they move down to the white t-shirt in my hand.

'Santiago de Compostela?' I ask, still trembling.

He points across the field to where a red backpack is just visible in the distance.

I retreat as another gunshot hits the sky.

Afternoon arrives before I find a hiding place for the t-shirt. My water ran out hours ago but I still haven't seen a fountain. The air is stifling hot. And I already have blisters on my heels from the hiking boots. Exhausted and hungry, I take shelter under the shade of a tree and lie against the bristly grass with my head against the backpack.

Something bites my shoulder. Then again, harder. I pull off my t-shirt and start whipping my back until whatever it was drops off or flies away. I must have slept for an hour — long enough for the sky to grow overcast. Again, I look for a place to bury my t-shirt, but the ground's too hard to dig a hole and there's nowhere discrete to hide it.

I have to keep walking. I have to get away from the trail.

The village at the end of the stage is filled with pilgrims. The main street doesn't have any bus stops or signs for public transport. I can't ask someone in a restaurant or bar in case they recognise me from my wanted notices. If the Policía Nacional aren't already here, it won't be long before a blue armoured truck arrives.

Desperate from thirst, I leave the street, hoping to find somewhere to fill my bottle. An open door leading into someone's kitchen almost tempts me to steal tap water, but I can't risk being seen.

A water fountain appears ahead. I drop my backpack, ready to put my mouth under its spout, but then I'm overcome by an urge to scratch my back. My fingers can't reach all the bites, but the ones I manage to touch only intensify the itching. I give up and walk towards the fountain.

Holding my empty bottle, I plead for cold water or something uncontaminated to quench my thirst. I press the button. Nothing. I push harder, but the button gets stuck and refuses to come out. Fuck. Some idiot must have disconnected the fountain from the mains.

I kick a stone across the street. It clatters into a red car with a body kit so low it's almost touching the road. Someone yells at me from a top window. I walk on, past the back of the buildings, until the next yellow arrow points away from the village.

A huge black cloud fills the horizon. While intimidating, it just sits there as though it hasn't noticed me. For a whole hour, the cloud is the only thing I experience. Nothing moves, not even the breeze which has forgotten how to blow. It's eerily quiet without the birds. But then comes the first rumble. A gust of wind sends a shiver down my arm. Within seconds, the temperature drops. A flash fills the sky. Thunderclaps follow. The storm has found me.

The downpour begins before I reach the next settlement. A steel fence saves me from a German Shepherd, but the animal refuses to stop barking as he throttles himself against his chain. I almost break my neck slipping on the wet paving stones, but I move quickly, searching for any form of cover.

A small albergue appears through the rain. The bites on my back seem to have multiplied and all I can think about is burning them under a hot shower. I walk inside through a narrow reception room, checking for any police notices containing my name and passport photograph. The communal kitchen is empty, so I put my head under the tap and gulp more water than I can swallow, until a loud voice demands what I'm doing here.

The Hospitalero points at all the mud I've brought into his clean albergue. I apologise and take off the hiking boots. Paranoid he's seen my face from the wanted notices, I comb back my wet hair and ask if he has a private room. He checks his register, dropping the frown on his face. I'm in luck. The room costs five times the price of last night's bed, but it's the only way I can avoid other pilgrims staying here.

'The bathroom is at the end of the hall,' says the Hospitalero, staring at my wet clothes. 'Please wash before you lie on the bed.'

The itching intensifies. There's no mirror in my cupboard-sized room but my hand finds at least twenty welts on my back which has already swollen up.

Voices fill the corridor. I wait for them to pass, then step out into the corridor hoping there's still hot water in the showers. A door to my left opens unexpectedly, revealing a man covered in tattoos with a towel around his waist.

'Ey, Bruno?' says a voice behind him.

Jesus Christ. The Italian brothers. They're here, staying in the room next door.

I run back to my room, almost slipping on the wet floor.

I listen through the wall, but no one says my name. Thank God they didn't see me. I'm still carrying my white t-shirt; the same t-shirt covered in Massimo's blood stains which Enzo saw a whole week ago on the night of the fiesta.

I'm trapped in this tiny room. I can't even use the toilet, let alone the communal kitchen where all the other pilgrims are preparing food. I haven't eaten all day, but the itching from the bites is worse than the pain in my stomach. What the hell bit me under that tree? If it was venomous, the poison must have already entered my bloodstream.

I lie face-down against the bed springs, listening to the rain against the window until my eyes can't stay open any longer.

DAY ELEVEN
FRIDAY 20 JUNE

My back is so raw it feels like all the skin has been stripped away. The urge is too much to resist. Again, I dig deeper with my fingernails, convinced that the itching will stop if I can just get under enough skin.

'Che cazzo!' shouts a voice through the wall.

Fuck. The Italians are still here; the boys whose fellow countryman I murdered outside that cabin.

Enzo must have told his brother about my white t-shirt. It's not exactly something you forget — how there's a guy walking the Camino with a t-shirt covered in blood right in the middle of a murder investigation.

The brothers must have seen my face on the police notices. Maybe they're responsible for my manhunt. Enzo directly challenged me when I said Massimo was drinking wine that afternoon. He even asked where the bottle had come from considering there were no shops on that part of the trail. And then I stupidly said I was worried he might have fallen off the edge of that cliff. Why would I have had any reason to worry about Massimo unless I had something to hide? Enzo must have connected all the dots. And if he hasn't yet reported his suspicions, he and Bruno will be on the phone to the police the moment they realise the murderer's staying in the room next door.

I pull against the window latch but it's sealed shut. Slowly, I step outside and peer down the corridor. The brothers' door is ajar. I'll never get past unseen. I have to wait until they've gone before I can escape.

Their conversation continues through the wall. I press my ear against the panel, waiting for one of them to say Massimo's name, but their Italian is too fast to understand.

A knock sounds on my door. I step quietly back towards the bed. The knuckles rap again. 'Out of your room,' says the Hospitalero. 'It's time for you to leave.'

'Un minuto,' I reply, trying to disguise my voice.

The Hospitalero moves on to my neighbours who must have closed their door. The banging becomes more impatient until one of the brothers shouts again.

The fist returns to my door. 'Por última vez, Michael.'

My bag is packed but I remove all the items just to kill more time. Again, the Hospitalero bangs on my door. Again, I say in Spanish that I'm not ready. I can't leave. Not unless I know for sure that the Italians have gone.

The door handle twists but I've locked it from the inside. 'Michael,' shouts the Hospitalero.

The next pound is on my neighbour's door.

'Fanculo!' shouts Enzo through the wall.

Seconds later, their door slams shut and footsteps disappear down the corridor.

Convinced it's safe to step outside, I unlock my door. Puddles of water fill the floor. The Hospitalero appears carrying a mop and bucket. He curses under his breath, but I move past before I can feel his glare.

A group of pilgrims dressed in full waterproofs stand huddled around the main entrance. I can't let them see me, but this corridor is the only way out of the albergue. I keep my distance and wait for them to leave. The main door opens and everyone steps back. Leaves blow inside and a door slams behind me. Faces turn around, including Bruno's at the front. I look away, hoping he hasn't recognised me.

The discussions resume in the doorway. Some say they'll wait for the storm to pass, but apparently this is the forecast for the whole day. Another pilgrim suggests asking the Hospitalero if he'll extend the check-out time which expired fifteen minutes' ago. The best strategy, they decide, is to send one person to negotiate. There's no time to react before Bruno nominates himself. I hold the itinerary pages in front of my face, although not quickly enough as his boots come striding towards me.

My chest is pounding. There's no way Bruno has forgotten me from the fiesta last week. He looked straight into my eyes that night when he finally opened the main door after breaking into the albergue.

Bruno's shaved head is within touching distance when someone calls back from the entrance. He turns around, still walking. 'Today we make party,' says a man dressed in a cape covering his face and whole backpack. Christ. It's Luc, the French guy from Estella.

I stand against the wall until Bruno disappears down the corridor.

I'm trapped between both ends of the building. Bruno will return any moment with news of the Hospitalero's rejection, but if I try leaving through the front door, Luc is bound to see me. I have to get into another bedroom and hope there's an unlocked window, but it's hopeless with all these pilgrims here.

'Benissimo!' shouts Bruno. 'We stay another night!'

The crowd surges towards me.

Luc is the first to run past, his hands raised until they meet Bruno's in celebration. Other pilgrims follow, not a single one of them noticing me. The storm, I suddenly realise, is the best thing that could have happened. If I walk the whole stage today, I'll get far enough ahead to never see these people again.

Two men remain behind at the entrance. Their waterproof hooded faces turn as I approach but I avoid looking up. I reach for the door handle, but then something catches my attention.

I stare at the object leaning against the wall.

'Go on,' says the tallest man, grinning under a mop of bleached hair. 'Try picking it up. That thing weighs a ton.'

I'm too shocked to respond. The staff is identical to Massimo's — from the colour of the wood grain to the metal tip at its base.

'Here,' says the other man, lifting the staff. 'Take it.'

My stomach turns at the thought of touching the staff. Surely it can't be the same one.

I reach for the door handle.

'Hey bro,' says the taller pilgrim, placing a rolled cigarette between his lips. 'You're not going out dressed like that, are you? Don't you have a jacket or something?'

I pull against the door. The rain is deafening and the sky isn't sky, just one black cloud covering the horizon.

'Alright then,' says the voice behind me. 'Adios amigo.'

I don't answer as I step out into the storm.

———

I walk for hours along the flooded trail. My blisters feel like there's a knife slicing skin off my heel, but I can't stop thinking about what I saw in that doorway.

Why didn't I just take the staff and destroy it?

But it couldn't have been Massimo's staff — not the same one I left outside the cabin with all my fingerprints on it. The police would have discovered the murder weapon long ago, even if I couldn't find it that night.

What I saw this morning must have been a similar model.

Either that or I'm losing the plot.

At last, a cafe appears through the rain. I must have covered enough ground to stop for lunch. No one else has followed me all morning and my energy is non-existent after missing dinner last night.

Condensation fills the windows. I open the door, wary of who might be inside, but the cafe is practically empty. My hiking boots soak the strips of cardboard leading the way to the bar. I sit in a puddle of rainwater, thanks to my shorts which I should have wrung out first along with everything else I'm wearing. An amphibian-looking creature is swimming in the pool on top of my backpack. I fish it out and unclip the main cover which floods the floor with more water.

Everything inside the bag is soaked: my jeans, t-shirts, underwear, sleeping-bag liner and travel towel which is covered in clumps of paper — pages which until this morning had been my Camino itinerary. I don't believe it. I've been carrying those pages ever since I set off on this journey; days before I threw that staff at Massimo's head. And now the sheets are ruined.

Fuck. How will I know how far I have to walk before I

finish today's stage and hopefully get the hell out of here? I have nothing to rely on except those yellow arrows pointing all the way to Santiago. I have no idea where I am right now, let alone the name of the nearest town or village with a bus station. How am I going to find somewhere to sleep if I have to spend another night out here? I can't risk a municipal albergue. Every Hospitalero on the Camino will have studied my face from the police's wanted notices. They'll catch me the second I step inside.

Voices emerge from across the bar. I look up, aware that I'm no longer alone.

Two pilgrims sit in the far corner; a strong jawed man in his fifties and a slight Japanese woman who must be half the man's size. I shove everything into my backpack, clip the cover and sit with my back to them.

I listen in on their conversation, hoping they haven't recognised me, until my food arrives. I thank the barman without looking up and sip the coffee as rain water trickles down my nose. The tortilla warms my stomach but I can't enjoy it knowing that other pilgrims are here. I check quickly over my shoulder, careful to avoid their eyes, until I see a pay phone on the wall. Before I can stop myself, I stand up and walk quickly across the wet floor. The couple must have noticed me. But this might be my last chance before they or the barman call the police.

It takes two attempts for my shaking hand to dial the correct number. Thank God I memorised her landline number. I drop the coins inside and press the receiver against my ear. Impatient from waiting for the connection, I can't resist glancing behind. The man at the table looks up. I turn away but his reflection gazes back in the window. Shit. He must have recognised me, even if I am soaking wet.

The third ring seems to vibrate through the handset, then

the fourth, and the fifth. A lump fills my throat. I'm pining for the sound of her voice. It's been weeks since we spoke — not since that morning she kissed my mouth and whispered goodbye outside her door. She has to pick up. It's Friday — the one day she works from home. This could be the last time I can say all the things I need to tell her before they lock me up.

Darling, there's something I need to tell you...

I've been killing myself over all the possible reasons why she sent that message. What if she realised she's been with the wrong brother all this time? Or maybe she's finally broken up with Alistair and has decided to join me on the Camino, after which we can both disappear together. But what if her news is more urgent; something she was desperate to tell me that moment before I threw away Alistair's phone?

I haven't stopped thinking about that night we spent together. But there was something else I should have checked with Jessica. I didn't wear a condom. It should never have happened, but things moved so quickly on the staircase that even when we did get to her apartment, we just carried on as before. And then everything was over quicker than I expected. Jessica said she'd just finished her period so it was probably okay, but I could tell she wasn't convinced, even when her menstrual app said her fertility rate was almost impossible. But what if her app was wrong? What if the news Jessica was so desperate to tell me is that she's pregnant? Pregnant with our child.

'Hello?' says a man's voice down the line.

My hand clenches the phone.

'Hello?' he repeats, this time with less patience. 'Alistair Pollock speaking.'

The two pilgrims stand up from their table. The woman heads to the door but the man walks straight towards me. His boots are made of broken-in leather, their holes all laced to the top. The rest of his clothing is also military-like: thick socks, khaki shorts and a backpack protected by a camouflage cover which encloses everything except for the shoulder straps around his huge arms.

I turn away, pretending to be deep in conversation. The pilgrim must have recognised me from the police notices. He's enormous. There's no way I'll get out of his grip when he tries to restrain me. The couple must have planned what to do the moment they saw me here. The Japanese woman is already outside, probably calling the Policía Nacional on her phone. I can't believe it. I've survived all this time — more than a whole week since throwing that staff — only to get caught by complete strangers sheltering from the storm. My knees give way. The phone slips from my ear until it falls to the end of the coil.

'Who is this?' yells Alistair's voice from the receiver.

I stare at the phone, waiting for the pilgrim's hand to clamp around my neck.

My heart is thumping. I have to put my brother out of his misery. He must be in a terrible state wondering who has been intercepting his Professional Misconduct emails. I have to tell him it was me. And then, if there's still time, I'll confess what I did with Massimo's staff.

I grab the phone, but not before the cafe door slams behind me.

Two figures move behind the fogged glass. I lean closer to the window until I'm sure it's really them. The pilgrim couple. They're leaving. I'm still safe.

Alistair's voice shouts down the receiver, demanding to know who it is.

I lift the phone to my mouth. My mind races through all the things I must tell him. But instead, I hang up the call.

I walk through the fields, trying to avoid the lakes flooding the land. The rain is falling harder than it's done all morning, but it's not as if I can get any wetter. After a while, I forget about my soaking body, heavy backpack and the blisters skinning my heels. As bad as I feel, today wasn't the right time to tell Alistair it was me who'd accessed his work emails. He'll be furious when he finds out I stole his phone, but it's better to tell him in person, even if it's inside some Spanish prison. And then, once I've had long enough to decide how to break the news, I'll tell my brother what happened that night with Jessica.

Darling, there's something I need to tell you...

The more I reflect on her message, the more convinced I am that she's pregnant. She must have known something was different in her body or at least felt the changes. Why else would she have used such distressed words? It was a plea for help. Desperation. And I ignored her. What if the police catch me before I find another pay phone? Maybe I won't have another chance to speak to her. Maybe after the arrest they'll deny me my right to make a phone call. Maybe the next time I see Jessica, she'll be carrying a baby in her arms and I'll be a father behind bars.

My feet stop immediately. I stare at the sewage pipe across the field. The spout is covered in mud, but it's not gushing out water like all the other drains. It's the perfect place. No one will ever look inside.

My hiking boots sink into the squelching mud. I move slowly, trying not to slip or lose my footing until I reach the long narrow pipe.

I unclip my backpack. How it has taken this long to

dispose of the evidence I don't want to even consider, but I never want to see that white t-shirt again.

The smell is disgusting but I can't imagine anyone coming anywhere near this place. I take one more step, just to get close enough so I can't miss, but then the ground sinks beneath my feet. Sludge fills my left boot until it reaches my shin. Whatever I'm standing in makes me want to vomit, but I have to pull myself out before I sink any deeper. The suction is so strong that it almost swallows the hiking boot. I try twisting my foot, hoping this will release me, but then I lose balance and start falling forwards.

Desperate not to land face first into the raw sewage, I push off with my other foot. The mud releases the trapped boot, giving me enough momentum to lunge forwards in the only direction possible. My foot disappears into black water but not before I reach the sewage pipe with the same hand that's still clutching onto the t-shirt.

I lean against the pipe, desperate to breathe without that revolting smell entering my mouth. Rain splashes up from the pipe, but I pull myself up onto its concrete ledge. I lean over the rim, lift back my arm and throw the t-shirt inside. I peer into the darkness until I'm convinced it's disappeared. And then, gripping the pipe with both arms, I slide forwards, scraping as much muck as I can from my boots, legs and arms, until I reach the next field and the safety of the trail.

By late afternoon, the clouds finally clear. I've been walking for hours, numbed by the smell of sewage, even though I washed in every place I found running water. The route was mostly flat, not that this stopped every kilometre from feeling twice the distance as the mud weighed down my boots.

Somehow, I haven't seen any one else since those two pilgrims in the cafe. Hopefully, everyone else also took rest days to avoid the storm. With any luck, I'll never see Luc or the Italian brothers again.

The first rays of sun catch the outline of a small village in the distance. Without my itinerary, I have no way of knowing where I am, but even if there was a bus stop here, the driver would never let me onboard in this state. Albergue signs start appearing on the trail. It's difficult to know which one is the least discrete, but a small converted monastery on the other side of the village seems like the safest option.

I step through an arched doorway, checking for backpacks or any other sign of pilgrim life. I walk quietly along the stone slabs, carrying my filthy boots until I reach the end of the cloisters, where the Hospitalero is leaning asleep against the desk. The message board behind him is filled with information about the monastery's restoration programme, but there's not a police wanted notice in sight. I clear my throat loud enough to wake him. The old man seems flustered by my arrival, but quickly switches to English. 'Last night's pilgrims waited until lunchtime to leave,' he says, pausing after every other word. 'Right now, you are the only person staying here.'

My relief verges on euphoria until he asks what happened to me.

'You fell in a field?' he asks, staring at the mud on my clothes.

I nod, aware of the vile smell I've brought inside his albergue.

'You can shower, but first I need your Credenciales.'

The ink from previous albergue stamps has run across the paper, so he turns to a clean page and marks today's date and stage.

'Are you okay?' he says, looking up. 'You haven't stopped scratching since you arrived. Do you want me to check your back?'

I turn around and lift up my t-shirt.

'Right,' says the Hospitalero, his voice more serious. 'Let me show you the bathroom. After that you can come to the infirmary. But you must leave all your things here.'

The Hospitalero leads the way to the showers.

The hot water sooths the bites on my back, but I can't wash the smell of sewage from my skin, even with all the different bottles of shampoo and shower gels. I change into my wet jeans and a t-shirt and soak today's walking clothes in the sink which I then hang on the clothes rack.

The Hospitalero shows me to a small room containing a single bed, a King James Bible and a wooden crucifix on the wall. His silence is unsettling, even more so after I ask what he thinks caused the irritation on my back. He tells me to make myself comfortable and then disappears.

I cannot relax. The atmosphere in the room is suffocating, or maybe it's the cross on the wall. I killed a man. A religious man. A Christian.

'Okay,' says the Hospitalero, making me jump. He's wearing wire-framed glasses and holding what looks like a medical encyclopedia. 'Lie down,' he says, pointing to the bed.

He opens the pages, casting dust motes through the air. I twist my neck to see a photograph that must be thirty years old, judging from the haircuts and shell suits. The old man snaps on a pair of plastic gloves and prods one of my bites. I flinch, overcome with an urge to scratch myself again. He makes an unconvincing sound and returns to the encyclopedia, cracking its spine as he turns through more pages.

The Hospitalero clearly thinks I'm contagious. There's no

other reason he would have told me to leave my backpack outside. A bedbug infestation would be disastrous for his business. Forget the restoration programme. My untimely arrival could result in the health inspectors closing the monastery's doors for the whole summer, while they fumigate the cloisters and burn all the mattresses.

'Right then,' says the man, sliding the glasses up his crooked nose. 'The good news is that your bites are too big for bed bugs. You have more than a hundred on your back. Do you remember when you were first bitten?'

I describe what happened yesterday after I trespassed through the farmer's land.

'You had a siesta in long grass under a tree?' says the Hospitalero. 'And that was when something bit you?'

I nod.

The Hospitalero turns back to the index and starts flicking through the pages. 'Yes,' he says, speaking more to himself. 'Here,' he says at last, placing the book on the pillow. 'These are what your bites look like.'

The photograph shows a close-up of skin so blistered with boils that I cannot distinguish the body part.

'If I'm correct,' says the Hospitalero, long lines appearing across his forehead, 'you had an allergic reaction to ant bites. I think you slept on their nest.'

His smile doesn't make the itching any less severe. Irritated by his optimism, I ask which cure the book recommends.

'I have no idea,' he says. 'It doesn't say. But I'm sure we have cream in the medicine cabinet. Sleep here tonight, Michael. And if things don't improve before breakfast, I'll drive you to the hospital in Burgos.'

I spend the night in confinement. Whatever cream the Hospitalero rubbed into the bites was effective for all of three minutes before the urge to tear lumps out of my skin returned. I can't risk going to Burgos hospital, even if my reaction is serious. The first thing they'll ask to see is my passport. The receptionists won't waste any time calling the Policía Nacional the second they recognise my face from those wanted notices. If the bites are no better by morning, then I'll leave before the Hospitalero wakes up and just find a pharmacy tomorrow.

I drift in and out of sleep. The bites have made me feverish. My head is pounding. I need water. And then, before I know where I am, that same corrugated iron cabin appears on the cliffside.

'Hey you, pilgrim!'

Something breaks the silence — the sound of metal against stone.

'Me Massimo. Watsa your name?'

Again, the same sound echoes down the cloisters.

''It me, 'an' you walk away. But miss an' I 'it you.'

Tap. Tap.

'Don't be a fool, Michael. You musta respect the Lord. This is what 'e wants. What 'e demands.'

Tap. Tap. Tap.

'Throw the steek. 'it me, motherfucker!'

I wake immediately, Massimo's voice still trapped inside my mind. I sit up against the headboard and stare into the darkness.

Tap.

A shudder runs down my spine. That sound is unmistakable. Massimo's staff. It's here, right outside my room.

'Who's there?' I shout. 'Who is it?'

The door creaks open.

I reach quickly over the table, feeling past the Bible until my fingers touch the lamp. I pull its cord until I find the on switch. The bulb's faint glow illuminates the room. A shadow moves behind the door.

I stumble out of bed, knocking the lamp off the table. I run forwards, convinced that I'm about to confront Massimo's intense eyes. I pull the door handle and step out onto the cold stone, hands raised to protect myself.

But the cloisters are empty. There is no one there.

DAY TWELVE
SATURDAY 21 JUNE

'Good morning,' says the Hospitalero, opening the curtains.

I try to pull up the sheets but he's already standing over me. 'You've been scratching again,' he says, leaning closer to inspect my back. 'The bites have got worse. I'll lock up and drive you into Burgos.'

He leaves before I can protest.

My clothes reek from the sewage pipe, but I dress quickly and pack all my things. I have to leave before the old man comes back. The last place I'm going is some city hospital on a Saturday morning. I might as well walk straight into the Policía Nacional headquarters holding up my own wanted notice. I check the room to make sure I haven't left any signs that I was here, then grab my backpack. Something tears behind my shoulder. I wait for the excruciating pain of a torn muscle, but instead the backpack falls to the floor, its left strap still in my hand.

'That's bad luck,' says the Hospitalero in the doorway, car keys in his hand. 'Maybe you can find someone to repair it. But first you need medical attention.'

I explain that I've decided to keep walking, but he refuses to listen.

'But you can't leave the albergue,' I say, loud enough to make him step back. 'What about the other pilgrims staying here?'

'Other pilgrims?' the man replies.

'Yes. I heard someone in the corridor last night.'

The Hospitalero frowns. 'You're the only person who stayed here last night, Michael.'

———

Mud clumps around my hiking boots, adding more weight to what I'm carrying. My back is burning and new blisters fill my heels. Without the itinerary papers I have no idea how many kilometres I still have to walk. Maybe I should have accepted the old man's offer to drive me into Burgos. Even if he'd parked outside the hospital, I could have just got out of the car and carried on my way. At least I wouldn't have had to wade for hours through flooded fields with one strap around my shoulder and the rest of the heavy backpack in my hands.

If there's anything yesterday proved, it's that I can't go home. I thought I was going to throw up when Alistair answered the phone. What was he doing in Jessica's flat on a Friday lunchtime? As terrible as it sounds, I thought his time behind bars would be the perfect excuse for me and Jessica to fall in love, justifying any chance of a future we might still have with each other. But Alistair picking up the phone is not only proof that he hasn't been arrested, but also that he and Jessica are still very much together.

Jessica's *'Darling, there's something I need to tell you...'* has now become quite different to how I first imagined her saying it. What if she's told Alistair what happened that night? Or what if she decided to get an abortion?

My head is spinning. And I still can't process what I heard last night. The Hospitalero said it himself. No one else was staying in the monastery. So who the hell was stalking the cloisters during the night? I was convinced that sound came from his metal-tipped staff. Or did I just imagine it was Massimo, back from the dead?

Maybe I'm not only hearing things which aren't real, but also seeing things as well. The wooden staff on the morning of the storm, for example. It couldn't have been the same one I threw at Massimo's head. That albergue was more than two hundred kilometres away from the cabin. How could the same staff have travelled that far? The idea that another pilgrim just happened to find Massimo's staff and then decided to use it, oblivious to its role in the murder, is so far-fetched that I feel ridiculous even thinking about it. The detectives must have discovered the weapon not long after they found Massimo's corpse. It was too late in the evening for anyone else to interfere with the crime scene.

I must have just imagined it was the same staff leaning against the albergue door. I was already terrified that the Italian brothers would catch me in the corridor and call the police. Fear or paranoia has to be the only rational explanation for what I thought I saw that morning. There's no way it was the same staff. It's impossible. Just like the sounds I thought I heard last night.

Maybe this is proof that I'm losing my mind.

I can try to make as many excuses as I can, but nothing will change what happened outside that cabin. Massimo is dead. I killed him. I'll be a murderer for the rest of my life.

Maybe the nightmares will never end. Maybe his death will haunt me for ever. But there's only one way to find out.

It's a thought that's been lurking in my mind for days now, but one I can no longer ignore. Even if I reached Bilbao and went into hiding, this wouldn't solve anything. Massimo's death is my responsibility. I have to accept what I've done. And to do this, I cannot leave the trail. Instead, I will walk the Camino for penance and then hand myself in once I reach Santiago; providing the Policía Nacional doesn't find me first.

———

The yellow arrows point towards a road filled with motels and industrial estates. Burgos's outskirts seem to never end, but thankfully I'm walking on concrete after all the mud this morning. The trail leads into the old town, and as if by chance, past a shop filled with sewing machines in the window. I walk under a tinkling bell and drop my backpack on the counter. A young woman smiles and says something too quickly to translate. I hold up the strap and point to my torn backpack. She calls across the room where a man, possibly her grandfather, is at work behind a machine. He heaves himself up off the stool, ambles over, lifts my torn backpack strap, sighs and then returns to his seat. I make a stitching sign with my hands, trying to find the words in Spanish, but the granddaughter's expression is also one of finality. I pick up the backpack and follow my footprints back to the door.

'Señor,' says the girl.

I turn around, expecting her to tell me off for bringing dried mud into their family shop, but instead she hands me a sheet of paper. The handwriting contains a long name and the number seven underneath. 'Autobús,' she says, pointing at the number. 'Vamos juntos.'

She leads me through the Saturday crowds until we reach a main road. The next bus arrives before I can thank her properly. I show the driver the paper, but he pulls forwards as if racing against the clock. Barely keeping my balance, I find coins for the fare, but the driver waves me away. Other passengers watch me stumble down the aisle, no doubt confused why I'm carrying the backpack in my hands. The old lady I sit next to has either lost her sense of smell or chooses to ignore my stench of sweat and sewage.

The bus veers down a ramp and onto a dual carriageway, travelling at speeds I haven't experienced for weeks. Buildings blur past and the bus seats rattle against their frames. Fifteen minutes later, we stop outside a large shopping complex — one I'm sure I saw earlier on my walk into the city. 'Peregrino?' shouts the bus driver. Everyone turns around. The doors open and the driver points at the tarmac. The bus drives away, leaving me outside an entrance with the store name's lettering towering over me.

The electric doors jolt open, sending a wave of air-conditioning down my neck. I step into the store, which with its endless aisles of products seems to be the Aladdin's cave of outdoor living. The cooking equipment is better than most municipal albergue kitchens and I soon forget why I'm here. A red-haired employee asks if I need assistance, and realising where I'm from, starts speaking in perfect English. 'Hiking is on aisle nineteen,' she says, clearly keeping her distance from the smell of my clothes. 'Follow me.'

Despite the variety of every other item in stock, their backpack selection is limited due to a cancelled delivery. The only fifty litre bag available — the size which she assures me is the one I need — comes in bright purple. Sensing my hesitation at the colour, she unzips the pockets to demonstrate its built-in wallet and a grey waterproof cover. 'Try it on,' she says.

The soft padding presses against my back, sponging sweat from my t-shirt. It fits perfectly, even before I try the waist and chest straps. The woman adjusts the shoulder fastening and then pats the bag as if to say I'm ready. Still unconvinced by the colour, I ask why there's a hole in the right strap, but this isn't a hole, just a feeder for a water bladder. I ask if the water bladder is included, remembering the ones I've seen other pilgrims using, but she shakes her head. 'However, it's great value at eighty euros.'

Despite her sales pitch, it's the lack of an alternative which swings my decision. Eighty euros is a stretch — one I didn't factor in when I withdrew six hundred euros on my first day at Bilbao airport. But without a backpack, this Camino is over.

I spend the next ten minutes transferring all my possessions into the purple backpack. True to her word, I now have an extra third of space, along with side-straps for water bottles. The smell of sewage fills my old bag but thank God I'm not carrying the white t-shirt covered in Massimo's bloodstains. That sewage pipe was the only place I could safely hide the evidence. With any luck, that t-shirt will stay there for years, until the cotton decomposes and it rots away for good.

Avoiding the stares from other customers, I find the main checkout area. The new backpack's so comfortable it seems to soothe the ant bites on my back. I can't imagine how I carried my old bag all the way here from France, which now seems like the equivalent of having a flat wooden board strapped to my spine. Conscious of losing more time, I'm still drawn to the next aisle, past four-season sleeping bags, all-weather tents and cushioned hiking sandals which would definitely heal my blisters even if they cost twice the price of my new purchase.

The employee at the checkout takes my fully-packed backpack so he can scan the price tag. I insert my debit card into the reader. The price appears on screen and I type in my password. The machine processes the transaction. I look up, only to see my whole body on the CCTV system — everything from my face to my hiking boots.

'James?' says the assistant.

I flinch, wondering how he knows my name until I realise it's written on my card.

My debit card. Jesus Christ. How could I have been so stupid? Not only do the Policía Nacional have proof of my location from the store's security cameras, but anyone tracking my card payments will know I was here in Burgos at four o'clock on Saturday 21 June.

'Your card,' says the shop assistant, pushing it back across the counter.

The security guard stares at me from the main entrance. I can hardly walk straight, convinced that he or anyone else here has recognised my face from the wanted notices, but then a voice calls out from one of the aisles. I turn around, expecting to see more security, but instead it's the red-haired sales assistant. 'Here,' she says. 'You forgot something.'

She's holding my pilgrim shell; the same one I've been carrying since my first day in St-Jean. I unclip my waist strap but she tells me to turn around. 'There,' she says, fixing the shell to my new backpack. 'And I wanted to give you this.'

She hands me a bottle of body wash.

'It's ecological,' she says, stepping back. 'You can use it in the water fountains or rivers if you need to wash clothes or …'

Her strained smile is enough to finish what she really wanted to say.

I try to pay for the bottle but she refuses to accept any money.

'Buen Camino,' she says, as I turn back to the main doors.

I wait in the bus shelter, wary of the surveillance cameras monitoring my every movement. I can't believe I used my debit card in the store. What if I've already triggered a security alert to the Spanish police? What if they're already on their way to arrest me?

My old backpack smells revolting in the afternoon heat. There's no reason to keep it now that I have a bright purple replacement. I walk behind the shelter to a row of industrial waste bins. I check behind, hoping the security cameras can't see me, and throw my old backpack inside the container, just as the next bus comes into sight.

Dusk has settled when signs appear for the next albergue. I follow the yellow arrows, regretting my decision not to buy a head torch from the store or something to light the path. At some point I'm going to have to start walking at night or far enough to cover two stages every day. My face was all over the shop's CCTV cameras, but three hours on the trail must have extended my lead.

The signs point to a set of tall iron gates behind which stands an old stone building. The oak doors are unlocked so I enter, assuming someone must have seen me walking down the drive.

The walls are full of photographs; each displaying hundreds of students all standing in front of the building, which must be a school from the year plaques underneath each frame. I can't remember the last time I saw one of my wanted notices, but like last night's albergue, this one is also missing my photograph from the notice board.

The Hospitalero accepts my Credentials without looking up from her desk. Opening the booklet, she gives a speech about the boarding school, which serves as an albergue outside of term time. She stamps my documents and then explains how most of the facilities are out-of-bounds, including the swimming pool, main dormitories and the library in the tower. 'Thank you, Michael,' she says, returning the booklet.

She walks down the corridor, pointing to the few places I am allowed to enter, including the bathroom and laundry facilities which are down a curved staircase with iron banisters. Thirty bunk beds fill the sports hall, most of them covered in clothes, but there's not a single pilgrim in sight. I choose a bed in the far corner under the climbing wall and wait until the Hospitalero leaves. Relieved to finally have some privacy, I unpack my clothes which are still soaking from the water fountain outside Burgos. I must have used half of the ecological body wash, as everything in my new backpack reeks of eucalyptus, although it's certainly an improvement from the previous smell of raw sewage.

I can't remember the last time I experienced hot water, so I make the most of the shower, scalding the ant bites on my back at the highest temperature. Cleaner than I've felt in weeks, I change into damp jeans and a clean t-shirt, then hang all my wet items on a clothes horse in the laundry room.

I get lost exploring the school, until I find a walled courtyard full of pilgrims drinking wine. I turn around, hoping no one's noticed me, but a woman's voice tells me to join them. The other pilgrims all look up, including a face I recognise immediately. My eyes dart away but I can't stop staring at his

'Climb Kilimanjaro' t-shirt. What is Luc doing here? He took a rest day with Enzo and Bruno on the day of the storm. There's no way the Frenchman walked the trail that day. I would have seen him, that's for sure. How has Luc managed to make up all those lost kilometres in just a few days?

'Don't be shy,' says the same woman, as she pulls out a chair.

It's too late to reject her invitation, so I keep my distance from the main group, including Luc, who somehow doesn't appear to recognise me. I snatch glances around the courtyard, but I don't think I've seen any of these other pilgrims before.

The atmosphere is dominated by Luc, who's dressed in a pair of tight yellow shorts, and an American called Bret. Their conversation, which is more a competition of who can project their voices louder, centres around the other Caminos they've walked, including the Camino del Norte, the Primitivo and the Vía de la Plata. Bret describes how he once camped through the whole Meseta — the stretch of desert which apparently starts tomorrow and continues for the next two hundred kilometres — but before I can worry about this, Luc starts reminiscing about his winter Camino when he walked the Pyrenees through three feet of snow. Bret challenges the snowfall levels, before telling everyone about his expedition through the Andes when both Sherpas collapsed from dehydration. Luc retaliates with a story about how he reached 'Kili' carrying all his equipment without seeing another soul for days, but then two new pilgrims enter the courtyard. Both men stand up, offering their seats to the two almost identical women. The older and equally striking blonde asks who used all the hot water in the showers, prompting the males to lock horns while I remain silent.

The Colombian sisters split the group. I try to remain

discreet but this is difficult with the woman next to me who's from Dublin and training to be a nurse. 'What's that smell?' she says, wrinkling her nose as she stares at my t-shirt. 'It's like eucalyptus on steroids.'

Realising that I cannot pass on free medical advice, especially as my ant bites feel like they're on fire after the twenty-minute shower, I quietly explain the situation and lift up my t-shirt.

'Savage,' she says, stepping away as if I'm contagious.

The other conversations end.

My hives, the nurse announces, are the worst she's seen, not that this encourages any sympathy. She laughs when I show her the cream I took from last night's albergue and then breaks patient confidentiality by telling everyone about my siesta on the ants' nest.

The whole courtyard crowds around my back. The attention is overwhelming, but just when I think they've seen enough of my 'leprosy', as someone describes it, a flash blinds my eyes. 'Research purposes,' says the nurse, although sticking her tongue out for a selfie next to my bites isn't exactly professional. The welts, I realise from the photograph, have all joined together to create one giant rash with a thick blubbery texture.

The nurse disappears before I can make her delete the photo. She returns as Luc and Bret start comparing their own scars and war wounds. 'Here,' she says, pushing a packet into my hand. 'Take two tonight, then one every four hours. But no more than that, okay? They're stronger than over-the-counter antihistamines.'

Dinner turns into a social media frenzy with everyone sharing photos on their phones. I almost didn't go to the dining hall, but I was starving after missing lunch, and besides, it's not as if I could remain anonymous after my public medical examination in the courtyard.

It's been so long since I last went on Instagram that I hardly recognise the feeds around me. Everyone has posted stories about yesterday's storm; Luc's close-up of raindrops bouncing off his face the regrettable winner with eighty-nine likes, even if Bret accuses him of staging the shot under a collapsed gutter. Both boys are equally persistent in friend-requesting the Colombian sisters, and I leave just as someone suggests a group photograph in the dining room.

Blackout has already been enforced when I return downstairs to check my clothes in the laundry room. The shadows give the basement an eerie feeling. I can't stop thinking about that strange tapping which echoed through the cloisters last night. The sound has tormented me all day, but it couldn't have been Massimo. I was feverish from the ant bites. I must have imagined his metal-tipped staff striking the paving stones outside my room. The Hospitalero said it himself. There were no other pilgrims staying in the monastery.

Light fills the crack in the laundry room door. I step closer, my bare feet on the cold stone.

'What do you mean, you think he's the same guy?' says someone who sounds just like the nurse. 'You must have met hundreds of pilgrims on Camino.'

'I'm sure it's 'is face from the notices. 'Ee just now 'as a beard.'

My knees go weak.

'Which notices? What are you talking about, Luc?'

'The police notices. They don't 'ave any 'ere, but they were everywhere before. And 'is photo was on all the pages.'

'What did the notices say?'

'That they were looking for 'im.'

'Savage.'

I knock one of the photographs on the wall. The frame comes loose but I catch it before it falls. The voices stop. I stare at the light in the doorway, picture frame in hand, as I wait for Luc and the nurse to find me hiding outside. Seconds pass. But the door doesn't open.

'There's something strange going on,' says Luc, lowering his voice. 'I'm sure 'e was called something different when I met 'im in Estella.'

'What do you mean?'

'Like 'e was called James, or something.'

'So let me get this straight, Luc. You think the police are looking for Michael — the guy whose back is covered in ant bites — who also happens to be called James, because he's a suspect in the Camino murder?'

'Yes.'

'Fuck. Do you think we should call the police?'

'I don't know. Maybe.'

'God, that's made me feel all creepy. What about everyone sleeping upstairs? What if he tries to strangle us in our beds?'

My chest is pounding so hard they must be able to hear it.

'I think we wait 'til tomorrow,' Luc finally responds. 'Then we tell someone.'

'Well I'm not sleeping in the same room as him tonight. No fucking way.'

'We can sleep upstairs in the library,' says Luc. 'I checked earlier. The door's not locked and I found extra blankets.'

'Then let's go upstairs before he knows where we are.'

DAY THIRTEEN
SUNDAY 22 JUNE

I wake alone in the sports hall. The beds are empty and all the backpacks have disappeared. I don't believe it. How the hell have I overslept?

This is the last place I want to be after what happened last night. I'd barely hidden in the basement when Luc and the nurse left the laundry room. Terrified how they'd connected my wanted notices to the murder, I heard Luc ask why the photograph frame was on the floor, but thank God neither of them checked the next corridor. I waited in the darkness until their footsteps disappeared, but when I returned to the sports hall, I suddenly remembered all my wet clothes downstairs, at which point it was too late to go back. My plan to escape and walk through the night was ruined when I discovered that the main entrance was locked along with all the other rooms on the ground floor. With no other choice, I returned to the sports hall, determined to wake before everyone else, but the bites on my back were unbearable. I'd already taken two anti-histamines after dinner, but I took two more, just to make the medication work faster. And the last thing I remember, I was staring at the ceiling, slowly closing my eyes.

Sunlight reflects off the wood panelled walls. I walk quietly down the corridor, hiking boots in hand to hide the sound of my footsteps, until I pass an open door. I stop. The room is filled with computers — school computers, which must have internet connection. This is it; what I've been waiting for ever since I stupidly threw away Alistair's phone a whole week ago. I enter and slowly close the door. The computer in the far corner is already switched on. I select the 'alumno' option which then asks for a password. I type the word on the laminated card stuck to the desk. Miraculously, the screen loads.

I move the cursor, numbed by the novelty of using technology. Jessica's pregnancy has been on my mind for days, but I still can't believe how quickly it happened. I thought conception took weeks, months maybe. Jessica said she'd just finished her period and there was definitely no blood. That was Friday night. Three days before I started the Camino. Sixteen days ago.

I type 'Am I pregnant?' on the school keyboard and wait for the results to load. The first article seems as reliable as any other. Apparently, there are various symptoms for early pregnancy; sore breasts, fatigue, morning sickness — all of which Jessica might already have. I scroll past an explanation about the 'fertility window' until my eyes stop on the next line.

Fuck. It's right there in writing. Conception can take place only moments after sex. And the fertilised egg only needs five days to attach itself to the uterine wall.

Sweat runs down my arm. No wonder Jessica was desperate to talk. She mistimed her cycle. And now she's pregnant. Pregnant with our child.

Footsteps fill the corridor. I turn back to the screen, ready to log out but then the page refreshes. I stare, transfixed by the headline.

'*Italian man, 32, murdered on the Camino de Santiago.*'

Somehow, I manage not to retch. I wipe my face and try to focus on the words.

It's a British newspaper; one of those tabloids intent on scaring the life out of people so they can't leave their front door. I haven't been able to face reading anything about what happened that night, instead following the updates from the endless conversations in the albergue dorms. And yet seeing this headline in my own language, and in a newspaper that I've known my whole life, suddenly makes his murder feel more real.

'Michael! What are you doing here?'

I look up from the screen. The Hospitalero is standing in the doorway, hands clamped around her hips. 'It's ten o'clock,' she says, scowling. 'You should have left hours ago.'

'I just need a few minutes,' I say, trying to scroll down the article.

'Absolutely not! You must leave right now.'

The Hospitalero walks towards my desk. Her demeanour implies anger more than any other emotion. If Luc already told everyone that I killed Massimo, then surely she wouldn't be alone in the same room as me, let alone trying to throw me out of the albergue.

My eyes race down the screen. The information is limited, but the Spanish national police have stepped up their '*manhunt*', discouraging new pilgrims from starting the trail while the investigation is still ongoing.

The next sentence traps my breath.

'*The Italian man was pronounced dead outside an aban-*

doned cabin near Zubiri, almost fifty kilometres from St-Jean-Pied-de-Port.'

'Michael! This is your last warning. You must leave this instant!'

The Hospitalero reaches the end of my row. I can't let her see that I've been reading about Massimo's murder. It's too suspicious, especially after I refused to leave her albergue. I try frantically to find the 'delete history' tab, but the Spanish language settings are too complicated.

'I'm warning you,' she says, pointing with her finger. 'If you refuse to leave then I'll call the police.'

I reach behind the monitor and hold down the power button. The screen goes blank just as the woman stands over me.

'Get out!'

'Okay,' I say, grabbing my backpack. 'I'm leaving.'

I step out into the corridor. There's a basket on the floor containing my clothes from the laundry room. I reach down and start packing the items.

'I should have known those were yours,' says the Hospitalero curtly.

My underwear has acquired a musty, fungal smell, but at least they're dry for the first time in days. Other items fill her basket, including a pair of yellow shorts and flip flops; the same pair Luc was wearing in the courtyard last night. Surprised that a man so well-versed in the art of Caminoing has forgotten his possessions — particularly the flip flops, which are effectively verruca shields in the albergue showers — I take these as well. A slip of paper falls out of the shorts. It's a bus ticket receipt dated Friday 20 June. The day of the storm.

No wonder Luc overtook me on the trail even though he rested that day with the Italian brothers. Last night, he was bragging about how the monsoon didn't even make it into his top five hardest days on the Camino. The photograph he'd posted on Instagram with all those likes said '30km through light rain'.

But this ticket proves that Luc took a bus for that whole stage.

Still fuming, I lift the backpack over my shoulders and return to the main entrance.

The greenery is soon replaced with a flat brown landscape that bakes under the sun. The few shops I pass are all closed, today being another Sunday. Thirst overtakes hunger. Sweat drips from my forehead, connecting a wet circle around the front of my t-shirt. There hasn't been a single water fountain all morning. Warm dregs swirl around the bottom of my plastic bottle; the only supplies I have left.

I'm still in shock that Massimo has made headline news back home. How are the journalists going to react when they discover that a British citizen is the murderer? It won't be long before everyone knows I killed him. My face will be plastered over the media alongside all the other murderers and psychopaths. And no one's going to listen when I try to explain what really happened that night.

Fuck. Why did I have to go online? I could have just waited until Santiago before asking Jessica if she really was pregnant. But now, thanks to that tabloid article, I'll never distract myself from the murder.

What's going to happen when that Hospitalero checks my search history and realises I was reading about Massimo? She was furious when I refused to leave, but my desperation to read the article must have made her suspicious. I didn't even have time to reach the last paragraph. What if it gave more leads in the investigation; information I need to know. But none of this resolves the new problem I have with Luc.

I've been walking more than a whole Camino stage every day, anxious to extend my lead over all those other pilgrims from the first week who know me as James. But Luc's decision to cheat and take the bus has ruined everything. How does he even know my real name? I don't recall introducing myself after he sat with me and the Americans at dinner in Estella. But last night he was adamant when he spoke to the nurse that my name wasn't Michael. Worse still, he recognised my face from the Policía Nacional's wanted notices. It's irrelevant that those notices seem to have all disappeared over the last few days. All Luc has to do is show the police my face in the nurse's selfie with my ant bites and they'll have a direct match. My photo with the Hats on that abandoned sofa was bad enough, but this is far more serious. Did I really think I could walk all the way to Santiago without being caught? I hoped not shaving might disguise my appearance, but facial hair or not, last night's photograph is proof that I'm still here, walking the Camino.

———

A small figure appears in the distance under the wide sky. I'm relieved to learn that I'm not alone out here at the mercy of the Meseta desert. I could do with company after hours of walking alone through this barren landscape. That and water.

I ignore the blisters on my heels and start catching him up. The trance music booming from his headphones is loud enough to frighten every animal in a mile-wide radius and his backpack is filled with badges of flags from other countries. We draw level. I raise my hand, careful not to surprise the man who still hasn't heard me over the volume of his head-phones, but then I stop dead in my tracks. Luc stares straight back at me. He takes two quick strides before realising there's no way out of this situation.

Fuck. I should have guessed it was Luc from all the flags on his backpack. If I'd known it was him, I would have kept my distance regardless of my desperation for water. And now it's just the two of us, out here alone in the wilderness.

The conversation that follows is as empty as the scenery. I ask where his friend is, but when he removes the headphones and tells me to repeat the question, he pretends not to know who I'm talking about, as if last night's sleep over in the school library never happened. I ask about the nurse, letting on more than I should have, but Luc shrugs. 'Oo knows. I walk alone today.'

I feel an urge to congratulate Luc for actually walking instead of taking another bus, but I bite my tongue. It's far more important to know if they've already told the Policía Nacional my current location.

'Want to walk together?' I ask, as if there's any choice in the matter.

We cross a ploughed field containing just one drooping sunflower. I do my best to be friendly but this isn't easy with his blunt answers. I ask if he's injured, which Luc immedi-ately denies before realising that I caught up with him. He mutters something about an old ankle sprain from Nepal and starts describing the 'fascinating' ruins a few kilometres back, which were actually no more than a pile of broken bricks. Oblivious to my reaction, he launches into some speech about 'feeling' every step of the way, forgetting how his head-phones were drowning out every natural sound around him.

Despite his heavy breathing, Luc doesn't want to stop. My mouth is parched and a migraine fills my skull. Hoping he might offer me some water from the hydration tube hanging from his shoulder, I convince him to take a short rest. 'Fine,' he says, as if this is a great inconvenience. 'But just a few minutes.'

I drop my bag in the dust and make a show of downing the last drops from my bottle. Luc covers himself in factor thirty sun cream and says my neck's burned as he places the cream back into his bag. Still optimistic that we might trade supplies if not sun cream, I offer him some chocolate, only to realise that the bar has completely melted. He laughs when I try licking the goo from the foil and stuffs a handful of nuts into his mouth. He then polishes a perfectly round apple and takes large bites from the fruit until only the core remains.

Desperate from thirst, I play my final hand. 'Here,' I say, unclipping my backpack. 'I think you left these behind in the albergue.'

Luc stares at the yellow shorts and flip flops. It seems as if he's going to reject them, but then he snatches both items without so much as a thank you. He places the returned property into his backpack, takes a long gulp of water from his tube and gets to his feet.

'Do you have any spare water?' I ask, tilting my empty bottle to the ground.

'Enough for the next town,' he replies.

Luc takes another long sip, spits into his hands and splashes it onto his face.

'How much further?' I ask, so thirsty I can barely articulate the words.

'Maybe five kilometres.'

Hopeless from his lack of charity, I abandon all dignity. 'Please, Luc. I need some of your water.'

He sighs, unstraps his backpack and takes out an unopened two litre bottle of spring water. I reach out, convinced he's going to give me the bottle but Luc takes my empty one instead. He breaks the seal of his own fresh bottle and pours slowly into mine, although not without spilling a few drops for the ground to swallow. The sound of water is euphoric, but then, after the shortest of pours, Luc straightens his hand and returns my bottle.

I stare at the three fingers of liquid, ready to call him out on his joke, but then he places the mostly full bottle into his backpack. 'If there's one thing I've learned,' he says, staring into the distance, 'it's never leave without enough water.'

My hands could wring his neck.

A church tower appears on the horizon. The main street is lifeless except for three old men on a bench. I sway towards a green water fountain shaped like a lion's face. I drop to my knees, ready to drink from the animal's mouth. My thumb jams the button but nothing comes out. 'No tiene agua,' says one of the old men, as if it's been this way since he was a boy. I turn around, ready to offer Luc whatever price he demands for his two litre bottle of spring water, only to see his flags disappear down a side passage.

Unsurprised by his getaway, I wonder what's lured him from the yellow arrows. I'm so dehydrated I would drink my own piss if I had any. I stumble through the passageway into a courtyard with four plastic tables, one of which is occupied by the Colombian sisters from last night's albergue. Luc walks out of the cafe, carrying two bottles of water, one of which he gives to the girls as he joins their table.

I drop my backpack and walk towards the cafe.

'Nice bag,' says Luc, as though only noticing it now. 'Didn't know they made pink for men.'

I'm too exhausted to stop my legs from walking.

The waitress pours Coke over three large ice cubes which crack inside the glass. I neck everything until the cubes touch my nose. High from the sugar, I order two bottles of refrigerated water and return outside.

'You really had visions last time you walked the Meseta?' asks the younger sister, as I pull up a chair. 'What happened?'

Luc starts another embellished story which the girls seem to believe. Intrigued by the 'apparition' he saw two years ago, they ask what else he experienced alone in the desert. Luc gratefully delivers, emphasising every other word and inserting dramatic pauses so his ten words stretch beyond the minute mark. Not once does he lift an eye from either sister.

Before I can stop myself, I open my backpack.

'Hey Luc,' I say, interrupting the climax of his tale. 'I just remembered something.'

'What?' he says, glaring at me.

'I saw you drop this earlier on the trail.'

Luc stares at the slip of paper which I slide across the table.

'It's a bus receipt,' I say, more to the sisters.

'Bus receipt?' repeats the eldest.

'Yes,' I reply, looking straight into Luc's eyes. 'Luc might want to hide the evidence next time he tells everyone he walked thirty kilometres through a storm when he actually lied and took the bus for the whole stage. Anyway,' I say, standing up. 'Enjoy your walk. Maybe see you at the next albergue.'

Fuck. Why couldn't I have just not said anything? All I had to do was let Luc get away with his latest fabrication. But instead, I've given him an incentive to call the police and tell them my exact location. I've risked everything. And all because of my pride.

It's so humid I can hardly breathe. Reluctant to waste precious water, I take sweat from my chest and rub it across my face. I walk towards the sun, counting my steps aloud; first in sets of one hundred, then into the thousands. I have to continue past the next town and avoid Luc at all costs.

Branches appear in the distance. It's the only vegetation I've seen all day apart from that one sunflower in the scorched soil. I follow my feet, wasting steps as they zig zag along the trail. Ten, possibly fifteen pilgrims sit huddled under the tree, some with their backs against the bark, others lying in the thin shade. 'It's not far to the next town,' says a voice I haven't heard all week. I search for his face, but another one stares back through the crowd — the nurse from Dublin. I quickly look away. 'Would you like to join us?' he continues from somewhere under the tree. I shake my head and keep walking.

The path drops down into a valley with a sunken settlement at the bottom. The outpost comprises one main street with an old church, a few albergues and a restaurant with tables outside. Two men who must be in their sixties call me over. Before I can remember ever meeting them, they pull out a chair. I ask how much further it is to the next town but they tell me to sit. 'Here,' says the larger of the two men, filling a glass from their jug. 'Today is far enough. Drink.'

The beer quenches my thirst but I can't stay any longer — not with Luc and the nurse so close behind. I can't be here when they tell all the other pilgrims that it was my face in the police's wanted notices. I get to my feet, promising to buy the men a round next time we see each other, but then my knees buckle.

'That's enough walking for one day,' says the taller man, catching my arm. 'Give me your Credentials. I'll check you into the albergue.'

Too tired to argue, I do as he says.

The sound of an engine wakes me up.

'Welcome back, James!' says the man with the beer jug, patting my back with unnecessary force.

I shudder. How does he know my name?

'You were asleep for thirty minutes,' he says, laughing. 'Another pilgrim who walked past thought you were dead.'

The engine gets louder, echoing off the stone. The street seems too narrow for a vehicle, but then the front grill pulls into sight. One of the men asks me a question, but I'm too shocked by the blue armoured truck to hear what they say. The thick tyres stop outside the albergue. Two armed officers climb out. They enter the building. A tall man, presumably the Hospitalero, leaves the entrance and points towards me. The Policía Nacional follow his instruction.

'James Pollock?' says the younger officer, projecting his voice to the plaza.

'Yes,' I reply, ignoring the stares from all the other pilgrims.

'Come inside with us.'

MONDAY 23 JUNE

I wake on a hard mattress. Someone above shifts positions, creaking the whole bed frame as if it might collapse on top of me. Other beds appear through the darkness. Backpacks line the walls. And hiking boots. Somehow, I'm still here in the albergue.

Everything happened so quickly last night. The police officers escorted me across the street until we reached the albergue. I couldn't look anyone in the eye — those fellow pilgrims who I'd shared the trail with for the last two weeks — but I knew they were all watching me. The taller officer led me into a small reception area and pointed at a chair. He stood over me, the insignia on his shoulder directly in my face as his wider colleague, balding except for a moustache covering most of his mouth, called for the Hospitalero. Sweat ran down my back as they spoke to each other in Spanish. I couldn't understand a single word, but then they turned in my direction and laughed at the same time. The albergue owner returned with two empty glasses and a bottle of water. The officers took long gulps, their eyes still fixed on me as if they expected me to try something stupid, like run back out into the desert.

'Hablas español?' asked the officer with the moustache. His wide-set eyes examined my face, as though searching for my motive for murdering Massimo.

My chest was pounding so hard I thought I was having a heart attack.

'Vale,' he said, after I shook my head. 'We try Inglés.'

Scared stiff, I was just about to admit what happened outside the abandoned cabin, but then the door flew open and a figure entered carrying a backpack filled with flags.

'What did you say?' said the officer, ignoring the new arrival.

Luc's audacity to eavesdrop on my interrogation gave me a sudden rush of adrenaline. He'd clearly contacted the police and told them my location. But there wasn't a chance I was going to let him witness my confession.

The officer leaned forwards, filling the air with his cologne. 'Did you not see the notices?' he asked bluntly.

'Notices?' I replied.

The Hospitalero stamped Luc's Credentials so hard that I flinched. He then led the Frenchman to the staircase where Luc managed one last smirk before walking away.

'People is very angry,' the officer continued, clenching his fist on the table. 'You waste our time and resources — specially with the investigation.'

'Yes,' I replied, still no closer to understanding what the hell was happening.

The officer got up from his chair. 'You are lucky another peregrino call us,' he said, cracking his knuckles. 'Estella is far away.'

He checked his watch and spoke quickly to his colleague.

I also stood up, ready for the handcuffs around my wrists,

but the taller officer pointed at the chair and told me to sit. He then reached into his pocket. 'Tomad,' he said, throwing a booklet across the table.

The other officer had already opened the albergue door when I finally realised what had happened. 'Lose your pasaporte again, James,' he said, shaking his head, 'and we don't come. Entiendes?'

I stayed in the entrance until the blue truck drove away.

———

The bed frame creaks above, loud enough to force me out of bed. I have an urge to be outside; to let the dawn touch my face.

I feel my way out of the albergue. The sky's black curve is lined with the faintest blue at its base. I stand with my backpack and stare up at the stars. Cold air fills my lungs.

Despite everything that's happened, I'm still here on the Camino.

———

A broad-shouldered pilgrim walks towards an old lady struggling with her bin bags. He says something I can't hear and takes the load from her hands. Almost three times her size, he makes light work of the weight she's been dragging across the road. He lifts the sacks into a rubbish container, accepts the woman's gratitude, and then says goodbye.

I watch their interaction conclude, until I realise I should have offered to help her first. The guilt is still on my mind when I notice the pilgrim's enormous boots. I recognise them immediately — their broken-in leather and eye holes laced to the top. When they'd walked towards me across that flooded cafe, I was sure he'd recognised my face from the wanted notices. But now, high from freedom, I'm the one who approaches him. 'I saw that old woman struggling with her bags,' I say, looking up past his huge arms. 'But I didn't think to help her.'

The man looks down from his height advantage. Just as it occurs to me that he might not speak English, he shakes his head. 'On a different day, you would have helped her, not me,' he says in a voice fitting his size.

'I've seen you before,' he says, more a statement than a question. 'The storm. You were in that cafe.'

He gives me another of those intense stares he used that morning I tried to escape in the rain. 'I was going to ask if you wanted to join us,' he continues, 'but you seemed busy on the phone. You were brave to walk that day in just shorts and t-shirt.'

'Or stupid,' I interrupt, not that the man seems to hear.

'But then I realised I'd seen your face on those police notices. What was that all about?'

The man listens to my explanation.

'You're lucky they returned your passport,' he says, still studying my face. 'I must admit, I thought those notices had something to do with that Italian pilgrim in Zubiri. Terrible news,' he says, shaking his head. 'Anyway, I'm glad everything worked out. What's your name?'

'Michael.'

'Robin,' he says, clamping his hand around mine.

His grip tightens. I tell myself there's nothing malicious in his handshake, but I can't stop my cheeks burning. What if Robin remembers my real name from the wanted notices? What if his surprise when I explained what happened wasn't surprise at all, but suspicion as to why the Policía Nacional would go to such lengths to return a lost passport? What if he knows the truth? What if that's why he just referred so openly to Massimo?

I don't feel comfortable with Robin any longer. I need an excuse to walk alone.

'Let's walk together,' he says, his eyes locking onto mine. 'Today's not an easy stage.'

———

I'm trapped with Robin for hours. I answer his questions with vague responses until I ask what he does back home in Belgium. Relieved to avoid the subject of the Camino murder, I listen to him describe how he started his own organic farm after realising what was happening in many abattoirs. He spends the next ten minutes explaining all the ways he gave his cows the best lives he could. Cautious not to lose the thread of his digression, I ask more about the process. 'What happened next?' he repeats, as if I've said something foolish. 'I killed them.'

Robin recounts how he shot each cow in the head, lifted the animal on his tractor forks with a counter weight, and then skinned the carcass, carving all the meat from the bone. Without warning, I see Massimo outside the cabin, lying exactly where I left him. His flesh is rotting away, chunks of skin missing from where the maggots have burrowed inside him. And that staff is lying next to his corpse. The same staff I used to kill him.

Something grips my shoulder. 'Is everything okay, Michael? You've gone completely white.'

'I'm fine,' I reply, waiting for his hand to release me. 'So when was the last time?'

'The last time I killed an animal?' he says, as I gulp from my bottle. 'Last week.'

I choke, spitting water across the path.

'Are you alright, Michael? Do you want to sit down?'

My name's not Michael.

I shake my head.

'It happened just outside Puente La Reina,' Robin continues.

Puente La Reina. The same town where I met Enzo and Bruno; the Italian brothers who'd arranged to meet Massimo that night at the fiesta.

'This may sound strange, Michael, but when you've lived around death long enough, you start developing a sense of when a creature is in danger.'

My legs have gone numb.

'Last time it happened, I was driving down a small lane back home when I suddenly felt it in the air. I stopped the engine, got out and ran into the nearest field. That's where I found the dead cow lying next to her stillborn calf. The hedge in the lane was too high to see over, so there was no way I knew both animals were in danger until I found them. That day, I was too late. But when I had that same feeling outside Puente La Reina, I had to trust my instincts.'

Robin looks straight into my eyes.

What if he has those same instincts about me? What if he already knows I'm the murderer?

'The deer was lying in a ditch, his back legs both broken. Who knows how fast the car was driving when it hit the animal. The poor thing was exhausted, but it thrashed around on its front legs until it realised it couldn't escape. Then I climbed down into the bank and walked slowly towards it.'

Robin stares ahead.

'The deer watched me with its big trembling eyes. He knew he was defeated; that he couldn't go on living. So I placed my hand on his side, consoled him and then took out my knife.'

I shudder.

'I explained what I was going to do,' says Robin. 'The animal accepted its fate — like he knew his suffering would soon end. I placed the knife between his skull and Atlas Bone, and then pushed the blade through its nerves. The deer died immediately, without pain.'

Robin wipes a thick forearm across his brow.

'You know, Michael,' he says, staring at the sky. 'I never thought I'd have to kill anything on the Camino.'

My knees weaken. How am I still here? Last night, I was ready to confess everything to the Policía Nacional. Even when the officer walked towards the door, I was convinced it was part of their interrogation. How could they let me get away with murder?

'People talk about the twenty-one grams theory,' Robin continues. 'You know, how our weight reduces by this exact amount when our souls leave our bodies. But for me, death isn't about the soul departing. It's more the moment when life itself stops as the body releases its final breath.'

I drop to the ground.

'Take it easy,' says Robin, leaning over me.

Water splashes on my lips but I barely taste it. Massimo's soul had already departed when I stood over him outside that cabin. It was me who took his twenty-one grams. It was me who took his soul.

Robin mixes dehydration powder into his bottle and tells me to drink everything. The electrolytes jolt my senses. The sun glares against my eyes. I say I'm ready to stand up.

'Okay,' says Robin. 'But slower this time. And no talking. You must save your energy, Michael.'

'Credenciales,' shouts a voice in front of my face.

The Hospitalero, a stout woman with freckles, slams her stamp onto my documents. She demands five euros, her eyes already watching Robin who's standing behind me in the queue. The fact that she's charging one euro less than the standard municipal rate seems ominous, but everywhere else is fully booked and we're lucky that she's opened the overflow building.

'Mochila?' she asks.

I say that I've left my backpack next to the bed. The Hospitalero starts yelling at me. When I finally manage to compose myself, other pilgrims in the queue are also saying that they reserved beds with their backpacks. Incandescent, the lady marches us through the hallway which reeks of hiking boots, past a bucket collecting water from the ceiling.

We enter the main dorm where everyone else has also broken her cardinal rule. More shouting ensues. Luc greets me with a cold stare, shocked that I'm still here after he reported me to the Policía Nacional. He lowers his gaze, however, when the albergue owner grabs his backpack by the flags. Luc protests, but then she flings his bag across the muddy hallway, narrowly missing the bucket. Close to tears, he confronts the woman, arguing that her rule couldn't have been a rule if no one knew about it, but she retaliates with more abuse.

It's hard to hear over the noise, but Robin finally encourages the Hospitalero to step outside so they can find a solution. Luc says he's never been so mistreated in all of his seven Caminos, before trying to stage a mass walkout. Bret places an arm around Luc's shoulder; the former adversaries bonding over a common enemy. Robin returns, explaining that we must all leave our backpacks outside in the corridor. Order returns to the albergue. All forty of us share one bathroom — which includes the only loo in the building, although one without a seat or toilet paper. Shortly afterwards, we all descend on the village pub.

'You!' slurs a voice across the packed bar.

The nurse pushes her way through the crowd before I can reach the exit. 'You,' she repeats, her breath touching my face. 'How come you're still here?'

I ask what she means, resisting the urge to wipe the sweat on my forehead.

'We all saw you with those police officers yesterday,' she says, loud enough for others to turn around. 'So go on. What exactly did they want from you?'

Her eyes clearly disbelieve my explanation. 'Your passport?' she says, shouting over the bar which has returned to its previous volume. 'That's why the guards came out all this way looking for you?'

I nod.

'Savage.'

The nurse takes a gulp of her wine. 'You know,' she says, her lips almost touching my ear, 'I may have a tiny confession to make. So when the police turned up yesterday, it wasn't exactly by coincidence —'

'You called them, didn't you?' I interrupt.

She brushes away her fringe. 'Yes, but only because I thought you might be — you know — dangerous. I mean, just look.'

She pushes her phone into my hand. I stare at my photograph from the wanted notice. The face of a murderer.

'Hey!' she says, thumping my elbow. 'You're not listening. I said, why does it say James in the notice? Your name's Michael, right?'

'Yes — I mean no. Not exactly.'

My eyes hunt around the room, searching for any sober pilgrim within earshot. 'James is my middle name. The police must have got confused by my passport details.'

'Of course,' says the nurse, rolling her eyes. 'The guards were confused by your passport. Makes total sense.'

She moves the glass to her lips, her eyes relentless in their examination.

'Luc was convinced you were the murderer. But I knew he was wrong. You're not the type, Michael. You're too nice to kill anyone, aren't you?'

She shakes her head, as if to dispel whatever images had entered her mind. 'How's your back anyway? Still covered in hives?'

Before I can stop her, she pulls up my t-shirt. 'Look at that,' she says, pressing her cold hand against my back. 'They've all disappeared.'

It's true. For the first time in days, my back has stopped itching.

'Well then,' she says, pushing her empty glass into my hand. 'I think somebody owes me a drink, don't you? I'm Jessica, by the way.'

Last orders come and go. The barman throws us out and we stumble back to the albergue, which even the locals in the pub admitted is infested with bedbugs. I walk alone until I find everyone waiting outside. The albergue, it transpires, has been locked up for the night.

An older, but equally intoxicated pilgrim tries to talk Luc out of battering down the door, but just as he lines up his first shoulder charge, a crack of light appears through the hinges. The doorway opens revealing half of the Hospitalero's face. In a voice which couldn't be further removed from her aggressive stance earlier, she says that the ten o'clock curfew has been enforced and that we will all have to find some-where else to sleep tonight.

After a long stalemate, we finally reach an agreement thanks to the patient negotiation of a young Spanish pilgrim who's far too drunk to be talking. The door swings open, amid much celebration. The bucket is kicked over in the race for the one bathroom. A handwritten sign reading 'no bags in the room' is pinned to the bedroom door. Within moments, Luc changes 'bags' to 'hags'. The commotion continues until the owner returns in her nightgown, threatening to cut the power supply.

Unable to sleep, I wash in the freezing shower, praying the smear on the tiles is only mud. It's the first time I've left a shower feeling dirtier than when I got in, but then I realise my towel has disappeared, along with all my clothes.

Laughter emerges from the dorm. I ask Luc for my clothing but he refuses, clearly retaliating after how I humili-ated him in front of the Colombian sisters by returning his bus receipt. I walk towards the bed, covering my nakedness with my hands. Luc switches on the light and cheers fill the room. My clothes emerge from various parts of the dorm, before the Hospitalero appears in the doorway and gives us our final warning.

The blackout is short lived as flashlights point to Bret's bunk where he's entertaining a guest for the night. Some complain about the sucking lips while others add their own sound effects. I lie still on the mattress waiting for the bedbugs to arrive, but the only biting in the room comes from Bret's bed.

A round of 'buenas noches' are sent around the room, each person adding a new name in the darkness which everyone then repeats together. Nerea, Oihana, Max, Genevieve, Herman, Peio, Tom, Katarzyna, Pietro, Colin, Jill,

Begoña, Tim, Jon, Sarah, Andrew, Josetxo, Paulo, Hugh, Arantxa, Virna, Roberta, Dario, Janine, Alexia, Miguel, Monica, Dennis, Ian, Benedetta, Seb, Aritz, Marta, Perla, Lindsay, Maisy, Bobby, Marco, Chiara, Nancy and the Hospitalero all receive honorary mentions.

'Buenas noches, James,' says a French accent.

'Buenas noches, James,' repeats the room.

TUESDAY 24 JUNE

This has to end. The guilt's going to consume me unless I stop my mind from constantly returning to that cabin. Massimo made me do it. It was his choice. His risk. But I've become so obsessed with trying to remember everything that happened, I can no longer separate truth from my imagination.

New details keep forcing their way into my memories. Did that Christ tattoo cover his whole back? Did he only want a cigarette? Sometimes, I walk away as Massimo screams at me to throw the staff. And yet on other occasions, I stand over him, pinning him to the ground while I smash his face with the staff's metal tip. But regardless of what happens, the nightmares always end the same, with Massimo's lifeless eyes staring blankly at the sky.

'*Italian man, 32, murdered on the Camino de Santiago.*'

Why did I have to read that article? I know what happened. I know what I did. Nothing can change that.

The only way I can stop these thoughts is by finding distractions. Distractions like Robin's good deed when he helped that old lady with her bin bags. Even bad deeds will do. Bad deeds like the pilgrim this morning who forgot to switch off their alarm before going to the bathroom and woke everyone up at five o'clock, earning themselves negative points.

Camino Points. That's it. My distraction. An imaginary game rewarding morality and other pilgrim-like behaviour — things like marking the trail with stone arrows when the route isn't clearly marked; sharing water, plasters or supplies with anyone in need; helping someone who's lost or walking in the wrong direction; telling someone when they've forgotten to zip up their backpack; listening when someone needs to talk; being sympathetic when someone shows you their blisters; buying a stranger coffee; donating a bottle of ecological body wash when someone stinks of sewage; inviting outsiders to the communal table. The list is endless. Five points for every good deed; ten points for anything that goes the extra mile; and fifteen points for something that's really exceptional.

But this honours system must also punish bad decorum, anything immoral, wrong or just plain selfish; like rustling plastic bags in the albergue while others are asleep; not reciprocating when someone wishes you 'Buen Camino'; disturbing the trail with loud music; leaving toilet paper in the bushes; making false arrows to mislead other pilgrims; hogging plug sockets in the dorms; wasting hot water in the showers; pissing in the showers; not showering; not washing your clothes so everyone has to sleep with the stench of your sweat; taking a bed that's already reserved; theft of any nature; under-paying at a donativo albergue; not washing cutlery in the shared kitchens; watching TikTok videos without headphones; farting in the dark; and most punishable of all, snoring.

I will start with minus one hundred Camino Points for murdering Massimo and deduct a further fifty for sleeping with Jessica. I must collect as many Camino Points as I can before Santiago. And after that, I'll accept whatever fate I'm dealt.

———

I'm sitting outside a small cafe, when a young woman approaches my table. I look at the gold baubles hanging from her ears and then at my reflection in her oversized sunglasses. Her manicured nails enter an expensive handbag and take out a camera which she pushes into my hands. Before I can admire its extended lens, she says something in Spanish and disappears into the cafe.

The camera's on button triggers a montage on the LCD screen. Images of its owner appear, showing her walking past various Camino landmarks, including the monastery at Roncesvalles, the iron figures at Alto del Perdón, and the spires of Burgos Cathedral. The dates on the screen are all from the last two days. And then I realise what she's doing. She's pretending to walk all the stages while she's actually doing a fly-by tour of all the main attractions. Appalled that the woman's faking her own pilgrimage, I deduct her ten Camino Points and then select another folder; one containing multiple close-ups of a face striking the same sultry expression.

A pilgrim steps out of the cafe walking awkwardly in hiking boots. I return to the vanity project, moving past thick lips and manicured eyebrows until I find her main Camino photographs. The clunking footsteps approach my table but something on the screen catches my eye. I lean closer. The albergue boot rack is like every other one I've seen, but there's someone else in the shot; a tall, blurred figure standing in the far corner.

My chest starts pounding. The man must have entered the frame at the exact moment the photograph was taken. But there's something about his appearance which raises the hair on my neck.

I zoom in. The image isn't focused, but what I see is undeniable; a shirtless man with a shaved head reaching for something behind the boot rack.

A hand snatches the camera.

I look up, shocked by who I think I've just seen.

The woman is barely recognisable, her face stripped of make-up and ear weights, but despite the running top and bright yoga trousers, the make of sunglasses gives her away. She places the camera on the table and lowers herself onto a seat, crossing her badly-laced hiking boots.

The LCD screen continues to display the same blurred figure next to the boot rack. I lean closer, trying to make out any distinguishing features, but the woman snaps her fingernails. She drags the table into the road, repositioning its contents along with the coffee cup which she rotates until the brand name is visible. She then moves a Camino guidebook into the shot and cracks its spine so the middle pages remain open. Still eyeing me suspiciously, she returns the camera to my hands and then gives the signal.

My subject strikes a series of poses ending with the coffee cup suspended inches from her lips. I take far fewer pictures than she desires, determined to return to that one image which is now all I can think about. The woman gazes pensively into the distance until a car horn breaks her concentration. She tells the vehicle to wait while she returns to her hand-on-chin mock-Rodin posture. The driver winds down his window and starts yelling.

I lower the camera and scroll through the Spanish options in search of the main photo gallery. The woman shouts at the man in the car, not that I'm listening. At last, I locate the most recent set of images but the boot rack is nowhere to be found. The driver offloads one last round of insults then accelerates away in the dust. I frantically press the same button until the boot rack finally returns. And then I see those same bare feet.

Fingers snatch the camera from my hand. The woman glares at the image and then shouts at me for looking at her photographs.

My back is covered in sweat.

A taxi pulls into the square. The woman climbs into the back seat and waits for the driver to close the door. The engine starts, but then she gets out and runs past the table, almost rolling her ankles in the hiking boots.

I'm so desperate to see the photograph again, that I almost steal the camera from the back seat, but then she returns carrying a pair of high-heeled shoes. The taxi drives away, denying me of my last opportunity to confirm whether it really was him in the photograph.

A cash machine. The situation regarding my finances has been on my mind for days, but I swore there was another fifty euro note tucked inside the one I used to pay for breakfast. Maybe someone opened my money belt in one of the albergues, but pilgrims don't steal. There's the possibility I was short changed when I paid with a previous fifty, but waiters and shop assistants must be used to dealing with the different colours and sizes of notes in their own currency; unless the mistake was intentional. But the more I think about it, the more probable it is that I've already spent almost all of the six hundred euros I withdrew from that cash machine in Bilbao, even though Santiago is still more than two weeks away.

My budget of twenty euros a day was always going to be optimistic, especially after that first private albergue, which at twice the price of a municipal is now a habit I can no longer afford. And then there's all the restaurant food. Confident that more calories meant more kilometres, I've been eating two slices of tortilla for breakfast and Menu Peregrinos for lunch. With the drunken tipping, I must have exceeded thirty-five euros a day, which doesn't even include the eighty euros I spent on a bright purple backpack. Without Alistair's phone to check my bank balance, I've been watching the wad of cash disappear without once trying to limit my spending. But now there's no hiding from the situation.

The cash machine seems reluctant to accept my debit card, as though wary of foreign plastic, but then it suddenly swallows my card. Nothing happens. I'm terrified that the card's gone for good — my one source of income, shredded into thousands of tiny strips — but then a message arrives on screen asking for my password. My fingers remember the four-digit code but it takes two attempts with the upside-down keyboard. I gamble with the various choices until I find the English language setting and then the balance option. The machine asks if I want 'Print or screen'. I select the former.

The vidiprinter slowly edges out the ticket which it then holds onto as though challenging me to accept. My eyes fall on the bottom line. I read again from the top, convinced there's been a mistake.

How is it possible I only have one hundred and fourteen pounds left in my overdraft? Was I really so extravagant in that first week? But those salad days couldn't have accounted for everything, unless I've racked up some serious bank charges from using my card abroad.

The cash machine asks if I want to make a withdrawal. I

type a one, another one, and then a zero on the keypad; the last of my funds, minus the additional four euros.

Fuck. Why didn't I arrange a payment plan with Greg and Dev? I should have made our bet conditional on them paying the thousand pounds in instalments, either quarterly or at the halfway mark. They could have funded this entire trip, paying for pilgrim menus and putting me up in private albergues where I only had to sleep with eleven others in a room.

The machine considers my request, but there's no sound of counting money.

A new message appears on screen. The transaction has a six euro fee; four from my own bank, and a further two from the Spanish ATM. Six euros. That's the price of a whole night in a municipal albergue.

I return to the main menu, although not before the screen taunts me with its next message, asking if I still want to continue. I take the next best alternative and withdraw one hundred euros, accepting the bank fees. Two fifty euro notes emerge, one with a gash down the middle that's bound together with Sellotape.

I hide the notes in my money belt and follow signs to the next municipal albergue.

―――――

Compared to yesterday's cattle shed, tonight's accommodation is surprisingly hygienic. The mattress doesn't have any unidentifiable stains and the bathroom has three loos all with toilet seats. I follow the aroma of garlic down the hallway. The sight of so many pilgrims in the kitchen makes me turn back, but then someone hands me a plastic cup.

'Prost,' says a man with a belly protruding from his t-shirt. He slaps my back as I swallow the wine. Introductions follow, including those from tonight's chefs, Thilo and Jürgen, who add herbs and every other jar they can find into their homemade sauce while a huge cauldron of pasta boils away. There are too many names to remember, but I don't recall their faces and most importantly, no one seems to recognise mine. Thilo pours a different carton of wine into my cup. I make an excuse about leaving to buy more supplies, but he says three euros will be more than enough to cover costs.

'Sit down, Michael,' he says, sipping sauce from the wooden spoon. 'We eat now.'

Food arrives as everyone bangs their cutlery on the table. The enormous quantity soon turns into second and third portions, although this doesn't stop ice-cream and apple pie from appearing. For the first time that evening, conversation slows. And before I can stop, my mind returns to that blurred image on the woman's camera.

It's the only thing I've been thinking about all day — that somehow, that giant, shirtless, bare-footed figure standing next to the boot rack really was him. For a moment this after-noon, I almost convinced myself he was still alive; that I wasn't a murderer. But who was I fooling? Massimo is dead. He's never coming back; not after what I did to him with that staff.

There must be hundreds of men with shaved heads walking the Camino. And his bare feet didn't prove anything. He was standing in front of the boot rack, for God's sake. That's why he was there in the first place; to put on his hiking boots before starting the day's stage. I must seriously be losing the plot if I actually believed it was Massimo.

'So who's ready for shooting stars?' says someone across the table.

All the conversations about walking with full stomachs must have gone over my head, as it turns out everyone's going to sleep for just a few hours, before waking for the meteor shower that's happening tonight.

'You must join us,' says Thilo, gripping my shoulder. 'We leave at four am. And bring lots of water. There are no fountains for twenty kilometres so we must beat the sun. Tomorrow is the hottest day of the year.'

I sit lost in the languages around me. Tonight's meal was the most fun I've had all Camino, at least until I started thinking about Massimo. How many other nights have I missed out on, all because I was terrified of being caught? With less than a quarter of my savings left and four hundred kilometres still to walk, I finally feel part of something. I award everyone at the table five Camino Points, myself included, and ten to the man who pours the last dregs of wine into my cup. Seduced by the moment, I ask where we are, if only to remember the town where I had my Camino epiphany. Someone answers, but the name is lost on me.

'Carrión,' shouts another pilgrim across the table. 'You know, carry on, like Queen.'

'Queen?' I ask, but Jürgen has already got to his feet. He holds his palms flat and in a baritone, sings the opening lines of Bohemian Rhapsody. Before I anticipate the next part, he reaches the ballad section.

A chill runs down my neck.

Someone pulls me into the circle of arms linked around the table. I try to escape but a hand pulls me back. Everyone raises their voices, not a single one of them aware of my terrible attachment to Freddie Mercury's words.

Tears fill my eyes. I'm trapped inside their bond. And it's true. I have killed a man.

Their arms tighten as the song reaches its climax. The

final refrain arrives with Jürgen on his knees, hands clasped together and pleading to the ceiling. The imaginary gong sounds in my head.

I fall into my chair, unable to look beyond the floor.

And then it's over.

Except it isn't.

Because everything matters now.

WEDNESDAY 25 JUNE

'Michael. You awake?'

My eyes open just as Massimo's head hits the ground. A figure is standing over me in the darkness. 'Leave me alone,' I shout, pulling myself back to the wall. 'Leave me alone!'

'Relax, Michael. It's me. Thilo.'

He switches on the light. The dorm is empty except for the German who sits at the foot of my bed. I wipe the sweat from my forehead. Thank God no one else heard my nightmare.

'Are you ready for the meteor shower?' he says, frowning. 'Everyone's outside ready to leave.'

It must be four o'clock; still two and a half hours before sunrise. What am I supposed to do when I finish the stage before midday? I can only afford municipal albergues and my budget is dependent on cooking in the shared kitchens. But Luc can't be far behind. And the longer I spend on the trail, the more likely the chances that I'll bump into someone who knows me as James. I can't risk people knowing that I've been lying about my name. Not with the investigation still ongoing. I still can't believe the Policía Nacional issued all those wanted notices just to return my missing passport. But it won't be much longer until they realise I killed him.

'Just give me twenty minutes,' I say, pulling up the bed sheets.

Thilo switches off the light. He disappears down the corridor, although not before telling everyone that I won't be joining them.

I turn over and try to fall asleep, but all I can see is Massimo's bleeding head. Pilgrim voices pass under my window. This is the only meteor shower I'll get to experience in my life. I won't see the night sky again for years, maybe decades, after they lock me up in some Spanish prison. I can't waste the precious time I have left.

I drag myself out of bed, pack my things and then leave the albergue.

———

I stare up, shivering from the cold. An infinite number of stars hang above. This is the earliest I've woken all Camino, but I feel fresh after only a few hours' sleep.

I follow the road out of town. It's impossible to know where I'm going but the route's mostly straight. A headlamp would help considering I still manage to get lost in the daylight, but there's something exhilarating about trusting my senses in the dark. The night is bewitching. I feel a connection — one that doesn't fit into words. It's as though I'm the only person here. Like I've left all my troubles behind. I take small steps, straining my gaze at the sky in search of any movements above. Something slips through the corner of my eye but then disappears before I was sure it was ever there.

Time seems to have acquired a new measurement, its minutes moving faster than I've known. 'Don't rush your Camino,' said Robin when we parted two days ago. And yet I've been doing the complete opposite ever since I set off from St-Jean. I've been counting down every kilometre, not once appreciating the unique moments of each day. My urgency has only got worse since I promised to finish this pilgrimage. I've become obsessed with walking four and a half kilometres an hour, regardless of the inclines or thirty-five degree temperatures. I've been on auto-pilot for weeks, following my legs for long stretches without noticing anything. There are times when I'm so focused on the trail, that when I do look behind, I don't recognise the landscape I've just walked through. Days are anonymous, except for Sundays when all the shops are closed. I've been so fixated on following the yellow arrows that I forgot why I'm here. But under these bright stars, the Camino is alive. My senses are sharpened. All I have to do is walk. Walk until my morning shadow grows shorter and the sun overtakes me so that it casts my mark on the land behind. I will think, drink, eat and sometimes talk, before reaching the next bed at the next albergue. And then I will wake early and repeat everything all over again.

I have just enough money. One hundred euros in notes from the cash machine, forty-seven euros change from the last fifty note, and eight pounds in my overdraft, minus the six euros for last night's bed and three for the communal dinner. One hundred and forty-six euros. There are seventeen stages left. If I walk a stage and a half every day, that gives me a daily budget of ten euros. It doesn't offer choices, but it's enough. Enough for a banana for breakfast, bread and ham for lunch, and a shared meal in an albergue for dinner. There'll be no more luxuries; no more Menu Peregrinos, private albergues, or fiestas. I'll channel all my efforts into making the most of the time I have left. And maybe, I can let myself pretend, at least until Santiago, that I didn't kill Massimo.

There! A streak of light across the sky. My first shooting star. Five Camino Points. And then a snail shell breaks under my boot. My second Camino murder. Minus five Points.

Darkness concedes to dawn.

The meteor shower dies for ever.

I complete the stage just as the sun has climbed the sky. It's not even one o'clock — a record considering I normally walk until the evening — but today's heat is different; a suffocating humidity that burns the air before it reaches the ground. This is far enough. I'll make up more kilometres tomorrow.

My blisters ache as I approach the municipal albergue. Inspired by the thought of an early shower and a bed to rest, I reach the entrance. The Hospitalero must have forgotten to remove the 'completo' sign from yesterday because the albergue can't already be full.

A shadow falls across the door, followed by heavy breathing down my neck.

'You've got to be shitting me,' says a loud voice that makes me flinch.

The man pulls open the door which I thought was locked. I follow his large boots into the main dorm. Most of the beds are occupied but there are ten or so in the far corner, all with 'reservado' signs on their mattresses.

'Knew it,' he says, wiping an arm across his red face. 'Fucking Downton.'

He shoves the nearest bunk, almost toppling the bed. 'You!' he says, fixing his blood-shot eyes on me. 'You're one of them, aren't ya?'

I ask what he means but this only aggravates him more. His arms are wider than my head, his feet size twelves. 'So which one are ya?' he says, towering over me. 'Upstairs or Downstairs?'

I'm too exhausted to deny whatever he thinks I've done.

'So ya not in Downton?' he asks, after I say for the third time I'm walking alone.

I shake my head, still oblivious to what this means.

His stare fades. 'At least one of ya Poms out here isn't,' he says. 'Here, I'm Dale.'

His handshake crushes my fingers. 'Good to meet you, Michael.' he says, turning his bleached eyebrows to his phone. 'Says here the next alberg's five clicks away. We need to keep moving before others arrive. I've got some tinnies on me. My way of apologising.'

Dale sets a hard pace but the warm beer loosens my tired legs. 'Downton', I learn, is his name for the group of English teachers who are moving 'like some biblical plague' from one albergue to the next. 'Shame ya selectors didn't send them out for the last Ashes,' he says, cracking open another San Miguel which foams down the can. My reminder of Jonny's drop goal earns me a second beer and a four-lettered term of endearment.

At twelve euros, the private albergue is a dent on my finances, but the next municipal is a whole stage away and the beers have gone to my head. Dale seems to know most of the pilgrims sitting in the garden which contains the only plant life I've seen all day. The Aussie introduces me to everyone, including two physiotherapists from Valencia who supposedly work miracles with their massages. 'And he's not in Downton,' says Dale, landing a hand on my shoulder just as I'm convinced no one here already knows me as James. 'Mike's one of the good guys.'

'I've seen what Downton are doing,' says a Scandinavian woman with arms covered in tattoos. 'Every day they choose someone to go ahead and reserve all the beds so the others can stop for lunches and long drinks breaks. I can't count how many times I've been turned away from an albergue even though it's only half full. I could literally kill them.'

The garden falls silent.

I stare at the tattoo on the woman's shoulder. It's the face of a young girl with stitches sewn through her lips, a spiderweb across her forehead and a blossomed rosebud behind her ear. But it's the eyes I can't stop looking at; those wide, childlike eyes which are gazing back at me as though they know exactly what I've done.

'Here,' says Dale pushing a phone into my hands. 'You'll like this one, Mike.'

My eyes stare at the screen as I enlarge the image. It's me alright — or rather my back, covered in hundreds of ant bites, and Jessica, the Irish nurse, grinning in the foreground. Somehow, neither Dale or the others recognise me, possibly because of my thinner beard in the photo, but I still deduct Jessica five Camino Points for breaking patient confidentiality.

My photograph prompts various conspiracies; one pilgrim accusing me of spreading a bedbug epidemic which has closed several albergues over the last few stages. Dale shares the image with friends back home but my back apparently went viral earlier this week.

'Well,' says Dale, opening another beer. 'At least it's a distraction from the other story.'

He frowns when I ask what he means. 'You do know about the Italian who got knocked off out here, don't ya, Mike?'

The effect of the beer immediately wears off. My face is burning but I manage to hold eye-contact. 'Of course,' I reply, aware how all the other conversations have stopped. 'I just thought they'd caught the murderer by now. It happened two weeks ago, right?'

'You haven't been following the news?'

Dale stares back as I explain my situation. 'Who doesn't take a phone with them on Camino? You gone troppo or something?'

I try to describe my bet with Greg and Dev back in London but Dale's too wired to listen. 'I've had mates back in the Alice calling up just to check I'm alright. Apparently, they're no closer to finding out who did it. Thought I'd left those crazy bastards back o' Bourke, but here we are, walking through the desert, with some nut on the loose.'

One of the girls tells Dale to shut up but he refuses to drop the subject. 'I wouldn't worry. He must be well off the trail by now. Anyway, the Camino's too important for tourism for the Spanish to let him off the hook. Fourteen years in the can. That's what they're saying.'

'He?' I interrupt. 'How do you know it wasn't a woman?'

Dale's glare makes me look away. 'Look, Mike,' he says, raising his voice. 'How many sheilas do you know could smash some bloke's skull in with a weapon?'

'Dale!' someone yells.

'Anyway,' he continues, 'last I heard, forensics had a match for the fingerprints inside that cabin as well as the foot-prints outside —'

'Someone make him stop,' says the Scandinavian, whose Day of the Dead tattoo is still watching me.

'All I'm saying,' says Dale, 'is that it won't be long before they catch that psycho and throw away the key. And all the better for it. Righto,' he says, finally breaking his stare. 'Who's hungry? I could murder some grub.'

THURSDAY 26 JUNE

I dream I'm back in the same London meeting room where we had our work appraisals. Air-conditioning sterilises the oxygen. Gone is the view of the east end building site, replaced now by a thirty-storey building whose glass panels reflect the seventies monstrosity I'm trapped inside. Bottles of spring water line the cabinet but their caps are too tight to open. Pages fill the places at the main table. I recognise their grid layout; the categories ranging from one to five and the comments box below. The same jagged signature has signed off every form, the ink from the firm's pens still wet. The sheets are identical; all replica copies of my final appraisal when the Managing Director said he was letting me go.

A shadow appears behind the frosted glass. I drop to the ground, convinced that it's him. A pair of imitation brogues pass the lower transparent screen. He must have seen me, but instead the footsteps continue towards the open-plan office. The Hanging Bell starts ringing with deafening tolls. I open the door wide enough to see a young graduate pulling the rope. The sound can only mean one thing. Money. My old colleagues give him a standing ovation, clapping as though they are lining their own pockets. They are all wearing new suits.

I take advantage of the diversion and slip through the door. The Managing Director has started his speech about quarterly profits, his voice no longer grave in the manner he reserved for my weekly reviews. I crawl behind the desks towards the exit. My backpack has doubled in weight, the Lycra shorts tighter than usual. It must have rained as my trainers are coated in mud. I reach the end of the corridor but instead of the main staircase I find the men's toilets. I open the window above the sink but it's too high to jump with the traffic four floors below. I lock myself in the furthest stall and take out Alistair's phone. The screen is still cracked from where I dropped it outside Massimo's cabin. Eight fifteen say the digits in the top corner. What am I doing in my old office this early? I never arrived before half nine; the latest time permitted by the Employee Handbook which no one bothered to read.

Fuck. I can't let anyone know that I'm here, hiding in the staff toilets. Security took my key card months ago, so the first thing they'll want to know is how I got inside. And then I'll have the shame of explaining what I'm doing with my life. What do I say? Lie about retraining as an arms dealer or confess that I'm walking some pilgrimage through Spain because I couldn't think of anything better to do with my life? I consider sending Greg or Dev an SOS, but they'd never live it down how they had to bail me out of my old office, dressed in Lycra shorts and carrying a purple backpack.

Time drags slower than it did at my old desk. No one, thank God, comes in to use the toilet, but I still haven't decided how to respond if someone knocks on my stall and asks who's inside. Alistair's phone has said it's nine twenty for the last ten minutes. If I hide here all morning, I'll have to kill another three hours for the lunch club to go downstairs. But even then, there'll still be others taking calls on the main floor. The office won't be empty until well after six.

The temptation of social media is too much to resist. It's marvellous to be back, even though nothing has changed. Wedding montages, holiday snaps and new home owners' house keys all pop up, before I see a selfie of that same pilgrim faking her Camino by travelling around by taxi. My chest is pounding. I'm desperate to know if that giant, shirt-less figure with bare feet has appeared in any more of her photographs, but then the feed refreshes and a different face fills the screen. Jessica. My Jessica — no, Alistair's girl-friend. She's just shared a photo from a spa day with her girl-friends. I enlarge the image, dying to see if the baby bump is visible, but she's wearing a long white dressing gown tied around her waist. I read every comment, but there's no mention of a pregnancy next to the three hundred likes. I start trawling through her profile, clicking on every status she's posted in the time we've been apart. I don't know how I've survived this long without Instagram. It feels like months, years almost, since I saw Jessica's photos and read her anec-dotes about London life. But then I see her and Alistair posing in front of a sunset on Hampstead Heath. And the fantasy comes crashing down.

Eleven thirty. I can't stay here a minute longer. If I had a lighter, I could set off the sprinklers, but there's only one emergency exit and it leads out into the side street where the company's nominated fire officer ticks off everyone's names on the register. A hoax fire drill would be the equivalent of staging my own execution. I'd be marched out of the building and led straight into my public humiliation. There'd be one hell of a bill to pay for all the damage. I doubt the insurance policy covers vandalism by jaded ex-employees, turned Camino pilgrims. I take one last breath and walk out of the toilets, ready to announce my return. Except he beats me to it.

'Well, well,' says the Managing Director, projecting his voice across the office. 'Look who it is. James Pollock. And he's forgotten to wear trousers!'

Blank faces stare up from their screens, while others turn back to their computers, including the new graduate who's taken my old desk. The Managing Director steps forward. He must have bathed himself in cologne and there's so much hair gel on his scalp that I can practically see flies circling overhead. 'Why don't you do us all the pleasure of explaining why you're back in our office,' he says, staring with vacant eyes. 'And while you're at it, maybe you can explain why you're carrying that pink backpack?'

I can't speak. None of the excuses I'd practised in the toilets now seem acceptable.

The photocopiers start churning out sheets of paper. I ask what's going on but the Managing Director waves his signet ring at the nearest machine. The feeder is stacked with hundreds of printouts. I pick up the first page. It's the same British newspaper that I read online in the boarding school albergue. My hands dig deeper through the pile but the pages are all the same. '*Manhunt for James Pollock, Camino murderer*,' reads the headline above an enlarged image of my passport photograph.

'Everyone knows what you did, James,' says the Managing Director. 'Or should I say, Michael.'

Policía Nacional storm the office. I try to explain what happened outside that cabin, but they crush my wrists with handcuffs and lead me towards the exit.

'See you in fourteen years,' someone shouts across the office. 'Unless they throw away the key.'

A hand grips my shoulder. I pull away and hit something hard.

'Jeez, Mike,' says a voice in my ear. 'You didn't half cack yaself.'

Light fills the room. But instead of my old office, I'm back in the albergue.

Dale is standing next to my bed. 'What was all that about?' he says. '*He made me do it*! That's what you were shouting.'

I wipe the sweat from my forehead, too shocked to respond.

'*It wasn't me. He made me do it.* That's what ya kept saying, Mike.'

'Must have been a bad dream,' I reply.

'Of course,' Dale interrupts, his eyes fixed on mine. 'Just a bad dream.'

Silence fills the dorm. There's no way he's going to keep his mouth shut about what just happened. Every pilgrim walking this stage is going to know about my night terror before the end of the day. It won't take long for someone to put two and two together.

'Anyway,' says Dale, walking towards the door. 'Downton just walked past. Time to get going if ya want a bed for tonight.'

He gives me one last stare then leaves the room.

I'm tired of these straight paths without vegetation or shade. There's no texture. Nothing to distinguish this flat, yellow landscape. Nothing new to touch my senses. Every kilometre only leads to more emptiness.

I can't stay in the same albergue as Dale again. It was bad

enough he brought up the murder investigation, but that was before he witnessed my nightmare.

Christ. What if I shouted Massimo's name in my sleep? What if I confessed to killing him with that staff? I thought I'd covered my tracks by wearing these hiking boots, which are literally tearing the skin off my feet with blisters. But what if Dale's information was true? What if the forensics already have my fingerprints from the crime scene?

Fuck. Why did I go into Massimo's cabin? And to then pull on the door handle because I thought he'd locked me inside. I literally gripped onto that metal handle as hard as I could before I yanked it open. I must have left perfect prints behind.

I can't afford any more mistakes. My social evenings in the albergues are over. I have to go back to being anonymous. It's the only way I'll reach Santiago and finish this cursed pilgrimage.

———

I continue beyond the end of the stage, as far as possible from Dale and all of last night's pilgrims, until I find a six euro bed. The Hospitalero recommends the local restaurant, but it's an extravagance I cannot afford. There's an old packet of spaghetti and some dry herbs in the kitchen cupboard, so I head to the village shop for extra ingredients. The family-sized can of tuna is out of my budget, although there's a cheap corned beef alternative on the back shelf.

I should have checked the albergue's cooking facilities, as the plug-in electric hob emits a cloud of smoke when I switch it on and the saucepan has a burn at the bottom which has worn through the enamel. The boiling water turns the pasta black and flakes come away from the pan as I drain its contents into the sink. The corned beef is coated in a thick gelatine-like substance which slops out of the tin in a tube-shaped serving. I slice the rubbery meat and try to hide its stench with oregano.

I manage to eat half of the bowl before it starts confusing my stomach. Three glasses of water can't cure the sickness in my gut, so I stare out of the window and watch the baby swallows race in and out of the rafters, until their high-speed acrobatics increase my urge to vomit.

A tall, bald man in his early-forties enters the kitchen and starts barking financial instructions down his phone. His vocabulary reminds me of the time Alistair tried to explain the difference between a management buy-in and buy-out over Christmas lunch one year, but just as I start thinking about my brother's professional misconduct accusation, the man's voice returns, its previously uncompromising tone now replaced with something more tender.

'I know, babe,' he says, as though his threat to axe a colleague three minutes earlier came from an entirely different person. 'I miss you too, but I'll be back home soon.'

Light catches the silver wedding band on his left hand. 'We'll do something special to celebrate — drive into Toronto or spend a week at the lake house.'

He turns back to the kitchen door. 'Look, more people just arrived. Let's chat tomorrow. I know. Okay.' And then, as if pushed to say it, 'I love you too.'

The man ends the call, grimaces at my half-eaten bowl of dog food and leaves the empty kitchen.

I lie in the dark, listening to the corned beef in my stomach.

The swallows have stopped singing and everyone in the dorm can hear my digestion.

Something outside triggers the light sensor in the lane. The room starts spinning. I lie still in the orange light and try to ignore the churning in my belly, but this only increases the nausea. Vomit fills my mouth. I catch most of it in my hands but the room starts revolving faster. I retch again; my body's final warning.

I run through the room, trying to remember the way down the corridor.

Light escapes from under the bathroom door. I twist the handle but it's locked. I run back down the corridor, both hands around my mouth. There are no plastic bags in the boot rack and the rancid smell of hiking boots makes me gag.

The kitchen is too far away upstairs. I'll never reach the sink in time.

My insides must be coated in that slimy gelatine from the corned beef. Visions of the food factory enter my mind, its shirtless employees scooping up lumps of mince with their bare hands from a revolving conveyor belt. I pound on the bathroom door, pleading with whoever's inside to finish their business. No one answers.

I lean against the door with my shoulder, trying to prise it open, until a woman's voice says 'one more minute'.

Sweat runs down my face. My stomach lurches, its contents reaching the upper walls of my stomach. The woman's promise of one minute expires. I run back down the corridor in search of the main entrance but then the bathroom door finally opens. I see her shadow return quickly to the dorm. I burst through the door, past a bald man who is washing his hands in the sink.

My vomit hits the porcelain. I direct chunks of undigested food into the toilet, retching from the pain. A second wave follows, which must come from another chamber inside my stomach. I heave until there's nothing left.

Tears fill my eyes as I stare at the orange water. Something is floating in my vomit. It's made of latex with a knot tied at the end.

I look back to the sink in time to see the Toronto banker's face leave the mirror.

'Darling, there's something I need to tell you...' says Jessica's voice in my mind.

I spit on the used condom and pull the chain.

DAY EIGHTEEN

FRIDAY 27 JUNE

León's street lights appear in the distance, almost bringing me to my knees. I'm exhausted, completely sapped of energy. A fast-food advertising board lines the footbridge over the motorway, the Camino's yellow arrows replaced with two-for-one hamburger deals. I haven't eaten anything all day; not since last night's corned beef.

I felt so weak this morning that I almost cheated. The bar which filled my water bottle had a timetable with all the buses heading into the city. *'Who's going to know?'* said a voice in my head — the same one that's started telling me to pretend I didn't kill Massimo. *'But then everything will be wasted,'* said a different voice, presumably what's left of my conscience. *'You must walk the whole way. There's nothing left for you after Santiago.'*

The solitude of the trail is broken by crowds and traffic. I'm desperate to escape, but walking any further this evening will finish me off. Albergue signs in the old town lead to a converted monastery. I check-in at the main desk with the Credentials and climb the stone staircase. Too tired to undress, I take a bottom bunk in the corner of the large room and collapse onto the mattress.

A moan fills the dorm. I lie half-asleep, waiting for someone else to help this pilgrim who's clearly in distress. The low, whimpering sound is impossible to ignore. My head is throbbing, probably from dehydration, but eventually I get to my feet.

Light filters through the slats in the closed shutters. I follow the sound past rows of empty bunks, my mind conjuring images from that cliffside which I wish I couldn't see.

I step on a creaking floorboard. The moaning stops. It's just the two of us alone.

The stench of urine takes me straight back to his abandoned cabin. I can almost hear the wind scraping the branches; almost sense that steep drop in the darkness. I can't stop thinking about what Robin said when he sensed that dying deer in the ditch. Death is close to this room as well. I can feel it all around me.

A figure is lying on the top bunk, covered with a white sheet.

I can hardly breathe. The body. It looks just like him.

Slowly, I raise my trembling hand and lift the sheet back from his head.

In the darkness, the man's face looks just like his. I can't believe this is happening. That he's really here. I pull the sheet further back.

The eyes jolt open.

'Michael,' says his weak voice. 'Is that you?'

I shudder as his scabbed arm reaches out towards me. I recognise the man, even though I cannot place him. My lungs feel crushed. Did I really think it was Massimo? He's dead. I killed him. He's never coming back.

'You don't remember me,' whispers the man. 'Your shorts. I helped you find them.'

'Iñaki?'

I stare at the skin stretched across his ribcage. He looks famished, his skin so mottled that it couldn't have seen sunlight in days.

'I didn't get more heroin, if that's what you're thinking. But I really need some.'

He tries to lift himself from the bed but there's no strength in his arms. 'Help me to the bathroom. Please.'

I support Iñaki's weight along the corridor until we reach the empty bathroom. The sharp light exposes the welts on his arms. I undress him and hold his hand as he steps into the shower. The water is freezing but he stands underneath, rubbing soap on his body until his lips turn blue. I turn off the tap and wrap a towel around his shoulders. We return slowly to the empty dorm where he sits trembling on a chair. I strip the soiled sheets from his bed and open the large windows, hoping this will circulate fresh air in the room.

The lost property basket has a pink Hawaiian shirt and grey tracksuit bottoms covered in paint stains. The clothes look ridiculous but they lift Iñaki's spirits. 'I need food,' he says. 'Can we go outside?'

The stone staircase hurts his legs but after two rest breaks we finally reach the bottom. A group of pilgrims in the foyer look up from their card game. Instinctively, I look away, convinced that someone might recognise me from the first week, but no one says my old name.

Iñaki takes a pair of trainers from the boot rack. I stare at them, not quite believing what I see. My old skate shoes. How the hell are they here? I hid them in that ecological albergue where my wanted notice was pinned to the message board. That was the last place I saw Iñaki. Christ.

He must have pulled back the boot rack and found my old trainers stuffed against the wall. They were supposed to have stayed undiscovered there for years; at least until Massimo had long been forgotten. But there's not a chance of that now.

'Like my shoes?' says Iñaki, looking up as he ties my old laces.

I can barely speak. My footprints were all around that cabin. If the Policía Nacional find Iñaki wearing my old trainers, they'll immediately think he's the murderer. I have to get those shoes away from him.

'There are hiking boots in lost property,' I say, reaching for the trainer he hasn't yet laced around his foot. 'Let me find you another pair.'

Iñaki shakes his head.

'But they're falling apart,' I interrupt. 'You'll never get to Santiago wearing those.'

'No, Michael,' he says, snatching the trainer from my hand. 'They're perfect for my blisters. Come on. Let's leave.'

───────

We wander through the old town, stopping every time Iñaki's legs tire. My stomach has recovered from last night's food poisoning, but we need to find somewhere cheap considering I promised to buy dinner. The fast-food chain with the two-for-one burgers can't be far away, but after ten minutes, Iñaki gives up and drops to the pavement.

The restaurant across the road is open, although the smartly-dressed Friday clientele isn't exactly our scene. I sit next to Iñaki and stare at his shoes. I should have destroyed my trainers while I still had the chance. I'll have to steal them from the boot rack when Iñaki goes to bed. There's no way I can let him walk in those shoes; not with the murder investigation still ongoing.

Metal shutters clatter open behind us. A feral-looking boy walks outside and asks if we're hungry. Iñaki accepts, clearly relieved at not having to walk any further. There's one other person inside the restaurant; a large, dark-haired woman, who's presumably the boy's mother. She drops a stack of plates on the bar, mutters something under her breath and hands me a laminated menu. Three courses for nine euros is the cheapest I've found all Camino, but eighteen euros is fifteen percent of my remaining funds. I suggest leaving, aware that the two-for-one burgers will cost half the price, but Iñaki's decided what he wants to order.

The boy returns with a bucket and mop. I wait for him to lay a table or set up the plastic chairs, but instead he starts flooding the floor with chemicals. The fan above our table must be on its highest setting, the blades rattling as though warning us of our imminent decapitation.

'Pablo!' yells the woman at the bar. She cuffs the boy on the cheek and sends him over to our table with wine and two plastic cups. The bottle slips out of his hands. It rolls to the edge of the table, seconds from smashing on the floor before Iñaki's reflexes somehow intervene. The boy stabs the corkscrew into the top and starts twisting until the cork splits. Unaware of his mistake, he starts pumping the bottle-opener's arms, but the cork refuses to move. Pablo grips the bottle and pulls until his face turns red. Without warning, the corkscrew flies out of his hands, landing halfway across the room.

The boy turns to his mother and then to our wine bottle, where the half-severed cork remains trapped in its neck. Pablo pushes his finger into the hole. The cork lands in the wine where it floats on the surface. He fills our plastic cups to the top, the cork still bobbing inside the bottle, and then takes our orders.

Iñaki and I both have the mixed salad which comprises of an unthawed lettuce, green tomatoes and a boiled egg which needed three more minutes in the saucepan. My patience, however, expires when the main course arrives.

'Buen provecho,' says the boy, as if he genuinely believes we're going to enjoy Salmonella poisoning.

From the smell, it's obvious the cod is undercooked, but then I poke it with my fork. The flesh slips away, revealing a pink layer underneath.

Dinner was supposed to be my good deed — at least ten Camino Points — but even Iñaki seems hesitant to eat. I call Pablo over. The boy shakes his head and says there's nothing wrong with the fish, although I suspect this is more from his fear of displeasing the chef. After more persuasion, he takes both plates back to the kitchen. Mother follows son through the swinging doors. Our plates return thirty seconds later, steam wafting from the sodden fish which smells worse than before. Iñaki raises a fork to his mouth, chews suspiciously with his black gums, then spits out the slimy fish. He apologises, but it's me who's more embarrassed. Iñaki doesn't have any money. And for eighteen euros, we'll both be leaving on empty stomachs.

I need to use the toilet, but the thought of walking past the kitchen is too much for my imagination. Who knows what else they're cooking up in there, or how many rats are scavenging through the bin bags? I lean forwards across the table. 'Iñaki?' I whisper.

He looks up from the pink fish.

'Want to get out of here?'

A smile fills his lips. 'You mean leave and not pay?'

'Yes.'

Iñaki stands up, placing a rolled cigarette in his mouth. He makes a smoking gesture to the woman but she's too busy watering down the wine to notice.

'See you in the albergue,' he says, hobbling towards the door in my old trainers.

I sit quietly, trying to time my escape. The fact that no one else has walked into the restaurant seems to explain our dining experience, but without other customers it's going to be hard to leave unnoticed. And the woman still hasn't left her place behind the bar.

The fan pushes the stench of fish through the restaurant. I was supposed to earn Camino Points in buying Iñaki dinner, not cheat a struggling family business. Iñaki left five minutes ago; surely long enough for him to get to safety. Any longer and the mother will get suspicious. I push away the plate, wondering if I'm up to faking a violent episode of food poisoning. Surely she won't follow me outside if I shove my hands down my throat and start retching? Then again, why go to all that trouble when I could just run? I'll have long made it across the street, past the real restaurant opposite and out of sight, before she even made it around the bar.

The woman asks me something in Spanish, presumably about where Iñaki has gone. I shake my head and check my wrist even though I'm not wearing a watch.

'Pablo?' she yells.

The boy doesn't respond. She slams down a tray of cutlery and walks towards my table, nearly slipping in a puddle of bleach. Her hands collect both plates. Oblivious to our untouched fish, she asks what we want for pudding. She glares back when I ask her to repeat the options. I choose the chocolate mousse and order fruit salad for Iñaki. The woman yells my order to the door, but there's no answer.

'Pablo?'

Again, she calls his name. Again, he doesn't answer.

'Joder!'

She kicks open the kitchen door. By the time it swings back, I've already left the restaurant.

The adrenaline carries me through the old town. It's difficult to find my bearings with everyone outside eating tapas and drinking wine. I get lost down an alleyway, but then the passage leads out in front of the Cathedral. After numerous wrong turns, including one past the fast-food chain with the two-for-one burgers, I find a yellow arrow. Other markers guide me back to the monastery which is now mostly hidden in darkness.

Iñaki is sitting next to the boot rack, his pink Hawaiian shirt half unbuttoned. He looks at me blankly and then to the group in the courtyard. Pablo is standing next to a large man wearing chef whites, presumably his father. Two police officers walk towards me. The taller man, with a shaved head, asks for my Credentials. He snatches the booklet from my hand and turns to the first page.

'Michael Evans,' he says to his colleague. 'El mismo nombre.'

I ask the Hospitalero what's happening, but it's clear from his expression whose side he's on. 'This is not your first time is it, Michael?' says the old man who checked me into the albergue only hours earlier. He shakes his head when I ask what he means. 'The first time you lied about your identity.'

The room starts spinning.

'I don't understand,' I say, clinging to any chance of an escape.

'The credit card you stole in St-Jean-Pied-de-Port,' says the Hospitalero. 'You pretended to be Michael Evans and used his card to pay for restaurants and hotels in the first week of the Camino.'

'What are you talking about?' I say, barely controlling my voice. 'You think I stole someone's credit card?'

'Then why are you using Michael Evans' Credenciales?'

'I lost my documents,' I say, trying to ignore the police officers as they surround me. 'But then I found Michael's Credentials outside Logroño — that was after the first week. Tonight was the first time I didn't pay in a restaurant. I swear that's the truth. My real name is James Pollock.'

The Hospitalero explains everything to the officers in Spanish.

'So your name is definitely James Pollock?' the old man asks again.

'It's true,' says a voice on the staircase. 'His name is James. We met on the first day.'

The officer grips my arm before I can turn to the man who just spoke.

Iñaki looks at me briefly and then turns away. He knows now that I've been lying to him this whole time. He knows I'm the same person from the photograph on the wanted notices; that same face which Iñaki said looked like my doppelgänger.

Shame burns my face. Our friendship is over. And any moment, the police are going to see the shoes on Iñaki's feet. No one else on the Camino is wearing those trainers; the same trainers whose footprints were all around Massimo's cabin.

'They want to see identification,' says the Hospitalero. 'Your real one, James.'

The officer takes the passport from my hand. His eyes study my personal details and move on to the photograph. The conversation continues in Spanish.

'So you admit you ran from the restaurant without paying?' the Hospitalero translates.

'Yes,' I reply, staring at Pablo's father who looks like he wants to punch me. 'And you would have done the same if you'd seen the food they served us —'

'Now's not the time for sarcasm,' the Hospitalero interrupts. 'The officers are going to take you both to the police station for written statements.'

'Iñaki's innocent,' I interrupt. 'It was my idea. I told him to run.'

'No, James,' says Iñaki, with more conviction than he's shown all evening. 'I must come with you as well.'

'Iñaki will stay here then,' says the other officer in perfect English. 'But if you are who you say you are, James, then you better have a good reason why you've been lying about your name.'

Handcuffs clamp my wrists.

I look back to the staircase and catch Joseph's eye. *See you in Santiago, Saint James* says his voice in my head.

DAY NINETEEN
SATURDAY 28 JUNE

I wake on the small bed in my cell. It's too dark to guess the time but my body has become attuned to waking before sunrise.

My thoughts backtrack to last night. As soon as we'd arrived at the police station, the officers took me out of the truck and led me through a side entrance behind tall security gates until we reached a small interview room. They then told me to sit at the table and closed the door, locking it from the outside. However long they left me in there I couldn't say, but I knew they were watching from behind the one-way mirror. Finally, the two officers returned, switched on the recording equipment and sat on the opposite side of the table.

'Let's start by confirming your identity,' said the English-speaking officer, fixing his eyes on me. 'What is your name?'

'James Pollock,' I replied, clenching the edge of the seat with my fingers.

'Speak into the microphone.'

I stared at the equipment in front of me. 'My name is James Pollock.'

The officer unbuttoned his cuffs and put his elbows on the

table. 'I want you to tell us everything that happened after St-Jean-Pied-de-Port.'

'What do you mean?' I asked, trying to ignore the coffee on his breath.

'Think carefully, James. This is your one chance.'

They already know, said the voice in my head. *They know you killed him.*

'I'm sorry,' I said, my eyes moving to the other officer whose silence was more intimidating. 'I don't understand what you want me to say.'

The officer leaned forwards with his thick forearms. 'Tell us where you stayed between St-Jean-Pied-de-Port and Logroño.'

'Where I stayed?'

'Yes,' he said, raising his voice so that the interview room felt more enclosed. 'Is that a difficult question, James?'

'No,' I replied, trying to ignore the sweat on my armpits. 'You want to know where I stayed in my first week.'

Staring at my hands, I spoke slowly, remembering my chronology out loud while the second officer took notes. When I couldn't remember a place name or albergue, the first officer searched for images on his phone, dictating the names into the microphone before asking me to confirm that these were the places where I stayed.

'And then you found Michael Evans' Credenciales,' said the officer. 'Not in St-Jean-Pied-de-Port, but on a bridge before Logroño? That was Tuesday the seventeenth of June.'

'Yes,' I said, too confused by the dates to know if this was the correct day.

His face made little effort to conceal his suspicion. 'And that was after you lost your own Credenciales in…'

'In Los Arcos,' I said, repeating the same lie I'd just told them. 'At least I think I lost my documents there.'

The officer's gaze sharpened, clearly aggravated by my interruption. 'In Los Arcos,' he said, as if completing his original sentence.

I shuddered as his eyes turned to his colleague's notes.

'So, James. You found another pilgrim's Credenciales just one day after you lost your own? Would you agree that this was... convenient?'

'I don't know,' I said, shaking my head.

'He doesn't know,' said the officer, repeating my answer into the microphone. 'So why James, did you decide to use Michael Evans' Credenciales instead of replacing your own lost documents in Logroño?'

Perhaps it was the pressure of having to support my previous lie, but my answer was surprisingly well-improvised. Under the glare of the interview room's lights, I explained how there wasn't time to buy new Credentials in Logroño as I needed to find an albergue that evening which wasn't already full. But then, before I realised what I was saying, I confessed about my wager with Greg and Dev.

'Let me get this correct,' said the officer, stretching his fingers across the table. 'You decided to use Michael Evans' Credenciales because you needed stamps from every stage to prove to your friends you walked all the way to Santiago?'

'Yes,' I replied, possibly too quickly. 'I didn't want to lose the prize money.'

'Prize money?' he interrupted. 'How much is this?'

'A thousand pounds.'

'A thousand pounds?' he repeated. 'Would you say that money is important to you, James, or that you might be tempted to steal from someone else; a credit card, maybe?'

'I didn't steal Michael Evans' credit card if that's what you're asking.'

The officer leaned closer. 'So you say, James. But didn't

you worry that something might have happened to Michael Evans? That maybe, he might be in trouble?'

'No,' I replied. 'The thought never occurred to me.'

'The thought never occurred to you?' the officer interrupted. 'You never thought it was suspicious that someone lost their Credenciales on that bridge, even though an Italian pilgrim was murdered on the Camino just days earlier?'

I fixed my eyes on the officer's gaze. 'No.'

White light floods the cell. I cover my eyes and slowly sit up. The officer speaks too quickly for me to understand and then points to the door. He escorts me through the police station, past plain-clothed officers eating breakfast and down a corridor to the interview room from last night. He knocks on the glass, behind which the same English-speaking officer is sitting.

'Entrad,' says the officer.

He puts down his coffee and watches me through narrow eyes. His lips start to smile as though he knows why I pretended to be Michael Evans. Fourteen years. That's what Dale said. How will I survive that long behind bars? It's two of Joseph's seven-year cycles, for Christ's sake. Maybe it's not too late to confess what happened outside the cabin that night. Maybe the judge will reduce my sentence if I show cooperation. There might still be time to do something with my life when I finally get out. I can't keep up this lie for ever. At some point, they're going to find out what I did.

My knees weaken as the officer points at the chair. 'Son las seis horas y cuarenta y dos minutos de la mañana,' he says, speaking into the microphone. It's not even seven o'clock.

'Okay, James,' he says slowly, as if testing the sound of my name. 'We have talked to all the albergues where you say you stayed in your first week.'

The officer stares at me from across the table. His words are unsettling. He must have spoken to the Hospitalero in Zubiri and discovered that I turned up late that night with blood all over my hands.

'You will be relieved to learn,' says the officer, still watching me, 'that they all confirmed the dates you provided.'

This can't be happening. It's too easy. One of those albergues must have said I was acting suspiciously — the cult leader in that religious community who asked if I'd seen Massimo on the trail, or the Hospitalero in Estella who gave the police my missing passport.

'We also spoke to the restaurant,' says the officer, placing his thick hands on the table. 'The family is very upset. If they'd known about your thousand-pound bet, they might have asked for more than eighteen euros, so consider yourself lucky.'

My head is spinning. Any moment now and he's going to explain the real reason why they arrested me.

The officer exhales slowly. 'My colleague outside will collect the payment. They also have your backpack. But we have one last formality.'

He places a small electronic box on the table.

'What is that?' I ask, staring at the object.

'You didn't think we'd let you leave without taking fingerprints, did you?'

Jesus Christ. He knows what I did. All this time he's been taunting me, when he really knows I'm the murderer.

The fingerprint machine beeps as he switches it on.

'Will this go on my record?' I interrupt.

'For eighteen euros?' says the officer. 'You think we would give you a criminal record for running from a restaurant?'

My chest is pounding. I have no idea if he's being sarcastic or not. Why did I ask that question? How could I have been so stupid?

'Put your right index finger on the scanner.'

My hand trembles as I reach for the black box. One simple scan of its reader is going to seal my fate. The machine beeps again. I can't decide whether to push hard against the screen or to just rest my finger on the sensor, but either way, it's going to take a clear record of my unique, individual fingerprints; the same fingerprints which were all over Massimo's staff and the door inside his cabin.

I try to keep my hand still but it's as though the machine is reading my thoughts. And then, before I know what's happening, I'm leaning over Massimo's body as his lifeless eyes stare blankly at the sky.

'James?' says a voice, breaking my thoughts.

'Yes,' I reply, looking up at the officer.

'Did you hear what I said?'

'Sorry. I didn't get much sleep.'

The man stares across the table. 'I said, that's everything. You are free to leave.'

My chair legs scrape on the white tiles. I walk towards the door, careful not to move too quickly. I can feel the officer watching me; hear the breathing through his nose. I reach for the handle, but not before he clears his throat.

'One last question,' he says, still speaking into the microphone.

Hairs climb the back of my neck. Slowly, I turn around.

'Thursday the twelfth of June,' says the officer. 'That was your second day on the Camino. You stayed in Zubiri.'

The officer cracks his knuckles. 'According to the Hospitalero, you arrived after ten o'clock at night. She said you seemed nervous. Angustiado was the word she used. Distressed.'

The officer looks down at his notes. 'Why do you think she said that, James?'

'I was — yes, something did happen that day. I had some bad news. Bad news from home.'

'From home?' asks the officer, snatching onto my words. 'But how did you find out? You are walking without a phone, no?'

'Yes,' I say quickly. 'That was the problem. I had to find somewhere with wifi.'

'So you went online?' he interrupts. 'Do your friends know you broke the bet?'

'No. It was just once. There was something I needed to check.'

'Have you been dishonest about other things as well, James? Dishonest like when you left the restaurant without paying. Maybe dishonest with me in this interview?'

I cross my arms to stop them shaking.

'No. I just needed to check my emails that day.'

'And where exactly did you check your emails that day?'

The lump in my throat is choking my glands.

'It was in a village. They had a computer. I just needed to check something.'

'Something with bad news?'

'Yes.'

'And what was this bad news, James?'

'News from a friend.'

The officer glares across the table. My nerves are shot. I've exhausted all my lies. One more question and I'm going to crack.

He leans forwards to the microphone. 'La entrevista termina a las seis horas y cincuenta minutos de la mañana.' The officer switches off the recording equipment.

My hand somehow opens the door.

'James?' says the voice behind me. 'Aren't you forgetting something?'

I turn back to the interrogation room. My legs won't hold much longer.

'Your Credenciales,' says the officer, sliding the booklet across the table. 'You'll need Michael's help if you're going to walk all the way to Santiago, won't you?'

I take the booklet and leave the room, James Pollock's lost Credentials still hidden inside the money belt under my shorts.

SUNDAY 29 JUNE

I can't believe I've come all this way, walked more than half the Camino, only to sabotage my whole pilgrimage for the sake of eighteen euros.

How the hell did the police not match my fingerprints? There must have been a technical glitch with the scanner which stopped their forensic records from connecting me to the murder. Maybe they've only just realised. But what if they haven't? What if the staff I saw in that albergue really was Massimo's? What if another pilgrim found the staff on the trail and just picked it up? It seems ridiculous, but nothing is impossible.

But whatever happened to the murder weapon, the whole police force in León know that I stole Michael Evans' Credentials.

It was just my luck to find documents belonging to a pilgrim whose credit card was stolen on the first day. No wonder the thief left Michael's booklet on that bridge. They must have used his card until it was finally declined or reported as stolen. I never even intended to use Michael's documents until I accidentally gave that nun the wrong booklet in Logroño. But by trying to stay anonymous, I've become one of the most notorious pilgrims on the trail — second only to Massimo.

Thank God the officers didn't search me. It's bad enough they know I arrived late in Zubiri on the night of the murder. But the thought of those officers patting me down and finding my original Credentials hidden in my money belt is too much to consider. They would have known immediately that I lied about losing my documents. Who knows what I might have confessed when they interrogated me for stealing another pilgrim's identity just as Massimo's murder became international news. Perhaps I would have told them everything.

Fate has intervened. But I can't afford any more mistakes. Any association with my name will pin me straight to the murder. The only way I'll reach Santiago is if I stop being James.

I have to destroy my old Credentials. Tearing the booklet to shreds or burying it in the ground won't be enough. I must burn the pages and leave only ashes behind.

I lower my head under a small entrance. The entire village must all be cramped inside the cafe; ten wrinkled faces huddled around coffees and plates of toast. The owner stands hunched in the corner, carving slices of cured ham off the bone. One of the elders coughs to catch her attention. The old lady hobbles over and smiles with sunken eyes. She offers me a slice of ham which tastes delicious, possibly because it's the only thing I've eaten all morning. I order coffee, still holding the two euro coin which I'd only intended to use to buy matches.

Her liver-spotted hand tilts a glass under the coffee machine. She presses the button and disappears into a small kitchen. The glass fills quickly. I'm convinced it's going to overflow, but then the fizz of a matchstick steals my attention. The lights go out, plunging the cafe into darkness.

The old lady emerges, holding a large chocolate cake with one candle in the centre. A rendition of 'Cumpleaños feliz' fills the tiny room. The cake passes under all the faces until it reaches the birthday girl — Maria, I assume, from her name in the song. She pouts her lips and blows out the candle with a thin layer of saliva. Maria hugs all her well-wishers, including a tall man who kisses her wrist. Maria screams in delight and then pulls his face towards her, planting red lipstick on both of his cheeks.

The cafe owner pushes a thick slice of cake towards me and serves the coffee which has remained balanced at its precarious angle. She then disappears before I can ask for matches.

'Peregrino?' says a voice behind me.

I turn to a pair of piercing blue eyes. His nose, wide lips and thick jawline are all perfectly symmetrical; Maria's smudged lipstick the only feature out of place. He combs his fingers through a knot of tangled hair and offers me his hand. 'I'm Oscar,' he says, giving me nothing less than his full concentration.

'Michael,' I reply, wondering when this man — who belongs more at Paris Fashion Week than some Camino wasteland — is going to release his strong handshake.

I'm trapped at the end of the narrow room. The last thing I need is to meet someone who thinks we're going to become friends. I have to be anonymous on the trail; nothing less than invisible for the next three hundred kilometres until Santiago.

Oscar takes a large bite of birthday cake. 'How far you walking today?' he asks, licking chocolate off his thumb.

'As far as possible,' I reply, staring at the box of matches behind the bar.

'Same. I've got to reach Santiago by the sixth of July.'

Oscar takes out a battered leather wallet. 'Hey, we should walk together.'

His enthusiasm smothers any chance of an excuse.

He pays the old lady for two coffees and tells her to keep the change. I offer my two euro coin but Oscar shakes his head. 'Another pilgrim bought me breakfast yesterday, so just do the same for someone else tomorrow.'

I award him five Camino Points even though I'm desperate to walk alone. This guy's going to turn heads where ever he goes. I cannot be seen with him.

Oscar lifts a large green backpack over his shoulders. 'That your bag?' he asks, smiling at the purple material.

I nod, remembering how Luc laughed at the colour. 'I would have bought a man's backpack if they'd had one in the shop.'

'Only you can decide who your backpack's for,' says Oscar. 'Anyway, purple means you have imagination.'

He bangs his fist on the bar. 'The day's still young, Michael. Are you ready to start walking?'

I'm wary of revealing anything about myself, but over the next few kilometres Oscar shows a depth I hadn't expected. I can't remember the last time it felt so easy talking to some-one; not since Jessica, when we lay tangled under the sheets until it was time to leave. When I ask Oscar about the triangle tattoos he has on each wrist — one pointing to his hand, the other to his arm — he describes how their shape gives him balance. 'That's why I bought this backpack,' he says. 'Green is supposed to connect me to the ground. But I can't tell you how many times I've nearly given up this Camino.'

'So why are you still here?' I ask.

He stares ahead at the flat trail. 'Because I can't go home yet.'

'Why? Was it something you did?'

Oscar's laugh makes me flinch. 'Is that why you're here, Michael? Because of something you did?'

I feel my face burning. Moments pass in silence. Why did I have to make things awkward? I was doing so well pretending there was nothing to hide. Pretending I wasn't a murderer.

'It was a promise I made,' says Oscar at last. 'A promise to leave my father's house.'

He seems to consider his words carefully, describing how he'd anchored himself to his father's apartment in Bern, moving from job to job and making other false starts. 'So one day, I left his apartment, closed the door and pushed the keys through his letter box.'

Oscar laughs. 'I had no bag, no laptop, just my wallet, phone and the clothes on my back. But when I left that building, I promised I wouldn't return for a whole year.'

'That's why you have to reach Santiago in seven days,' I interrupt.

He nods. 'You're a good listener, Michael. The sixth of July is my one-year anniversary. I've booked a flight and told my father I'm coming home. But only to visit him. It's been a long time since we saw each other. Too long.'

Oscar stares into the distance.

'So what about you, Michael? Why are you walking the Camino?'

Before I know what I'm saying, I describe my job redundancy, how I hid in Alistair's house for months on end, and my anger with Greg and Dev for betting that I wouldn't reach Santiago. 'But I don't know why I'm still here, except for the thousand pounds. Because nothing has changed. And if anything, the Camino has only made everything worse.'

Oscar drops his backpack and sits on the ground.

'Everyone carries a stone, Michael,' he says, opening his water bottle. 'Your friends too. Their insecurities. The parts they wish they could change about themselves.'

'We've been friends for ever,' I interrupt. 'But I can't forgive them for what they said. I don't want to forgive them. And it makes me so angry all the time.'

'Then do what you don't want to do,' says Oscar. 'Forgive your friends. Forgive them the way others have forgiven you. It's the only way you'll find peace.'

I will never find peace; not after Massimo. I am beyond forgiveness.

'Your head and heart must be in line,' says Oscar. 'But your head must serve your heart, Michael. The heart must be your ruler.'

Oscar wipes sweat off his forehead. 'The mind can act like a crazy monkey; drive you mad and make you do terrible things — things you would never normally do, even kill out of anger or jealousy. What is it?' he says, interrupting himself. 'I can tell something is troubling you, Michael.'

Tell him what happened. He'll understand it was a mistake; that Massimo made you kill him. You can trust Oscar.

'My brother's girlfriend,' I finally reply. 'Something happened with us before this trip. She's the reason I had to leave London. Because I fell in love with her. And now she's pregnant with our child.'

My lungs release a long, slow breath.

'I don't know what's going to happen when I go home. My brother will never forgive me. It's going to ruin our whole family.'

Oscar stands up and hugs me. He squeezes harder, releasing more of my suppressed energy. 'Let it all out,' he says, rubbing my back with his hand. 'You're a good man, Michael.'

'No, I'm not,' I say, fighting back the tears. 'I've done terrible things.'

Oscar stares at my face.

I wait for him to ask what I've done that's so unforgivable, but instead he takes hold of my hand — the same hand which threw that staff at Massimo.

'We're all meant to meet each other for a reason,' he says, now gripping my forearm. 'The cafe this morning. This conversation. It's all part of your journey, Michael. You can end your suffering. But first, you have to forgive yourself. Can you do that? Can you forgive yourself?'

I swallow the lump in my throat. 'I'll try.'

'Life is too short,' says Oscar, staring at the ground. 'That Italian pilgrim who was murdered a few weeks ago. He was just walking the trail, living his Camino, when someone smashed him on the back of his head. Who knows when our lives are all going to end?'

'I know,' I say, stepping backwards. 'I'll do my best from now on. I promise.'

It's dark when we eventually stop at an albergue. The Hospitalero has two beds left which Oscar takes as a sign.

Ten euros is four more than my budget, but if I walk far enough tomorrow I'll reach Santiago earlier than planned.

The Hospitalero shows us the kitchen which has a gas hob, and next to it, a box of matches. She tells us to leave our backpacks under the staircase — presumably as a bedbug deterrent — then takes us upstairs to the main dorm.

We've walked further today than any other day I can remember. The chances of bumping into someone who knows me as James seems unlikely, but the last thing I need is for Oscar to find out I'm lying about my name.

I can still see Iñaki's face when the police arrested me as James Pollock. I feel terrible for being dishonest, especially after everything he's going through with his heroin addiction. If I'd been a good friend, I would have gone back to that albergue to check on him after the police released me, but I was too afraid he'd demand to know why I lied to him. I'd promised Iñaki that the man in the wanted notice wasn't me, even when he said the photograph looked just like my doppelgänger. But now he knows. And maybe he's worked out why I lied.

Fuck. What if Iñaki has exposed my secret? The guy's a recluse, but I hope he hasn't told any other pilgrims I've been calling myself Michael. Then again, who would believe him if he did say anything anyway? His arms are covered with needle marks and scabs. If anything, he's more a danger to himself. I just hope he hasn't relapsed. Someone could have easily tempted him to stay behind in León. And he's still wearing my old trainers — the same trainers whose footprints were all around Massimo's cabin. What if the police match his shoes to the crime scene? Going cold turkey would be a convenient explanation for sudden loss of control. But I wouldn't let them convict Iñaki for murder, would I?

I wait for Oscar to shower before returning downstairs. A

group of pilgrims are eating in the kitchen but I don't recognise them. I pretend to check the cupboards, concealing the box of matches I just took from the gas hob. I then open the back door and step out into the garden.

How have I walked all this way still carrying my original Credentials? I should have destroyed the booklet as soon as I became Michael. The Policía Nacional must have announced that Massimo died from a head wound. There's no other way Dale and Oscar would have both known such specific details about his death. Maybe the police have released an image of the murder weapon. That metal-tipped staff couldn't have been the same staff I saw before the storm. My paranoia must be getting worse. I was almost convinced this afternoon that the police were following us. After confessing about Jessica's pregnancy, I'd almost caved in and told Oscar everything that happened outside the cabin. But I can't afford any more moments of weakness. I can't tell anyone. Maybe not even when I reach Santiago.

My eyes adjust to the darkness. I follow the clothes line to a fence at the back of the garden. Laughter emerges from the kitchen but they can't see me out here. I kneel in the grass with my back to the albergue. I take the Credentials from my money belt. The booklet feels heavy, as though it has acquired a different weight. It has cursed my pilgrimage. The longer it exists, the greater the chances are that I'll be caught.

I strike a match. It bursts into flame but then the breeze blows it out. I strike another, shielding it with my hand. I lift the match towards my old documents.

'Saint James? Is that you?'

My body tightens.

Joseph. How has he found me again? I was so terrified about bumping into Iñaki, that I never thought Joseph, that same sixty-nine year old German who I've been unable to escape from ever since my first day, might actually have walked this far.

'You're burning your Credentials?' he says, rubbing his beard. 'Why?'

I turn around, still clutching the booklet in my hand. His face is just visible from the lights of the albergue but we're far away enough to stop anyone else from hearing him use my real name.

'Because I'm giving up, Joseph.'

He sighs. 'I don't know why you ran from that restaurant without paying, but you still have the chance to finish your Camino.'

'But I don't have the strength to keep going.'

The garden falls silent. What I said suddenly feels true. Maybe I don't have the strength to continue. Maybe it's all become too much.

'James,' he says, moving his eyes from the booklet to my face.

I flinch at the sound of my old name. Joseph knows I've been calling myself Michael. He confirmed this to the officers in León. Apart from Iñaki — wherever he is now, probably shooting heroin into his veins — Joseph is the only person this far on the trail who knows who I really am.

'You are not the only pilgrim who wants to give up,' says Joseph, shaking his head. 'Why else do you think I found you that morning in Estella? You might find this hard to believe, James, but it was me who nearly cheated that day. I was tired. My legs hurt and I didn't want to walk. So I went to the bus station to buy a ticket to the next stage. But then I saw you.'

Joseph places a hand on my shoulder. 'In that moment, I knew you were my sign that I had to keep walking.'

Wind rattles the clothes line. I wait for Joseph to ask what he's really thinking: why I've been lying about my identity all this time.

'What I'm trying to say, James, is that you helped me when I needed you. And now I want to help you. Today we passed Astorga. That means we finished the Meseta.'

He shivers from the cold. 'I don't know if you noticed, but I said hello when you passed all of us pilgrims sheltering under the tree after Burgos. That was the start of the Meseta. And today, after two hundred kilometres, we have finally left the desert together. Isn't that a strange coincidence?'

Joseph takes a short breath that catches in his lungs. He no longer seems like the man with the marathon runner's legs who I met in the Pyrenees. For the first time, I sense the toll this journey is taking on him.

'Are you alright?' I ask, after he has another coughing fit.

'I'm fine,' he says, waving away my offer of help. 'It's my back that hurts most. But I paid for a company to transport my backpack tomorrow. It's amazing really. You just put a label on your bag and they collect it early in the morning and take it to your next albergue. Which reminds me,' he says smiling. 'I took your backpack to the police station in León. I hope you don't mind. I just thought you might need it.'

My mind has gone blank. I never even wondered how the police got hold of my backpack after they arrested me. I thank Joseph, hoping he won't ask any more questions.

'This is the last part of the Camino, James. We are so close. Don't burn your Credentials. You can do this —'

'Hey, Michael,' calls a voice across the garden. 'Is that you out there?'

My face burns in the darkness. I try to ignore Oscar, hoping he'll go away, but then he steps out of the kitchen door. Somehow, he knows I'm here. And he's walking straight towards us.

Fuck. I can't let these two meet each other. It's bad enough Joseph knows I'm still calling myself Michael, but if Oscar finds out I've been lying about my name, I'll have a serious problem.

'One minute,' I shout, finally finding my voice. 'Just wait for me inside.'

Oscar stops halfway towards us. 'No need to shout,' he says. 'I just came to say our pasta's ready.'

My chest is pounding. I can't deal with this. I've used up all my lies. Finally, Oscar's shadow turns back to the albergue.

Joseph stares at me but I don't dare look at his face.

'Good night,' I say, walking away with the Credentials still in my hand.

Joseph doesn't respond.

MONDAY 30 JUNE

Oscar was the only person I could have walked with to Santiago. We were obviously chalk and cheese, and his obsession with Chakra colours, energy centres, and alternative medicine had started to grate on me. But I admired him even if his freedom was intimidating. Oscar would have balanced me just like the triangles on his wrists balanced him. But instead, I ruined everything.

It's all my fault. I was so paranoid Joseph would find me in the kitchen and call me James, that I told Oscar I needed to lie down. 'Heatstroke?' he said, still clearly offended at how I'd shouted at him in the garden. Oscar frowned, but then he offered to make me a juice using the mint leaves he had in his backpack. 'But you can't sleep on an empty stomach,' he said, after I turned down his herbal concoction. 'You need nutrients for energy, as well as protein and vitamins.'

I had to get away from the kitchen, but I shouldn't have reacted the way I did. 'Can't you just leave me alone for one second?' I said, forcing him to break eye-contact. 'I've got this far without your help. You're not my father. And I don't need your fucking advice about what to eat.'

My outburst shocked Oscar as much as the other pilgrims around us. 'Fine,' he said. 'I didn't mean to get in your way. From now on, I'll give you the space you need.'

Embarrassed by all the stares, I returned upstairs. Hunger cramps filled my stomach but I was terrified Oscar and Joseph would meet each other over dinner and start talking about me. My fear was completely irrational. It had been too dark in the garden for both men to see each other and there were at least twenty other pilgrims downstairs, so the chances of them meeting, let alone choosing to speak about me, were minimal. But I still couldn't rest, not even after Joseph hobbled into the dorm and slowly got into his sleeping bag.

I'd intended to wake early, apologise to Oscar and suggest walking the next stage together, but his bed was empty before sunrise. And the note he left on my backpack only made my guilt worse.

I knew it was his handwriting the moment I came downstairs and saw 'Michael' written on the folded page. It was just a few lines, but typical of Oscar, he managed to convey everything in the fewest possible words. He wrote how surprised he was by my behaviour, but also how he knew I would conquer my demons. That was it. There were no other words at the bottom, not even his name.

I left the albergue shortly afterwards, aware that Joseph would soon wake and come downstairs. But I spent the whole morning thinking about Oscar's last sentence.

Conquer my demons? If only he knew.

I have collected a new friend. He has one milky eye, the other as black as his fur. He stops every few moments and digs his claws into his mangy coat. I wonder when he's going to return home to the last village, but his panting mouth stays inches from my knee.

The landscape is changing, the dry shrubs replaced with trees and mountains in the distance. After a week of desolation, I feel overwhelmed by the greenery. I drop my backpack and eat the sandwiches I made from the albergue fridge. Stealing other pilgrims' food has dragged my Camino Points deep into negative numbers, but I was starving after missing dinner again last night.

The stray dog swallows the cheese before his tongue can register the taste. His good eye blinks as he begs for more, but I must save the rest for myself. I stare ahead, thinking about what Oscar said when he became too reliant on his father. I did exactly the same in London. Alistair's home was my safety net; an excuse not to be independent. For months, I lived the same day, every day. The routine broke my spirit. It left me without ideas, too uninspired to leave the front door. And it was all my fault. My brother never wanted me there, but he still let me live in his home. And how did I repay him? By sleeping with Jessica, the only woman Alistair has ever loved. And getting her pregnant.

A tall wooden pole with an iron cross stands against the sky. I climb the mound of rocks to where other pilgrims are standing. Hundreds of ribbons are attached to the pole, reds, yellows, greens, blues and other colours, all flapping in the breeze. A pilgrim throws a stone over her shoulder. My eyes follow to where it lands. 'Cusco', it says in black marker. Other stones also contain names, some belonging to places, others belonging to people.

I wait for the pilgrims to leave and then open my money belt. The stray dog hangs out his tongue, but I tell him now's not the time for more food.

Alistair's house key feels sharp against my fingers. I sit and start moving the stones in front of me. I then place it inside and seal the hole with other stones until the key is buried under the mound.

A small shop appears on the trail. I enter, just to buy chocolate or a cheap snack I can afford, but other items lure me to the wooden shelves. The label on a box of tuna says two euros. Two euros for six tins. That's almost one-third of the price in the last shop. I check the other items, still in disbelief. There are tins, cereal bars, biscuits and crisps, all with prices which must be twenty years old. I fill my arms with enough rations to last three days. The shopkeeper adds up the total on her calculator. 'Siete con noventa,' she says.

Seven euros, ninety cents.

My bank overdraft. It still has the eight pounds I couldn't withdraw from the cash machine. Whatever the exchange rate is, eight has to be enough to cover the cost of these supplies.

I ask the shop assistant if they take card, convinced there's zero possibility that they accept plastic somewhere this remote, but then she reaches behind the till for a touch-screen card reader. The woman taps my debit card. The machine beeps and processes the payment.

The stray is still waiting outside. He wags his tail when I show him the dog food. Oscar told me to return yesterday's favour by buying someone else breakfast, but he never said it had to be a pilgrim. I open the can and scrape the dog meat onto the ground. My companion swallows the food. For the first time all morning, he lets me pat his head. 'You can go now,' I say.

The dog sniffs the air and makes an expression that's almost a smile.

'Go back home.'

He gives me one last stare, turns around, and then walks back to wherever he came from.

I separate the shop items and open my backpack. A pair of pink yoga trousers are folded at the top, next to a sports bra and a pair of Teva sandals. My hands tremble as they dig further inside. The outline of a passport is in the security pocket — the same place where I hid my real pilgrim documents last night after Joseph stopped me burning them in the garden. 'Repubblica Italiana' is printed on the passport's front cover. I open the photograph page. A young woman with dark frizzy hair and green eyes stares back. An Italian woman called Virginia Ferrara.

Jesus Christ.

Virginia Ferrara must have taken my backpack from under the staircase this morning, thinking it was hers. There were no other purple bags in the luggage pile when I came downstairs. I never even thought to check it was my bag after I found Oscar's note resting on top. He obviously thought it was mine as well. And the weight is so similar that I never noticed a difference when I left the albergue at dawn. She also has the same white shell attached to the front strap. I have literally been walking for hours this morning, carrying Virginia's backpack without realising it was hers.

Fuck. This can't be happening.

My Credentials are inside my backpack — the Credentials which belong to James Pollock. Why the hell did I put my documents there last night? Maybe Oscar's talk about karma went straight to my head. Or maybe our argument made me think it was bad luck to keep the booklet so close to me as I slept. But whatever stupid reason made me move those cursed pages from my money belt for the first time this whole Camino, my original Credentials have now disappeared.

My chest is pounding. I haven't seen another pilgrim with a purple backpack all morning. Virginia must still be in front.

Christ. As soon as Virginia opens the bag and finds my Credentials, she's going to ask everyone if they've seen another pilgrim called James Pollock. Everyone on today's stage is going to know my name by the end of the day. What if Virginia explains what happened to the Hospitalero at the next albergue, who then decides to file a missing bag report, or worse, notify the police? How will the Policía Nacional react when they find out that James Pollock's Credentials have miraculously reappeared on the trail weeks after they supposedly vanished in Los Arcos? The officers who interrogated me in León will know I lied to them about losing my documents. I'll immediately become the main suspect in the murder investigation. The police have my fingerprints on their database, for fuck's sake. They won't even have to find me before they match my electronic prints to the evidence on Massimo's staff or the cabin's door handle. And if that's not enough evidence, they'll just need to analyse a sample of my blood and prove it contains the same DNA as the blood I left on that nail after I cut myself inside the cabin.

I walk as quickly as I can with my blisters, praying that Virginia's figure appears ahead. I search every cafe, restaurant and shop on the trail, asking if anyone's seen an Italian woman with dark frizzy hair who's carrying a purple backpack, but no one's seen her.

The irony could kill me. I murdered an Italian man on the Camino and now, after weeks of avoiding the police, I'm going to be locked away in some Spanish prison for fourteen years, all because an Italian woman called Virginia Ferrara bought the same purple backpack as me.

My mind starts racing.

What if Virginia isn't actually walking with my backpack? What if like Joseph, she used a courier company to transport the bag to the next albergue where she's staying? Last night or early this morning she could have easily attached the transportation label to my backpack instead of hers. If so, Virginia won't realise what's happened until she reaches her albergue and opens my backpack.

Maybe there's still time to avoid this disaster. I can't stop walking — not when there's a chance I might intercept my backpack before Virginia or the police discover James Pollock's Credentials.

The municipal albergue finally appears at the end of the stage. I enter the hallway, exhausted from walking all afternoon. I stop, stunned by the sign sellotaped to the front desk. 'Missing backpack' reads the printed line at the top.

I walk closer, still disbelieving my eyes. The sign has more writing underneath. It says my name at the bottom. My real name. James Pollock.

Thank God. Virginia must be here in this same albergue. I'm safe. I can still hide what happened, as long as we exchange backpacks and I can get the hell out of here.

I tear the sign off the desk and call for the Hospitalero, ready to explain that I'm the owner of the missing backpack, but then footsteps approach from behind.

'James Pollock?'

I flinch and turn around.

An officer in a blue uniform walks towards me. He holds up the same Policía Nacional wanted notice with my passport photograph printed underneath.

'James,' he says, moving his right hand to the holster on his belt. 'We've been looking for you.'

TUESDAY 1 JULY

A canoe-building weekend. That's how Alistair did it. He arranged every detail with his usual precision, surprising Jessica outside her Mayfair office that Friday morning after colluding with her boss so that she could take the day off. He drove her straight to the Cotswolds in a hired Jaguar convertible, checked into some overpriced bespoke Bed and Breakfast, and then revealed the reason for their surprise getaway. Alistair and Jessica did everything together. They chose the wood and then cut, carved, sanded and varnished it. If I'd known what Alistair had planned, I would have relished the prospect of them falling out during the process; my brother's incapability of doing anything with his hands making Jessica finally come to her senses and realise that a future with him was as desirable as a hammer blow to the thumb. But the instructor had never seen such perfect teamwork, from the moment they were blindfolded and selected the same timber from its scent, to the last stroke of the paintbrush when their shared hands finished the name they christened their Adirondack canoe. 'Jessica-Stair.' Boats are always shes.

As soon as the varnish dried, they took Jessica-Stair on her maiden voyage, drifting through the reeds and willow branches that Sunday afternoon until they reached a bend in the river where Alistair got down on one knee, no doubt with a towel to protect his chinos, and asked Jessica if she wanted to be Mrs Jessica Pollock.

Of course, she said yes.

Champagne emerged from the hamper my brother had stowed under his legs and the rest as they say was history.

The irony is so hilarious it breaks my heart. Alistair had been the first to ridicule my plan to walk the Camino, but what does he think he's going to do with some Adirondack canoe in central London? Take it for a punt down the Thames at the weekend? The only water it's going to touch is the dampness in his garage, where after years of decay, it'll finally succumb to rot. Apparently, it's true love.

Everything happened so quickly after the Policía Nacional officer escorted me into the albergue office. He pointed at a stool under a wooden crucifix, ordered me to sit and then picked up the phone.

My head was spinning, barely able to concentrate as he spoke. His cold tone informed his superiors that he'd found me, not a hint of victory in his voice despite being the one who had finally caught the Camino murderer.

'James Pollock, sí,' he said, raising his eyes at me.

The voice at the end of the line was too quiet to hear, but they must have given the officer instructions, as he took out a pen, wrote down a number and then hung up the call. A sense of calm transcended my body. If the officer had allowed me to speak, I would have confessed everything that happened outside Massimo's cabin, but instead, he lifted the receiver, dialled the number he'd written down and then pushed the phone into my hand.

I stared at the wooden cross until the line connected. 'Darling?' said a voice which it seemed like I hadn't heard for eternity. 'Is that really you?'

I was still shaking as the officer left the room.

'Thank God,' said my mum, tears filling her voice. 'Do you have any idea what you've put us through, James? Three weeks without even a text. What were you thinking?'

The adrenaline must have kicked in as mum then raised her voice and gave me the type of telling-off I hadn't received since I got lost in the supermarket when I was six years old. After weeks without hearing from me, mum had posted a desperate plea on Facebook asking if anyone knew of my whereabouts, to which Dev finally responded and came clean about our wager. 'Honestly, James,' she said, sobbing. 'What made you think you could walk all that way without a phone?'

When mum finally stopped crying, she admitted how she'd filled out a missing person report which the British police then sent to the Spanish authorities. But it was Alistair who'd tracked me down; accessing my online bank account and discovering my location; all thanks to the card payment I'd made earlier that morning in the grocery shop. 'Thank heavens for your brother's quick-thinking,' said mum, banging the final nail in my coffin. 'Ali's been acting strangely, although I suppose he has his reasons.'

I asked what exactly she meant, convinced it was something to do with his professional misconduct case which had completely slipped my mind, but then mum's voice interrupted me. 'I can't say how worried me and your father have been — especially after that poor Italian was murdered on your trek. The story has been all over the news... James? Are you there?'

'Yes,' I said, watching the police officer walk back into the room.

'I'm really worried about you,' mum continued. 'I know how lost you've been these last few months. But things will get better. I know they will. And you would tell me if there was something I needed to know, wouldn't you, James? You can always ask for help if you need it. There's nothing that cannot be repaired.'

The officer stared at me across the room. He was probably standing outside the door that whole time. Or maybe he didn't need to. Maybe the entire police force was tapping the call, recording every word. Maybe this whole conversation with mum was a set-up organised by the police so they could trick me into making a confession.

'Did you hear what I said, James? I'm always here for you. It doesn't matter what you've done.'

'I know, mum,' I said, trying not to look up at the officer.

'And call your brother, James. Please. Do it for me. I know you've had your differences, but he has something to tell you.'

The officer smirked when I hung up and asked if I could call one other person. He checked his watch and nodded slowly, his patience clearly expired from the time he'd wasted investigating mum's missing person report. But I wish he'd never let me make the call.

'Hello,' said Alistair, clearly suspicious of the foreign number. 'Who is this?'

'It's me,' I said, trying to hear over the noise in the background. 'James. What's going on? Do you have people at home?'

'Just a small gathering,' he replied in his typically coy manner.

Other voices emerged, including Jessica's laughter which immediately disproved my first suspicion that Alistair was throwing a farewell party before they sent him off to jail.

'You know you gave everyone palpitations after your disappearing act,' he continued. 'What were you thinking? Mum almost had a breakdown.'

Alistair showed little interest as I tried to explain my bet with Greg and Dev, instead gloating about how he'd discovered my location on the Camino by accessing my online bank password which his laptop had saved after the last time I used it to check my balance. 'EddieVedder1996?' he asked. 'Isn't that the guy you and Jessica saw last month?'

Flashbacks from Jessica's bedroom filled my mind.

'You need money, don't you, James? I've seen your bank account, remember? You've reached your overdraft limit. There's no way you'll finish your hike unless you —'

'What's this important news mum said you wanted to say?' I interrupted, humiliated that Alistair thought I was only calling him to beg for money.

'Hold on,' he said, as someone asked about ordering more sushi. 'What did you say?'

'The important news mum was talking about?'

'Jessica and I got engaged. I popped the question last weekend. Wait. Jessica's here right now. She wants to have a quick word.'

I tried to hang up but then that same voice I'd been so desperate to hear for weeks was finally speaking again in my ear.

'Hello?' she said, as I moved the phone between my hands. 'Are you there? James? Oh dear, bad line. I'll try another room to see if that's any better.'

Jessica's heels sounded on the wooden floorboards. There was nothing subtle about her excuse to speak in private. Alistair would be on to her in seconds.

'Oh good, you're back,' said Jessica, her voice louder than necessary. 'So how's everything going, you adventurer? Do tell.'

I wanted to ask what the hell she was thinking by accepting Alistair's proposal but all I could do was murmur words of congratulations.

'Thank you, darling,' she said. 'That's so sweet of you.'

After that, Jessica told me all about their trip to the Cotswolds and the Adirondack canoe which was now the centre-piece of Alistair's living room. 'But there's something else I need to tell you,' she said, her voice dropping to a whisper. 'The night we went to the show…'

The line cut out.

'Jessica?' I said, raising my voice. 'Can you hear me?'

'… I'm sorry James, but we both know it was a mistake. And I feel terrible about what happened.'

'So are you going to keep it?'

'Keep what?' Jessica responded.

'Our baby.'

'Baby? What are you saying, James?'

'I researched everything online,' I said, the words spilling out before I knew what I was saying. 'I know your app got it wrong. That it can still happen just after you've finished your cycle.'

'What are you talking about?'

'You're pregnant, Jessica. Pregnant with our child.'

'What? Of course I'm not. Don't be so ridiculous.'

'But your message. You said there was something you needed to tell me.'

'Yes. It was about that night,' she said, lowering her voice.

'So you're definitely not pregnant?'

'James!' she shouted. 'Ali's just come in. Here, I'll pass you over to him.'

'What was all that about?' said my brother. 'Jessica just ran out the room. What did you say to her?'

'Nothing,' I said, barely able to speak. 'She asked about the Italian who was murdered out here. I probably said more than I should have. It's been traumatic for everyone.'

'Right.'

In that moment, I could have been anywhere; no longer in that albergue with the police officer sitting opposite me. There was no way Alistair believed my lie about why Jessica was so upset. He'd entered the room too quickly. He must have heard her say it was all a mistake.

'James,' he said, interrupting my thoughts. 'I'm going to ask you something and I expect you to be completely honest with me.'

My chest was pounding. Alistair had worked it out. He knew everything that happened with me and Jessica that night.

'Did you take the phone from my bedroom?'

'What?' I replied, almost disbelieving his question.

'The phone,' he shouted. 'The one in my wardrobe.'

'I'm sorry, Alistair, but I don't know what you're talking about.'

'Look, James,' he said, raising his voice. 'I've got a lot of shit going on right now. Things I can't talk about. But I need to know if you took that phone. I know you went through my wardrobe when you were packing for your trip. And now that phone is missing. Did you take it?'

The email receipt from The Letter of Claim. Alistair

knows someone opened the document before him. He must have spent weeks worrying that his work emails had been hacked. It would have been on his mind the whole canoe-building weekend. The paranoia must have overshadowed all his excitement about their engagement.

'James, are you listening? Did you take my fucking phone?'

'Yes, Alistair. I took your phone.'

'Christ. And where is it now?'

'I don't know. I threw it away.'

'I'm being serious, James. Where is my phone?'

'I'm sorry but it's true. I threw it away.'

'Why are you still lying? What's wrong with you?'

'I'm not lying, Alistair. Why would I do that?'

'I spoke to the phone company this morning,' he said, his breath filling the line. 'They tracked the handset last time it was active. And it's exactly where you are right now —'

'But that's impossible,' I interrupted. 'I threw your phone into a bin weeks ago. I swear it's the truth. Is everything alright, Alistair? You sound really worried.'

'Of course I'm worried, James. Some of us have to live in the fucking real world, remember? Some of us actually have jobs. And that phone contains extremely confidential information. Do you realise how much shit I'm going to be in when my firm discovers you lost their phone gallivanting around Spain on some hippie pilgrimage? Not all of us can just run away when we fuck everything up, can we?'

At that point Jessica's voice returned and Alistair ended the call.

I stared at the wall, stunned by what had just happened, until the police officer cleared his throat.

'You can leave now, James,' he said, standing up to adjust

his holster. 'And don't waste our time. We won't be so forgiving if this happens again.'

That evening, I sat on a large rock in a field with thirty other pilgrims. We all sat in silence, watching the sun fall under the horizon. The light faded until the colours burned out of the sky. It was the most beautiful thing I've seen in my twenty-seven years. I stayed outside with the cicadas until the Hospitalero called me in from the field. And then I returned to the albergue, just me, my purple backpack, and a new thought which refused to leave my mind.

DAY TWENTY-THREE

WEDNESDAY 2 JULY

N othing has changed. Despite everything that's happened out here on the Camino, the world continues as usual back home.

Why would she choose to spend the rest of her life with Alistair? Their relationship was supposed to be some experiment where she attempted to play it safe until she finally came round to her senses. But to actually settle for my brother? Two years ago, he'd never had a serious girlfriend or dared dream about a canoe-building weekend which ended with him sliding an engagement ring on anyone's finger; let alone someone like Jessica's.

This is a catastrophe. A tragedy. The only consolation is that I'm not home right now for all the celebrations and arrangements which will inevitably consume the rest of the year. Thank God I don't have social media. The whole world will have already heard, courtesy of the inevitable Instagram photograph of the depressingly happy couple drifting along the river in their hand-built canoe, the ring on Jessica's finger perfectly catching the water's reflection, and 'I said YES' inscribed in the caption below.

This is not how we're supposed to end. Jessica can't marry Alistair. I'll spend the rest of my life tormented by love. Not plain, ordinary love, but a terminal, incurable love for the woman who's going to become my sister-in-law. This isn't like mediaeval times when you could just bash your older brother on the back of his head with a candlestick holder or accidentally spear him through the chest on some hunting trip, before swanning off into the sunset with your dead brother's widow on your arm. I'll have to suffer this way for the rest of my life. I'll watch Jessica slowly grow old, knowing that I'll never get over her, knowing that she was the only person I could have loved. Alistair will never be lonely. Whereas I have nothing to go back to, except fourteen years in prison for murder.

———

The path climbs up through steep woods. My knees are in agony and blisters fill my toes. The altitude hasn't been this high since that first day in the Pyrenees. A time before Massimo. A time when I still had purpose, or at least a reason to keep going.

I trick myself into believing I'll rest at the next turn, but my legs seem determined to continue. Still no closer to the top, I throw my backpack to the ground. Exhausted, I kick a rock over the edge, bruising my toe before the stone crashes through the branches below. I lean against a tree trunk and gaze into nothing.

Something enters my sight. Something swaying in the breeze.

I follow its thick fibres to a branch high overhead.

Before I know what I'm doing, my hands touch the tree. I pull myself up, scratching my knees on the bark and scraping off fungus with my fingers. I climb higher, the tree falling away in my hands as spores of mould fill my face. At last, I touch the branch. The timber creaks, but it's sturdy enough to hold my weight. I slide forwards on my chest, trying not to look down into the endless drop below. Finally, I reach what I saw from the bottom of the tree. I slowly sit up on the branch, my legs hanging either side of the rope.

What a fool I've been. Jessica never loved me. And why would she? What do I have that could ever make her spend the rest of her life with me?

The saddest part is that I actually wanted Jessica to be pregnant. I was desperate for anything to bring us together — like a child. Our child. But now all that remains is a memory of one night we had together.

Jessica didn't break my heart. I did that myself. But there are some people you never get over. Some people who make life impossible to live without.

The fibres feel coarse in my hands. I pull up the rope, coiling it between my legs until a knot appears at the end. Whoever made the noose must have had a wide skull, but there's enough slack to pull it taut around my neck.

The constriction hurts my throat. I can hardly breathe, disorientated by my lack of balance. Using the branch overhead for support, I slowly stand on both feet.

No one is going to miss me back home. They all have their own lives to lead. Lives they made for themselves.

I stare down into the clearing. The same stretch of pathway I walked earlier is still there, back when death wasn't even an idea. But death has always been here. It's followed me ever since I walked away from that cabin. Me. James Pollock. Not Michael Evans.

My knees are trembling but I can't back out. Not now.

I should have known this would all become too much. I

thought Camino Points might help but who was I fooling? The game is over. Nothing I do can change what happened. I killed a man. Killed another human being.

The guilt will eat me alive. Everyone already knows what happened to Massimo, even my own mother. Like she said, the story is all over the news back home.

'You would tell me if there was something I needed to know, wouldn't you, James? You can always ask for help if you need it. There's nothing that cannot be repaired.'

But mum was wrong. This can't be repaired. And what is she going to do when she realises her own son is a murderer; that I killed him?

Jessica, I could have got over. Maybe. But Massimo?

This rope is here for a reason. It was meant for me.

I stand straight, breathing slowly through a small gap in my mouth. The rope burns my neck but in a few moments this will all be over. I won't have to think about Jessica or Massimo again.

I tilt forwards.

The worst part will be the seconds it takes to reach the end of the rope. If I land hard enough, my neck should snap straight away, but if not, I'll have to hang there until I choke to death or lose consciousness.

Something chirps above my head. The sound breaks my concentration just as I start to fall. Instinct makes me grab the nearest branch. Somehow, it holds my weight.

I lean on my toes, arms straight as both hands clutch onto this one branch which separates my life from death.

A tiny bird walks through the leaves towards my hand. It puffs out its red chest and looks at me with its twitching black eyes. The robin opens his beak. 'What are you doing, Saint James?' it says, speaking in Joseph's voice.

Tears fill my eyes.

'You cannot end your life,' the robin continues. 'You have to reach Santiago. You have to live.'

I push off against the branch. The momentum carries me back to the tree. I grab onto the bark, gasping for breath.

My voice makes a terrible groan; a sound I never thought could come from inside me. The sound echoes through the valley until it dies in the distance.

The knot loosens in my fingers. I pull it over my head and drop the rope down through the leaves. I crawl back until I reach the tree trunk.

My friend watches me climb down. It's only when I touch the ground that the tiny robin leaves its branch and flies away.

The yellow arrows point towards a stone building at the top of a hill. A hand-carved sign half hidden under the vines welcomes pilgrims inside. Before I know what I'm doing, my feet leave the trail.

Every sound has a defined quality — the creaking gate, the long grass, the bees and wind chimes. I unlace the hiking boots and peel off my socks. Blisters cover my feet but the cold tiles in the entrance soothe my skin. The main room is filled with wooden furniture, plants, painted canvasses and piles of books. A draft from an open window cools the sweat on my spine. I follow the slanting sunlight until a figure moves through the dust motes.

'Bienvenido,' says her voice.

My mind sees Jessica but the face which emerges is softer, more natural. The woman speaks again but I can't process her words.

'English?' she asks, still watching my face. 'What is your name?'

'James,' I reply.

'Sit down, James,' she says, smiling. 'It's been a hard day. But you're here now.'

Bracelets slide up her arm as she lifts a jug of water. She fills one of the glasses and places it in my hand. The water tastes of salt but it quenches my thirst. 'Better?' she asks, as I swallow the last gulp. 'Can I see your Credenciales?'

A strange sensation separates my thoughts from my body. I open the money belt and give her my documents. She opens the booklet. I wait for her to ask why there are no albergue entries from the last two weeks, but instead she presses her wooden stamp on the page and writes the date. 'It's six euros for the night and another eight if you want dinner.'

I place six euros of loose change in her hand.

The warm shower removes dirt from my pores. It's been weeks since I thought about hygiene but I take the last clean t-shirt and underwear from my backpack. There's something odd about this room, but it's welcoming, not menacing. Maybe I feel it because of what happened in that tree. Or maybe it's this place. Or her. I stand at the foot of the bed, taking long breaths, until the smell of honeysuckle draws me outside.

I can't remember the last time I washed my clothes, but I scrub them thoroughly and wring out the last drops before hanging them on the line. The wet cotton sways in the breeze. Today could have easily had a different ending. Without that tiny robin, I'd probably still be hanging from the tree, waiting for some pilgrim to find me on the trail. I feel sick with shame. Ashamed that I almost gave everything away.

'Mind if I sit here?'

I turn around. She's barefooted, her dress touching the

grass. I must have been so confused earlier that I forgot to ask her name.

'Gabriela,' she replies, sitting on a small wooden bench. 'And don't apologise. Most pilgrims are exhausted when they arrive.'

'You speak English,' I say, still standing. 'But you're from Spain?'

'Yes,' she replies, laughing.

I stare at the clothes line, unable to think of anything normal to say.

Gabriela crosses her knees. 'When I first saw you, James, I thought you were one of those wild men walking the Camino. I guess it was the beard, your tanned skin and how your Credenciales only have a few stamps.'

She blows an insect from her shoulder. 'To be honest, I was surprised you even had hiking boots. You might as well have been walking without shoes and carrying one of those long staffs. What is it?' she says, reaching for my arm. 'Your face has gone white.'

'It's nothing,' I say, flinching. 'I'm just tired.'

Her hand lets go of my wrist as though she's sensed the reason for my reaction. Still haunted by Massimo's eyes, I pour the laundry bucket down the sink.

'We normally make a communal meal,' says Gabriela, standing up. 'But it's just you and two others tonight, and they've already gone out. You look like you're starving.'

She studies my face. 'You don't have to pay anything. The food has to be eaten. Anyway, it would be nice to have company.'

I sit at a long wooden table inside the albergue. Gabriela returns from the kitchen with bowls of salad, green beans, tofu and rice. She sits opposite, places both hands together and bows over her plate. 'Sorry, James,' she says, opening her eyes. 'I don't talk when I eat. It's my moment for reflection. But please, take as much as you want.'

After days of eating from tinned cans, the meal tastes like real food. I swallow quickly while Gabriela chews each mouthful.

I'm still shocked at how she said I looked like Massimo. She described him perfectly; everything except the razor burns on his head and the Christ tattoo on his back. She must know about his death. Everyone on the Camino knows what happened. And yet Gabriela has no idea that she's eating dinner alone with the murderer.

'Would you like to sit outside?' she asks, ending her silence. 'Dusk is my favourite moment of the day.'

Dusk. The time I killed Massimo outside his cabin.

Gabriela leads me into the garden to a swing bench filled with cushions. We sit under a blanket and watch the light fade.

Her perfume takes me back to my childhood. The smell is intoxicating. My mind wanders through old memories, desperate to place the scent until I remember where it's from. It smells like an action figure Alistair and I shared as children; back when we were almost friends.

How could I have slept with his fiancée? Even if he doesn't suspect anything — which is unlikely considering how Jessica dropped the phone and ran out the room — it's inevitable that Alistair will find out what happened. It's not the kind of secret you can hide for ever. Like murdering someone.

'Your neck is red,' says Gabriela, her face barely visible in the darkness.

Instinctively, my hand touches the burn marks from the rope.

Gabriela leans forward. 'What happened, James?' she says. 'You can trust me.'

It's obvious what she's implying. She must know I tried something stupid, but I can't let my mind return to that tree.

'Your perfume,' I say, trying to shift position on the bench. 'What is it?'

Gabriela pulls her legs up under the blanket. 'It's patchouli,' she says, still staring at my neck. 'Why do you ask?'

'It reminds me of something.'

'Something nice, I hope.'

I feel the warmth of her body. I have no idea how to respond.

'You walked the whole Camino here, didn't you?' I say at last.

Her face smiles. 'Yes. How did you know?'

'It was the way you welcomed me when I arrived. I knew you'd also felt the same.'

'That's very perceptive, James.'

'But then you stopped. And stayed here instead. Why?'

Gabriela's knees press against mine. She breathes slowly, as if deciding whether to answer. 'Three weeks ago, I climbed the same path you did today.'

Three weeks ago. Almost to the day that I killed Massimo.

'I was only going to stay one night,' she continues. 'But then something happened to me here in this garden. I was lying in the grass, the sun on my face, when I realised I didn't need to reach Santiago. The Camino had given me enough. I knew I'd found what I needed to find when I first started walking. But I wasn't ready to go home. So I asked if I could stay and work as a volunteer.'

'But we're so close to the end,' I interrupt. 'You never wanted to complete your journey?'

'Why is Santiago so important to you?' she says, crossing her arms. 'What do you think will change when you get there?'

I flinch, unable to ignore the sound of that staff striking Massimo's head.

'I don't know. But every day I see things I couldn't see before. The Camino has made me realise how free I've been all this time. And if I don't reach Santiago, I'll never know how this is supposed to end.'

My face burns in the darkness. 'But there's something else. Something I still haven't processed. Maybe never will.'

I try to swallow but there's no saliva in my mouth. 'There's another reason why I'm walking the Camino. Well, more than one. But the real reason is because…'

I stare at the stars, lost in the enormity of the sky above us.

'… because I fell in love with my brother's girlfriend.'

I look away. Whatever connection we had has now completely disappeared.

'My brother doesn't even know,' I continue. 'At least I don't think he does. And now they're engaged.'

Gabriela pulls the blanket around her shoulders. This must be the last thing she was expecting me to say. She must think I'm such a creep.

'Did anything happen between you? I guess something must have happened.'

'No,' I lie. 'Something nearly did, but…'

Fuck. I was so close to what I needed to say. But I'm too ashamed; too weak to admit what happened.

'Why do you like her so much, James? What makes her so unlike anyone else?'

I wait for an answer — except nothing comes.

'I don't know,' I say, shaking my head. 'Honestly, I don't know.'

'We all make mistakes,' says Gabriela. 'All of us.'

Except my mistakes are far worse.

'You said there was something you needed to find when you started the Camino,' I say, trying to ignore the thoughts in my mind. 'What was it?'

The darkness hides Gabriela's face, but I can tell she's crying.

I apologise, but she speaks over me. 'You were honest, James, so I will do the same.'

She shivers under the blanket. 'Like you, I also walked the Camino to escape someone.'

Her breathing is heavy. Her knees are shaking.

'There was a man in Madrid. He was intelligent, interesting, attractive. He travelled for work, leaving for weeks on end, or so he said... Everything happened so quickly. The things he said he felt for me. How we could spend time together without ever needing our own space. He started staying in my apartment when he was back in the city. He never said what he did, but I just accepted why he couldn't talk about his job. And then one day, months into our relationship, he said he was going to work in San Francisco, and that he wanted me to come with him.

'He wanted me to leave my whole life behind. Everything. He made all these promises about our future. That's what he kept calling it. And I started believing him. I was bored with my job. Bored with my life which felt so ordinary until I met this man. So I started making plans to leave. My friends thought I was crazy, especially as they'd only met him once because he was always so busy at work and the time we had together was precious, or so he said. But I was ready to change everything. Until one night, when I checked his phone while he was in the shower.'

Gabriela trembles.

'Obviously, I needed to know everything about this man I was going to change my life for. But I never thought I'd find those things on his phone.'

The bench stops swaying beneath us.

'He had a family, James. A wife and child. I saw the pictures, read the messages he'd sent about how much he missed them. When he came back, I was still staring at his phone. I told him to get out, but he sat on the bed and said there were things he had to say; things he'd wanted to admit for months but didn't know how. I was furious, but he convinced me to listen. He told me all these reasons why he couldn't leave his wife, even though he was desperate to start a new life with me. I was shocked. He'd lied to me all that time, living a double life, which was obviously why he said he was away on business when he was actually living with his family right there in Madrid.'

Gabriela wipes her eyes.

'I didn't leave my apartment for weeks. But he was persuasive. He sent flowers, wrote long letters about his wife's problems and how he couldn't leave her and their little boy. He was terrified she'd hurt herself. Or the child. Of course, it was all a lie, just like how he promised our lives would be different when we moved to America. But I started allowing him back into my life. First for coffee. Then a walk. Then dinner. And then, just a few weeks later, just as I was starting to believe he was still the same man I first thought he was, he disappeared. He literally disappeared.

'My life fell apart, James. I realised I'd made a huge mistake; a mistake that everyone could see, except me. The guy faked his whole life, literally invented everything about himself, and all to deceive me. I don't even know if he told me his real name.'

A shudder passes through my body.

'It took me months to trust anyone, James. But the Camino has taught me how to trust people again. There are good people here. People who are honest. Like you.'

I try to sit up, but I can't change position.

'We're not so different, are we?' she says, turning to face me. 'We both started the Camino to escape people who nearly broke us. And we still have time to heal.'

Gabriela touches my hand. She moves towards me. I almost do the same.

'I'm sorry,' I say, standing up. 'But I have to go inside.'

The bedroom door crashes into the wall. I look up from my bed, trying to make out the figure in the darkness, but then it falls against the nearest bunk. A woman's voice starts giggling as she pulls herself up from the floor. A man follows her into the dorm, kicking the door with his foot. They must know I'm here. It's a shared room. Not a private.

The woman slurs her words, laughing about how much they drank at dinner. 'Hey, where you going?' she says. 'Come back here and kiss me.'

The man walks into the ensuite bathroom and switches on the light. He lifts the toilet seat and relieves himself with the door still open. Again, the woman tells him to hurry up. 'One second, babe,' he replies.

Hairs climb the back of my neck. His voice. And that word. Babe. I've heard it before on the Camino. This isn't the first time we've stayed in the same albergue.

The bathroom light catches his face. It's the Toronto

banker, I'm sure. The same man who was in the toilet that night I threw up all the corned beef onto his used condom. The same man who only hours earlier that evening had promised his wife he would fly home soon so they could spend a week at their lake house.

At last, he switches off the light, still oblivious that I'm trying to sleep in the corner. The woman shrieks then accuses him of stealing the blanket. Finally, they fall silent.

It's too late to go back to the garden. Gabriela was probably only waiting for these two to return before locking up. But maybe she's still sitting on the bench outside. Maybe I could check if she's still there.

A sound emerges from across the room. I convince myself that it's not what I think it is, but then the same sound returns. The man's breathing grows faster. 'There,' he whispers. 'That's it, babe. Keep going. You're so good at that.'

They must know I'm here. They're only three beds away.

'Want me to keep going?' says the woman. 'Or we could just fuck instead?'

I smother my face with the pillow, but not before I see Jessica on top of me, her breasts against my chest.

The bed frame creaks as if it's about to collapse under their weight.

I stare at the ceiling but I can't stop looking into Jessica's eyes.

The headboard crashes against the wall. 'Yes,' moans the woman. 'Jesus Christ. Right there. Don't stop.'

Jessica puts her arms around my neck.

'Harder,' says the woman three beds away. 'Fuck me harder.'

I can't stop looking into her eyes.

'I'm going to come. I'm going to —'

Her body trembles.

I throw the sheets off the bed and run to the door.

THURSDAY 3 JULY

T hick mist covers the trail. This must be the highest I've climbed but I can't see more than ten feet in front. The last pilgrim said this was the most spectacular view on the whole Camino; not that there was anything to take in as he shouted over the howling wind. I stub my toe against a rock, bursting another blister inside my hiking boots.

I still haven't recovered from what happened last night. When I woke at sunrise, the gruesome couple were snoring away in each other's arms. The room reeked of sex, no longer the tranquil place it had been before they arrived. I threw everything into my backpack, desperate to forget their performance, only to then see the woman's breasts hanging over the bedsheet as I reached the door. Do they have no shame? She knows the Toronto banker is married from the wedding ring on his finger. And does he not care about cheating on his wife? Has the freedom of the trail tricked him into thinking his conscience doesn't apply out here? And yet I'm no different. How did I think I could just forget what happened that night with Jessica? Alistair's girlfriend. My brother's future wife. I'll carry the disgrace for the rest of my life. And to make everything worse, if that's even possible, I've finally realised something I always chose to ignore. I never loved Jessica. I just loved the idea of being in love with her.

Sitting under the blanket with Gabriela last night, I felt something I desperately needed to feel. For the first time in years, I allowed myself to like someone else. I'm convinced we had a connection. Maybe she felt it too. But I was too afraid to tell her how I felt. Because like the man who betrayed Gabriela, I'm also living a double life, one as James Pollock and the other as Michael Evans. And like that man in Madrid, I am also a complete fraud.

From the moment I woke this morning, I felt an urge to tell Gabriela everything — how Massimo made me throw that staff at his head; how I only used Michael's Credentials by mistake until those police wanted notices forced me to take on his name; and how I almost hanged myself from that tree. I walked into the albergue kitchen, terrified at how Gabriela would react but also determined to confess what happened. But instead of Gabriela, someone else was preparing break-fast; a man, presumably the Hospitalero. When I asked where she was, he said it was her day off and that she wouldn't be back until tomorrow. The best I could do was write a note, but it makes no difference if she reads it or not. It's too late. That chance has disappeared. And anyway, it's not as though we could have continued anything once I'm locked up behind bars.

———

A head stone appears through the fog. 'Galicia', says the carved writing beneath a cross. I lean against the marker and try to catch my breath. I never thought I'd get this far. The last region on the Camino. The last region I'll walk as a free man.

The wind ripples a sheet of paper held by a stone at the marker's base. A scratched two euro coin rests on top of the note. 'Buy coffee,' says the smudged ink. 'Share kindness.'

I push on through the rain, past cattle with clanking bells around their necks. If Oscar left the coin on the marker — which is just the kind of thing he'd do — then he can't be too far ahead. I have to apologise for shouting at him that night Joseph stopped me burning my real Credentials. It's the least I can do to thank him.

Cottages with thatched roofs appear through the mist. Determined not to lose Oscar, I ignore the blisters on my heels until I see a sign advertising breakfast for the same price as his donation. It feels so long since I ate anything from a cafe that the temptation is too much to resist. I give my order to the barman and sit next to the log fire. The coffee warms my insides. I spread two packets of butter and marmalade across the toast, ignoring the newspapers at the end of the bar.

A middle-aged woman dressed in a pink rain jacket walks towards me. 'Excuse me,' she says in English, emphasising her vowels. 'Are you walking the Camino?'

I swallow my mouthful and nod.

'May I ask how far you are walking today?'

I shake my head.

'You don't know?' she says, staring down the bridge of her nose.

I take a large bite of toast and stare into the fire. I want to enjoy the luxury of breakfast in a cafe, but she won't take the hint, instead lecturing me on how all the Camino markers in Galicia count down the kilometres left to Santiago. 'And tell me where exactly you started your Camino.'

I respond, mid-mouthful.

Her lips straighten, as though she's going to pull me up on my manners. 'But St-Jean-Pied-de-Port is not the official start of the Camino, is it?'

Her wellington boots don't have a speck of mud on them. I slurp my coffee and say in no uncertain terms that St-Jean is indeed the start of the Camino Francés.

'Ah!' she says, jabbing her finger in the air. 'That's where you went wrong. You said the Camino Francés. But that begins in Le Puy.'

Taken aback by her gritted teeth, I explain that today is my twenty-third consecutive day of walking and if anyone knows where the Camino begins it's me, considering I've walked all the way from the start.

'I'm afraid you're wrong,' says the woman.

She unzips a tiny backpack and takes out a glossy brochure. 'I'm making my pilgrimage by bus and we started our journey in Le Puy. Here,' she says, pushing the magazine into my hands. 'This is the official itinerary my tour company provided. If you check the index, you'll see I'm right.'

Her manicured fingernail makes an imprint on the top line. According to her magazine, the Camino Francés starts in Le Puy, wherever that is.

The butter has melted through my toast but I've lost my appetite. The bet I made with Greg and Dev was to walk the whole Camino. But if this brochure is correct, then St-Jean-Pied-de-Port isn't the official start of the pilgrimage. Greg will have undoubtedly researched this already and prepared his argument for how I forfeited the wager and am not entitled to the thousand-pound prize money when I reach Santiago. Why the hell did nobody tell me about Le Puy twenty-three days ago? If I'd known where to start the Camino, I would never have met Massimo. He would never have made me throw that metal-tipped staff at his head. I would never have become a murderer.

'Of course, all of this will be included on your Compostela,' says the woman, closing her travel brochure.

'My Compostela?'

'You don't know about the Compostela?' she says, shaking her head. 'The Compostela is the certificate you receive at the end of the pilgrimage. You have been collecting stamps in your Credentials, haven't you?'

'Yes, but —'

'When you present your documents at the Pilgrim's Reception Office in Santiago de Compostela, they verify your identity and check you have all the required stamps to prove you completed your pilgrimage. After that, and providing you fulfil their criteria, they present you with a certificate containing your full name and the total number of kilometres you walked. They even write your name in Latin. What is that on your neck by the way?'

'My neck?'

'Yes,' she replies. 'You have red marks around it. Like grazes.'

'No idea,' I say, touching the rope burn from the noose.

The woman checks her watch. 'It's time I got back to my tour group. We have strict safety protocols after what happened outside Zubiri a few weeks ago. You do know that an Italian pilgrim was murdered there on the Camino, don't you?'

'Yes,' I interrupt. 'I know all about him.'

'Well then,' she says, placing the brochure into a tiny backpack. 'Buen Camino, as us pilgrims say. And may I suggest that next time someone asks where you began your pilgrimage, you say St-Jean-Pied-de-Port, not the start of the Camino.'

'Michael Corleone?' calls out a voice across the albergue reception area. 'Is that really you?'

Jesus Christ. How could I have been so careless? For weeks, I checked obsessively for any pilgrims I already knew whenever I entered a new albergue, but I must have let my guard down, convinced that I'd walked further than everyone I met in that first week. And yet to my horror, the Hats — those three men from the UK who I met with Iñaki in that convent, and who took the photo of the four of us all sitting together on that abandoned sofa in the middle of the trail — are somehow here in the same albergue.

I flinch as the boys greet me. 'I hardly recognised you with that beard, pal,' says Cowboy, placing his hand on my shoulder. 'And you've lost a ton of weight since we last saw you, what, nearly two weeks ago?'

'Long enough for you to get a new backpack and some hiking boots,' says Panama, frowning. 'So how've you been, Michael? We were wondering what happened to you after we saw your face on all those police notices. What was that all about, anyway? And why did the notices say you were called James?'

My chest is pounding. I can't believe the Hats recognised my face from the wanted notices. I broke down in front of them that night in the chapel when the nun asked why I was walking the Camino. What if they told the police how I reacted that night? What if they told the police I was calling myself Michael? That was right around the time Massimo's murder was first reported in the media.

Panama crosses his arms, still waiting for my answer.

Checking that no one else in the albergue is listening, I explain the story of my missing passport, lying about how the police called me James, my middle name, but Panama seems unconvinced. 'It's lucky they found you,' he says, scratching his chin. 'For a while we were worried it might have been to do with …'

'What?' I ask, my voice starting to crack.

'This is going to sound ridiculous,' Panama continues, still avoiding eye-contact, 'but we thought it might have been related to that Italian who was murdered in our first week.'

I manage a short laugh, more out of desperation, but Panama grimaces.

'Sorry,' I say, shaking my head. 'I still can't believe they haven't caught him yet.'

'Him?' interrupts Baseball. 'Who says it's a he?'

My face is burning. I don't know how to respond — if responding is what an innocent person would do in this situation.

'I disagree,' says Panama, finally breaking his concentration. 'According to the reports, the police are convinced the footprints outside the cabin belonged to a man.'

Cowboy claps his hands loud enough to make me jump. 'Enough of that chat,' he says smiling. 'Got any plans for dinner, Michael? The guidebook says there's a wee place for octopus nearby. Got to try the local speciality when we're in Galicia, right?'

I can't think straight. Iñaki is somewhere out on the trail still wearing my old trainers. The trainers whose footprints were all around the crime scene.

A hand squeezes my arm. 'You're knackered, pal,' says Cowboy. 'Go lie down. The restaurant is on the main street and we'll stay til closing.'

I tell the Hats I'll catch up with them later, but Panama doesn't respond. He's on to me, I know it. Fuck. Why did I react that way when he asked if my police notices were connected to Massimo? Only some twisted psychopath would have laughed about someone's murder. Panama must suspect something. Maybe he's wondering if I killed Massimo. Maybe he already knows.

I say goodbye, but Panama walks slowly to the door.

'Remember, Michael,' says Cowboy, the only Hat who turns around. 'Nae vino, nae Camino.'

The Hospitalero doesn't have change for my last twenty euro note, so she disappears in search of coins. The albergue door opens behind me. I stare into the office, aware of the hiking boots walking towards me.

'Ey! Look 'oo it is,' says a loud French accent. 'And 'e's still carrying that pink backpack.'

I shudder at the sound of his voice. Luc. How is he this far along the trail? I was supposed to have out-walked him days ago, unless the cheat took the bus again.

'Look what I found,' he says, tapping a two euro coin on the desk. 'Some idiot left it on a stone with a note saying me to buy a drink and leave money for someone else. No way. This pays for my first beer. Tonight, I make party.'

The Hospitalero returns before I can prise the same two euros from Luc's hand which I left earlier on the trail. 'Here,' she says, handing back my change. 'You're in bed seventy-four, James.'

'James?' Luc interrupts. 'But last time your name was Michael.'

I look away but I can see Luc staring back through the corner of my eye.

'I knew it! You are changing names, aren't you?'

I walk away before Luc can make any more of a scene.

I lie on my bed at the back of the dorm. After my honesty with Gabriela, I was ready to go back to being James, but if Luc opens his mouth, I'm going to have serious problems. I can't believe he's staying here in the same albergue as the Hats. And he's still clearly resentful about how I humiliated him by returning his bus receipt after he lied about walking through the storm. He was convinced my wanted notices were related to Massimo's murder. I can't risk Luc spreading any more rumours. And I can't have him telling other pilgrims that I've been lying about my name. Not with the investigation still ongoing.

I can't decide what to do. I'm too exhausted to leave the albergue and keep walking, and anyway, I've already spent my budget on tonight's accommodation. Luc's plan to drink at the bar should keep him away until the curfew. If I find a quiet place outside, I might still be able to keep a low profile.

The crowd of pilgrims in the garden almost sends me back to the dorm, but they're all too absorbed in their phone screens to notice my arrival. I soak my laundry, wasting time in the far corner. It's too early for dinner but hopefully most of them will be eating out tonight so I can have the kitchen to myself. I hang my clothes on the line, checking discretely for who else is outside. It's hard to see with their backs turned, but most of them seem to be pilgrims I haven't met before — people who probably started walking days before I left St-Jean, but who I've now caught up with.

One main group talks about the days ahead, but apart from them and a girl strumming a ukulele, everyone else is silent. Oscar is nowhere to be seen. Maybe he didn't donate the two euros I spent on breakfast after all. I can't believe Luc found my replacement coin. He's probably propped up at the bar right now, drinking the beer I bought him with no intention of passing on the goodwill.

A cheer wakes me from my doze. I couldn't have been asleep in the grass for long, but most of the pilgrims are watching the main group laughing and hugging each other. They take a few moments to settle, after which a tall man with tribal tattoos blindfolds himself and turns his back to the others. A girl with big hair and Lycra bottoms walks behind everyone until she stops behind a blonde girl and taps her on the shoulder. One at a time, the group creeps towards the man with the blindfold. The whole garden stops what they're doing to watch. Three girls take the lead. They move closer until they're within touching distance of their target. The blindfolded man stands perfectly still, even when the girls start to giggle. Together, they reach forward from different angles, until the blonde shoves the man's shoulder. The girls fall back and hide themselves in the main group.

The man removes his blindfold. He turns around and searches for the one who can't keep a straight face. 'You!' His tattooed arm points at the wrong girl. She shakes her head. The blonde girl steps forward and the group celebrates again.

The girl in the Lycra bottoms walks towards me. My chest starts pounding. I recognise her immediately. It's Carolina, one of the Americans I had dinner with in Estella — that same evening the police came to the albergue and asked for everyone's Credentials. I look away, hoping Carolina won't remember me. She reaches up to the washing line and unpegs a coral-coloured t-shirt hanging next to my wet laundry.

'Hey!' she says, looking at me straight in the eye. 'We've met before, haven't we?'

I ask if she's mistaken me for someone else, but she's adamant that she knows me. 'When was it?' she asks, running a hand through her frizzy hair. 'God, it seems like ages ago. Estella! We had dinner together — you, me, Eric and Amy. I've forgotten your name.'

She smiles as she waits for my answer.

Christ. Who was I that night? James or Michael?

'Yo, James!' yells a voice across the garden.

I shrink into my skin. Now everyone here knows me by that name.

'At least someone remembers,' says Carolina, laughing. 'And mine?'

She shakes her head when I pretend not to remember. 'I can't believe you've forgotten. It's Carolina.'

'Red Coat!' says Eric. 'Come over here.'

My legs can't move. After hundreds of kilometres on the trail, have I really ended up at the same albergue as the Americans?

'Don't sit by yourself,' says Carolina. 'Come join us.'

Eric welcomes me with a handshake. 'Nice beard,' he says, still clenching my hand.

I feel him sizing me up with his eyes. Eric's on to me. It was obvious that afternoon when we sat under the tarpaulin in the middle of that field. He'd challenged everything I said; and not just why I'd thrown away my phone after starting the Camino. But it was something else he'd brought up which was far more serious. My white t-shirt. The t-shirt I'd worn on the twelfth of June. Eric said all three of them had seen me try to throw away the t-shirt that afternoon we met in the church plaza — the same white t-shirt which Eric said was covered in stains — stains which the girls were convinced had looked like blood. Even after I'd lied about the marks coming from a bathroom floor, Eric was still not convinced. They were all 'on edge', he said, Eric's exact words. 'On edge after what happened to that Italian'.

'So how good are you at murder?'

Eric punches my arm as I flinch. 'You're totally out of it, James,' he says, laughing. 'I meant the game, obviously!'

Amy steps in and explains the rules, but I can't concentrate. I have to get out of here.

'... and then someone hits the person with the blindfold, who then has to guess who's the murderer,' she says, crossing her arms. 'If the victim guesses incorrectly, they're dead. But if they work out who hit them, then the murderer loses their life.'

'Ey, guys! What you playing?'

Fuck. This can't be happening. Not here. Not now.

Luc strolls across the grass, carrying a litre bottle of beer. He smiles at the girls, making no attempt to notice me.

It's too late to make excuses to leave. I'm trapped.

'Alright then,' says Eric. 'Frenchie takes the blindfold. Everyone ready?'

Luc ties the material over his eyes. The rest of us stand in a line as the last murderer walks behind us. Her hand taps my shoulder. 'Okay, Michael,' whispers her voice in my ear. 'You're the murderer.'

I shudder. How does she know I was Michael?

'Go,' she whispers, pushing me forwards. 'Kill him.'

Luc places the beer bottle on the ground and extends his arms. The movement turns my stomach. All I can see is Massimo's face behind the blindfold.

Eric breaks ahead of the group, his hand already raised. The rest of us move slowly forward together. My legs can barely walk.

We stop inches behind our target. I point to my chest, signalling my role, but Eric shakes his head. Before I can stop him, he brings down his hand on the back of Luc's neck.

The slap stuns the garden. Luc howls in pain and knocks over the bottle of beer. His neck is filled with the outline of a large red handprint. I'm so shocked that I forget to slip back into the main group.

Luc removes the blindfold. 'Fuck you!' he shouts. 'Why you slap so 'ard?'

I try to explain that it wasn't me, but he's seething with anger. 'Come 'ere, you fucking idiot. I fight you right 'ere in front of everyone.'

'I did it,' says Eric, raising his voice. 'I hit you. Sorry. My bad.'

Luc points his finger at my face. 'Fuck you, James, or Michael, or 'oo the fuck you call yourself today.'

'Calm down,' says Eric, trying to position himself between us. 'Let's get a drink and call it quits.'

'No,' Luc shouts, wiping tears from his cheek. 'Ee's a liar! A fucking liar! 'Ee's been doing this all Camino. Lying about 'is name.'

Eric grabs Luc by the arm and leads him towards the albergue.

Everyone is staring.

I wait for the game to continue, but the group slowly leaves. Stunned by Luc's reaction, I walk past all the other pilgrims and return to the dorm.

FRIDAY 4 JULY

'Leaving already, Michael?'

The voice startles me. I didn't think anyone else was awake, but Cowboy must have been in the kitchen while I packed my bag in the corridor. He knows I was planning another quick escape, just like the last time I abandoned the Hats on the trail. I almost ignore him and walk towards the exit, but the silence implies that he's the only one here.

I peer through the doorway. Cowboy is sitting alone, pouring milk into his cereal. Of the three Hats, he seemed most willing to accept my explanation about the police wanted notices. He's always been friendly. We'll talk for a few minutes; long enough for me to appear innocent, before we never see each other again. Finally, I respond to his question, making an excuse about needing fresh air.

'There's scran if you're hungry.'

His voice is flat, as though he knew I was going to leave without saying goodbye. I ask what he means until he points at the breakfast in the far corner.

My stomach aches from hunger. I waited hours for

everyone to finish cooking last night, too ashamed to show my face after Luc's shouting, but then the Hospitalero locked the kitchen before I could find any leftovers.

'At least take some fruit,' says Cowboy. 'Might as well stock up for the road.'

I stare at the breakfast buffet. Who knows how far I can walk on an empty stomach, but I can't sacrifice a free meal; not with fourteen euros left to my name. If I'm quick, I'll still be able to make food without anyone else seeing me.

I walk to the main table, overwhelmed by the plates of ham, cheese, sliced tomatoes, bread, biscuits and a large fruit bowl. I make four sandwiches and carry as much as I can back to Cowboy's table.

'How far you walking today, chief?' he asks, staring at the food piled on my plate.

'No idea,' I reply. 'Guess I'll see how I go.'

Another pilgrim enters the kitchen. I bite into the sandwich, chewing as quickly as I can. A slice of tomato falls onto the floor but I shove it into my mouth. There's barely time to swallow before the next pilgrim arrives. And then another.

I have to leave before Luc turns up, but my body demands food. I scrape two packets of marmalade across the next slice of toast and gulp down more coffee.

The silence with Cowboy becomes awkward. He must be just as suspicious of me as the other Hats, even if he's not showing it.

The banana skin snaps as I peel it open. My mind fills with visions of my broken neck swinging from that tree, until more pilgrims arrive. Some sit alone, while others chat together, although too quietly to hear. They're talking about me, I just know it. My confrontation with Luc must have been the only gossip from last night.

I glance behind, checking for any witnesses from the

garden. Luc went ballistic when he thought I'd hit him. Everyone heard him accuse me of using different names on the Camino. It's hard enough trying to remember who knows me as James and who knows me as Michael. All it's going to take is for one pilgrim to report me to the police.

I fold serviettes around the other sandwiches, but then Cowboy looks over my shoulder. 'Morning lads,' he says, raising his eyebrows.

Panama places his hat on the table and walks to the buffet.

'Jeez, Michael,' says Baseball, staring at my plate. 'Forget second breakfast. That's enough to feed an army.'

Panama returns with one slice of toast.

'That all you're having, pal?' asks Cowboy.

'It's all that's left,' Panama responds, still refusing to make eye-contact.

Hairs prick the back of my neck. I offer the Hats my sandwiches but they both decline. Others at the breakfast buffet stare at my plate. They don't have anything to eat either. My face is burning. Has my situation really forced me to stoop this low?

A hand grips my shoulder.

I turn around, expecting to find Luc ready to drag me outside, but tribal tattoos fill the thick arm. 'Morning, bro,' says the man from yesterday's game in the garden. 'How d'you sleep?'

The kitchen falls silent. Paranoid from the attention, I ask what he means.

'So who's Massimo?' he asks, grinning with his teeth.

Coffee spills from my mug. My voice denies all knowledge of that person, but I know the words lack conviction. The man stares back until his lips start to twitch. 'You sure you don't remember?'

This is it. The end of my journey. The end of everything.

'Oh Massimo!' he says, in a high-pitched voice. 'Massimo!'

Someone in the corner erupts with laughter.

'Missing someone back home?' he asks, clenching my shoulder. 'No worries. You'll soon be back together, just you and Massimo.'

I can't breathe.

'But if you get lonely before then,' the man continues, 'you can always scream out his name in the dark. I'm sure no one else minds if you wake them at three in the morning.'

His hand releases my shoulder.

I can't look up and see who else is here. We all slept in the same dorm. Everyone would have heard me shouting Massimo's name; everyone including Carolina, Eric and Amy. They won't have forgotten how they caught me trying to throw away my t-shirt the day before the murder was front page news. There's not a chance they won't connect both events; not when the girls were convinced they saw blood on my shirt.

'Alright,' says the man with the tattoos, checking his watch. 'Six fifteen. Want to walk together, or prefer to keep it just you and Massimo?'

He slaps me on the back. 'Just playing with you, James. Buen Camino.'

The man leaves the kitchen.

My chest is pounding.

'What did he call you?' asks Panama.

I shove the sandwiches into my backpack, pretending not to hear.

'That bloke just called you James,' says Panama, loud enough for others to hear.

'Did he?' I respond. 'He must have made a mistake.'

'But you didn't correct him,' says Panama. 'And he's not the only pilgrim calling you James. There was a French guy in the restaurant last night. He was really angry with you — kept telling everyone you were lying about your name. What was that all about? You are called Michael, aren't you?'

'Look guys,' I interrupt. 'Luc's been pissed off with me ever since I told everyone he took the bus through the storm when he pretended to walk that day. He's the fucking liar. I wouldn't believe anything that comes out his mouth.'

I walk to the sink and fill my bottle. My hands are trembling. No one else in the kitchen is speaking. They all know I'm using two different names. Christ. What if Luc told the Hats he thinks I'm a suspect in the murder investigation, just like he told the Irish nurse weeks ago in the boarding school? I can't believe I screamed Massimo's name in my sleep. How has no one said anything? Have they even realised he's the dead pilgrim? Maybe the police haven't released Massimo's name yet. I've been too terrified to read the Spanish newspapers, but maybe they're honouring the family's wishes to keep their son's name confidential until the murderer has been caught.

Water overflows from my bottle. I can't risk any more time here. Not when Luc's going to turn up any moment.

'It's okay, Michael,' says Cowboy, making me flinch. 'You can stop checking the tap. It's turned off.'

I walk quickly past the other pilgrims to the Hats' table. I lift the backpack over my shoulder and say goodbye, but neither Panama or Baseball respond.

It's no longer safe to sleep in dorms with other pilgrims — not if I'm going to scream out Massimo's name in the night.

When did the trauma consume me? Am I so used to the nightmares that I don't remember them anymore? At first, the dreams always led me back to that cliffside where everything played out exactly as it had happened. Massimo walked towards me, stared at the money belt under my shorts, demanded a cigarette, disappeared inside his cabin and then pushed his metal-tipped staff into my hand, after which he lay on the ground, a huge gash in his head and eyes staring blankly at the sky. But then my dream projector started adding other details I knew weren't true. The corrugated iron cabin became a wooden house. Massimo started wearing shoes. And then a suit. One night, he regained consciousness as I leaned over him, so I had to finish the job with the staff until I was sure he was dead. Since then, there have been no limits to the ways I've killed Massimo. The last time I remember, I loaded weights on the back of Robin's tractor and lifted Massimo off the ground with the hay bale spear through his chest. I was standing in a field, wearing Jessica's apron and skinning strips of flesh from Massimo's corpse with a butcher's knife. But it wasn't the blood spurting across my face which woke me that night gasping for breath. It was because no matter how far I sliced into Massimo's back, more layers of skin always appeared underneath; each one with the same tattoo of Christ's mournful eyes staring back at me.

And the nightmares don't end with Massimo. Ever since Alistair got engaged, I've started living another scene in my sleep. I wake in Alistair's bed, next to his wife, but the small boy who runs into the room and climbs up onto the bed doesn't belong to my brother. The three of us eat breakfast together in our Clapham home; me, Jessica and little Oscar, before we leave for the meeting. We drive across London, park the Jaguar convertible behind the security gates and show our Credentials to the staff in the visitors' centre. I tell

Oscar to stay quiet as the prison guard reads out the rules — the same rules we've already heard countless times — after which we follow the uniformed man into the hall where Uncle Alistair sits hunched over a table. He's been attacked again, probably by some murderer or another lifer. I ask how he's doing, unable to look at his broken nose. Jessica gives Alistair her hand — the same hand he held when they made their vows at the altar. My brother smiles and says these visits are the only thing keeping him alive. Alistair thanks me for acting as Oscar's father. He stares into the three-year old's eyes, desperate to tell the boy that he's his real father. But Alistair has no idea. No idea that I've replaced his old life. No idea that Oscar is actually my son. And no idea that Jessica has already conceived our second child.

I can no longer control my thoughts, even when I'm awake. And it's not just the obsessive ticks, like checking every tap is turned off or how I stare at the ground every time I stop on the trail, convinced that something has fallen out of my backpack which proves James Pollock was there.

The guilt is driving me insane. I can't pretend it isn't happening. The signs have always been there. The night I heard his staff tapping along the cloisters in that monastery, only to learn from the Hospitalero the next morning that I was the only pilgrim staying there. The morning I saw Massimo's staff leaning against the albergue door. The blurred image on that woman's camera screen of the giant, shirtless man with a shaved head and bare feet standing next to the boot rack.

Massimo has been following me this whole time.

And it's only so long until he finds me.

Gabriela was the last person who could have saved me. There was a moment in the garden that night when I thought I was going to tell her everything. I was desperate to confess what I'd done. But then she told me about the man who betrayed her by living two secret lives; one with her, and the other with his wife and child. After that, how could I pretend I was not a fraud myself? Maybe something could have happened between us if I hadn't killed Massimo. Maybe we would still be together; either out here on the trail or back in that albergue working as volunteers. Gabriela taught me how it felt to have a connection with someone. A genuine connection; not what I thought I had with Jessica. But Gabriela has gone for ever. And I'm not sure if I can trust my memories of her anymore.

What if Gabriela was just someone I invented after Jessica's engagement? Jessica. Gabriela. Their names aren't so different after all.

Who knows if anything is actually real anymore.

I still can't comprehend how the police aren't on to me. Or maybe they are. Maybe they've been playing with me all this time. The evidence is overwhelming. My fingerprints were all over Massimo's staff; those same fingerprints which the officer took on the electronic machine at the police station in León. They have everything they need to convict me. Even if for some freak reason the fingerprints don't match, they still have my DNA from that nail in Massimo's cabin. My own mother even stitched me up with the missing person report she sent to the authorities. How is it possible I've got this far? How am I still out here walking the Camino?

What if everyone else on the trail already knows? Panama was certainly suspicious of me; and that was before I shouted Massimo's name in the night. It was bad enough last week when Dale heard me yelling in my sleep, but I never said Massimo's name out loud, or I hope I didn't. But last night I literally confessed what I did to the whole albergue.

Too many people must suspect me now.

The Hospitalero in Zubiri, who saw Massimo's blood all

over my hands before she wrote my real name and passport details in her register.

The Hospitalero in the boarding school, who must have checked my internet search history and realised I clicked on that British newspaper's website with the '*Italian man, 32, murdered on the Camino de Santiago*' headline, before she threw me out.

The telecoms company for Alistair's phone must also be involved. Alistair was convinced I still had his handset, but I threw it away weeks ago. There's no way the phone company tracked the handset to my exact location, as Alistair claimed. The phone company must be working with the Spanish detectives, British intelligence, Interpol, or whoever the Italians have sent after me. Maybe they're all collaborating together, doing everything they can to lock me away for the rest of my life.

It's becoming hard not to suspect every coincidence that's happened to me on the Camino. The 'M' shaped password on Alistair's phone. How I lied to Massimo outside the cabin and said I was Michael — the first name that came into my head that night; and which also happened to be the name in the Credentials I found on that bridge outside Logroño. What if Michael Evans' Credentials didn't just appear there by accident? What if someone left the booklet, knowing I would pick it up and start calling myself Michael? What if it was Luc, the Hats with their 'Michael Corleone' comments, the police, or even Joseph?

Like Luc, Joseph knows I've been switching identities. What if his trademark 'See you in Santiago, Saint James' has always been a warning that he wouldn't let me out of his sight? I can't help thinking how easier things would be if Joseph wasn't still out here. If he somehow, just disappeared. Luc too.

Fuck. Why did I leave Massimo outside the cabin? I should have dragged his body into the woods, buried it under a mound of rocks, or hidden it somewhere no one would have found until I'd reached Santiago or flown home. Maybe I would have read about the Camino murder years later after I'd forgotten all about Massimo. His corpse would have decomposed, the albergue records all destroyed and the Hospitaleros long gone. Thursday 12 June would have been banished from the archives of history. I would have been safe.

But maybe I still can be safe. That's what the voices are saying; the quiet voices which have started speaking louder.

'Mike's one of the good guys,' Dale said. But what if I'm not? What if I've been the complete opposite all this time and no one suspected me?

Or maybe they did suspect me, but couldn't say this out loud.

Oscar knew there was darkness inside me. It was right there in his note. 'I hope you learn to conquer your demons, Michael.'

Thank God I didn't tell Oscar about Massimo, even though I was desperate to clear my conscience. I could have ruined everything.

And Oscar isn't the only pilgrim who sensed my wickedness. Iñaki said something similar that night in the albergue when he saw my face on the police wanted notice. 'He's like your doppelgänger. Your evil twin.' Iñaki's exact words.

Iñaki, like Joseph, also knows my real name is James Pollock, not Michael Evans. He heard everything I confessed to the police officers that evening in León before they arrested me. All this time I've been hoping Iñaki can beat his heroin addiction. But if he relapsed, or God forbid something worse happened to him, then at least...

Maybe I am dark. Or worse.

Maybe I am evil.

I chose to throw that staff at Massimo's head. I didn't have to do it. I could have walked away. But I did exactly what he asked. And part of me enjoyed it.

Throwing that staff released an adrenaline I've never experienced at any other time in my life. Something happened when that staff left my hand. Something I haven't been able to admit until now. As I watched the staff soar through the air and come down towards his head, I felt something I never thought I would feel. And while I could never confess this to anyone, I actually enjoyed throwing that staff at him. It was easy to kill Massimo.

My shadow looks different under the sun. It's darker. Heavier.

Is this what happens when you kill another human? Does the devil come to claim your soul? He owns me already. There's no way I'm not going to hell after what I've done.

It's too late for redemption. Maybe whoever left the Credentials on the bridge knew this already. Maybe they were only trying to help.

Without Michael, I would never have got this far.

And there's no reason for me not to just keep on being him. We're not so different after all. Some people even think he's me, or I'm him.

Michael didn't kill Massimo.

And Michael doesn't have to hand himself in when he gets to Santiago. Michael can still take Massimo with him to the grave. No one else would ever have to know.

Together, we can still get away with murder.

SATURDAY 5 JULY

I walked two stages yesterday. I wouldn't have had the energy without those cakes I found behind that bakery's door. It was wrong to steal from a local business, but I'm sure they wouldn't have minded if they'd known how hungry I was.

Twelve hours later, I arrived at the municipal albergue only to find it was full. With pus oozing from my blisters, I followed the notices to the village hall which was also offering pilgrim accommodation. Three euros to sleep on the floor was steep, but I took extra mats from the cupboard and found a discrete place in the corner. The 'kitchen' sign next to the microwave was clearly a joke, as there were no plates, cutlery or running water, let alone any packets of free pasta which I've been living on all week. What they did have, however, was a pair of blunt scissors.

The stench from the drains led down to a small windowless bathroom. After Luc's confrontation and my nightmare in the dorm, this was the only way to remain anonymous. And so with the cracked mirror as my guide, I quickly set to work.

The first snip was so loud I thought I'd taken off my ear

lobe, but as the pain failed to arrive, I grabbed another fistful of hair.

It seemed inevitable I'd nick the back of my neck, but I managed to hold the blades straight. My head appeared to shrink by half its size, while the beard only grew thicker. Whenever a pilgrim knocked on the door, my raised voice scared them away.

After the satisfaction of the initial purge, things started to get frustrating. What I really needed was a pair of clippers or someone to stand behind and cut everything evenly, but after a period of fixed concentration, my hand finally slipped.

The pain was so intense that someone outside asked if I needed help. Without any toilet paper I couldn't stem the bleeding, but from what I felt with my fingers, the wound clearly needed stitches.

Gripping onto the sink, I tried to use the reflection in the mirror, but I couldn't see how far I'd sliced into my ear with all the blood pouring down my neck. My only option was to tear a strip off my t-shirt and apply pressure until it eventually stopped bleeding.

The banging on the door became relentless, so I threw the clumps of old hair into the bin and wiped the blood on the sink with my hands. Ignoring the stares from those waiting outside, I returned to my sleeping mat, unrecognisable to the other pilgrims who'd seen me less than thirty minutes earlier.

The stone markers taunt me as they count down the remaining kilometres. Every number seems to creep higher than the last, as if whoever measured the distance just wanted to torment me.

I don't know why I'm still walking, except for stubborn

pride. If the Le Puy lady was right, then I don't have enough albergue stamps for my Compostela certificate in Santiago. With my stamps split between two different Credentials, the officials at the Pilgrim's Reception Office will never believe that just one of us walked all the way from St-Jean. It's not as if they'll write both our names in Latin and let us share a certificate for our combined efforts. Even if I do escape and board a flight to London, I'll never be able to prove to Greg and Dev that I walked the whole Camino. This journey has all been for nothing. And every step leads to an ending I don't want to discover.

The heat is rising. There were rumours last night that today would reach forty degrees, but I hadn't expected it to get this hot while the sun was still low. The cut behind my ear is throbbing, although the wound seems to have finally clotted. My sleeping mat was covered in so much blood that I had to hide it at the back of the village hall's cupboard. My ear clearly needs stitches or something to stop it getting infected, but the police will be on to me in seconds if I check into a public hospital.

Sweat drips down my body. I try cooling my face with moisture from my chest, but there's not enough breeze to ripple the grass. I'm down to the last dregs in my bottle. I should have found somewhere to replenish my supplies instead of gambling on just half a litre of yesterday's water. The last drops taste more like molten plastic. I don't have any saliva. And whatever thoughts I had of drinking my own urine end when I piss dark yellow fluid.

Finally, I reach the next village. My relief on finding a fountain is short lived as the pipes are disconnected. I could strangle the idiot who decided it was a good idea to deny pilgrims drinking water, but there's a small grocery shop on the main street. I step inside, only to discover that the bottles of water all cost two euros and it's an extra fifty cents for anything refrigerated. The shopkeeper barely blinks when I accuse him of exploiting pilgrims with his fridge tax, but he suggests trying the bar at the end of the road.

I walk into the establishment and give the barman my order. He returns with a bottle that's half the size of the ones in the shop. 'Tres euros,' he says.

I put my crumpled plastic bottle on the bar and ask him to fill this instead.

He shakes his head.

I unscrew the cap and again ask for tap water.

The barman takes the next customer's order.

I explain that I'm a pilgrim, walking the Camino de Santiago, but he pretends not to hear.

My hands start shaking. I have drunk from every kind of water source on my pilgrimage: public fountains, private albergues, municipal albergues, kitchens, bathrooms, garden taps, strangers' homes, cafes where I didn't eat, restaurants where I didn't eat, fresh spring water pouring through a hole in a rock, and even from a five-star hotel. But I've never been more desperate than now.

I wait for the barman to return and then repeat my order.

'Tres euros,' he says, pushing his refrigerated bottle towards me.

I tell him that I want free water.

He tells me to use the fountain.

I say that the fountain is not working.

The barman walks away, but I catch his arm. After a short struggle, he slips out of my hold. 'Agua gratis,' I say, pushing my bottle into his hand. He shakes his head and points to the door. 'Fuck you,' I shout. 'Fuck you, you fucking fuck.'

I leave the bar through a trail of glaring customers.

There's no saliva left in my mouth. I should have asked for water from the pilgrims in the last village, but I scared them away when I kicked over the bar sign. The sun is burning all the oxygen in the sky. I overheard some pilgrims saying they were going to stop at midday because of the heat, but that was hours ago. The trail is completely empty. Everyone else must have given up as well. The seventy-five kilometres marker takes an eternity to drop to seventy-four. I walk until my knees can't support their weight any longer. I tilt forwards but my hands aren't quick enough to break my fall.

Fingers touch my face. However long I passed out for I can't tell, but I'm too weak to retaliate when the hand lifts my chin. Cold liquid runs down my throat. It must be water, but it tastes like something otherworldly.

I squint with my eyes. A tall figure blocks the sun. I can't focus on anything beyond his calloused hand holding the bottle to my lips. I swallow everything, entranced by his voice whose words I don't understand.

Slowly, I start to sit. A smile creases the corners of the man's eyes. He's dressed in robes which must have once been white, his face and hands the only visible parts of his body.

'Where are you from?' I ask.

'I am here,' he says, now in English.

I try to thank him but I can barely speak. 'James,' I manage, pointing to my chest.

'Ismael,' he replies.

His calm aura is all around me.

I try to stand but he slows my movement with his hand.

His eyes return to the horizon. Fingers in mouth, he blows a sharp whistle. Three sheep dogs come bounding towards us through the field. They kneel at their master's side and drink from his cupped palm.

Ismael places a hand on my shoulder.

'Buen Camino, James,' he says.

I stare into the distance. But when I turn around, the shepherd has disappeared.

———

The next village has so many pilgrims that I can't understand where they've all come from. Unsurprisingly, the municipal albergue is full so I return to the main street.

Santiago is two days away and I only have nine euros left. I'd planned to sleep rough once the temperature dropped, but I don't have the energy to walk any further.

My thoughts about sleeping on a bench are interrupted by a sign sellotaped to a door. *'Only pilgrims with two hundred kilometres,'* reads the handwritten sheet.

A voice welcomes me inside. Sheltering from the humidity, I say that I can't afford a private albergue, but she explains in English that it's five euros a night. 'This is a place of refuge, not money,' she says, staring at my torn t-shirt. 'Sit down. You're exhausted.'

The woman returns with water which I down in one gulp. She refills the glass and asks for my Credentials. The zip on my money belt catches against something, possibly my passport, but I pull harder until it opens. I give the Hospitalero my documents. She opens the first page then closes the booklet before checking the other stamps. 'You've come a long way, Michael.'

The relief is overwhelming. I can stay here tonight. I don't have to keep walking.

I unlace the hiking boots and let my feet breathe. The right boot has a tear at the back which explains why I've been walking all afternoon with gravel under my heel. The hole is wide enough for two fingers but the Hospitalero says a South African called Magriet might have tape to repair my boot. From what I gather, Magriet is tall, broad-shouldered and has a scar across her cheek, according to how the Hospitalero runs a finger across her face. 'She's in the garden,' the woman adds, reassuringly.

I swallow more water and ask why there are so many pilgrims outside.

'That's why we have our sign on the door,' the Hospitalero replies. 'Many come to walk the last hundred kilometres for their Compostelas.'

She smiles when I ask why. 'Because certificates are important to some people. Now go rest,' she says, staring at the blood stains on my t-shirt.

Lightheaded from standing too quickly, I walk into the bathroom and find the switch on the wall. A figure appears under the flickering bulb. I shout out his name, my hands raised in defence before the light becomes permanent.

'Everything alright?' asks the Hospitalero outside, but I can't respond.

I stare at the reflection, my chest pounding.

Slowly, I touch my face.

The man in the glass does the same.

I walk closer, still staring into the mirror.

For a second, I was convinced it was really him, but up close, the resemblance is startling. With my short hair, torn clothes and tanned skin, I look just like him.

I undress, still watching the reflection. I knew I'd lost

weight from the slack around my shorts, but weeks without eating properly must have shed at least two stone from my body. My face is gaunt, the bony ribcage disproportionate to my thick beard. The only food I ate today were berries from a tree and the bread I stole from that village shop charging fifty cents extra for cold drinks.

Finally, I feel safe enough to turn my back to the mirror. The hot shower cleans the sweat from my skin. There's no body wash in the stalls but I use soap from the dispenser, careful not to open the wound behind my ear.

I unclip my backpack, dripping more water onto the floor. I must have forgotten to collect my clothes the last time I did laundry as there are no t-shirts, underwear or travel towel inside. I almost punch the wall until the voice in my head reminds me that I was going to throw everything away in Santiago and buy new clothes there instead.

I change back into my torn, blood-stained t-shirt and Lycra shorts, but Massimo has returned in the mirror. Unnerved by the hard eyes watching from behind the glass, I reach into my backpack for James Pollock's Credentials. I push the booklet into my money belt which I clip around my waist, then leave quickly before I see the reflection again.

A woman fitting Magriet's description is sitting under a tree in the garden, writing in her notebook. She has the same features the Hospitalero described, except the scar on her cheek is longer and more defined. She lowers her pen as I introduce myself, her stare consistent even after I explain why I'm here. 'Tape as in Sellotape?' she repeats. 'Why do you need tape?'

Her hand snatches my hiking boot, but instead of examining the split, she turns over the heel and measures its width between her thumb and first finger.

'Where did you buy these?'

Her bluntness catches me off guard. 'London,' I lie.

'Doubt it,' she says. 'This is a South African brand.'

'I don't know what you mean,' I reply, trying not to sound unsettled, 'but I bought the boots in London. And I just need to repair them so I can finish the Camino.'

'Where exactly in London did you buy them?' she asks, standing up. 'I was there last month, but couldn't find a shop with this brand.'

At full height, Magriet is taller than I expected. Taller than me. Almost as tall as him.

'I don't remember,' I say, trying to banish Massimo's corpse from my mind. 'But I definitely —'

'Of course, you don't remember,' she says sarcastically. 'But wherever you bought them, they clearly weren't specialists.'

'Why not?' I ask, wary of how she's looking at the stains on my t-shirt.

'Because they're at least a size too big for your feet.'

I have to leave right now. There's something not right about how close she's standing, as though she's taking my measurements in her mind.

'You cut your hair,' she says, staring at my head. 'Or at least tried to.'

I shake my head and smile.

'Something amusing?' she asks.

'I don't know who you are, but I don't have to explain anything to you. And anyway, it's more practical to have short hair for the Camino in summer.'

Magriet points her finger at me. 'You had weeks to cut your hair, go to a barber if you wanted to, but instead you did a hack job with scissors just days before Santiago. You cut yourself as well,' she says, gazing at the wound on my ear.

She leans closer, hardening her eyes.

'It's going septic. But the real question is why you were in such a hurry to cut off all your hair.'

'I think we're finished here,' I say, looking at my boot which she's trapped under her arm. 'The Hospitalero said you had tape, but clearly that isn't going to happen. I'm going to take my boot from you now.'

'I've seen you before, haven't I?' she interrupts.

'I don't remember,' I reply, trying to ignore the wound that's itching behind my ear. I don't believe it's infected. She's only trying to rattle me. 'It's possible, I suppose. We're a small community of pilgrims, after all.'

'Wrong again,' says Magriet. 'There are hundreds of pilgrims walking these last stages, possibly thousands. Anyway, I'm sure I saw you weeks ago. Now where was it?'

It's obvious what Magriet means. She must have seen my photograph on one of those police wanted notices.

'Tell me,' she says, opening her notebook. 'Where were you on Thursday the twelfth of June?'

Thursday the twelfth of June. The day I killed Massimo.

Sweat runs down my spine.

'Well,' I say, pretending to think backwards. 'On the twelfth of June, I was sitting at my desk in London. Now I need to fix my boot, so if you don't have any tape, you can give me back my shoe and I'll find someone else instead.'

'Not so fast,' she interrupts. 'If you were in London on the twelfth of June, then how did you get here so quickly?'

'I started walking from León.'

'León? Why did you start there?'

'Because I only have two weeks off work. Not everyone has time to walk the whole Camino, do they?'

'And which day did you fly to Spain?'

The gash in my ear is throbbing. Why am I putting up

with this? If she's going to try and keep my boot, then I'll take it straight from her hand.

'Come on,' she says impatiently. 'Time clearly matters to you and your important job. So which day did you fly out?'

I can't think straight. What day is it today? It must be the fifth of July. There were some Americans on the trail yesterday celebrating Independence Day. So how many days ago was León? That was the night I ran from the restaurant with Iñaki; the night the police arrested me and then took my fingerprints. How long did it take to walk here from León? A week, maybe? Possibly less?

'The twenty-eighth,' I say, snatching at the nearest number. 'Now give me back my boot.'

'The twenty-eighth of June,' she repeats, returning to her notebook.

I flinch as she writes down the date.

'So you walked all the way here, from León, in one week?'

This is bullshit. Who does she think she is?

'You must have done some serious training beforehand. What was it you said you did in London?'

'Look, I don't know what you mean,' I say, trying to ignore the sweat on my face, 'but I wasn't here when that Italian was murdered.'

'Murdered? Who mentioned anything about a murder?'

'Well it's not exactly a secret, is it?' I interrupt. 'Everyone's been talking about it for weeks. The twelfth of June. That's when they think he was murdered.'

'Who thinks that's when he was murdered?'

'The newspapers. It was all over the news when I flew out.'

'But the autopsy only came back this week — when you were already here, walking the Camino.'

I try to swallow the lump in my throat. 'Why are you so interested, anyway?'

Magriet places both hands on her hips. 'Let's just say that after thirty years as a homicide detective in Jo'burg, you start taking interest when some Italian gets his head smashed open on your retirement trip. Now show me your Credentials.'

'My Credentials? Why do you want to see them?'

'Because I don't believe you started walking from León on the twenty-eighth of June. And I want to know your name.'

'This is ridiculous,' I say, touching the money belt under my shorts. 'I'm not showing you my documents. You're a normal pilgrim. I don't care what you did before —'

'The thing about murderers,' she interrupts, 'is that they know how to manipulate the truth. The sickest ones believe their lies. We've all read the reports how it might have been some local, but come on. A local on a cliffside next to that cabin? And to moer him on the back of the head? Why not just push him over the edge? That way you know you've done the job properly. That they're never coming back.'

Massimo's eyes stare blankly at the sky.

'If you ask me,' says Magriet, 'the murderer's still out here, hiding in plain sight. He probably thinks he's safe — that after weeks on the Camino, he's disguised himself among all the other pilgrims, probably changed his name and identity as well. He thinks he can walk straight into Santiago just like everyone else. But that's where he's wrong.'

A smile forms across her lips.

'I've seen it all before. The murderer always makes one mistake. Something so small they don't even realise. You see, to catch a killer you have to enter their mind, think what they're thinking, anticipate that one moment they slip up.

'Here,' she says, pointing across the garden. 'This very

albergue. The murderer walks into town, sees all the crowds and thinks he has to move on for the night. But then he passes this place and sees the sign on the door. Only pilgrims with two hundred kilometres. Jackpot, he thinks to himself. He walks inside, thinking he's safe, but what he doesn't realise is how meticulous these albergues are in checking pilgrim ID. Some albergues give lists of all their guests to the police so they can monitor which pilgrims are staying where. Not everyone is walking with good intentions, you see. And then…'

Magriet slams her hands together.

'You didn't half jump,' she says, smiling. 'And you've gone completely pale, like you've just seen a spook.'

'Magriet?' calls a voice from the albergue. 'La cena está lista.'

I'm trembling so much that I can't look at the Hospitalero as she walks towards us.

Their conversation continues in Spanish. I try to follow the words but they're speaking too quickly. León is mentioned, Roncesvalles too. They're talking about my Credentials, I know it.

Jesus Christ. I showed the Hospitalero Michael Evans' Credentials. She knows my first stamp was from St-Jean, not León like I told Magriet.

Their conversation ends. The Hospitalero looks at me then walks away.

'Take your boot,' says Magriet. 'We'll continue this after dinner, Michael.'

SUNDAY 6 JULY

I ran the second Magriet turned her back. She was clearly guarding the entrance, so I jumped the fence and cut through the side streets, checking that no one was following me on foot or by car. I had to sacrifice the backpack, but my passport, bank card and both Credentials were still inside the money belt under my shorts.

It was humiliating how quickly I caved in to her interrogation. I had weeks to practise my alibi, literally weeks, along with hundreds of kilometres, only to bottle it the moment Magriet sized me up with her stare. How will I escape the police in Santiago if I'm foolish enough to walk up to a retired detective sitting under a tree in an albergue garden? I literally presented myself to her on a plate. And the way she smiled at the end when she called me Michael, taunting me with how easily she'd learned my name from the Hospitalero. It's irrelevant that Magriet doesn't know who I really am. She knows my face, height and full description. And she also knows that I lied about starting my pilgrimage in León.

Christ. Why did I panic and say I didn't have time to walk the whole Camino? I should have told Magriet it was none of her business, but I was complacent, convinced that my short hair had disguised my appearance. Those fucking hiking boots. None of this would have happened if the Hospitalero hadn't said Magriet could repair the hole in the heel. And trust my luck that the same boots I took weeks ago from that ecological albergue also happen to be some specialist South African hiking brand.

I can't stop thinking about what Magriet said about the albergues sending lists of their guests to the police. It was obviously a threat; a warning that they already knew I was there, or would know the moment the Hospitalero informed them. The police in León must have told every officer in the area that there's a pilgrim called James Pollock using Michael Evans' Credentials. What if the officer told the Hospitalero that I'm walking the trail with two different names? Magriet will already know that I'm James Pollock. All she needs to do is find me and the game's up.

But what if Magriet was lying? Not every albergue could have sent records of their pilgrim guests to the police or I would have been caught weeks ago. But if it's true, then it explains why that Hospitalero in Zubiri recorded my details in her register when I turned up late outside her door after killing Massimo. And it was the same with Gabriela —

Jesus Christ.

I gave Gabriela my Credentials.

My real Credentials.

She wrote everything down; my full name, address and passport number.

Me. James Pollock.

Fucking hell.

Why did I tell Gabriela my real name? Why of all the people I've met, did I have to be honest with her? She knows everything about me. Literally everything after our night of confessions under the stars. If what Magriet said was true, then there's no reason why Gabriela wouldn't have told the police I was staying in her albergue after she stamped my documents. There were only three of us staying there that night — me, the Toronto banker and his Camino lover who spent most of the night trying to break the bedframe in our dorm. Even if Gabriela didn't tell the police, the albergue owner could have told them I was there the next morning when Gabriela had already left for her day off.

How could I have been so stupid? What if the police already know that after weeks of disappearing from the trail, James Pollock has finally reappeared in Galicia, just days away from Santiago?

It's like Magriet said. The murderer always makes one mistake.

I couldn't sleep last night in the forest. The trees creaked and mosquitos whined in my ear, which true to Magriet's diagnosis seems to have gone septic with pus oozing out of the wound. I was so cold in just shorts and t-shirt that my body kept shivering me awake. Every time my eyes opened, I expected to see beams of torchlight searching through the canopy, but the only thing that found me curled up on the ground were biting insects.

And before I knew if I was still awake or dreaming, I was back in Alistair's home.

I stepped out of the shower and reached for my towel. The cotton felt soft around my body. I touched my face but there was no stubble, let alone a full beard. The cut behind my ear had vanished, so too all the blisters on my feet. It was as though I had never walked a day on the Camino; that I'd never walked past his abandoned cabin.

'You'll be late for your meeting, darling,' called out the voice in the bedroom.

I wiped away the condensation on the mirror, checked my reflection one last time and turned around.

Tap.

The sound shook the whole bathroom. I closed my eyes. *He made you do it*, said the voice in my head. *It wasn't your fault*.

Convinced that the sound was just in my imagination, I walked to the door.

Tap.

I turned around just as the cabinet mirror swung open on its hinges.

Walking through the shower steam, I closed the cabinet.

He died years ago. No one ever found out. Forget it ever happened, James.

'Darling,' said the same voice outside. 'You'll be late if you don't get a move on. I've got to take the little monsters to nursery, remember?'

I walked back across the bathroom to the door.

Tap. Tap —

The third strike shattered the mirror.

'What was that?' she called out.

I tried to respond but a strange noise filled the room. The mirror above the sink. Somehow, it was vibrating, as if an electric current was passing straight through it. My fingers reached over the sink and pushed the mirror shut. The vibrations stopped.

It must have been the mirror — the same mirror Alistair bought years ago before they locked him away in prison.

I bent down to collect the shards of broken glass. The

children would soon wake up and walk into the bathroom with their bare feet. I'd have to ask their mother to check for any pieces I hadn't found.

Tap.

I looked up as the mirror again slammed into the wall. More glass fell from the frame, but then the cabinet door swung back by itself and clicked shut.

I walked towards the sink, in disbelief of what my eyes were seeing. Something sharp cut my foot but I walked closer, amazed at how not a single scratch filled the glass. The reflection was complete; the four toothbrushes all in their cupholders and Jessica's toiletries on the shelves. Only something was missing. Me.

I pinched my arm but there was no sensation. I dug my fingernails into my wrist, but again, nothing.

Tap.

I looked up at the mirror.

'Michael,' said a tanned face, grinning back with white teeth. 'Remember me? Or maybe yousa forget?'

The staff's metal tip crashed through the glass.

The pain was excruciating, but I must have lost consciousness before my head hit the floor.

Her scream woke me up, except when I came around, I was no longer inside my body but staring down from the ceiling. Jessica was kneeling on the floor, crying as she reached over my body to check my pulse. Two children appeared in the doorway, still dressed in their pyjamas. 'Daddy,' they cried out. I tried to assure them that everything was fine, but nothing came out of my mouth. Jessica's hands started gripping my shoulders. I tried to move but my muscles wouldn't respond.

'James,' she screamed, her voice in my ear. 'Please, darling. Wake up! Wake up!'

That was when my eyes opened and I found myself alone in the forest, covered in leaves and still clutching onto my passport.

Thuds fill the ground. There's no time to hide, so I lie still, hoping the trees will camouflage my body. It's almost dawn, early enough for the first pilgrims on the trail.

It's Magriet, I just know it. Few others could make as much noise as the feet stomping towards me. I stare through the branches, waiting for her hand to reach down and drag me up by the throat. Sweat runs down my forehead. I feel an urge to wipe it away, but I'm lying on both hands and any movement will expose my position.

The boots grow louder. I strain my eyes, trying to ignore the sweat drop hanging on the edge of my nose. A backpack passes through the leaves. It's just like the one I left behind in the albergue, only this version is grey and has a sleeping mat attached to the straps. The adrenaline makes me lift my neck. It's not her. I'm safe. Thank God.

I wait for the footsteps to disappear and then finally stand up, brushing the dirt off my body.

I can't waste any more time. Magriet must have realised that I escaped and returned to the trail. I should have hiked through the night or at least given myself a head start before sunrise. Who does she think she is, appointing herself as chief murder investigator? And her arrogance to accuse me of making the mistake of staying in an albergue for pilgrims who'd walked more than two hundred kilometres. Magriet's probably been staying there all week, taking notes on any potential suspects. She has no right to poke her nose into my business. Massimo has nothing to do with her. Anyway, Massimo made me throw that staff at him. He would have hurled it straight at my head if I hadn't followed his orders. One of us had to die that evening. And he made that decision for both of us.

Fuck Massimo. I'm the victim, not him. I didn't have to go back to the cabin and look for him that night, but I still did it anyway. I did everything that was expected of me.

Massimo has ruined my Camino, but I refuse to let him ruin the rest of my life. Why should I hand myself in when I reach Santiago? I did nothing wrong. I only did what he told me to do. What he demanded.

Maybe Massimo wanted to die. No. He wanted to die; that I'm convinced. Why else would he make me throw that staff at his head?

I'm innocent. And I've come this far.

I don't have to tell anyone what happened.

All I have to do is erase it from my memory. Pretend it never happened.

But first, I have to get the hell out of this country.

The hole in my right hiking boot is full of stones. I pull it off and try walking in one shoe, but the height difference makes this impossible. I sit down and unlace the other one. Before I can stop myself, I throw the first boot into the nearest bush, and then the other one as well. The left boot lands with a thud, but the right boot catches a thicket, where it hangs clearly visible from the path. I reach through the branches, cursing my stupidity, but the thorns are too sharp and I can't stretch far enough.

That one hiking boot is proof that I was here. Magriet

held the same boot in her hand. I can't leave it there; not when she's going to turn up at any moment.

I try throwing stones at the boot and then search for a stick long enough to unhook it, but this only makes me more frustrated. Eventually, the sound of other pilgrims forces me back onto the path.

───────

My speed has reduced, even without the weight of my backpack. The ground is sharp on my bare feet and I stub my toe against a root which splits the toenail.

According to the last marker, Santiago is still fifty kilometres away; too far to walk in half a day, even with some obsessed ex-homicide detective breathing down my neck. I have four euros remaining; hardly enough for breakfast let alone two days of walking. I'll have to beg or steal when I get to the city, maybe before then.

And I still haven't planned my escape once I reach the end. A public pay phone would be too easy to trace, so I'll have to borrow a pilgrim's phone instead. Greg will be furious if I interrupt him at work, so I'll call Dev and fake my excitement on finally completing the journey. Hopefully, he'll bring up the thousand pounds so I don't sound desperate, but if not, I'll have to swallow my pride and ask for the money. Alistair will have no doubt told them about our conversation earlier in the week, so they must suspect I'm close to the finish line. I just hope they don't try arguing that the Camino starts in Le Puy. Even if Greg withholds his share until he sees me in person, Dev might be decent enough to transfer his amount directly into my bank account. Five hundred pounds will be more than enough to pay for a last-minute flight back to London. With any luck, I'll find an internet cafe in

Santiago and buy a ticket for the same day. If not, I'll have to find a cheap hotel and quarantine myself inside the room in order to avoid Magriet, the police or anyone else waiting outside.

Before I fly, I'll go to a barber's, buy whatever I need from a pharmacy for the wound on my ear, splash out on some new shoes and clothes, and do whatever else I need to eradicate every trace of my five-hundred mile pilgrimage. I'll have to trust fate when I pass through airport security. I'll have to use my real passport, but I might slip through the net. If anyone talks to me on the plane, I'll pretend to speak another language or fall asleep. And then, when we finally touch down on home soil, all of this will be over. I'll go back to being James Pollock; back to a time before I ever met Massimo.

I just hope Dev pays up so I don't have to sleep rough in Santiago. I can't face calling Alistair for help. He'll only start banging on again about his missing work phone and how he's convinced I'm still walking around with it on the trail. My brother's paranoia about the court case must be consuming him. But I refuse to let Massimo do the same to me.

Two brown leather shoes stick out onto the path. I tell myself it's only the hunger pains making me see things again — like yesterday when I thought the tree root was a horse's head, or when I saw that man dressed as a mediaeval knight with a hawk perched on his chain mail — but then I see the body.

The mottled legs are covered in thin wispy hairs. I assume it's a man although the rest of his body is hidden in the long grass. Christ. This is just my luck to find another dead man on the Camino.

I stare down at his corpse. He can't have died long ago — yesterday evening at the latest, probably after the last pilgrim left the trail. The heatwave must have been too much for him; either that or a heart attack.

The shoes are too obvious to miss from the trail. Fuck. Why couldn't he have chosen to collapse further inside the field or somewhere else out of sight? It was almost daylight when I passed through the last village. Other pilgrims will soon arrive and they'll definitely call the police to report what they've found. The police will start asking questions. And it won't be long before one of the villagers says they saw a man with short hair and torn clothes walking without shoes or a backpack.

I lean further into the grass, careful not to touch him with my feet. Just one strand of DNA could pin me to a second investigation.

The body has made a perfect imprint in the grass. Its face belongs to a man, probably in his late seventies going from the lines on his forehead. I close my eyes and try to think of something Oscar might say if he was standing here, but before I finish paying my respects, something grabs my ankle.

I pull back but the corpse's hand tightens.

For a few terrifying seconds, it seems that I'm trapped in the rigor mortis of his locked muscles, but before I can detach myself from the dead man's grip, a head emerges from the grass.

He looks at me straight in the eye, pulls himself up with my hand and says something I don't understand. I'm still trembling when he sets off in the direction of the last village.

The trail is packed with school children. I have no idea where they've come from, but they walk in large packs, yelling and chanting songs in Spanish. I should be grateful for more safety in numbers, but their joy infuriates me. Who do they think they are, enjoying the Camino? They have no idea what I've endured these last twenty-six days. I push through the crowds, but with bare feet I have to concentrate on every step. My speed reduces. Magriet is going to catch me unless I walk faster.

Cramp fills my legs. Initially, it's a distraction from my raw blisters and the wound in my ear which was itching so much that I couldn't resist scratching, but the pain gets worse when I try stretching out the muscles. I get past another gauntlet of teenagers, only to find myself stuck behind a bald man dressed in brand new hiking clothes. I tell him I'm going to overtake but he hogs the middle of the narrow path. I raise my voice in case he's deaf or can't hear over all the noise, but after two failed attempts to pass, I realise he's blocking me intentionally.

The trail bends right, creating just enough of a gap to move in front. We draw level, his walking poles now in my side-vision. I increase my strides but the path starts to drop. One of his poles lands close to my bare foot. At first, I think it's accidental, but then he stabs the next pole inches in front of my toes. Our bodies brush before he manoeuvres himself in front.

My hands become fists. That idiot almost spiked my foot. One of those poles would have ended my Camino less than fifty kilometres from Santiago. He would have ruined everything I've sacrificed.

I reach out for his backpack.

Violent thoughts fill my mind; thoughts like throwing this weekend pilgrim to the ground and stabbing his own feet with those walking poles.

My fingers graze the bag straps.

I was capable of murder last time. I could do it again.

I throw myself forwards, desperate to grab onto his backpack, but the man drives both poles into the ground, propels himself down the slope and away from my grasp.

I'm still shaking when I reach the next two pilgrims in front. Who knows what I would have done if I'd caught that idiot with the walking poles. Maybe I would have lost control all over again; just like when James threw that staff at Massimo.

I overtake, but then the older pilgrim says something I haven't heard for days. 'Buen Camino.'

Unlike all the others behind us, he doesn't stare at the cuts on my feet or try to keep his distance. 'Do you speak English?' he asks. I look at the boy who's young enough to be his son and nod. 'The Camino's changed, hasn't it?' says the man. He then grants me the rarest of expressions. A smile.

It feels so long since my last conversation with someone other than myself that I can barely string a sentence together. The two Americans also started in St-Jean, although they set off days before me. 'You've done well to catch us,' says the father, clearly trying to ignore my infected ear. 'Then again, I never thought we'd make it this far.'

He shakes his head when I ask what he means.

'You heard about the incident, right?' he says, lowering his voice as we pull back from the boy. 'We almost called off the whole trip. I didn't want to keep walking with Noah here knowing there was some murderer on the loose. And they still haven't caught him. Hold on,' he says, interrupting himself. 'That Italian must have been killed around the time you were walking that stage. It was just outside of Zubiri wasn't it, not far from Pamplona. Some cabin on a cliffside.'

Massimo's dead eyes stare up at the sky.

'Why aren't you wearing shoes?' Noah interrupts. 'And where's your backpack?'

The man apologises for his son's directness, but it's a relief to change the subject. Before I know what I'm saying, I explain how I started the Camino with all my equipment until I decided to walk like the pilgrims of old. My lie sounds convincing until the boy becomes more confident.

'But don't your feet hurt?' he asks, staring at my black toe which lost its toenail earlier this morning. 'My feet are full of blisters and I'm wearing hiking boots.'

'Why don't we walk together?' says the father, breaking his awkwardness with a laugh. 'But I must warn you, the rest of our family's flying out from Minnesota tonight, so we've got to reach Santiago by tomorrow morning. You don't mind walking quickly, do you?'

I nod without making eye-contact. This is fate. It's exactly what I needed. If Magriet reported me to the police, then they'll be looking for a man walking into Santiago alone. But if I enter the city with this father and son, I might just go unnoticed.

'I'm Ethan,' says the man.

His smile forces me to respond.

'What about you, Michael?' he asks. 'Got any brothers or sisters?'

I check the path behind, just to make sure Magriet's not there. 'No. I'm an only child.'

Three teenage boys run out of the albergue, towels wrapped around their waists. They go to the side of the building where steam is wafting out of an open window. Together, they lift a large bucket and tilt it through the window until screams fill the shower. While I'm relieved that the albergue is full, Ethan is anxious to find a place before sunset. He phones other albergues using his Camino app, but these are also fully booked, the hotels as well. The last call, however, lasts longer than the others.

'Okay, guys,' he says, rubbing his son's shoulder. 'They have a few beds left but don't take reservations. It's four kilometres. Do you think you can do it?'

Our urgency leaves no time for talking. Other pilgrims seem equally desperate for accommodation but we overtake twenty others before a gravel track leads up to a building on a hill. A man, presumably the Hospitalero, starts walking towards us holding a sign that says 'completo'. He says in English that they're full for the night, but then he stops mid-sentence and stares.

A shudder runs down my spine. The Hospitalero has recognised me, I know it. I've seen that look before; the look of fear in his eyes.

Fucking hell. What if the police have issued more wanted notices with my face on the pages? They could have easily driven out here earlier and warned the Hospitalero that the main suspect in the Camino murder has been seen in the area. Or maybe they didn't have to. Maybe the police posted my face online and it's been shared on all the WhatsApp groups and Camino forums.

Fuck. This is all Magriet's fault. She must have called the police. The police already know I'm using two different names. Everything that happened when they arrested me in León will be on file. And they'll know it's James Pollock as soon as Magriet says Michael Evans is the murderer.

'We spoke an hour ago,' says Ethan. 'You said you had beds for the night.'

'No,' says the Hospitalero, still watching me. 'The beds have gone.'

I look back to the trail. I have to leave immediately. The Hospitalero will call the police any second.

'Those hammocks,' says Ethan, pointing to the field. 'How much to sleep there tonight?'

The Hospitalero finally breaks his stare. 'Six euros each. And two more for blankets.'

I look at the hammocks. I'm desperate to rest. Maybe I was just being paranoid. Maybe the Hospitalero was only staring at the pus on my ear, or because I'm walking bare-footed and not carrying anything. Surely the Hospitalero wouldn't have offered us a place to stay if he'd seen my face on a wanted notice? Unless he's buying more time, or following the police's instructions on what to do if the murderer suddenly turned up at his albergue. Either way, I'm exhausted. I don't have anywhere else to go. And of all these people, it's Magriet who I have to avoid. Magriet still has to overtake all those pilgrims we passed to get here. And even if she does walk this far, she'll see the 'completo' sign at the end of the gravel track and have to find somewhere else for the night. Santiago is less than thirty kilometres away — short enough to never see her again.

'Are you happy to sleep outside?' says Ethan's voice.

'Sure,' I reply, still staring across the field. 'Why not.'

I open my money belt and pretend to search for the six euros but Ethan pays for all three hammocks, blankets included.

'Don't worry about it, Michael,' says Ethan. 'This one's on me.'

I challenge his generosity, aware that I don't have the money to repay him, but then something steals the breath from my chest. My fingers dig deeper into the money belt but it's not there. My debit card. It's gone.

Nausea turns my stomach. I unstrap the belt from my waist and take everything out of the zipped pocket. Where the fuck has it gone? That strip of plastic decides my whole fate. How am I going to escape if I can't access Dev's money? How am I going to buy a flight home?

My mind races through all the possible places I might have lost it until I'm convinced I know where it is. Yesterday evening. That was the last time I saw my bank card — when I unzipped my money belt to pay for that albergue for pilgrims who'd walked more than two hundred kilometres. Jesus Christ. What if my debit card fell out onto the floor when I gave the Hospitalero Michael's Credentials?

Noah asks if I'm alright, but I don't answer. That bank card has my name on it. My real name. James fucking Pollock's name. If that Hospitalero has found it, then she already knows my real name. And Magriet as well.

There's not a chance I'll go undetected at Santiago airport after she's reported me to the police. And even if I do get as far as London, they'll still come looking for me. This night-mare will never end.

'Is this what you're looking for, Michael?' says Noah.

My heart jolts. I grab the bank card and check the details. It's mine. Thank God.

Ethan glares at me until I realise why he's angry. I apolo-gise to Noah for snatching the card from his hand, but his lip is shaking. He's a young boy, no older than eleven. What if

Alistair has a boy one day? Is this what they'll be doing in the future, walking the Camino together, just father and son?

'Why does it say you're called James?'

I flinch.

The boy stares up at me, waiting for my answer.

'James,' I reply, aware of Ethan's silence, 'is my family name. In England, we write the surname first.'

I quickly return the bank card to my money belt.

'Is that why you have two Credentials?' says Noah, pointing to the ground.

'What? No,' I say, feigning a laugh as I pick up both booklets. 'It's a long story. I lost my Credentials in the first week so I had to buy a new one. But then I found it again at the bottom of my backpack.'

'The same backpack you threw away?'

'Credenciales,' interrupts the albergue owner, checking his watch.

Hairs climb the back of my neck. I can't open both booklets to find the one with Michael's name. It's too suspicious, especially after the lie I just told the boy.

I stare at the two Credentials. Both documents have the same front cover and worn edges. Fuck. Why didn't I make one more distinctive from the other? I've had weeks to tear off a corner or mark one in a way that differentiates Michael's Credentials from James'. And now one mistake could expose everything.

The Hospitalero mutters under his breath. But before I can decide which booklet to give him, he takes the nearest Credentials from my hand.

My legs feel weak. How will I lie again if he's holding James Pollock's Credentials? All three of them will know I lied about my name — Ethan, Noah and the Hospitalero. What will happen when the Hospitalero sends the police a list of all the pilgrims staying at his albergue this evening? A list of names which includes James Pollock?

The owner turns through the Credentials. My chest is pounding. His eyes study the dates until he reaches the last page. He presses his stamp onto the paper. 'Michael,' he says, closing the booklet.

My hand shakes as I take back the documents.

The Hospitalero stares at me one last time and finally leaves.

I thank Ethan for paying for my hammock, but he doesn't respond. Shortly afterwards, he and Noah head off to shower in the main building.

———

I lie in the hammock, covering myself with the blanket. Enough time has passed for the police to arrive, but no one else has walked up the gravel track. Maybe the Hospitalero didn't recognise me after all. Maybe the police haven't issued new wanted notices for James Pollock.

But even so, it was still a mistake to stay here. Ethan already asked if I'd walked the same stage as Massimo on the day he died, but then I stupidly said I'd lost my Credentials in the first week. Ethan must have seen straight through my lie about why I ditched the backpack and hiking boots. Everything I said would have triggered his suspicions. What if he already knows I killed Massimo? What if that's why he and Noah have spent so long in the showers? Because they've gone to call the police.

'Completo,' says the owner's voice behind me. 'No beds.'

I open my eyes. It's almost dark, the last light clinging to the sky.

From the silence that follows, it seems that these arrivals

have accepted the news and returned to the trail, but then footsteps crunch the gravel.

'Cuánto cuesta dormir en una hamaca?'

I shudder from the woman's voice. Even speaking in Spanish, I recognise her accent.

The owner gives the same price; six euros for a hammock and two more for blankets.

'Bueno. Dos hamacas.'

I twist my neck, still hidden under the moth-eaten blanket. Two pilgrims cross the field. I recognise the figure at the front. She's carrying something in her hand, something which looks distinctively like the same hiking boot I threw into the brambles this morning, but my attention moves on to the backpack which her partner is carrying — a backpack filled with badges of sewn-on flags.

Fuck. This isn't happening. These two can't have met each other. It's just a nightmare that's happening while I'm still awake.

I lie still, desperate to hear their conversation.

Magriet and Luc leave their backpacks by the hammocks and then walk back across the field straight towards me. I slide deeper into my hammock.

'And you're certain it was him?' says Magriet. 'The same man from the police notices?'

'Yes. One day 'e was James, the next 'e was Michael. And 'e 'ad a big nightmare in the albergue. Massimo, Massimo, 'e was screaming. It woke everybody up.'

'And he was wearing sneakers when you first met him?' Magriet interrupts. 'Sneakers, not hiking boots?'

'Yeah. Everybody was calling 'im the guy in those shoes.'

'Then we must find him before he reaches Santiago.'

Luc walks straight behind my head.

I'm covered in sweat. I can't believe they didn't see me. But I have to leave before they come back from the albergue.

'Hey, Michael,' says Ethan, startling me. 'Who are you talking to?'

'No one,' I reply. 'Just thinking aloud.'

I watch Ethan from the corner of my eye. I'm embarrassed that he caught me talking to myself, but he seems agitated. Maybe he just called the police to tell them I'm here. Maybe that's why Noah hasn't come back — because Ethan told his son to wait in the albergue until the police arrive.

I look back to the main building as Magriet and Luc disappear inside.

Ethan rests against the wooden post of my hammock. 'Is everything alright, Michael?' he says. 'You seem a bit... on edge.'

'No. Everything's fine.'

'Well, if you're hungry, Noah's making pasta in the kitchen.'

I analyse the tone of Ethan's voice. There's nothing to suggest he's lying about his son cooking. Maybe I was just being paranoid. But I can't afford any more mistakes.

Again, Ethan invites me to eat with them. My stomach aches but there's not a chance I'm stepping into that albergue; not with its two latest guests inside.

'I'm fine, thanks,' I reply.

'Okay,' says Ethan, frowning. 'You know where to find us if you change your mind.'

He leaves, just as Luc returns across the field.

Tap.

The sound jolts me awake. I stare at the black sky, not wanting to believe what I heard. But then it comes again.

Tap. Tap.

The staff's metal tip moves up the gravel track. I can't free my arms from the blanket.

Tap. Tap. Tap.

His smell is all around me; that same stench of piss and sweat.

I tell myself it's not real — that it's just the guilt trying to consume me, but then a hand rests on the wooden post behind my head.

My hammock sways from side to side. The sky is so black that I can't tell if my eyes are still open. But I can hear his breathing; the long, slow draws of breath entering his lungs.

Gimmie cigarette.

I wait for those intense eyes to appear through the darkness. But then the hand releases the post above my hammock.

The footsteps return to the path.

Tap. Tap.

Massimo slowly disappears. But he'll come back tomorrow.

He always does.

MONDAY MORNING 7 JULY

The blanket is soaking wet. I don't remember it raining but I must have fallen asleep at some point. I shiver under the mouldy cover, breathing its spores. There are no stars above, just darkness.

I'm still haunted by last night's visitor. I couldn't have shouted his name as the screams would have woken Ethan, Noah and the whole albergue even from out here in the field. Jesus Christ. Magriet and Luc. They're here, less than fifty metres away in their hammocks.

I untangle myself from the blanket and step onto the wet grass. Pain fills my shins. I grit my teeth, but it's as if hundreds of knives are all stabbing through the bone. I wince and bend down to drop my last coins into Ethan's hiking boot. I'm four euros short, but it's the best I can do.

It takes forever to return down the hill back to the trail. I thought my feet would be the problem but thirty kilometres to Santiago is going to be impossible with these shin splints, let alone moving quickly enough to outwalk Magriet and Luc.

A head torch in the distance gives me something to follow

until it disappears into the pitch-black. I try swinging my arms for warmth but my clothes are soaking from the blanket. Gravel cuts into the blisters on my bare feet. I waste precious moments trying to find the next Camino marker in the darkness. My fingers trace the shape of an arrow carved into a stone post. It points away from the track and into another field. I look back to the albergue, convinced I'll see beams of torchlight. But Magriet and Luc are not following me. Yet.

The forest adds more layers to the darkness. It's hard to keep a straight line as I feel out for branches or other signs that I've strayed from the trail. The softer ground does little to help my shins. I try everything to reduce the pain, taking small steps, side steps, and walking backwards, but it feels like the bone is protruding through my skin.

An eerie silence fills the air. I can't stop thinking about the last time I walked through a forest at night, when I'd climbed back up that cliffside only to discover that his body had disappeared from outside the cabin.

Finally, the canopy clears. The horizon is the darkest shade of blue until a slither of light pricks the sky. The slither becomes an arc. Then the arc becomes a circle.

The sun climbs so quickly it threatens to outrun the day. Burning black rings swirl around its circumference before a layer of blue appears underneath.

Clouds drift over clouds, their pink, turquoise and gold colours making fish scales in the sky. The trees come alive with birds. Ants move around my feet carrying loads to wherever they're going.

My last morning has begun.

There are more people in the next hundred metres than I've seen in the last four weeks. Some carry backpacks with sleeping bags underneath, but most carry drawstring bags which can't contain more than a water bottle. A few, like me, aren't carrying anything.

I try overtaking the hordes but there are too many of them. Hiking boots without a single scuff cover their feet. Walking sticks rest on shoulders, their sharp ends pointing at the next person behind. Every moment is recorded on their screens — selfies with farm animals, videos of ukulele singa-longs, and armies of teenagers marching with home-made banners as Reggaeton blasts through their speakers. Laundry detergent purges the air. Graffiti messages fill every wall space. Someone's phone GPS announces the exact distance to Santiago.

Again, I check behind, but there's no sign of my stalkers.

The engraved kilometre plaques have all been pulled from their markers, presumably stolen souvenirs for those walking for certificates. It's so loud I can't hear myself think. No sooner do I overtake one group, then the next one appears in front. And then the next.

These imposter pilgrims make me feel more alone than I've felt all Camino. Where were they four weeks ago? Have I really walked all this way to share an ending with thousands of tourists?

Maybe Greg was right. What have I achieved by walking across Spain? I have nothing to go back to. No job. No future. No ideas. And I've done something terrible. Something that can never be reversed.

How did I think I could just return home and forget everything? I threw a metal-tipped staff at his head, for God's sake. I killed him. I'll have to live with this for the rest of my life. I'm a murderer. Nothing will ever change that.

Massimo is going to visit me every night unless I hand myself in. I must confess what happened outside that cabin. I owe that much to his family. They deserve to know what I did to their son. They need closure. A way to mourn his death. And it's my duty to accept the punishment once I reach Santiago. There is no other alternative.

***

Motorway fumes fill the air. An Alsatian tries to tear its chain from the wall, desperate to maul my ankles. Pop-up stalls sell cheap Camino memorabilia. An airplane almost scrapes the trees overhead before landing behind an air traffic control tower. Everywhere, pilgrims desperately fill their Credentials with enough stamps for their certificates.

***

Finally, the ground plateaus onto a lookout point. I know what I'm going to find, but still the moment feels surreal.

I walk through the field, past all the people taking photographs. And right there, after eight hundred kilometres and twenty-seven days of walking, I stare down through the mist at Santiago de Compostela's Cathedral.

The Camino is ending. And so too my life as a free man.

***

The concrete gives way to cobbled streets. Tourists sit on terraces, unable to distinguish one pilgrim from the next as we arrive in droves. I constantly check behind, determined not to let Magriet or Luc deny me of these final moments. They must be waiting further ahead. Everyone's walking the same route, presumably straight to the Cathedral. If I continue this way, Magriet will catch me. But I refuse to let her interfere. I'm doing this on my own terms; first with my conscience, then with the law. And so for the first time all Camino, I abandon the yellow arrows.

I stagger through the old town until I reach a small plaza packed with people. The crowds make me feel more exposed than I've felt this entire journey. Magriet and Luc could be hiding anywhere among all these faces, just waiting to restrain me until the police arrive.

Tall stone steps lead up to the back of a grand building. It must be the Cathedral as there's no other reason why a security guard would be standing outside. He crosses his arms and watches the square. If Magriet alerted the authorities, then they'll all know what I look like from my passport photograph.

I climb the far end of the steps and wait against the back wall. A group tries to enter through the tall wooden doors, but the security guard leaves his position and tells them to use the main entrance. Their diversion lets me slip behind his back.

My feet touch the Cathedral floor. The temperature drops, sending a chill up my arm. There must be hundreds inside, even though the next Pilgrim's Mass doesn't start until midday.

The hum of voices echoes up to the vaults. I almost feel anonymous until a man wearing a pink polo shirt and chinos stares at my blistered feet and then at my chest under the torn t-shirt.

I walk towards a large incense burner hanging from the ceiling but my legs give way. I fall against the nearest pew and yell out in pain. No one else seems to notice unless they're too ashamed to watch. I lower myself onto the seat, gripping my shins which feel like they've shattered under my skin. Bowing my head, I slowly disappear from those around me.

Words leave my lips; words I never thought I'd use with my own voice.

I pray for Massimo's parents, then for his family and loved ones. And then, once I've exhausted the list of Massimo's mourners, I ask for my own forgiveness; forgiveness which I know I don't deserve.

The Lord's Prayer comes as easily as the last time I said it as a child — a time when I never thought I would kill someone.

'Our Father, who art in heaven, hallowed be thy name —'

Tap.

I tighten my eyes, refusing to hear that sound which has haunted my entire journey.

'Thy kingdom come; thy will be done; on earth as it is in heaven.'

Tap. Tap.

'Forgive us our trespasses,' I say quicker, 'as we forgive those who trespass against us —'

The metal tip strikes the paving stone. It sounds perfectly real; as if it's not only in my imagination but right here inside the Cathedral.

'And lead us not into temptation; but deliver us from evil —'

Tap. Tap. Tap.

The staff. It's coming straight towards me.

I slide off the pew, down onto the floor. My shins are in

agony, but I'm determined to finish the prayer before he finds me.

'For thine is the kingdom, the power and the glory —'

The staff strikes the stone at the end of my row.

'For ever and ever.'

The whole pew shakes.

'Amen.'

His stench is all around me. I glance to my left but I already know who's there.

'Please, Lord,' I say, burying my face into my arms. 'Make him stop. Make him go away.'

Unable to bear it any longer, I turn to the giant sitting a few feet away.

'What do you want?' I ask, my voice trembling.

Massimo stares up at the altar, his huge hand gripped around the staff. Tears run down his cheeks, but he mumbles words in Italian as though oblivious to my presence.

'You,' I say, louder, staring at his soiled rags. 'Why won't you leave me alone?'

He turns slowly in my direction. A thick scab covers the skin where the staff pierced his head.

'Help me, Michael,' he whispers. 'They come now.'

My body is paralysed.

This isn't happening. This isn't real. Massimo didn't just speak to me. He's dead. I stared into his eyes as he lay on the ground outside that cabin. There's no way he could have survived that staff smashing into his skull.

'Who?' I reply. 'Who is coming?'

Heavy footsteps fill the aisles.

Massimo digs his fingernails into the side of his shaved head and looks behind. 'They 'ere, Michael.'

I follow his gaze. The pews are empty. All the tourists and

pilgrims have left. It's only me, Massimo and maybe twenty armed police officers inside the Cathedral.

'Take,' says Massimo.

He slides something across the pew.

'Me watch yousa throw away phone in bus station,' he says quickly. 'So me take phone from trash. Password same as your name, Michael. So me use phone.'

Hairs climb the back of my neck.

'Me try tell you me alive, Michael,' says Massimo, wiping sweat from his forehead. 'But me afraid. Afraid because what me do.'

A loud voice tells us to stand with our hands behind our heads. Other armed police close in around us.

'James Pollock?' demands the nearest officer.

I stare at the gun pointing towards me. It feels like it's the only object that exists. The Cathedral, police and the giant standing next to me are suddenly all insignificant.

I try to speak but the voice is trapped inside my body.

The gun moves from me to Massimo and back again. I focus on the face behind the weapon. He can't distinguish me from Massimo. Our torn clothes. Cut skin. Bare feet. To the officer, we are exactly the same.

'James Pollock?' he says, louder.

A shadow fills my mind. I want to know what the officer is capable of. I want to know if he will lose control and pull the trigger, just as I lost control and threw the staff at Massimo's head.

'This is your last chance,' says the officer.

Massimo hardly moves. I can almost hear his thoughts. He doesn't want to respond either. He also wants to die. But I won't let that happen.

'Me,' I say. 'I am James Pollock.'

The officer walks forward, his gun pointed at my head. A

hand grips my neck, forcing my head down. Handcuffs clamp my wrists. Someone pushes me along the pew.

'No,' says Massimo. 'Not Michael.'

I try to stop but the hand shoves me into the aisle.

'Not Michael,' shouts Massimo. 'Me you want. Me kill Alessandro.'

'Qué has dicho?' says the officer behind me.

Massimo's scabbed feet step into the aisle. The officers turn their guns on him, not that Massimo seems to notice.

'Alessandro my friend,' he says, his voice starting to crack. 'But then 'is 'ead go strange. And 'e say throw steek at me.'

Massimo lifts the staff above his head as if he's about to throw it at the officers. I can't believe what he's doing. He's going to be shot dead right here in the Cathedral.

'Me say, No, Alessandro,' says Massimo, thumping his chest with his fist. 'Me no throw steek. But Alessandro get angry. So me throw steek at 'is head. An' then 'e die.'

Massimo drops the staff. It lands hard on the stone paving and rolls away.

'Me 'ide Alessandro in cabin. But then 'e come.'

Massimo points at me.

'Michael was sign from Dio,' he says, bowing his head. 'Dio tell me what to do. So me say, Michael you musta throw steek at me. But Michael no want. So me get angry. Throw steek, me shout. Finally, Michael do it. But steek no kill me. Steek only make me sleep.'

I can't believe what Massimo's saying. And that name. There's something familiar about it — as though I always knew it was the word Massimo kept repeating under his breath when he returned from the cabin, made the sign of the cross against his chest and then demanded I throw the staff at him.

Alessandro.

'Finally, me wake,' says Massimo, scratching his arms. 'So me find place for Alessandro near cabin an' then walk all Camino for my brother. An' for Dio.'

Massimo shakes his head. 'Me carry steek all the way so me never forget. But Alessandro always 'ere,' he says, jabbing the side of his skull. 'Alessandro never forgive me.'

A guttural sound escapes from Massimo's mouth.

'Me never forget my friend,' he says, tears filling his voice. 'So me make rope in tree. Me make rope because me want to die. An' me stand in tree but then Dio say, No Massimo, you musta go Santiago before inferno.'

Massimo wipes his face and stares up to the vaults. He releases another howl which fills the Cathedral. Then he walks towards the officers, his hands raised.

'Me kill Alessandro, not Michael. Michael good man.'

The handcuffs release my wrists. Within moments, the officers restrain Massimo and lead him past the other pews.

'Me sorry, Michael,' he says, trying to turn around. 'Me watch yousa come back to cabin that night. But me 'ide. Me 'ide because me afraid.'

Even from across the aisle, I can still stare into the depths of his eyes. And I hear something in my mind. A word that seems to come from Massimo's soul. *Michael.*

I shudder.

The officers push Massimo forwards. Our eyes separate. And the bond, or whatever it was that existed between us, dies.

'Me follow you all Camino, Michael,' shouts Massimo. 'The storm. That monastery you sleep with bites on your back. Last night in hammock. Me want to say you no kill me. But me afraid. Do yousa forgive me?'

My knees can barely hold my weight.

'Michael,' he screams. 'Do yousa forgive me?'

'Yes,' I say, straining to catch his eye through all the police who have surrounded him. 'I forgive you.'

'Addio, Michael. My brother.'

Massimo disappears into the sunlight. The tall doors close shut. And I am the last person left inside the Cathedral.

MONDAY AFTERNOON 7 JULY

Sunlight blinds my eyes. I close the Cathedral door and hobble down the steps. I can't decide where to go, so I wander along the cobbles, past market stalls and buskers until I find the main square. Hundreds are gathered there, most of them pilgrims. Instinctively, I move straight for one of the side streets, desperate not to be seen, but then I stop and turn around. It doesn't matter if Magriet finds me. The man I killed is alive. Massimo didn't die.

I try to blend in but everyone is staring at my feet and torn clothes. Some stand for photos with their backpacks in front of the Cathedral, while others sit in groups, presumably those they shared this journey with. I feel completely overwhelmed. Together, we have all walked this pilgrimage across an entire country.

I move through the crowds until my shins can't carry any more weight. Staggering towards the nearest stone column, I collapse to the ground. The pain is excruciating. I straighten my knees but this only makes everything worse. In the end, I just lean back against the pillar until the stabbing starts to fade.

I don't know where to begin, let alone comprehend what happened inside the Cathedral. But today, for the first time in four weeks, I am innocent.

'Saint James?' says a voice in front of me.

Hairs climb the back of my neck. I shield my hand against the sun, in disbelief that he's actually here. And yet somehow, I always knew Joseph would find me.

'You cut off all your hair,' he says. 'I almost didn't recognise you.'

I stand too quickly, my shins almost giving way.

'You're hurt,' he says, taking my hand.

'It's nothing,' I say, flinching. 'Just tiredness.'

The skin under Joseph's eyes has sagged, but something else about him is different. Maybe it's the lines across his brow or the white hairs in his beard, but it's as though he's aged years since we met at the start of the Camino.

'I'm sorry, James,' he says, placing his hand on my shoulder. 'Last time I saw you, I forgot to say see you in Santiago. Oh well. We're here now. That's what's most important.'

Before I can stop myself, I embrace him in my arms. I'm covered in dirt and sweat but he doesn't pull away. I squeeze tighter, overcome by the release of emotions.

How could I have had those terrible thoughts, wishing Joseph wasn't there on the Camino, just so I could get away with murder? He's supported me this entire journey — that first day in the Pyrenees when he talked about seven-year cycles; the morning in Estella when he caught me trying to buy a bus ticket to Bilbao; the night in León when he confirmed my identity after the police thought I'd stolen Michael Evans' credit card; that same night he took my backpack to the police station after they arrested me; the evening he stopped me burning my real Credentials; and that day I hung Massimo's noose around my neck, ready to fall from the tree, until that tiny robin landed on the branch next to my hand and spoke in Joseph's voice, telling me not to end my life.

I would never have reached Santiago without this sixty-nine year old German, who has always watched over me despite my failure to appreciate him.

'What a strange morning!' he says, as I release him from my arms. 'Did you hear they arrested the man who killed that Italian pilgrim in our first week?'

'Yes. I know him.'

'You know him? How?'

'He's called Massimo,' I say, too ashamed to look at Joseph's face. 'But he's not a murderer. Well, not intention-ally. He's not so different from me.'

Joseph frowns. 'I don't understand what you mean, James.'

Tears fill my eyes. I have to tell him. He's the only person who'll ever understand.

'I did something terrible, Joseph. Something I...'

He catches my arm as I fall. 'That's it,' he says, lowering me to the ground. 'Relax. Take all the time you need.'

Joseph raises his bottle to my mouth. I drink until I can't swallow any more. My balance returns, my breathing too. And then, sitting on the warm paving stones in front of the Cathedral, surrounded by all those other pilgrims who for weeks I tried to hide from, I confess what happened that evening I walked past the abandoned cabin on that cliffside.

Joseph sits in silence.

'Let me understand,' he says at last, lowering his voice. 'You arrived at the cabin, just after Massimo hid the body? Alessandro's body. The Italian who was murdered on the Camino. But Massimo saw you. And he made you throw the same staff at him, because he also wanted to die?'

My hands are trembling. Everything makes sense. Why Massimo was shocked to find me on the trail that evening. Why he kept looking back to the cabin where he'd hidden the body. Why he kept slapping his face as he prayed to the sky. And why he was determined to suffer the same fate as his friend who he'd killed only moments earlier.

'You walked this entire way, James, because you believed the Italian who was murdered was Massimo? Because you thought you killed him?'

'Yes.'

I can't swallow. I know what Joseph is thinking. To him, I'm still the murderer.

'You never read the news, or knew the name of the real pilgrim who died?'

I stare at the cracks in the paving stones. My head is spinning. If I hadn't been so terrified of seeing Massimo's face all over the news, I would have known what everyone else already knew.

Who knows when Alessandro's body was identified. Maybe it wasn't much longer after I read that newspaper headline in Estella. How is it possible that neither Luc, Magriet or any other pilgrim ever referred to Alessandro by name? It would have changed everything. I would have realised Massimo was still alive weeks ago; not here at the end of my pilgrimage. But I was too frightened to confront what I'd done. And the denial pushed my mind into its darkest corners until I almost ended everything.

The silence becomes unbearable. That morning in Estella's bus station. Joseph said the police were asking for anyone with information to come forward. He asked if I knew anything that would help the murder investigation. But instead, I denied all knowledge of what happened.

Why is Joseph still sitting next to me? He must be deciding what to do, or how he's going to find the police and tell them what I did.

'I should have confessed, Joseph. But I was terrified. And the guilt almost killed me.'

I wipe my eyes, but it can't stop the tears running down my face.

'I was convinced the police would catch me, even before they took my fingerprints in León. But they never connected me to the murder. Because Massimo was still on the trail, still carrying the same staff I thought I'd used to kill him.'

'And that is why you used Michael Evans' Credentials,' says Joseph.

I can't look into his eyes. I lied to everyone. I'm a complete fraud.

'At first, I used Michael's Credentials by mistake. But then those police wanted notices started appearing on the trail, so I used Michael's documents to hide.'

Joseph doesn't respond.

'It was inevitable that someone would realise what I was doing and report me. Some pilgrims knew me as James while others thought I was Michael. But even when I was arrested for running from that restaurant, the police still let me walk free. After that, I made a pact that I would reach Santiago and then confess to the murder. But I became obsessed. I started believing I was Michael.'

A weightlessness fills my head.

'I thought I was losing my mind,' I say, finally looking up. 'Massimo's ghost was haunting me. I heard his staff in my nightmares. That sound. Tap. Tap. Tap. It drove me mad. I saw him in another pilgrim's photograph. Found a staff that looked exactly like his — that was his. But I wasn't hearing or seeing things. Massimo was there all along, following me on the trail, just like last night, when he stood over my hammock as I pretended to sleep.'

My back is covered in sweat.

'I did a terrible thing, Joseph. I lied to you and so many others; all because I thought I killed him. I'll never forgive myself.'

I stare at all the pilgrims in the square. I can't relate to anything they're feeling in this moment. We have walked entirely different Caminos.

'You say you were going to tell the police when you reached Santiago?' says Joseph, at last.

'I think so. But I'm not sure.'

'Maybe I would have done the same.'

I stare at the lines around his eyes. 'What do you mean?'

He touches my arm. 'None of this was your fault, James. Massimo made you throw the staff at him. You had no choice.'

'But I tried to get away with murder, Joseph. My mind was consumed with dark thoughts. Thoughts about hurting others. And hurting myself. I still have them now. They're still inside me.'

'And you don't think I have bad thoughts as well?' he says, shaking his head. 'We all do. But you just have to learn how to silence them.'

'How?'

'All these pilgrims,' he says, gazing across the plaza. 'Imagine they represent all the thoughts we have. Good thoughts. Bad thoughts. Everything. Close your eyes.'

I do as he says.

'Now would you stand up and follow one of these pilgrims out of this square?'

'No.'

'Then accept these bad thoughts exist, James. But don't follow them.'

I open my eyes as more teenagers enter the square, chanting and waving their banners.

'Isn't it wonderful they get to enjoy this moment as well?' he says, smiling. 'How special we can all share it together. It's why I come every year.'

'Hold on, Joseph. How many times have you walked the Camino?'

He stares at his long fingers. 'This is my sixth time, I think.'

'Your sixth? But why didn't you say anything before? Why did you pretend you'd never walked the Camino when we met on the first day?'

Joseph laughs. 'Because every time is different.'

'And you never get bored?'

'Maybe one day I will understand the Camino and stop walking. But until then, I continue my pilgrimage.'

We sit and watch all the pilgrims. Four weeks ago, I set off from St-Jean, but the time that's past feels more like months. And despite all those days on the trail, I know I've wasted this entire Camino. It's obvious from the joy in all these pilgrims' faces. I never embraced this journey the way they embraced it. I made Santiago my objective when I should have experienced every moment of every day. And I sacrificed friendships with people I would never have met anywhere else. This whole pilgrimage has been about people. People who will forever be attached to specific mornings, afternoons, evenings and nights. It's taken me five hundred miles to realise this, but those opportunities have now all disappeared. The pilgrims I met have all disappeared. And so too the yellow arrows which always pointed me in the right direction.

My hand grips around Alistair's phone. 'How did you know what to do with your life, Joseph?' I ask, my voice starting to crack.

'Now that's a question,' he says, wiping his forehead. 'But the truth, James, is that I never really planned anything.'

'But you have a wife and children. How did you know you wanted a family?'

'Well,' he says, straightening his back against the stone column. 'One day, my wife was in the bathroom and she says,

'Oh Joseph, I think...' and then she walks into the bedroom pointing at her stomach. I say, 'I see', and then nine months later, we have a baby boy.'

He pauses. 'Then three years later, I'm lying in bed when my wife again calls from the bathroom. 'Oh Joseph,' she says, 'I think...' and then she walks into the bedroom pointing at her stomach. I say, 'I see', and then nine months later, we have another baby boy.

'And then three years after that, I'm still in bed when 'Oh Joseph...' says my wife from the bathroom. 'I think —' 'Okay! Okay!' I reply. And then we have another baby boy.'

Joseph laughs. 'Nobody knows where to begin, James. There are as many ways as people.'

A vibration fills my hand. I must have switched on Alistair's phone as the cracked screen lights up. Somehow, after all that time with Massimo, it still has a few percent of battery. 'Sorry, Joseph,' I say, lifting myself up from the ground. 'I have to call someone. Will you wait for me here?'

Aching from my shins, I walk down a cobbled slope away from the Cathedral.

Instinctively, my thumbs dial his London number.

I should have done this weeks ago. I made a terrible mistake. But it's not too late to clear my conscience.

The dial tone rings five, maybe six times, before I realise it's Monday afternoon and he's not going to be home. I try to decide what message to leave but then the tone cuts out mid ring.

'Hello?'

I almost drop the phone.

'Hello?' repeats her voice. 'Anyone there?'

'Jessica,' I say, clearing my throat. 'It's me.'

'James! How wonderful to hear you. Oh my God, you're in Santiago, aren't you? I can't believe you reached the end! You know we pinned this enormous map of Spain across the kitchen door to follow your progress. Hold on, one sec...'

Another voice appears in the background. One I recognise straight away.

'Ali's here,' says Jessica quickly. 'I know he'd love to congratulate you. We're both so excited to see you. So much has changed since you were last home.'

I flinch as the phone changes hands.

'So you made it?' says Alistair, his tone strangely enthusiastic. 'It's quite an achievement to walk all that way, James. Well done.'

I stare at my bare feet, trying to breathe slowly. I don't remember my brother ever congratulating me, but I can't delay this any longer.

'Alistair,' I say, trying to centre my voice. 'Can we speak in private? There's something I have to tell you.'

He's going to be heartbroken. This is going to destroy his marriage before it even begins. Our whole family will be devastated. They'll never forgive me. My parents, grandparents, aunts, uncles, cousins. No one will ever speak to me again.

'It's about my work phone, isn't it?' Alistair interrupts.

'What?'

'That's what you were going to say, James. You wanted to apologise for lying about throwing away the phone. But I knew you always had it. That's why I didn't have the phone blocked. I couldn't leave you alone out there without a phone, especially with some murderer on the loose. But forget it. Everything's all been resolved.'

'Resolved? So they dropped the misconduct charges?'

His breathing fills the receiver.

'Sorry, Alistair. I didn't mean to read your emails. But I

was really worried when they threatened to have you struck off and sent to prison —'

'Like I said, James, that's all over now.'

'So you're still going to be made a partner at your firm?'

'No, they had me struck off.'

'Shit, Alistair. I'm really sorry.'

'It was my fault. I let work take over. But things happen for a reason. And it's time for some changes. Jessica and I have decided to leave London. We want to buy somewhere in the countryside.'

The countryside? This doesn't sound like Alistair. He's being too open; too nice. And there's something odd about how his misconduct accusation has just vanished into thin air. None of this makes sense. I'll have to read his work emails after this call and find out what's really going on.

'Listen,' says Alistair abruptly. 'Greg and Dev came around last weekend. They were really concerned, especially after that Italian was murdered on your hike. They've been trying to get hold of you for weeks. I know everything — your thousand-pound bet to walk the Camino, or whatever it's called. Anyway, they asked me to tell you that they paid the money into your account. And Greg says he's sorry, whatever that's about.'

A smile pulls the corners of my mouth. Maybe Oscar was right. Maybe my friends were trying to help. Just with a few hard truths.

'And there's something else,' says Alistair, his voice more urgent. 'Something important.'

Fuck. He's too shrewd not to notice how awkward Jessica was when we spoke moments ago. He must suspect something happened between us.

'You know I've always admired you for doing what you want in life, James, even when I didn't exactly show it. But I want that to change. There's a lot I can learn from you. And I was wondering how you'd feel about being my best man at the wedding.'

A shudder runs down my spine.

'Yes, Alistair. Of course I'll be your best man.'

A message appears on his phone. The battery is flashing but another notification fills the screen; a message from someone called Maxine. I stare at the first line, shocked by what it says.

'Can I call you back later, Alistair? The phone's about to die.'

'You don't want a quick word with Jessica? I know how close you are.'

'Not right now,' I say, flinching.

'Fine. But don't forget that phone, James. Work are still furious and they want that handset back. In fact, just switch it off when we end this call. Put it in your bag and bring it home safely. Do you swear you'll do that?'

'Yes,' I reply, before hanging up the call.

The battery is on two percent but it's enough to open the message.

'*What do you mean you can't see me anymore, Alistair? Six months and then you dump me over text. I don't give a fuck if you're engaged. And if you think my misconduct accusation was bad, just wait for what's next...*'

The 'M' shaped password on Alistair's phone. Maxine.

I scroll up to her previous messages but the phone starts vibrating.

It's Alistair again. Fuck.

'Hello,' I answer, holding the phone to my good ear, but the voice immediately speaks over me.

'James, it's me.'

'Jessica? What is it? Why are you speaking so quietly?'

'There's something I need to tell you. But you can't ever tell Alistair. Do you promise?'

'What is it?'

She pauses. 'God, I can't believe I'm saying this. I'm —'

The voice cuts out.

I check the screen just as the battery dies in my hand.

'James? Is that you?'

I turn around, stunned by the sound of her voice. She walks towards me, a green backpack hanging from her shoulders. Before I know what's happening, I'm locked in her embrace.

'Gabriela,' I say, breathing her patchouli. 'What are you doing here? You said you'd never go to Santiago.'

'I know, James, but that note you left was the sweetest thing I've ever read. And when I realised you'd left, I knew I couldn't stay in that albergue any longer.'

Her face is glowing. How did I ever think I was in love with Jessica?

'That night in the garden,' says Gabriela, moving her hand to my wrist. 'You said every day you saw things you didn't see before. And that if you didn't reach Santiago, you'd never find out how it was supposed to end. What is it? Why are you laughing?'

'I'm not. It's just what I said was so —'

'I'm being serious, James. You made me realise the Camino wasn't over. And that I had to see you again. Why are you frowning? Is this weird?'

'No,' I say, moving my fingers between hers. 'It just feels like I've been someone else this whole time.'

'Then who are you, James?'

She places her hand on my arm. The same arm which threw Massimo's staff.

'You cut off all your hair,' she says, stepping backwards.

'And that ear is definitely infected. God, you probably think I'm some stalker.'

'No, Gabriela. I'm so happy you're here. I just can't believe it's all over. I'm not ready to stop walking yet.'

'Then we don't have to.'

'What do you mean? This is the end of the Camino.'

'No, it's not,' she says, smiling. 'There are still three days to Finisterre. It's meant to be the most beautiful path. They used to call it the end of the world. Do you want to walk together?'

'Yes. But don't you need to rest? And what about your Compostela?'

'My Compostela?' she interrupts. 'You really think I want some certificate that says I walked the Camino? Didn't you learn anything?'

Her eyes stare into mine.

'Then come on, James! You need someone to check your ear. And we're not leaving until you buy some shoes. Your feet look terrible. At least those marks on your neck are starting to heal. What happened to you anyway?'

'It's a long story.'

'Then you can tell me all about it later.'

'Okay,' I say, looking up at the Cathedral. 'But I need to say goodbye to someone first. Promise you won't go anywhere.'

Gabriela locks her fingers around mine. 'I promise.'

I hobble back into the square. Moments ago, I was desperate to buy a phone charger and read Alistair's messages with the woman he was having an affair with, but that's now the furthest thing from my mind.

I can't believe Gabriela's here. I'll tell her everything. There'll be no more secrets — not after what she went through with that man in Madrid. I'll confess what happened outside Massimo's cabin, and then how I found those other Credentials and pretended to be Michael. I just hope Gabriela will understand like Joseph did. Thank God, she's always known me as James. I'll never not be myself again. And if we make it to Finisterre, or further, then I'll tell her everything that happened with Jessica and whatever it was Jessica was so desperate to tell me before the phone died.

I walk through the crowds, trying to remember which column we sat underneath earlier. I've got to thank Joseph. He's changed my whole Camino, possibly the next stage in my life.

The square is even busier than before. I move around a group sitting on the ground but then a pair of shoes step in front of me — a pair I never thought I'd see again.

I stare at my old trainers and then at the same tracksuit bottoms and pink Hawaiian shirt from the lost property basket in León.

'Iñaki,' I shout. 'You made it.'

He looks up, as though shocked to hear his name.

I try to ignore the scars on his arms, but he seems healthier since we last saw each other. I'm amazed he's here; that somehow, he's still alive.

'You thought I relapsed, didn't you?' he says calmly. 'I nearly did. I needed heroin so bad it almost killed me. But like you said, I made it. Although for me, this is the beginning.'

His smile makes it impossible not to hug him.

'I lied to you, Iñaki,' I say, looking into his eyes. 'I'm sorry. My name is James, not Michael. And I am the same person from the police wanted notices. But you already knew that, didn't you?'

'Yes,' he says, placing both hands on my shoulder. 'But there's something I have to tell you as well. The night they arrested you in León. I should have gone with the police, not you.'

'What are you saying?' I interrupt. 'That was my fault. I told you to run from that restaurant without paying.'

'No, James. It was my fault. That night, the police were looking for me.'

'For you? Why?'

'Because I was Michael Evans.'

'What? You're Michael Evans? The same Michael Evans whose Credentials I found?'

'Not exactly,' he says, shaking his head. 'But I pretended to be Michael, just like you.'

'I don't understand. What do you mean?'

Iñaki looks around to check no one else is listening.

'When I left the hospital I didn't have any money, so I hitched to St-Jean. But before I started the Camino, I went into a bathroom to fill up my water and there by the sink was a wallet next to all this expensive hiking equipment. I heard this English guy in the toilet, but no one else was there. So I opened the wallet.'

Iñaki crosses his arms.

'I only wanted to take a few notes,' he says, lowering his voice. 'Just enough for an albergue or some food. But then I saw all these credit cards inside. And before I could stop myself, I took one. And some fifty euro notes.'

He stares at the ground.

'I was desperate, James, but I really needed the money. The first time I used the credit card I was terrified, but then it actually worked. For some reason, the man didn't cancel the card. I guess he had so many that he didn't realise it was missing. But then I got addicted to using it. I stayed in this amazing hotel in Pamplona and ate the best meal I've ever had. So I bought new Credentials and said my name was

Michael Evans — the same name on the credit card. I pretended I was using the card to hide from my family after I escaped the hospital, but really, I was just hiding from myself.'

I can't believe what Iñaki is saying.

'In the end, I knew I'd get caught,' he continues. 'So I went back to my old name and started sleeping in albergues. That's why I threw the credit card off that bridge before Logroño and left the fake Credentials there — the same Credentials you must have found that same day.'

Iñaki shakes his head. 'I thought it was just a coincidence when we met in that convent and you said your name was Michael. But then I saw your real name on the police notice at the next albergue. And when the police arrested you in León, I saw your Credentials and realised you were using my old documents. The ones that said Michael Evans.'

My hands are trembling.

'But that night in the albergue,' I interrupt. 'You saw the police notices with my photograph. You knew the police were looking for me and that my real name was James. Why didn't you say anything?'

'Because whatever happened, and whatever they thought you did, James, I knew you were still a good person.'

Iñaki wipes the sweat on his forehead. 'I felt terrible when they arrested you. That's why I told the officer I had to come to the police station as well. But then they said only you had to go. After that, I left the albergue because I was terrified they would find out I stole the credit card and pretended to be Michael Evans. I felt terrible for betraying you, James. It's the reason why I'm here. Because I had to find you and say sorry. Do you forgive me?'

This is all too much to understand.

'Yes, Iñaki. Of course I forgive you. But I let you down. I

should have gone back to that albergue after the police released me. But I kept walking, even though I knew you needed help.'

Iñaki grips my shoulder. 'Then we must both forgive each other. Deal?'

'Deal.'

He checks the watch on his wrist. 'Sorry, James, but I have to catch my bus. I must go home and start again. But thank you for everything.'

Iñaki disappears through the crowds. It's impossible to comprehend everything that's happened, but there's still one person I have to find before I leave with Gabriela.

I reach the stone column but he's not there. I look around, convinced I must have gone to the wrong place, but Joseph's not at the next pillar, or the one after that.

I don't even have his email address or telephone number. All I know is that he lives in Stuttgart, has a wife and three sons, and has walked the Camino six times. I have to tell him what he's meant to me — how if it hadn't been for him, I would never be here right now.

I search the square until I accept that he's gone. It's getting late. I can't leave Gabriela waiting any longer.

'Goodbye, Joseph,' I say under my breath. 'Buen Camino.'

ACKNOWLEDGEMENTS

I would like to thank the following for their support and inspiration: Jane Corry, Nancy Warren, Ian Burton, Bill Bidder, Giles Bidder, Lucy Bidder, Millie and George, Hannah Dennison, Orlando Murrin, Richard D. Handy, Jon Herbert, Virginia Modafferi, Seb Coles, Herman Cloete, Miguel Álvarez, Oscar López, Alex Paget, John Brierley, Arantxa Martínez, Philip Charter, Eric, Carolina, Amy, Perla, Andrew, Alba, Colin, Hugh, Tim, Tom, Bobby, Genevieve, Hubert, Aritz, Iñaki, Janine, Maria, Max, Oihana, Idoia, Jacques, Ascen, Katarzyna, Begoña, Virna, Omar, Peio, Olly, Stephen, Jill, Pietro, Sarah, Marta, Miriam, Elena, Paulo, Ro, Javier, Rashina, Josetxo, Finn, Lis, Monica, Rut, Ana, Mariado, Jamie, Monika, Lindsay, Maisy, Hans, Ignacio, Luke, Scott, Kaila, Alberto, Safiya, Nadine, Marco, Café Iruña, and anyone else I may have forgotten to include.

If you enjoyed reading Murder On The Camino and could take a few moments to leave a review that would be really appreciated.

To stay in touch and hear about upcoming releases, please visit willbidderauthor.com

Murder In The Adirondacks, coming 2025.

Will Bidder

Printed in Great Britain
by Amazon